PENGUIN BOOKS

THE TWELFTH DIALOGUE

Tom Petsinis is a novelist, poet and playwright. He was born in Greece in 1953, emigrated to Australia in 1959, and has since lived in Melbourne. After graduating from the University of Melbourne, he taught at a number of high schools, and presently teaches mathematics at Victoria University of Technology. He is married with two daughters.

Tom Petsinis is the author of two previous novels, *Raising the Shadow* and *The French Mathematician*, which has been published in England, America, Italy and Germany and was shortlisted for the New South Wales Premier's Literary Award. He has written and directed a number of plays, including *Salonika Bound*, *The Drought* and *The Picnic*. *The Drought* won the Wal Cherry Playscript of the Year in 1993 and was shortlisted for the Victorian Premier's Literary Award. His four collections of poetry are *The Blossom Vendor*, *Offerings: Sonnets from Mount Athos*, *Inheritance* and *Naming the Number*.

ALSO BY TOM PETSINIS

Novels
Raising the Shadow
The French Mathematician

Plays
The Drought
Salonika Bound
The Thief
The Picnic

Poetry
The Blossom Vendor
Offerings: Sonnets from Mount Athos
Inheritance
Naming the Number

TOM PETSINIS

THE TWELFTH DIALOGUE

Penguin Books Australia Ltd
487 Maroondah Highway, PO Box 257
Ringwood, Victoria 3134 Australia
Penguin Books Ltd
Harmondsworth, Middlesex, England
Penguin Putnam Inc.
375 Hudson Street, New York, New York 10014 USA
Penguin Books Canada Limited
10 Alcorn Avenue, Toronto, Ontario, Canada M4V 3B2
Penguin Books (NZ) Ltd
Cnr Rosedale and Airborne Roads, Albany, Auckland, New Zealand
Penguin Books (South Africa) (Pty) Ltd
5 Watkins Street, Denver Ext 4, 2094 South Africa
Penguin Books India (P) Ltd
11, Community Centre, Panchsheel Park, New Delhi 110 017 India

First published by Penguin Books Australia Ltd 2000

1 3 5 7 9 10 8 6 4 2

Copyright © Tom Petsinis 2000

All rights reserved. Without limiting the rights under copyright
reserved above, no part of this publication may be reproduced, stored
in or introduced into a retrieval system, or transmitted, in any
form or by any means (electronic, mechanical, photocopying,
recording or otherwise), without the prior written permission of both
the copyright owner and the above publisher of this book.

Design by Ellie Exarchos, Penguin Design Studio
Typeset in 11/15 Cochin by Midland Typesetters, Maryborough, Victoria
Printed and bound in Australia by Australian Print Group, Maryborough, Victoria

National Library of Australia
Cataloguing-in-Publication data:

Petsinis, Tom, 1953– .
The twelfth dialogue.
ISBN 0 14 027936 9.
I. Title.
A823.3

This project has been assisted by the Commonwealth Government through the
Australia Council, its arts funding and advisory body.

www.penguin.com.au

The author is grateful to the Australia Council for a residency at the B. R. Whiting Library in Rome, where the final draft of this novel was completed.

For my father

the FIRST dialogue

Another six-aspirin day, concedes Sonya Gore, owner of the second-hand bookshop BIBLIOPHILE. Grimacing, she reaches for a slim paperback from a pile on the counter. Early in the morning she drove to a market on the other side of town, where, compulsively selecting from the vast range on offer, she filled two large suitcases almost to bursting. She considers the paperback for a moment, a collection of poems. Does it have any worth? What price should be set on it? She confronts the same dilemma over each book: how to reconcile intrinsic worth with a realistic price. As though a sixth finger, the cigarette in her right hand releases a line of smoke that curls and twists and spirals into a cursive script, covering her face with its uncoiling before drifting away to infiltrate the pages and add meaning to books pressed hard against each other on the shelves. If only this were an ideal world. Books would be free, or at least of equal worth. As it is, she must view them as commodities and appraise each for its resale value. Poetry! she now admonishes herself, scratching away the fossilised remnants of a silverfish on the title page. If only she had seen the circular coffee stain on the back cover. What possessed her to buy it? She knows only too well that poetry does not sell, particularly self-published work. Was she perhaps drawn by the cover, a charcoal sketch of a burnt tree with its roots in the sky? Or by the sound of the author's surname, Pepel? Turning pages almost as brown as fallen oak leaves, she notices an old train ticket, the sort that disappeared years ago. She is about to throw it away, but is checked by a whimsical thought: the book has travelled through time on this ticket, and is perhaps yet to reach its final destination. How far and how much longer will it travel on this ticket? she muses, replacing it precisely in its outline on the page.

In the chilly pre-dawn dark, as stalls were being set up and vendors of all sorts playfully cursed each other, the sentiment of several poems appealed to her and, without thinking, she dropped the book into her suitcase. Prudence, she now counsels herself. Be more circumspect in what you bring into the shop. This business requires an intuitive feel for prevailing tastes and trends, a sixth sense for books that flit from hand to hand. To survive the present recession you must be resolute with books crying for sympathy. Avoid pity that offers long-term shelter to self-published authors. The downhill road to bankruptcy is littered with good intentions. And this book of poems? It will find a place among the established poets and remain there until it is culled and taken back to a market – a painful but unavoidable practice necessitated by a chronic shortage of space.

Three years ago, when Sonya leased the vacant building between what was then a butcher and a bank (both now vacant), there were few second-hand bookshops in this part of town and business was brisk. At thirty, after seven years of teaching English to adolescents who were more interested in McDonald's food than Macbeth's words, she resigned, took out a second mortgage on the house she had bought the previous year, and became self-employed. The change was just what she needed: a spark to a withering life. Miserable in teaching from the very outset, she had doggedly persevered not in the hope that things would improve with promotions and seniority (in fact, she never applied for positions of responsibility), but more from the grim reality that she possessed no other skills or talents. Apart from the obligatory meetings and exchanges about unruly students, she had little contact with the other teachers, preferring to spend the lunch hour at her desk bent over a novel, or strolling the elmed paths of a nearby park, her face concealed by the covers of a book. Who knows, she may have endured another thirty years of quiet misery, but for the sudden and random attacks of panic she felt at the approach of her thirtieth birthday. Each attack triggered a shower of white stars that shot into her field of vision, and when they subsided a headache struck its spike between her eyes. The attacks culminated in a feeling of burnout, which made the very thought of packing her black briefcase a nightmare. Stress, her friends said. She ought to take a holiday, be more outgoing, meet someone who would sweep her off her feet. To Sonya, a holiday was nothing more than a temporary escape; as for a man, she much preferred the company of books. And that was precisely where her cure lay.

Within a week of resigning, the panic attacks stopped and she felt ready for a new life. Methodical by nature, she had studied a number of likely suburbs and shopping strips, researched the demographics of the area, spoken to shopkeepers, and settled on a single-storey building with a large front room, a smaller back room with an open fireplace, and exposed brick-work on the internal walls. The landlord, Lev Simkin, was a seventy-year-old tailor whose own shop was nearby, on the same street. After they had agreed on the terms and conditions of the lease, Simkin offered Sonya a few words of advice, speaking with a lisp. In business your best friends were paper and pen. The devil's haunt was the human mouth. Black on white, he said, venting his anger at the previous tenant, an accountant who had been charged with embezzling clients' funds and sentenced to four years' imprisonment, leaving Simkin considerably out of pocket (though thankful the fellow had not set fire to the building in a desperate attempt to conceal the evidence of his crimes).

As the shop was being painted and fitted with shelves, bookcases and a glass counter, Sonya exchanged her car for an older-model van and set out to learn her new trade. Taking notes all the time, she quickly made contacts and got a feel for the buying and selling price of different types of books. Her sources of supply were advertised in newspapers or picked up by word of mouth: markets, church fairs, second-hand stores that sold everything from clothes to furniture, garage sales of people shifting house, estates of souls who had moved from this world to the next. Having completed her homework, Sonya went about indulging her passion for books in a way she had experienced only in dreams. She bought two large, sturdy suitcases from a nearby church-run welfare store and embarked on an exhilarating shopping spree, filling the shop with cartons of books. Over several nights, losing all track of time and sustained by coffee and cigarettes, she arranged her purchases on the new pinewood shelves, transforming her life in the process. On the day the signwriter smoothed the final brush-strokes to BIBLIOPHILE on the front window (she had studied his list of scripts and decided on Gothic in gold, set in a crimson block), she stood behind the counter, happy and proud at what she had accomplished in such a short time. The smell of pine, paint and paper mingled in the shop. Neatly arranged on the new shelves according to subject and author, her books were ready for business. When the signwriter came in for payment, his white overalls spotted with colour, he complained that his was a dying craft. Computers, he said, as she counted the notes into his palm. Sure they could laser print peel-off-stick-on signs for half his cost, but such signs were impermanent, their letters wrinkled and cracked, lacking not only the body of paint but the human touch. The sign on her window would last a lifetime and draw customers, he said.

With turnover increasing each month in the first year, Sonya comfortably met her outgoings, made her repayments on the bank loan, and still had enough left over as clear profit. Comparing this to her life in teaching, she could scarcely believe her present happiness and capacity for work. Work? The word had all kinds of unpleasant associations. Her present activity was a pleasure, a passion – the profit was quite ancillary. Immersed in the business, surrendering herself to the charm of books, she felt no need to socialise with her small circle of friends. Books, novels in particular, had always been her joy. Whenever she recalled an important event or a defining moment in her life, it was always in terms of the book she had been reading at the time; not just the title and text, but the very texture of the pages, the feel of its weight, the smell of its paper. Now, surrounded by the objects of her desire, there was no need to seek happiness elsewhere.

The honeymoon lasted nearly two years, and then, almost overnight, the country's economic climate changed: the air became heavy with recession, while the more gloomy forecasters were warning of depression. Suddenly second-hand bookshops were springing up everywhere, proliferating like mushrooms in damp conditions. Two others opened on the same street, not more than a few hundred metres from her. Takings declined, falling to a level where she barely made a wage. Investigating the larger of the two shops, she was disgusted by what she found. The bearded, dishevelled proprietor had no feeling for what he sold, or he would not have housed books in such a dismal place. The fellow had no doubt taken advantage of a cheap lease (the only things flourishing in the city were the FOR SALE and FOR LEASE boards on once-thriving premises, with an obvious sale in every lease), knocked together some rough shelving, and taped a sign on the window announcing BOOKS BY THE KILO. Her disgust turned to anger. Books were not cabbages: they were not meant to be bought, consumed and discarded. A voracious reader from an early age, Sonya had always cherished her books and as a child would spend hours arranging and rearranging them on a plywood case her father had built. The permutations of colours and titles seemed endless, and each arrangement was like a new collection. At times she would read the titles aloud, as though that particular arrangement of sounds were the key to a world of adventure, the 'Open Sesame' of a story yet to be written. This place would not last long, she consoled herself. The fellow was obviously an opportunist, cashing in on the misfortune of people caught out by the recession, forced to sell not only their books but all they owned. He did not have her love of books. Her view of the shaggy proprietor was vindicated by a pile of comics in a corner of the shop. She detests them and refuses to sell them, despite their present popularity as collectors' items, and the fact that a few have acquired something of a cult following. Her dislike goes back to childhood: even then, possibly because of her advanced reading level, she considered herself above comics. They were intended for those with a feeble imagination, for whom illustrations were needed to flesh out the text and make the wonder of words come to life.

Straightening up from writing in a notepad, the fellow rotated his head a few times, jerked it this way and that, accorded her a thoughtful look, then returned to his work, scribbling as though inspired. A writer, she thought, and her antipathy toward him subsided. As an avid reader it was only natural that she had also wanted to be a writer, but her one serious attempt ended in failure. She was twenty-one and had just completed her first placement as a student–teacher. The three-week experience had gone well, at least on the surface, with an encouraging report from her supervisor; on a deeper level, however, she felt as though she were being inexorably drawn toward an abyss. Desperate, she suddenly saw writing as her means of salvation. The outcome, completed in six months, was a turgid Lolita-type novel in which a teacher was seduced by one of his students, a mischievous girl who, disliking school, decided to test the power of her newly-awakened sexual prowess in a destructive game against him. Devastated by four or five rejections from publishers, she gathered all the copies of the manuscript together with the intention of burning them. She put them in a tin drum and, wanting a quick end, sprinkled them with kerosene. But she recoiled from the match's impish flame, terrified by the finality of fire, as though she were about to cremate part of herself. Instead, she took the manuscripts and buried them in a compost heap, beneath rotting leaves, fruit and vegetables. A week later, when the paper had putrefied without trace of a word, she forked the stinking refuse into the flowerbed, amongst the flourishing roses and rhododendrons.

Sonya stares at her reflection in the O of the shop's name on the window. She has already taken four aspirin, the last two at lunchtime, and she is determined to overcome her headache through intense work. Mind over matter, she thinks, turning to the suitcases. For the next three hours, she wipes each book with a soft cloth, feels the texture of its paper, inhales its particular mustiness, flicks away the remnants of the odd insect, and blacks out the names of previous owners and prices. Then, using all the experience gained in three years of buying and selling, she prices each with a small yellow sticker on the spine.

Finally, she pushes aside the last pile of books, crushes her cigarette in the overflowing tray, blows a few flakes of ash from the glass counter, and slips the packet of aspirin from her jacket. Now, as the winter evening tightens its grip on the city and rain begins to fall, darkness presses against the front window, enhancing the reflection of ceiling-high shelves that appear not quite perpendicular, Sonya rubs her left temple and gazes at the white tablets in the hollow of her palm. Tiny eggs in a nest of wrinkles, she thinks. After a deep sigh that seems to take the stuffing out of her, she tosses the tablets into the back of her mouth and swallows them with a gulp of cold coffee. Soon the tiny eggs will hatch in her knotted stomach, releasing two angels of mercy that will spread their wings, flutter through her veins, hum their way through the labyrinth of her brain and silence the merciless demon chiselling at her temple.

A fire engine screams past, gleaming under the orange streetlights. Inside, chewing casually, a young fellow in the back seat is buttoning his coat. Stepping over books piled on the floor, she goes to the doorway, drags in the stand marked BARGAINS and locks the door. She stands there for a while, staring now at her features circumscribed by the O, now through them at the street glistening with misty rain. The two parallel lines across her forehead have become more prominent in the last year. Splashes of orange, red, green colour the bitumen. A truck groans past, shaking the front window. The reflected shelves sway, as though about to topple and bury her in books. Her eyes are a haunt for purple shadows. A cherubed clock behind the counter chimes six. Simkin will be here soon. Across the street a brightly lit FOR SALE OR LEASE board stands on the verandah of an empty shop. Next to this, the once-fiery sign PLAMEN'S GRILL has been almost obliterated by smoke. The restaurant burnt down last month, and through the gaping upper-storey windows the blackened roof-beams stand out against the night sky. The other three businesses in the row of two-storey terraces appear to be faring better. There is no shortage of customers to the betting agency; in fact, the number of gamblers appears to have increased in direct proportion to the depth of the recession. Punters are always loitering around the entrance, littering the footpath with tickets and cigarette butts. The bread shop is also doing well, providing punters with crispy French sticks and a little fresh hope between races. Last summer a body piercing salon opened in the building on the end. An artist worked on the front window for days, painting an eagle and a snake caught in a ferocious struggle.

From the gathering dark a face appears and presses between the letters on the window, smiling crookedly. Sonya turns the CLOSED sign outward. A claw with numerous rings clatters on the glass. Sonya recognises an old woman who comes to the shop from time to time to sell books and exchange gossip. Tonight, though, with the headache becoming sharper, Sonya rattles the sign at her. The woman points to an old-fashioned shopping trolley with which she roams the streets and lanes in the area, rummaging here and there, collecting anything that might be of value. The books she brings are generally of no interest to Sonya, though she is sometimes pleasantly surprised by the offering. No, she now exhorts herself. She bought several hundred this morning and sold about forty. The woman opens the trolley's cover and invites Sonya to look inside. What has she found this time? Perhaps a classic long out of print? Chastising herself, she opens the door. The woman pushes her four-wheeled trolley inside, complaining that winter was not this cold when she was a girl. She was sixteen when she got her first overcoat. Now she wears two and still cannot get warm. Chuckling, she dips into the trolley and places the books on the counter. The odour of marijuana rises from them. She found them in a back lane, all in a rubbish bag. The young people who have invaded the area respect nothing, she complains. What with their pink hair, torn jeans, and pins through their noses there is no telling boys from girls. They live like gypsies. Six months here, six there. And every time they move, out go half their belongings. They have it too easy, she scowls. Things were different back in the old days when honest families lived in this area. People had respect in those days – respect for work, for their appearance, for their belongings.

Rubbing her temple, Sonya inspects the offering at a glance: novels, books on the occult, three or four battered texts on mathematics. She already has several copies of Dostoyevsky's *Crime and Punishment* and one of Tolstoy's *Resurrection*. Should she buy the ones on the counter? They are in good condition. The woman smiles and adjusts her unevenly buttoned overcoat. A few drops of rain flick onto Sonya's hands as the woman shakes a red umbrella. She selects seven or eight titles and pushes the others back. Her wrinkled face contracting in disappointment, the woman tosses the unwanted books into the trolley. Sonya rings open the cash register, scrambles out a few coins and drops them in an extended palm that closes like a mousetrap. Outside, the woman opens her umbrella, waits for a break in the traffic, and hobbles across the colourful street, where she straightens her overcoat and enters the betting agency.

Sonya removes the day's takings from the register and goes to the back room. She prods the dozing fire and throws in a few scraps of black, damp wood. Thank heaven for aspirin: the pain in her head is not as strong. Simkin is due any minute. Sitting in a faded armchair with protruding springs, she prepares the rent money. A few dollars short. She should have listened to reason and not opened for the old woman. Now she will have to squirm in explaining the shortfall to Simkin. She lights a cigarette, leans back and closes her eyes. No sooner does she feel a tingle coursing through her body than she starts and sits upright. Voices again. Is it due to the headaches she has been having? Is it her imagination playing tricks? Or the fact that business is slow and she is spending more time alone? It has happened a few times in recent months. At first, nothing more than the rustle of a page, as though someone were leafing through a book on the other side of the shelves. Had a customer entered without her knowledge? It turned out to be nothing more than a draught sneaking in through the gap under the front door. Then the sounds became a whisper coming from the back room, where she keeps drama, poetry and religion. When she went to check, the whispers gave way to sap wheezing in the fireplace. She began to play classical music when things were too quiet. This dispelled the sounds, but only temporarily, for they returned with more distinctness than before.

She goes to the front – nothing. Cars swish past on the wet road. She checks the door and finds it securely locked. But slipped under the door is a large gold envelope with her name handwritten in a neat blue script. No address, no stamp. Is that what made her start, the sender shuffling at the door? She is about to open it, when Simkin appears and taps on the window with the handle of his umbrella. Pressing the envelope to her breasts, she opens for the old tailor, with his familiar measuring tape around his neck. As they walk to the back room, he inspects the shop, darting glances from under eyebrows well overdue for a trim. At their first meeting he informed Sonya that he preferred to deal directly with his tenants, rather than relying on agents, who more often than not did very little to justify their commission. And so at six, on the sixth of each month, he came not just to collect the rent, but to judge for himself the state of his tenant's business. Sonya recently exercised her option and signed a new lease for a further three years, though not before Simkin interrogated her at length about her ability to meet commitments. Times were bad, he said. Businesses were closing all over the place. Things would get worse. He had seen it before in his fifty years since coming to this country from Bulgaria. Business was like musical chairs: while people were running around, happily wheeling and dealing, there was a seat for all. But when bankers and politicians pulled the plug and the music stopped, people found themselves not only without a chair, but without trousers and backsides. He had been burnt a couple of times himself: a tenant's once-thriving business fails, they declare themselves bankrupt, and the poor landlord is left with an empty building and a lease not worth the paper it is written on.

They sit in front of the fire and exchange small talk about winter's sudden onset. They have missed out on autumn this year, says Simkin, playing with the end of the measuring tape. It is his favourite season. The sound of maple leaves scuttling over bitumen reminds him of Bulgaria. As a child in Sofia before the Second World War he would run through the quilted blanket of poplar leaves covering the cobbled streets. From their numerous chats, Sonya has learnt that Lev Simkin was born in Sofia, where his father and grandfather, who had originally come from Salonika, were also tailors. His ancestors, Spanish Jews, or Sephardic Jews as they were more commonly called, had been forced by the Inquisition to leave Catalonia. Knowing of their talents as craftsmen, merchants and scholars, the Ottoman Sultan Bayezid the Second invited the refugees to settle throughout the Turkish empire. His grandfather had a prosperous business in Salonika, making fezzes for Jews, Muslims and Christians. In those days if men wanted to advance in their trade or profession, they had to show their loyalty to the sultan, which meant wearing a fez with a black tassel. The fez-making business declined with the fall of the Ottoman Empire. When the Turks were driven from Salonika in 1912, grandfather Simkin moved the family and settled in Sofia. He must have had a sixth sense of what would happen thirty years later. In 1943 the large Jewish population of Salonika was rounded up by the Nazis and sent to the concentration camps. For some reason the Bulgarian government, an ally of the Germans, interceded on behalf of its Jewish citizens and saved them from the gas chambers. When the fascists were defeated and the communists took control of Bulgaria, the Simkins left for France, from where, with only a bundle under his arm, the twenty-year-old Lev Simkin came here.

The springs squeal as he sits more upright. And business? he asks in a deeper tone. Are books selling? They are moving, Sonya replies, giving him the rent. He licks a finger and flicks deftly through the notes. The envelope on her lap, Sonya studies the handwriting, but is unable to put a face to it. Simkin's eyebrows fall, his lower lip glistens. The rent is short. She is quick to apologise. She will make it up next month, or tomorrow if he prefers. He frowns. A calendar month is a long time in business. Anything could happen in this uncertain climate. Would he like a few books instead? Simkin closes his eyes and raises his chin. Is business really all right? he asks, twisting the ends of his eyebrows. Her right palm raised to the fire, Sonya swears that books are moving, not as well as she would like, but enough for the outgoings. Simkin nods and reminds her of his losses from the accountant. Sonya tells him that her takings have suffered a setback due to other bookshops opening in the area. They will not last long, she assures him. They are nothing more than fly-by-nights. He nods, unconvinced. How is your business faring? she continues. He points out that times of recession benefit him. People cannot afford new clothes so they alter and mend what they have. Not only this, the young people now moving into the area are very fond of buying recycled clothes, which of course require mending and alteration. Our businesses are similar, says Sonya. You clothe the body and I clothe the soul with ideas. He muses a moment, then takes out a receipt book, scribbles a few things, tears out a page and extends it to her. The shortfall? It can wait until next month, he says, standing. At the front door he wishes her good night, with the hope for a better month to come. She clicks the lock, checks it several times, turns off the lights in the front of the shop, and hurries to the back room.

Opening the envelope with a paper knife, Sonya counts nine handwritten sheets. On the first, in capitals executed by a hand sure in the use of a fountain pen, she reads, THE FIRST DIALOGUE. She turns quickly to the last page – neither an author's name nor an explanatory note. Perplexed, she sits and prods the fire. The textured pages are unlined, but the writing sits perfectly horizontal; the words have a gentle forward slope, while the spacing between them is uniform. At arm's length the script might easily be mistaken for the work of a computer – a printout of an italicised font. Examining the first page under the bare overhead bulb, she can discern the texture of ink in each letter, the movement of the nib, the slight tremor (revealing as a fingerprint) in the hand of the anonymous author. It suddenly strikes Sonya that the writing is so meticulous the author could not possibly have produced more than one copy. But why send the original? And in such a way that it might easily be irretrievably lost? A serious writer would have used a word processor and sent a printout, or at least a photocopy. Has the author mistakenly sent the original in place of the copy? Will he or she realise the mistake and come to the shop first thing in the morning? Enough speculation. She lights a cigarette, draws deeply, and blows the smoke aside. The answer to the mystery might lie in the work itself. And suddenly she feels the familiar tingle of excitement at the knowledge that the front door is locked and she is deliciously alone, without commitment, free at last to enjoy the voluptuous pleasure of reading, to surrender fully to the body of the text resting on her lap.

As your itinerary permitted only twelve days in this sprawling city, you decided to spend the first in the famous Museum of Human Thought. No, it's not a library, but a vast network of annexes housing paintings, statues and countless glass cases containing manuscripts, first editions, and personal belongings of great thinkers. After eight hours of wandering through Kafkaesque corridors and plodding up and down Escheresque staircases, you took yet another wrong turn and found yourself in a room full of busts and statues of Jewish thinkers. Exhausted, feeling faint from hunger and heat, you sat on a wooden bench opposite a barred window. You had seen enough for one day, and now your only thought was to revive yourself for the long journey out of the museum and back to the pensione. Drinking the last mouthful of mineral water, you shoved the plastic bottle into your backpack and looked around the room. A female attendant in a blue uniform was sitting on a stool in the corner furthest from you. She was about thirty, but her slight build gave her a girlish look that seemed incongruous with her position of responsibility. The pallor of her face was contrasted by short black hair and the almost horizontal line of her black eyebrows. Her eyes seemed to have a permanent squint, and her thin lips were tightly sealed. As you were the only other person in the room, she examined you with a sharp look and lowered her eyes to an open book resting on her lap. A wave of languor coursed its way up from your throbbing feet and spread through your body. Outside, excited swallows were slashing the faded, denim-blue sky with their black wings. Sunlight was losing its grip on domes and bell-towers, slipping from terracotta roofs and stucco walls, releasing louvred window-shutters.

A bronze bust of Karl Marx, like that above his grave in the Highgate Cemetery, stood on a pedestal to the left of the bench; to the right, a full-size replica of Michelangelo's Moses. His horned head turned to the side, Moses was staring fiercely out the window. Marx looked directly ahead with a dour expression.

Feeling as though unsinewed from your body, you stretched out on the bench, using the backpack as a pillow.

The attendant was too absorbed in her book to bother with your impropriety. You would rest for a few minutes, long enough for the lethargy to pass, then go. Outside, swallows were twittering ...

– I was beginning to think this moment would never come, says Marx.

He moves his grizzly head from side to side, as if a bronze collar has just been removed from his neck. Moses turns slowly from the window.

– God has finally seen to it, he replies, with a pronounced lisp.

– You attribute too much to God, my friend.

– More and more each day.

– The world has changed since you led the Jews out of Egypt.

– Man is still man, Karl, and God is ...

– Still the boss.

– I would have said: I am that I am.

– God's not responsible for this conversation, Moses. If we must give thanks, it should be to this young tourist, whose fatigue has made this moment possible.

– You reduce everything to your lowest denominator – man.

– We're the tourist's daydream.

– Nonsense!

– Keep your voice down, please. If the tourist wakes, it will be the end of our conversation, and we may have to wait another hundred years for a suitable go-between.

Moses muses with a frown, pressing the tablets closer to his body with a bare right arm, while twirling his beard with a powerful right index finger. Marx looks around, pondering the tessellated tiles on the floor.

– *Who is this tourist?* asks Moses.
– *That's the Australian flag on the backpack.*
– *Australia,* reflects Moses. *They say the wilderness there is even harsher than the deserts we experienced in the Passover.*
– *That wilderness would've tested your faith.*

Chuckling, Marx turns his head to a window overlooking the capital city, the streets bustling with commerce and traffic.

– *They call it the Lucky Country,* says Moses.
– *Migrants and refugees have flocked to it.*
– *Seems deserts and Promised Lands go together.*
– *That's one way of looking at it,* Marx nods.
– *I'm tempted to wake our friend and ask about Australia.*
– *You'll become a block of marble if you do.*
– *I want to test your theory.*

Turning from the window, Marx focuses on Moses again.

– *Let's finish our conversation first.*

With the eyes of an eagle Moses gazes out the window, over the rooftops, at an aeroplane moving across the desolate sky, bringing more tourists to the capital. Marx observes him for a moment, his beetle-black eyes partially concealed by bushy, overhanging brows.

– *You're always looking into the distance, my friend. What do you see out there?*
– *All right, Karl, let's talk.*

He places the tablets on his lap and brings his left foot beside his right, assuming a more relaxed position.

– *That's more like it,* beams Marx. *I've been staring at you for the past hundred years, and that left foot of yours has reminded me of a sprinter poised in the starting-blocks for a hundred-metre dash.*
– *It's a habit from the old days.*
– *As for the tablets, I've cudgelled my brain to work out*

whether they're the first lot or the second. I've studied your expression, your gestures, the folds of your robes – all to no avail.

– The third lot.

– There's no mention of a third lot in Exodus.

– I smashed the first lot in anger and disappointment at the sight of the Golden Calf. The second lot, identical to the first in all respects, haven't been seen since they were placed in the Ark of the Covenant. These, the third lot, also identical to the first, were chiselled by Michelangelo.

– I'm perplexed by what exactly Michelangelo had wanted to express when he depicted you in that ambiguous moment.

– I can't speak for the sculptor.

– Did he want to show you the first time you came down from the mountain with the tablets or the second?

– Let's not waste time on idle questions, Karl.

– You're right, Moses. Let's consider our similarities.

– Shouldn't we commence with our differences?

– We'll consider those later.

– Very well. We're both Jews.

– We've both wandered around.

– Both of us have been moved by a vision.

– Neither of us set foot in the Promised Land.

– Yes, Karl, perhaps that's where we're most alike. God directed me to the top of Mount Nebo, pointed out the Promised Land, and said that I would never set foot there.

– And I, Moses, never set foot in a communist state.

They contemplate the irony of their respective situations for a moment.

– I have accepted my disappointment, says Marx. It was the work of chance or blind fate. But you, Moses, don't you feel cheated by your God?

– My work was done, Karl. I wasn't needed in the Promised Land. My role was that of a guide, not a founder of countries and cities.

– I've never been able to relate to your God. He was far too unpredictable, too irascible, too inconsiderate of the human condition. I mean, take that incident outside the inn, just after God had chosen you to lead the Jews out of Egypt. We have it on your authority that God wanted to kill you. Why did He turn against you like that, Moses?

– Was that the incident with my wife and son?

– Have you forgotten it?

– It happened a long time ago, Karl. My memory's very misty about certain things.

– It's in your book of Exodus, chapter four, verse twenty-four.

– I haven't opened those books of mine in ages.

– I've read that bewildering passage so many times, I know it by heart. 'And it came to pass by the way of the inn, that the Lord met him, and sought to kill him. Then Zipporah took a sharp stone and cut off the foreskin of her son, and cast it at his feet, and said, "Surely a bloody husband art thou to me".'

– Yes, yes, I remember the incident now, and in particular the look of reproach on my wife's face.

– Did God really want to kill you, or is it all symbolic?

Moses ponders a moment. The broad span of his forehead creases with deep lines.

– Well, I suppose God must have been angry with me. You see, I was still new to my mission, still uncertain of God's expectations. At the same time, I was also a recent husband and father. Family life and missionary zeal don't mix well at all. I suppose God was angry with me because

I'd allowed my family to interfere with divine purpose. In any case, there were no more threats once I sent my wife and child back to her father.

— Yes, sighs Marx. A family can be a burden to the visionary mind. I could have publicised my ideas more widely but for the responsibilities toward my family. That's not to say I didn't love Jenny and the children. No, it wasn't their fault they had to share me with my work. An angry God wasn't breathing down my neck, so I never sent them back to Germany. They travelled with me wherever I went.

His head sinks forward, his beard fans across his chest. Absent-mindedly, Marx continues as though talking to himself.

— Jenny was a very patient woman. We lived in debt all our married life. We moved from one boarding house to another, with one landlord after another threatening us with eviction. Three of our children died because I wasn't able to provide a comfortable home. Little Edgar was six. The poor boy shrivelled away before my very eyes, and I could do nothing for him. Guido and Franziska died as infants. Am I to blame for the death of my children, Moses? Should I have given up my political theories and found a job in some English factory to provide for them? I was driven by an idea, Moses, just as you were driven by your God. I wanted a better future for all children, not just for my own. The family is so often the deepest pitfall for idealists and Utopians. Too many minds soon enough forget the welfare of mankind and direct their thoughts exclusively to the welfare of their families. The ideal is replaced by the particular; the future is replaced by present concerns. No, Moses, I couldn't abandon my work, even though my struggle against capitalism cost me three children. You know, I enshrined those children in my heart. I saw them as *martyrs for a better world. Their death gave me the strength and courage to continue my work.*

A sigh wheezes through his whiskers as he bites his lower lip. Moses adjusts his sandal-strap. Marx straightens his stocky shoulders, as though throwing off a weight that has waylaid him.

— The future demands its sacrifice, he nods.

— I've thought deeply about your work, Karl.

— And I yours.

— There are great differences between us.

— There's only one difference: God.

— You're right. God sets us apart as distinctly as substance and shadow.

— Who's the substance and who's the shadow?

— God is the sun.

— Let's leave God aside for a moment and consider our respective work from a rational point of view.

— But ...

— Please, Moses, bear with me while I outline my impression of your work. The Jews were an oppressed people in Egypt. Suffering in servitude, they baked bricks and carted stones for Pharaoh's conceited building projects. You witnessed the injustice and sought to free your people. Put in a nutshell, you wanted to rescue your people from slavery and lead them to a place where they could exercise their free will and develop their own national and religious identity. Do you agree?

— With reservation.

— My aspirations, Moses, were exactly the same as yours. Change a few names and it becomes evident that the circumstances which prevailed in my time were identical to the circumstances which moved you to action. I mean, 'Jews' can be replaced with 'proletariat', 'slavery' with 'exploitation',

'Pharaoh' with 'capitalism', 'Promised Land' with 'communist state'. You sought to liberate three or four hundred thousand Jews; I, hundreds of millions of oppressed people all over the world.

– We can't leave God out of our discussion, Karl.

– We worked and died in the name of freedom, my friend. In the end God makes no difference.

– That's precisely where we differ, Karl. There's no freedom without God. Those who espouse that kind of freedom run the risk of replacing one form of slavery with another.

– All right, Moses, let's talk about your God. I suppose you're my forerunner in many ways, not least in the age-old question of God. The Jews had lived in Egypt for generations, during which time they had come under the influence of Egyptian polytheism. I'd argue that their perception of divinity was identical to that of the Egyptians, a fact supported by the incident with the Golden Calf. And then you appeared on the scene, full of the fire that rose from the burning bush, your ears still echoing with the voice of God, who announced himself as 'I am that I am'. You opposed Egyptian polytheism and idolatry and advocated one unknown, unseen God. All great movements arise as a reaction to the existing order of things: your monotheism could only have arisen in a place like Egypt. I see your greatness, Moses, not in the fact that you led a tribe of ragged, dusty Jews across the desert, but in that you offered them a new perception of divinity and a radically different explanation of reality. And how did the Jews come upon the idea of one God?

– Revelation.

– Reaction, my friend. The great law of motion and change. I would argue that your monotheism dates back to Akhenaten, the pharaoh who reacted against the Egyptian *pantheon and worshipped the solar disc as the one God. Akhenaten's cult may have been short-lived, but the seed of his idea spread and found root in the heart of men like Abraham.*

— You're very eloquent, Karl.

— I addressed countless gatherings in my time.

— My lips were never circumcised, if you'll pardon the expression. I've always had this speech impairment. As you know, God chose Aaron to be my mouthpiece.

— It's precisely this sort of detail that makes your God a contradiction to the rational mind. I mean, if He could turn your rod into a snake, why didn't He repair your speech defect so that you could transmit His words directly to the people? Why did He use Aaron as an intermediary, thereby having His words twice removed from the source?

— You're forever questioning, Karl.

— My skull's a cave full of writhing questions.

— I could well ask why Engels chose to be your supporter and co-worker? Why his abundant material resources were needed to help promote your ideas and theories? You see, I could continue asking why without end.

Marx nods, conceding the point.

— I see it this way, Moses says, and the powerful sinews in his neck are like the strings of a harp. I maintain that God chose Aaron to assist me in His work, while you would say that good fortune brought Engels to your aid. Simply a change of terms, as you put it before: chance in place of God.

— You're my forerunner, Moses. You sought to lead people away from the worship of Golden Calves, to belief in an unseen God.

— And you, Karl, sought to lead mankind from one God to a state of godlessness.

— *I carried your work to its logical conclusion.*
— *Godlessness was never my work.*
— *I'm your legitimate heir, Moses. I've brought to completion what you commenced thousands of years ago. You took mankind from polytheism to monotheism, and I ...*
— *From monotheism to nihilism.*
— *We both sought to free mankind, my friend. You gave the Jews the abstract idea of a God without form, whose name was I am. I've simply extended your abstraction to the point where there's no need to refer to God. The human mind has evolved since your time; it seeks a freedom commensurate with its present state of consciousness. I've proposed a freedom those ancient Jews would have found impossible to comprehend, and yet this freedom would have been impossible without you. God is a concept, a product of the mind, an idea that is constantly evolving, just as ideas about the physical world evolve. Consider the ideas of that Jew over there.*

With a sideward nod he indicates the corner opposite the attendant. Moses looks over his shoulder at a glassy bust of Einstein staring dreamily into space.

— *His abstract equations and theories, which evolved from the finger-counting of your time, have presented a new view of the universe. Gravity is no longer gravity, but an attribute of the curvature of space.*
— *Does it really matter whether a thing falls because of gravity or the curvature of space? What difference did it make to the people of Hiroshima whether the bomb fell because of gravity or curvature? And what's the relevance of your new physics to those people still suffering the after-effects of the bomb's fall?*
— *I could well ask you the same question, Moses. Where's the truth of your God to the millions of Jews killed by the*

Nazis? How could your God have allowed such a thing to happen? In fact, doesn't the holocaust render your God obsolete? Isn't it reason enough for rational minds to recoil from the idea of God?

– The holocaust occurred precisely because the Nazis turned away from God, proclaiming themselves the super-race, the supermen, the gods of the new order. That's the inevitable result of your nihilism, Karl. In the absence of God, man aspires to the role of God, or the state is worshipped as God – either way, the consequences are catastrophic. Stalin sacrificed millions of Russians on the altar of the communist state. Pol Pot did the same in Cambodia. In more recent times we've had the atrocities in Tiananmen Square and Romania. The list goes on, Karl. No, there's no humanity or freedom without God.

– And what of wars in the name of God? The holy destruction by the Crusades? The blessed bloodbaths between Jews, Muslims and Christians?

– Wars are fought in the name of God, not in the spirit of God. The Egyptian priests used idols to subjugate people; leaders today use names for the same end. Perhaps true freedom lies in going beyond names.

– In going beyond God?

– God, Allah, Yahweh.

– Perhaps a global God.

– I would have said universal.

– Let's be honest, Moses, there's no freedom in either the name of God or the spirit of God. Consider the free world, as the West referred to itself during the Cold War, where your God is supposedly most at home. This free world retards and oppresses the so-called Third World in order to feed its insatiable appetite for consumer products. Economic slavery –

that's what your God relies on to maintain a comfortable mansion. The situation is no different from the plight of the Jews in your time. Pharaoh's whims were realised by countless broken backs. I'm amazed that millions of people make pilgrimages to the Pyramids each year and stand before them in reverential awe. The truth is they are monuments of horrible violence, testaments to gross inhumanity, the ancient equivalents of Auschwitz.

– That's a valid analogy, Karl, but it doesn't address the fact that the Berlin Wall has come down and communism in Russia and Eastern Europe has failed the people.

Marx's shoulders fall and a painful expression creases his face as though a blow to the stomach has snatched his breath.

– I can't help thinking of my children.
– They're in God's care.
– Was their death for nothing?
– Communism is dead, Karl, not their spirit.

With the red sun now just above the domes and rooftops, evening light streams in through the barred window, covering the statues and busts in the room with a soft glow, making them more life-like. Marx looks thoughtfully around the room, turning his head so that his shadow sometimes glides over the tourist on the bench, sometimes disappears in the larger-than-life shadow of the man of God.

– Communism is not dead, he says.

There is now a deeper resonance in his voice, as though his words are coming directly from his chest, bypassing his larynx.

– It was first practised a little over eighty years ago, Moses. And in China, where it's still robust, a mere fifty. In historical terms, communism is still in its teething stage.

People have yet to grasp it in an ideal sense. They still consider it foreign, as going against human nature, something imposed from without. But, in time, when capitalism consumes itself to death as it inevitably must, the truth of communism will triumph and people will embrace it as the new God, and through it build a heaven on earth.

— In an economic sense?
— In a human sense.
— What about spiritually?
— That comes from physical freedom.
— You still believe in your theories?
— As I believe my children's death wasn't in vain. There's no other salvation for humanity. Though my eyes well with tears at the present chaos in Russia, I'm certain it's only a temporary setback. In fact, it's analogous to the problem you encountered convincing the Jews to accept your ideals. As your memory appears vague on certain points allow me to remind you of a few things written by your own hand. When you first asked Pharaoh to allow your people to go three days into the wilderness to worship their God, he reacted by making life even more difficult for them. Suddenly they had to gather their own straw for the manufacture of bricks, a chore which had been done by others. The Jews admonished you for disturbing the status quo, which at least had been bearable. And even when you'd parted the Red Sea and led them into the safety of the wilderness, they complained to you of hunger and thirst. They would have returned to the flesh-pots of Egypt and forgotten the Promised Land, if not for the manna that fell from the sky. Finally, when you went up to the mountain, they became frightened, like children left in the dark, and crafted the Golden Calf because they thought you'd abandoned them. They would have reverted to idolatry if you hadn't come

back with the tablets and chastised them for their foolishness. People haven't grasped my ideal, Moses. The majority are still in the wilderness, somewhere between Egypt and the Promised Land. The people in the countries you mentioned are experiencing the same anguish that led your people to raise the Golden Calf. You see, my friend, there's still a tendency to prefer the security of slavery, to the uncertainty of freedom. My ideal is the only answer to the question of human freedom. It will lead mankind from the bewildering chaos of the present and into the Promised Land — a state without slavery, human exploitation, God. Religion, as the right arm of capitalism, imposes the last and most subtle form of servitude. Mankind's ultimate freedom will come when all religions have been swept from the face of the good earth.

A quick reflex by Moses saves the tablets slipping from under his arm. Frowning, he opens them and reads to himself for a moment. Marx smiles wryly, shaking his ponderous head.

— You've moved a long way from your forefathers, says Moses, closing the stone tablets.

— My forefathers?

— The Jewish people, the Jewish faith.

— I renounced my forefathers because of their God, and I object to some of today's Jews on the grounds of their collusion with capitalism.

— You sound anti-Semitic.

— Anti-Semitic, anti-Christian, anti-Muslim.

— And you, a Jew?

— I know the Jewish mind from within.

— And the holocaust?

— Perhaps those ancient Greeks were right: a person's fate is determined by their character. The Jews have always *proudly and defiantly considered themselves the chosen race. When the Nazis rose to power and proclaimed themselves the chosen race, the conclusion was inevitable: the world couldn't accommodate two chosen races.*

— So, Moses sighs, the faith of the Jewish people is responsible for the holocaust?

— You tell me, Moses. Why did the holocaust happen if the Jews are the chosen race and not just a self-proclaimed chosen race? If there is a God, and if the Jews are His chosen people, why didn't He prevent the holocaust? After all, we have it on your authority that He opened the Red Sea and destroyed Pharaoh's vast army. Why then didn't He make the Reichstag collapse on Hitler and his henchmen? I see in the holocaust indisputable proof of the non-existence of God. In fact, the holocaust should mark the definitive death of God. If we're to learn anything from the holocaust, it should be that the idea of God also went up in smoke in those gas-chambers. The crucifixion of a Jew established one calendar; the extermination of five million Jews should establish another calendar — one that counts the years from the death of God and the beginning of man's freedom.

Moses turns to the window, rubs his horned brow, then fixes Marx with the same fierce look he must have directed at the Jews when he came down from the mountain and witnessed their recalcitrance.

— And yet, Karl, what you're advocating hasn't happened. It's been more than fifty years since the holocaust and the Jews haven't buried God together with their dead. The Nazis have been destroyed, while the Jews are still flourishing in their faith. I see that as indisputable proof of God's existence.

— And the five million deaths? How does your God justify them, Moses?

– *I can't speak for God.*

– *Unless He chooses to speak through you?*

– *He hasn't spoken to me in a long time.*

– *Because He no longer exists.*

– *What about these?* asks Moses, spreading his large, veined hand and laying it flat on the tablets.

– *Mohammed claimed he wrote the entire Koran on instructions from the angel Gabriel. Joseph Smith's* Book of Mormon *is supposed to be a transcription of certain golden tablets revealed to him by the angel of God. Who does one believe, Moses? Which alphabet does God use? Hebrew? Arabic? English?*

– *So, you'd destroy everything I worked for?*

– *Just as you destroyed polytheism.*

– *And in place of God you'd establish the Great Nothing.*

– *Humanity.*

– *I don't possess your eloquence, Karl. I can't defend God with words.*

– *There's nothing to defend. God's imperialism is over. The time has passed when religion made people senseless with its opium-like qualities.*

– *And in place of religion people are turning to real opium.*

– *That's capitalism exploiting the vulnerable.*

– *I'm not an economist. You see things in terms of gold, while I see them in terms of God. The Jews wavered in the wilderness; they made the Golden Calf and worshipped it with song and dance, just as they had done in Egypt. But the word of God prevailed, and they reached the Promised Land.*

– *The Promised Land! How permanent was it? After the Romans and the Ottomans, the Jews were scattered throughout Europe and the world. The holocaust wouldn't have occurred* if those early Jews had really found their Promised Land. And now, after the holocaust, the Jews have found their Promised Land once again, to which they're migrating from everywhere. But it's a very uncertain Promised Land, surrounded by nations making territorial claims. How long will it stand before the Jews are scattered again? History is full of recurrences.

– History is all retrospective, Karl. As a Jew, I've no sense of historical time, therefore no feeling for what you call history. I see events teleologically – in terms of final causes, not temporal effects.

– Final causes, or final solutions?

The attendant folds the corner of page 136, closes the book and walks towards them with quiet, rubber-soled steps.

– We haven't got much time, Moses. She's coming to wake our young tourist.

– We've got all the time in the world, Karl.

– It may be another hundred years before we speak to each other again.

– A hundred, a thousand, it makes no difference.

Marx looks anxiously over his shoulder.

– One more thing before she wakes our young friend.

– What?

– Those horns on your brow – what do they mean?

Moses rubs the two small protrusions and smiles.

– They're ...

The swallows were twittering outside.

Closing time. The attendant was standing over you, clutching the book to her breast. You sat up and rubbed your eyes. She went back to her position in the corner. Harnessing yourself with the backpack, you felt refreshed, ready for the journey to your pensione. A red tinge appeared over the rooftops and swallows darted across the barred window. You looked *at your watch: barely ten minutes since you lay down. Did you dream? You weren't sure, though it felt as if you had. Walking out with the spring in your step considerably revived, you stopped before the attendant and, without thinking, asked how far she'd read. The look in her brown eyes was homely as chestnuts on a winter's night. She opened to the page folded in the right corner.*

Page 136, she said, warily. You thanked her with a smile and left, intent on a hearty meal and a good night's sleep, before setting off early for your next destination.

Sonya throws her cigarette into the fireplace, at a small flame struggling to free itself from a black nail bent almost into a question mark. Feeling the bond paper's texture, she taps the sheets on her thighs and hugs them to her breasts. She is now more perplexed than before. What is she to make of this? Why has it been sent to her? It is an intelligent piece, and well written, but she is not a literary critic. For her the pleasure of reading lies not in analysis and commentary but in the exchange between text and thought, the engagement between eyes and words, the contact between page and fingertips. What was the author's intention in addressing this to her? And what is she to do with it now that it has been read? If it were a book she could place it on a shelf, but a nine-page, handwritten short story?

In glancing up at her faint reflection dwarfed in a bronze ornamental pot on the mantelpiece, she shuffles the sheets and looks down to find the passage describing the attendant. She reads it again, slowly, and this time each word adds to a growing sense of self-recognition. Suddenly the resemblance is unmistakable. She is the attendant! A feeling of disorientation unsteadies her for a moment. Why has she been placed in that setting? Is the author an acquaintance? Or a customer who has studied her furtively from between the shelves? There are several writers among her regular customers. Is one of them playing a game? Teasing her with all this unnecessary mystery? Is there something in the tourist that might provide a clue to the author's identity? She shuffles the sheets again: apart from youth, there are no other distinguishing features, not even a reference to gender. But perhaps the mystery will be resolved tomorrow, when the author, realising his or her mistake, comes to ask for the manuscript.

the SECOND dialogue

Autumn is the cruellest season, reflects Sonya, gazing through the letters of BIBLIOPHILE. The elms along the street are tattered, threadbare, with limbs black from recent rain. Yellow, brown and red leaves swirl in a dance of death. Like mischievous streetkids they gather and loiter in doorways, harass pedestrians, rush happily in the wake of speeding cars. Freedom comes at a price, she muses, for both leaves and flesh.

   A week has passed and no one has come to claim the manuscript. She has read it closely several times, looking for a key to its mystery, and with each reading she has been drawn deeper into the text, as though her presence as the attendant is more than incidental. If nothing else, the intrigue has helped take her mind off the recession. She has been observing her regular customers more intently, looking for a hint of the anonymous author: a tell-tale glimmer in the eyes or quaver in the voice. She has even initiated conversation, letting slip a detail or phrase from the story in the hope of evincing a reaction, but nothing.

In the last few days she has focused on the newer customers: one may be a writer who has just moved into the area, visited the shop once or twice, and found a suitable model in her for the attendant of the story. The area has attracted many end-of-the-millennium existentialists, men and women in their twenties and thirties with earrings, studs, shaved heads, tattoos. Quite a few have visited the shop in the past week, all looking like avant-garde artists and writers. Conscious of order and cleanliness, she cringes at the dishevelled look of these customers. A lover of books, she is often reluctant to part with her dearest possessions – a necessity that has always irked her, but more so now that so many of her customers have this god-forsaken look about them. Sometimes she comes close to refusing a sale not only from an attachment to her books, but because of a customer's grubby appearance. She always breathes a little easier when her books are bought by fellow bibliophiles – people who never crack a spine or dog-ear a page, who shelve their books in a quiet, dry, ordered place, and for whom reading is as necessary as eating. Profit is not everything. She prices her books fairly (too cheaply according to some customers), and nothing gives her more satisfaction than knowing her children will find a place in a good home.

She brushes cigarette ash from the counter and greets Lou Cape, a regular customer and writer of humorous short stories. His last visit to the shop was over a week ago. Is he the author of the manuscript? Experimenting with a new style? Testing his work on her? Morose, in his mid-forties, he takes off a tweed cap, combs back his thinning hair, and begins his usual complaint in a voice bleaker than a crow's call from a winter tree. His wife of more than twenty years left him a few months ago, accusing him of being domineering and repressive. Taking their two children, she wanted nothing more to do with him, and their only form of communication regarding children, property and divorce has been through fax and email. Frank in his condemnation of her, he has shown Sonya several faxes and even downloaded some of their email correspondence as proof of the woman's callousness. Despite the turmoil in his life, he has continued to work on his stories. Better to write than be written about in the obituary column of the newspaper, he said, with a chuckle that sounded like footsteps on crushed rock.

After an outburst at the treachery of women, followed by a blast at a legal system that regards men as monsters, he concludes with a condemnation of feminists, whose hysterical cries for freedom are destroying family life, as surely as the wild Bacchic women in Euripides's play destroyed the family of the unfortunate Pentheus. A shadow settles on his face and the bony plate over his broad forehead becomes even more prominent. The recession is hitting publishers, he frowns. A recent collection of his short stories has been rejected by two publishing houses, not on literary merit, but simply because the genre is not selling well. Market surveys have shown that people prefer longer fiction, with a comic touch, perhaps in order to forget the depressing economic climate. Taking the hint, he has started work on a novel about an eccentric public servant who acuses his superiors of subverting his efforts at promotion.

But Cape is finding the longer genre difficult. He holds up his left thumb and thrusts a gnawed fingernail toward Sonya, as proof of his frustration. He curses the day he decided to be a writer. Look, he says, removing his cap. Head like a half-plucked chicken, bags full of darkness under his eyes, and he could show her a case of haemorrhoids to compare with the arse of Mount Etna, for which the only relief is to sit on the toilet for hours, with the laptop on his knees. He sleeps badly, suffers headaches, has no social life. Why? To entertain others, make them laugh and lull them to sleep at the end of the day – in short, so that others may derive pleasure from his pain. Since starting on the novel, he has thought deeply about the relationship between writer and reader. Perhaps the writer – the one driven not by money but by necessity – is a kind of martyr, sacrificing health and happiness so others might have a little joy in their lives. The true writer is a tragic hero, often hiding behind a comic mask.

He envies Sonya. He was a reader, too, as a younger man. In fact, he weighed his decision to marry against his love of books. He took Aristotle's *Ethics* on his honeymoon. In bed in the hotel room, absorbed by Book Ten – 'Pleasure and the Life of Happiness' – he glanced at his new wife in turning the page, hoping she would take a little longer at the dressing-table, where she sat in a lilac-coloured camisole, removing her mascara after a night at the theatre. With a few pages left, he was racing to finish the chapter when, having revived her fading perfume, she slipped in beside him. She lay still for a moment as he followed Aristotle's lively thoughts expressed in supple prose. It was only when she turned on her side and caressed his thigh that he felt compelled to put down the book, closing it on a fragrant bookmark she had bought for his birthday. And once again he curses her treachery and laments at how many more books he would have read if he had not married. Since becoming a full-time writer, he has had to forego reading because there is simply no time. If only books were sold with a package of time on the front cover: three hours for *Heart of Darkness*, two full days for *War and Peace*. He still enjoys visiting bookshops, loves to browse and perhaps select a dozen books, though in the end he will leave with one or two, more often than not with none, depressed by the thought that there is not enough time to read them. And he quotes a passage from Ecclesiastes: 'To the making of books there is no end and study is a weariness to the flesh.' But he disagrees with the wise Solomon. The line should have been: Writing is a weariness to the flesh, while reading is its sustenance.

When Sonya draws a stack of books closer to her and rustles the pack of yellow stickers for pricing, Cape takes the hint and moves off to a back shelf containing the Classics. He is not the anonymous author, she concludes. And his frankness? Is it simply a case of her being a sympathetic listener? Some men are better able to express their emotions to female acquaintances than close male friends. But there is something else beneath Cape's churlishness, something more than the need to be assuaged by female sympathy: a feeling for her as both a woman and a bibliophile. But even if he were to overcome his reticence and ask her out, she would decline, though in a way that did not hurt his feelings. Apart from finding him physically unattractive, she is too immersed in her business to become involved with a man. The recession is tightening its grip. She will have to work longer and harder, with single-minded determination, in order to survive the squeeze.

A young woman enters in a denim jacket, jeans torn at the knees and army boots whose toes have been worn through to bare steel. Her hair is cropped short, close to her pale scalp, and numerous rings fringe the perimeter of both ears. Rummaging in the deep carpet-bag strapped over her shoulder, she asks for the section on Theatre and, without looking up, slips off to the back room. The word ARMAGEDDON is written in calligraphy on the back of her jacket.

Shaking his head, Cape returns to the counter with a few books and spreads his left hand flat on the glass. There's my likely readership, he whispers. She is probably unemployed, with all the time in the world for books. He must suffer his haemorrhoids, so the likes of her can sit in a cosy cafe all day, smiling over his stories. He pays for Thucydides's *The Peloponnesian War*, Marcus Aurelius's *Meditations* and Plato's *Republic*. No fiction for him, he says, tucking the books under his arm. Would he like a bag? No – he likes to carry them the way the French carry their bread. Sonya wishes him well with his novel. He darts her a glance. She looks forward to reading it. Biting his fingernail, he is about to say something, but turns abruptly and strides out onto the windy street, leaving his moist hand-print on the glass.

From the convex mirror located in the top corner of the door frame Sonya is able to survey customers in the back room. Theft has been increasing over the past year, while her efforts at prevention have failed. She tried making customers leave their bags on hooks near the entrance, but this met with objections, refusals, and accusations of infringement of civil liberty. Next she asked customers whether she might glance into their bags on the way out. This was also unsuccessful: some complained it was an invasion of personal property, while others, the more vocal, insisted that a glance constituted a search, for which the law required a warrant. In the end, wanting to avoid a confrontation that might result in bad publicity (all that she needed was a few know-alls to call her a fascist, and the young impressionables out there would never set foot in the place again), she dispensed with bags and searches, and installed the small convex mirror as both a third eye and a deterrent.

Perhaps knowing it is unlikely to sell, Sonya has not shelved Pepel's book. She keeps it on the counter, picking it up from time to time to enjoy a poem, the way she enjoys a cigarette. The poet's images and brooding tone have made an impression on her. How is it that art can transform the melancholy into enjoyment? Perhaps a poetic sensibility is similar to the mellow autumn light that sweetens the sour grape.

Glancing up at the mirror, Sonya is jolted: the distorted figure in the back room slips a book into her bag. Her first reaction is to confront the thief, but she quickly checks herself. The woman might claim she intended to pay on the way out. Strategies for handling the situation flit through her mind. Call the police? No. She went through that in her first encounter with a thief. Interviews, reports, charges, court, closure of the shop for the day – a costly exercise. When asked by the magistrate why she had stolen the book, a computer manual, the girl replied in a faltering voice that she was a computer junkie and had spent all her money on upgrading her system. She had needed the book desperately, as others needed a fix, to access the Internet and trip out on the information highway. The magistrate, an elderly woman with a tinge of purple through her hair, listened solemnly, though a hint of a smile appeared to tug at the ends of her lips. On a few occasions she darted a castigating glance at Sonya, as if reproving her for dragging the unfortunate girl through this ordeal. In the end, the magistrate reprimanded the first-time offender, ordered her to return the book and undertake ten hours of community work, and used her discretionary power to waive a conviction. Sonya left the courtroom feeling guilty. As she stood on the front steps, the griffins at the arched entrance to the courthouse seemed to snarl in retribution.

The second time it happened, she decided to handle it herself. A stocky man in his early twenties entered the shop, browsed for a few minutes, and then, in full view of Sonya, began stuffing books into a loose-fitting jumper tucked into his trousers. She was taken aback by his casual manner: it was as though he were picking apples from a backyard tree. She left the counter and demanded he return the books. He confronted her with a defiant look and replied that he had a right to the books as surely as he had a right to breathe. Sonya threatened to phone the police. He snickered, turned, and shoved another book down his jumper. She would give him one more chance. He called her bluff. As an anarchist he was not afraid of the law, he said, thrusting out his barrel chest expanded by the books. He had every right to take as many as he pleased. Knowledge came from the great pool of the universal mind, and as such it was humanity's common property. He rejected patents and copyrights. Ideas were not private possessions. A poem was never the work of an individual author, but arose out of a language and tradition, and so belonged to the community. Likewise, a formula discovered by a mathematician belonged to the world because it arose from a language and body of knowledge common to mankind. An idea was a natural phenomenon, like light, and it should be accessed freely by mankind. If people did not wake up to the truth, the day would come when governments, in collusion with large companies, would put a tariff on sunlight, just as they had tariffed water. Had she heard of Nikola Tesla? No? He was an electrical engineer, a genius who invented transformers and generators. But most of his work has been deliberately kept in the dark by those with vested interests. He studied and researched the physics of electromagnetism and calculated that the earth's electro-magnetic field afforded an inexhaustible supply of energy. He made drawings and plans of how this energy could be accessed freely, without cables, just as microwaves were received by satellite dishes. This energy, or light, or the presence of God – whatever one chose to call it – would free mankind, allowing individuals to realise the fullness of being. But, of course, governments and companies remained in power by herding and harnessing mankind. They had denigrated much of Tesla's work and ridiculed his vision of a free society. And those who dared to speak out were hounded and silenced. Mankind's salvation and empowerment lay in ideas and knowledge, whose repositories were books. Therefore, rejecting governments, legislators, and the myth of private ownership, he was expressing his God-given right by helping himself to a few books.

The force of his conviction, the flow of his words, put Sonya on the defensive. She offered to sell him the books at cost price. He laughed. She would gladly loan them to him if it were a question of money. He did not need permission to take what rightfully belonged to all. If he put them back she would take the matter no further. Had she not understood a thing? he flared. And did he not realise that she was running a business, not a half-way house for anarchists? He accused her of succumbing to publishers and profiteers, of trading in light, spirit, ideas. He should get real. And she should become ideal. Was he going to return them or not? Look at the sunshine, he said. The letters of BIBLIOPHILE glowed in the afternoon light. He would go to a park, sit on a bench, and read at his leisure. With that, he turned and walked out. Sonya was about to run after him, but reconsidered: better a small loss than an unpleasant scene.

How many books has she put in that bag bulging with what seem her worldly possessions? There, she is at it again. Sonya moves closer to the mirror and observes the woman with a mixture of apprehension and fascination. Having taken a book and flicked through it, the woman looks around. This is the pivotal moment: should I? A tingle passes through Sonya. The woman calmly slips it in her bag, adjusts her jacket and emerges from the back room. Sonya is determined to get the better of her, as though a victory here will save the business from ruin. But what if she is an addict? What if she has shot up just before coming to the shop? You could not take ten steps on the footpath without seeing a thin syringe. She might be a walking time-bomb. A wrong word, an accusing look, and she might explode in rage.

Casually, Sonya looks up from the black and white postcards of literary figures along the bottom of the counter and asks if she can be of any assistance. Pressing the bag to her side, the woman accords Sonya a look heavy with eyeliner. There was nothing of interest, she replies in a surly tone. Would she mind if her bag were checked? Her eyes are startled blackbirds. Expecting her to make a dash for the door, Sonya steps out from behind the counter, taking a hefty cookbook with an immaculately presented dining table pictured on the cover, just in case things get out of hand. To Sonya's surprise, the woman lowers her head, reaches into the bag and removes three books – all from the Religion section, not Theatre, as Sonya expected. She could not help it. Her head hangs penitently, earrings tremble. She has tried to overcome it, sought psychiatric counselling, but it always gets the better of her, like an irresistible temptation. Her eyes brim with tears. Kleptomania – that is what her psychiatrist calls it. And it is always the same thing – books on religion. She felt much stronger after the last session, certain that she would at last get the better of it. She came to the shop to test her resolution, nothing more. But the moment she entered, the demon within her began stirring. In brushing her eyes, she smudges black liner over the sides of her face. Sonya plucks three tissues from a box on the counter and gives them to her with a few words of comfort. Alone in the back room, with no one watching, she felt that dreadful temptation drawing her to the shelf. She tried to resist, even as her hand went out, but the instant her fingertips touched the spine of *The Cloud of Unknowing* she was doomed.

In a twinkle of that tear trembling on the thief's penitential lash, Sonya is twelve again, an only child, a student in an overcrowded inner-suburban high school. The onset of menstruation has made her quieter, withdrawn, distant from family and friends. Frightened and confused by the powerful stirrings in her growing body, she feels as though she is being uprooted from all that she has known. Books are her only refuge: a place where she can retreat from the surrounding chaos and still find that part of herself that is not subject to change. During the summer holidays she seldom leaves the house, finding comfort and company in a set of *Children's Encyclopedia* bought by her father at a trash-and-treasure market. Only a few months ago she was outgoing and enjoyed tennis, now she is most at home in the vast world between the bright red covers with gold letters along the spine. She likes their particular smell, the feel of their glossy pages, the colour plates of gemstones, flowers, butterflies and other collections from the natural world. A good all-round student before the holidays, when school commences again she switches off from everything except English. Her mathematics teacher, a softly-spoken man with sideburns cut at a sharp angle, scolds her mildly upon discovering her with a novel instead of a textbook. He informs her parents of her disinterest. She resigns herself to failing the subject, despite their threats. The teacher accepts the situation and does not bother her, unless to ask good-naturedly from time to time what she is reading.

An unmitigated curse for most of the girls in her class, the monthly period is nothing short of a blessing for her. She feigns sickness or exaggerates her stomach cramps in order to stay home from school. With both parents at work she has the house to herself, to read without interruption. Propped on a couple of pillows, she spends the day in bed, a book on her budding breasts, giving herself fully to her passion, losing all track of time, even going without lunch. Her passion is like an illicit affair. Is it right for her to be in bed with a book, while her mother is standing at an assembly line, gluing insoles into a thousand pairs of shoes? Is it right to indulge in this forbidden pleasure, while her father toils at the abattoirs, slitting the throats of electrocuted sheep, hooking them up by the hind leg, sending them off to be skinned, disembowelled, frozen? Her parents are working for her sake, while she plays truant in order to read. Guilt soon gets the better of her, though passion continues unabated.

Books are expensive for the daughter of working-class parents, they cannot sit comfortably in a house that is still mortgaged, they are a luxury when bills cover the kitchen table. Books can be borrowed from the library and returned by the due date, but seldom bought, unless prescribed by school, and then they should be covered in cellophane and cared for, so they may be re-sold at the end of the year. Books should be studied, used as stepping stones to a good job, perhaps a profession, they are not ends in themselves, and must never be enjoyed. Enjoyment of books is for the privileged, like an after-dinner glass of port; the poor must learn from life and must be content with their bread and beer. Yes, her parents discourage her from idle reading. It will ruin her eyesight, not to mention the adverse effects on her health due to lack of exercise, and she used to be so good at tennis, had a copybook backhand. They forbid her reading after dark. Her silence worries them. She must remain in the livingroom, make conversation, talk about shool, boys, anything. She bows to their wishes and sits through hours of television, chaffing, desperate to return to her books. But when the televison is turned off and the house is silent and dark, she cries hot tears, dissolves in them, and curses that the eye is not a solar element, absorbing light by day and emitting it at night. One afternoon she finds her father's torch in the shed – a long silver tube that accommodates four batteries. This is her salvation. Now she welcomes the dark. The pleasure of reading is greater than ever because it is forbidden. She has made a retreat for herself, a cocoon, a private world. With the blankets over her head and the torch between her knees, she reads until sleep catches on her lashes.

The possession of a book intensifies, makes more personal the reading experience, especially when it takes place under her blankets at night, in secret. A book borrowed lacks this intimacy. But where is she to find the money to buy and own the books she craves? She is on her way to the public library not far from her place. It is housed in the Town Hall: an old building modelled on an ancient temple, with a broad sweep of stairs leading to a row of columns and a wide entrance. Dark oak shelves line the walls from floor to ceiling. Afternoon light falls lazily on a table where a few pensioners shuffle newspapers. A boy, his face raw with acne, is flipping through catalogue cards. The silver-haired librarian is processing returned books. Sonya browses for a while, wanting to borrow a hundred books, but restricted by a limit of three. Her attention is caught by a title gleaming on a dark-red spine: *Grote's History of Greece Vol.1*. She pulls it out from its pressing neighbours. The cover is impressed with the profile of an ancient warrior, circumscribed by a few circles, all within a floral design. She passes her fingertips lightly over the impression. Closing her eyes, she takes in the dry, earthy smell of thick pages. The spine creaks like an old wooden gate as she opens the front cover. A lithograph of the author faces the title page: an imposing figure with fluffy side-whiskers, a scroll in his right hand, his left resting on a thick tome. How long has it been since George Grote last saw the light of day? Since he looked into a reader's eye? She notices a sign: BOOKS ON THIS SHELF NOT FOR LOAN. But she wants this book, not to borrow for two weeks and return, but to possess for the rest of her life, to read it at her leisure, and in reading feel and smell its body.

Suddenly a current of excitement tingles up her spine and spreads to her shoulderblades. Her heart beats strongly, blood hisses in her ears. But what if she is caught? The old librarian will not suspect a thing. She goes behind a shelf and slips the book between her bare skin and jeans, concealing it with a loose shirt. Taking three other paperbacks, she goes to the counter, her stomach throbbing against the hard cover. The librarian peers at her over his glasses. He admires her appetite for books. She swallows, but regrets it immediately, fearing it has given her away. He smiles kindly. The joy of reading belongs to youth and old age, he says. The middle years are too busy for a true appreciation of books. Leaning over the counter, she can hardly breathe, while the hard edge of the book's cover hurts her stomach. The librarian stamps the first loan. Suddenly she must go to the toilet. He stamps the second, taking time to read the back cover. It must be the book pressing against her bladder. The third has been borrowed so many times it needs a new leaf. She is about to burst. Wishing her happy reading, he places the books on the counter. Face licked by tongues of flame, she nods and hurries to the toilet at the end of a corridor lined with honour boards full of golden names. In the cubicle, she slips out the object of her desire and notices a pinkish impression of the warrior's profile on her white skin.

She becomes even more daring, stealing not only rare books from the library, but new ones from the local newspaper shop, popular with students after school. The girls browse through magazines of the latest fashions and pop stars, while the boys flick through sporting heroes and cars. The owner, whom everyone calls Boss, is a thin, middle-aged man with owlish features. He patrols the shop with brisk steps and darting eyes, now and then scolding a student for mistreating or misplacing a magazine. Despite his diligence, theft and pilfering are rife. A group of boys from her class has devised a scheme whereby a few divert the Boss with a minor disturbance, while another sneaks out with a pornographic magazine wrapped in cellophane. They shuffle it about in class, passing it from hand to hand under the desks, occasionally flashing it at an unsuspecting girl who blushes at their laughter. She feels sorry for Boss, but is unable to control this impulse to slip away with a book. And it is so easy, as all his attention is directed at the magazine stands.

Elbows bruised from supporting his head on the table, her father has been unemployed for six months and each day the arcs of despair under his eyes grow darker. Her mother is working longer hours in order to make ends meet. The cloud over the house is becoming more oppressive, without a sign of dispersing. And now her crime has started to become painful: guilt's claws tear at her even when she is alone. But she must balance her love of books with respect for her parents. It is not right, this illicit pleasure of reading a stolen book with a stolen torch. Perhaps it is nothing more than diversion, titillation – no different from the experience of those who read comics, Mills and Boon romances, pornographic magazines.

It is difficult to overcome, this desire to possess a book's body and soul. She slips out with *Crime and Punishment* from the school library. This will be the last one, however – no more stealing. And suddenly this thought becomes a conviction, though not from fear of being caught, but from an overpowering feeling of sadness at the sight of her mother preparing tomorrow's work lunch, cutting her sandwich diagonally with a serrated knife.

Sonya is moved as much by the woman's confession as by the tear quivering on her eyelash. She understands her need to possess books, but it will lead to trouble if it is not overcome. If business were better she would allow her to keep the books, in the hope of there being something beneficial in them: a page or even a passage that might give her strength to resist the urge to steal. The woman nods and promises to try harder. Sonya invites her to come and browse whenever she likes, for as long as she likes, without obligation. Hugging the carpet-bag with one arm, the woman wipes her eyes with a black-stained tissue and leaves, steel-capped boots scraping at each step. She crosses the street, stops for a moment in front of the burnt restaurant to light a cigarette, and enters the body piercing salon.

In returning the stolen books to their place on the shelves, Sonya is taken aback by another gold envelope, this one protruding from the Theatre shelf. She is certain it was not there before the woman entered the shop. Is she the anonymous author? Sonya slips it out from between *The Theban Plays* and *The Frogs and other Plays*. The woman was edgy, high-strung. She asked for the Theatre section, but stole from Religion. And this envelope? Was she a courier for the anonymous author? If so, why this intrigue?

Another hour to closing time, but the day has been quiet and a last-minute flurry of customers is unlikely. Sonya locks the front door and returns to the back room. She throws a few scraps of wood into the fire and lights a cigarette with a splinter. The wind has strengthened. Loose strands of barbed wire scratch against the tin fence in the backyard. Builders are working overtime next door: hammers clatter, a circular saw screams. The bank operated for years, before even Simkin moved into the area. Things are not good when banks start closing, he remarked dolefully not long ago. Vacant for more than six months, it finally sold at auction. A notice was taped on the window two months ago: an application to open a funeral parlour. As if business was not bad enough! People feel uneasy walking past a funeral parlour, some would think twice about entering a shop next door to one. What sounds like a sledge-hammer thumps on the other side of the wall, rattling the window, swaying the light. The property on the other side of her shop is still vacant. What will it become? Will she survive the recession? A protracted sigh fills the room with cigarette smoke. Reading her name on the envelope, she feels a sense of unease at the thought of an anonymous hand writing her name, as though she were vulnerable to something sinister. She opens the envelope and draws out a small pile of carefully handwritten pages, nothing else.

Having left the bustling flea-market, with its throng of sweaty tourists moving in slow motion, its hawkers singing from craft shops and souvenir stands, its waiters inviting passers-by into their cool taverns, a man walked with measured steps up a roughly cobbled lane that rose steeply toward the Acropolis. Tall as the statue of Apollo which Praxiteles completed last winter, he wore a cap made of young vine leaves to protect his bald, well-proportioned head from the abrasive sun. He stopped beside a window with pelargoniums blooming in clay pots, and shielded his eyes in looking up at the sacred hill. The upper section of the Erechtheum was just visible above the surrounding wall: beautiful against the sky scoured metallic blue, the heads of the Caryatids appeared as though they were balancing a book instead of the marble pediment. Taking his bearings for the remainder of the journey, he set off again, picking his way over the uneven stones. Cicadas chirruped from shrubs and bushes on the rocky side of the Acropolis. A second man appeared from a side lane, looked around in distress, and called to the first.

– Themachos! Wait!

Stocky, wearing a short tunic drenched with sweat, he hobbled gingerly up the lane. The first man turned gracefully on the ball of one foot, as though performing a slow dance, and waited for the caller.

– What is it, Xanthipes?

Hands on knees, gasping, he was unable to reply.

– You're redder than the setting sun.

Regaining his breath, Xanthipes straightened up and wiped his brow with the loose end of the tunic tucked under his arm.

– Don't make fun of me, Themachos. I've been looking for you all over Athens. What a day! The hottest summer in years. I shouldn't be running around like this, not at

my age. Callimachus has warned me. The old ticker's not too regular these days. Ah, the things we do for our young friends. Hades take them! Such friendship! Mention it to Socrates next time you see him.

Frothy saliva sealed the corners of his mouth, sweat reddened his eyes, and his hairy chest heaved like a blacksmith's bellow.

— *Let's sit for a while, Xanthipes.*

They walked across the lane to a quiet courtyard surrounded by small workshops producing souvenirs and handicrafts. A mulberry tree laden with fruit and loud with cicadas provided welcome shade. Like the laughter of children, water trickled from a pipe into a marble trough. It was siesta time and the craftsmen were sleeping at the back of their shops. Xanthipes revived himself at the tap, moistening the end of his tunic and applying it to the back of his head. Water dripped from his grey-streaked beard as he sat beside Themachos on a wooden bench around the base of the tree.

— *Feeling better?*

— *I thought my temples were going to burst.*

— *Why are you running around on a day like this?*

Themachos removed his vine-leaf cap and brushed a few dry mulberries from the bench.

— *I left home this morning thinking to spend a few hours with the boys in the cool of the local taverna, when I ran into young Polyxeros. That's when all my troubles began. I've told you about Polyxeros, haven't I? A real scholar, that young man. He's going to be a big brain some day, and Zeus has endowed him with broad shoulders to carry weighty ideas. I told him about the Symposium — just as you related it to me, but it wasn't enough for our* scholar. He stopped me this morning and begged me to chase you up for a few more details about that heady evening. As I'm fond of the young man, I set out for the Agora, thinking I'd find you there. Well, Themachos, six hours later, a trip to Eleusis, my best pair of sandals wrecked, almost a heart attack to boot, and I've finally managed to track you down.

– You should have saved yourself the trouble, my friend. I told you everything about that night, exactly as it happened, every word that was said on the theme of love.

Xanthipes looked up at the leafy tree and shook his head, causing a few droplets to fly from his beard.

– Cicadas! Hades take them! Night and day! Enough to drive a man crazy.

– They're doing what they know best.

– My young friend's not interested in love, Themachos. I'm not referring to his personal life, although sometimes I think he's so intellectual he looks contemptuously on relations of any kind. No, what I mean is, he's not interested in carnal love. Damned cicadas! They're scrambling my brains! What I meant to say is, my young friend's particularly interested in the last part of the Symposium, after the differing accounts and opinions on the true nature of love.

– Then he's interested in nothing, Xanthipes, for when Alcibiades concluded his eulogy to Socrates we went home.

– But didn't you say that when the majority had either fallen asleep or left, Socrates, Aristophanes and Agathon were still passing the wine around, discussing tragedy and comedy?

– By Zeus, you're right!

– Polyxeros wants to know what they discussed.

Themachos turned thoughtfully to the side for a moment in recollecting that night. His composed gaze rested on a mask-maker's shop: brightly coloured comic and tragic masks hung from the lintel of the open doorway, while the craftsman, naked from the waist up, lay sprawled on the work-bench at the back of the shop, sleep gurgling from his open mouth.

– It was a long time ago.

– Please, implored Xanthipes, chewing on a mulberry. I praised your memory and promised to provide him with what he sought. You know what young people are like today: one disappointment and they're heartbroken.

– It was a mid-winter's night. We gathered to celebrate Agathon's first prize for a tragic work at the Lenaea drama festival. The night seemed endless, and the wine kept flowing. I must have dozed off for a while, for when I woke with a start to the sound of cocks crowing, Socrates was asserting that a skilful tragedian could write a rip-roaring comedy, and that a competent comedian could write tear-jerking tragedy. Having thrown the cat among the pigeons, he stretched out on the couch and waited for Agathon and Aristophanes to commence, those ass-like ears of his twitching with suppressed mirth. You know, Xanthipes, that's the only time I've ever seen Socrates use his mouth for wine instead of words.

– What was said, Themachos? And please, be brief. My wife's going to give me an ear-bashing worse than these damned cicadas when I get home.

– As I recall, Aristophanes was about to start, when he erupted in another burst of hiccups which called for a jug of water. Agathon took over and said they must first examine the nature of tragedy and comedy in relation to existence, not aesthetics. Having drowned his hiccups, Aristophanes agreed. As though by reflex, both turned to Socrates, expecting him to add something, but their eager look met with a broad grin from which they turned to each other in mutual surprise. And then, somewhat rhetorically, Agathon asked how it was that tragedy had arisen as an art form. The answer, of course, lay embedded in the word itself: tragos, *a he-goat or satyr, and* aeidein, *to sing,* which combined to produce a singing satyr. The ancient satyr-plays were the forerunners of Aeschylean tragedy. But how had something as frivolous as a satyr-play given birth to Prometheus Bound? *The satyr-plays themselves had arisen from singing, dancing and merry-making — from the influences of Dionysos, for whom the satyr Silenus was a faithful attendant. Through Dionysian revelry our ancestors were able to subdue the fears that threatened the newly awakened rational mind. Empowered by the potent trinity of wine, song and dance, they broke through the walls of individual existence and attained union with the gods and the forces of nature, which in turn gave them the strength to confront the dread at the core of existence. As the rational mind evolved and our ancestors became more cultured and civilised, they developed a more temperate way of looking into the abyss, through tragedy — the synthesis of wine, song and dance.*

As Themachos spoke Xanthipes took off his sandal and examined the broken strap. A thin, black-haired woman appeared from one of the workshops, placed a handicraft on the section of bench away from the speakers, and drank a few handfuls of water. Her dark eyebrows gathered as she squinted across the courtyard at a white-washed house with potted pelargoniums on the windowsills. A figure sat crouched on the top step, partly covered by shadow. The woman shook her head and reached up on tip-toe for some berries, accentuating her shapely calf muscles. She washed her sticky hands, sat on the bench, and bowed over an embroidery hoop with a piece of material stretched skin tight. Taking a needle from the top of her tunic, she set to work, deftly piercing the material back and front.

– And then Aristophanes reminded Agathon that what he had said about the origins of tragedy applied equally to comedy. He also began with etymology: the word 'comedy' was derived from komos, a festive revel, and aeidein, to sing, from which it followed that comedy originated from songs of revelry, in other words the ancient satyr-play also. He argued that song and revelry had provided our ancestors with a means of overcoming, albeit temporarily, the crushing burden of existence. They had managed this not by passive contemplation, as tragedy would demand, but by making fun of the gods and everything that threatened them with extinction. Revelry, a sense of wellbeing, an abundance of healthy emotion, was later transformed and structured into comedy. Laughter, the essence of revelry, became the expression of comedy. Tragedy was a perverse fascination with pain and death, which of course led to a pessimistic view of the world; comedy, on the other hand, celebrated health and life, promoting vigour and optimism. And once again they turned to Socrates, expecting him to throw his argument behind one or the other, but the crafty sage was now frowning, deep in thought, and it was impossible to determine whether he was contemplating the present discussion or something completely different.

Themachos glanced at his companion, to see whether he was still paying attention. Head resting against the tree-trunk, Xanthipes was staring into the depths of the tree, mouth open like a trap waiting to snap on a plump berry.

— Please, continue, he said, without changing his position.

— Agathon asked whether tragedy or comedy had come first. Tragedy, replied Aristophanes. The early writers had a ready stock of plots and themes in the myths, most of which were full of death and destruction. With little creativity and imagination they worked these well-known myths into a dramatic form. Far more imagination was required to write comedy, for which there were no precedents in our traditions. It was, therefore, the natural successor to tragedy — the drama of the future. All our bright young dramatists were writing in this vein. There was already a school known as the New Comedy, which was producing work that made even his own appear outdated. Agathon then asked Aristophanes which tragedian he most preferred. Aeschylus. Why? Because he had been a pioneer. Very well, Agathon continued. If tragedy was morbid and life-denying, as Aristophanes maintained, why had Aeschylus chosen to express himself tragically at precisely the time Athens had defeated the vast Persian army, when democracy was beginning to burgeon, when art and architecture were starting to flourish, when there was a tremendous feeling of vitality and confidence, when the future was full of hope and possibility? If what Aristophanes had said earlier were correct, Aeschylus should have written comedy. Everything in its turn, countered Aristophanes. Tragedy had arisen before comedy because the mind of our ancestors was closer to the mythic. A new sensibility was required for comedy, and tragedy provided the groundwork for that sensibility by transforming life into art. But where tragedy portrayed life in a natural sense, comedy recreated it and stood it on its head, transforming suffering to laughter. Agathon disagreed. The emergence of tragic art should be seen in the light of Athenian history, he said. It began with Thespis, who staged the first tragedy at the Great Dionysian Games; it had found prominence in Aeschylus, at a time when Athens was gaining strength and security; it rose to perfection with the early works of Sophocles, when Athens was at her peak; and it began to decline in our generation, at a time when Athens was being morally and materially depleted by the ravages of the endless Peloponnesian War. The conclusion was inescapable: the greatest tragedies were written when Athens was vigorous, prosperous, free of epidemics and the threat of invasion. He had dredged his brains over this apparent paradox, and concluded that youthful strength and vigour were the preconditions for great tragic art. When a culture was young and strong, artists were not afraid to look deeply into the soul. In expressing our fears, they rendered them less terrible; in presenting our nightmares on the stage, they freed us to enjoy the light of day. Tragedy was this: the confrontation between the human and the more-than-human, with freedom as the prize.

It was now the hottest part of the afternoon. The stones in the courtyard shimmered. Having sharpened their weapons, the cicadas were clashing in a furious battle. A blackbird drank from the trough, raising its yellow beak in thanks after each sip. Xanthipes grimaced, probed a hairy ear with his little finger, and flicked away a dark coagulation of sound from the end of a longish fingernail.

— But Aristophanes would not be denied, continued Themachos, raising his voice a little. He also used cultural and historical factors to defend his position. Athens had *freed herself from Doric oppression by means of nothing more than the kore's smile. Light as a butterfly on stone, the wistful smile on the faces of those youths had been the precursor not only of comedy, but the very Golden Age of Athens. The curve of those lips was a bridge from the old to the new, from stone to marble, from death to life. For him it was that smile, not the cry of Aeschylian protagonists, which symbolised strength and defiance. It was a smile which said: I am equal to fate and the gods; which declared: I have overcome the gods; which announced: there is only man and death – and I laugh at death. That first tentative smile now found its fullest expression in comedy. Agathon protested that Aristophanes disposed of the gods far too easily. The old oak must make way for the new, Aristophanes countered. Today comedy ridiculed the demi-gods, tomorrow it would bare its arse and fart at the Thunderer himself. Agathon cautioned him about such talk, saying the Athenians would punish him for it. Aristophanes laughed. The Athenians no longer believed in all that tripe. Yes, he had been brought before the Areopagus on a charge of blasphemy, but the Athenian elders had acquitted him. Why? Because the temple had become a hollow institution. The dazzling splendour of the Parthenon blinded the faithful to the emptiness inside. These days, people would much rather laugh at the gods in comedies than struggle up the Acropolis to make offerings to non-existent gods. And if some still persisted in that practice it was because old habits died hard. Agathon reflected for a moment. Unlike comedy, the essence of tragedy lay precisely in a belief in the sacred, a feeling that there was a force shaping human destiny. This feeling permeated the great tragic plays as surely as a drop of wine coloured a jug of water. The tension found in the* greatest works was the pull between the human and the more-than-human. That certainly was the case with Aeschylus, said Aristophanes, accepting the wine-bowl from Agathon. But society had changed. The gods had lost their grip on the human heart, and it was the playwright's duty to represent the change. The later works of Sophocles, those of Euripides, Agathon's prize-winning play — they all had a hollowness about them. Agathon's work was technically and structurally competent, but it lacked inner tension for the simple fact that audiences no longer responded to the sacred. The gods in contemporary tragedy were nothing more than contrivances, machines that maintained action and provided a satisfactory denouement. The works of Euripides demonstrated this perfectly. His tragedies would become very relevant social dramas if he but stopped dragging the gods into them. Ironically, his extensive use of plot, social themes and characterisation had served to kill tragedy. And Aristophanes repeated what he had said earlier: comedy was the natural successor to tragedy.

The woman raised her needlework and examined it at arm's length: embroidered in blue the Attic letters sigma and gamma were circumscribed by the hoop. She licked the end of a red thread, passed it through the needle, and bowed over the letters. A spear of light passed through the tree and found her left kneecap, revealing a pink scar.

— Tragedy was undergoing a crisis, Agathon frowned. There were no more than a couple of thousand at his play. Yes, it had been chilly, but the cold had never deterred our ancestors. Comedy was certainly popular at the moment. Aristophanes always played to a full amphitheatre. A riot had broken out when Peace was performed because people couldn't get a seat. A statue of Athena was pushed off its *pedestal and trampled by the angry mob. It showed that people were craving for comedy, smiled Aristophanes. The poor Athenians were tired of bloodshed, of capricious gods, of family curses, of suffering and destruction. Horror had become so much a part of daily life people did not want to see it on the stage. Athens was not the place it had been fifty years ago: the Peloponnesian War had emptied our coffers and spilt the blood of our best youth. Not only this, we suffered that disastrous loss at Delion, we endured an epidemic the likes of which had never been seen, and if all that wasn't enough, Alcibiades was now running around raising money and support for a fleet to invade Syracuse. Athenians had stomached enough tragedy: they needed diversions, entertainment, laughter. A good laugh was better than a good shit — it cleaned the insides and promoted wellbeing. Comedy, both a relaxant and a laxative, made people feel lighter, brighter, more optimistic about facing tomorrow. Athenians wanted to laugh at their gods, at their public figures, at their poets, at their morals and ethics. They would much rather see Procleon offering his floppy phallus to a flute-girl so that she could pull herself up onto the stage, than Oedipus blinding himself with a pin. It was far preferable to laugh with tears than cry with blood. Laughter, not pain — that was what Athenians needed. He was sick of hearing how tragedy was cathartic, how it cleansed impure emotions through association with its hero, how it made people more human by providing insights into our darker nature. It was all nothing but rhetoric and sophism! He wouldn't swallow a word of it! The facts did not attest to it. He had observed the people leaving the theatre after Agathon's play: their faces were pale, as if the blood had been drained from them, and more anguished than the mask of a tragic hero. They were silent, brooding, burdened by dark thoughts and emotions. He had not seen one person who had undergone a liberating experience. Tragedy had had its day. It was time for comedy and social drama – Euripides stripped of the gods. By this time, Xanthipes, I started to feel drowsy again, but I resisted the pillow, expecting Socrates to interject at any minute and win the day in his inimitable manner.*

   – And Socrates said nothing all this time?

   – He just sat there, opening his mouth only when the wine-bowl touched his fleshy lips.

   – Was he tired, Themachos?

   – Tired! The man's indefatigable. No, his eyes were wide open and those ears of his were like an ass's that hears a she-ass braying.

   Xanthipes stood and, wearing one sandal, hobbled to the tap, where he slurped from cupped hands and washed his face with a noisy splutter. Themachos, meanwhile, gazed at two masks hanging from the lintel of a workshop. One was tragic, its mouth a crooked circle shaped by the cry, Ah. The other, painted brightly, was a comic mask. Though the colours and expressions were very different, Themachos was struck by the similarity in the shape of the mouths. The mouth of the comic mask was also a circle, shaped by the universal, Ha. A faint breeze moved the masks, making them touch and click.

   – Well, Themachos, what happened after that?

   – The conversation flowed, together with the wine.

   – After so much wine I'd have thought them incapable of speech, let alone conversation.

   – We Athenians are incorrigible talkers, Xanthipes.

   – To a fault, I often think.

   – To drink and think – Dionysos and Athena. What more could a man want?

— My wife's going to be in a real pickle when I get home, Themachos. How did Agathon counter Aristophanes?

— They both turned to Socrates, as though each expected a verdict in their favour, but when he simply scratched his hairy armpit in a preoccupied manner, Agathon asked Aristophanes whether the chief aim of theatre was to provide entertainment. The aim of all art was enjoyment, replied Aristophanes. Temporary diversion, Agathon snapped. Art was about creating illusions, Aristophanes continued. The theatre was a dream-world, and the dramatist a creator of public dreams. Plays were performed at night to enhance their dream-like quality. Writers of tragedy presented the public's worst nightmares: fears, dark passions — the very things people wanted to forget. If there was pleasure in tragedy, it was perverse, akin to the feeling of waking from a nightmare. Writers of comedy presented a dream from which the dreamer would rather not wake, Agathon persisted. Was it simply a coincidence that the Golden Age of Athens — a time of abundant vitality and creativity — had also produced the greatest tragedies? No. Tragedy, the nightmare, as Aristophanes called it, promoted the wellbeing of the state. Our ancestors were healthier than us because they confronted their darkest fears and transformed them into art. Their freedom, greatness, the very source of their art, all stemmed from a childish innocence that faced the nightmare, looked into the abyss, and said yes to life, yes to the divine, yes to the future. Presenting the nightmare on stage, making it public, was not an exercise in catharsis, but an acceptance and reconciliation of human and divine, present and future, life and death. The replenished wine-bowl came to me again, but, not wanting to interrupt Agathon, I passed it on to Aristophanes without a word.

Tragedy was the supreme art form of a strong, youthful culture which accepted the sacred and sought to raise mankind to the divine. There was no better example of this than Aeschylus's Prometheus Bound. *Here Aristophanes interrupted him, passing the bowl to the attentive Socrates. Mankind had outgrown the gods. We did not need them meddling in our affairs. What good had they ever done? If one considered the facts, they had a very poor track-record. They were responsible for the Trojan War and the dreadful consequences of that protracted affair. As for Prometheus, the gods were responsible for his plight, just because he had wanted to make life easier for us mortals. They had lived their comedy on Mount Olympus, while gloating over mankind's tragedy – a tragedy instigated by them! Our generation was overcoming the gods, and where there were no gods, there could be no tragedy. This new freedom would allow us to express ourselves as we liked, and the truest expression of freedom was laughter. The greatness of the Athenians would be seen not in that they made an art of death, as the Egyptians had done that far more grandly, but in that they celebrated life and laughter. Agathon countered: laughter dissipated the force of consciousness. Aristophanes said that too much consciousness burdened us with pain and guilt, destroying the spontaneous, the spark of life. Agathon retorted that the effects of comedy could be achieved by using a feather on the sole of the foot. Aristophanes replied that tragedy concentrated energy inwardly, leading to self-destruction. Agathon said comedy was hedonistic. Aristophanes countered that tragedy was morbidly ascetic. Agathon pronounced that comedy reduced man to a bestial state, as shown not only by the names of Aristophanes's plays but by the presence of monstrous phalli* on stage. At this point Aristophanes said that they might hit the shuttlecock back and forth all night, without settling a thing. At the very outset of their dialogue he had pointed out that comedy had its origin in komos, a word remarkably close to cosmos. At certain times of the year — such as religious days in honour of Dionysos — our ancestors had been allowed to revel, to shatter the sense of self and unite with the orgiastic spirit of Dionysos, the universe's great generative force. Priests and priestesses knew that society's wellbeing depended not on repression but controlled expression of mankind's instinctual nature. Since then civilisation had imposed greater restraint on the instinctual, and though it no longer found expression in orgiastic revel, it continued to exist in comedy. I must confess, Xanthipes, by this time drowsiness was getting the better of me and I had to prod myself awake to follow the conversation.

They both turned to a middle-aged man who walked wearily across the courtyard and stopped in front of the mask-maker's shop.

— A foreigner, sighed Xanthipes.

— He looks Macedonian.

— How can you tell?

— He hasn't got a beard.

— Sightseeing in this heat!

The man examined the masks hanging from the lintel: first the comic, then the tragic.

— Which one will he buy? asked Xanthipes.

— Neither. He'll never wake the owner at this hour.

After knocking on the half-door and calling in heavily accented Attic, the man shook his head and plodded out of the courtyard.

— Where was I? asked Themachos.

— Aristophanes was saying the instinctual nature of man found expression in comedy. You see, Themachos, I'm trying to grasp everything word for word, to satisfy my young friend.

— As I said, drowsiness was pulling at my eyelids and I had trouble following the conversation. Aristophanes turned to Socrates, hoping for a sign of approval for his last argument, but that Silenus-faced sage wouldn't be drawn into the role of judge: he raised his hairy shoulders and reclined on the couch, content to remain a silent spectator. Agathon finished the wine in the bowl, wiped his glistening moustache, and argued again that comedy arose when a culture was in a period of decline. Having lost her vigorous strength, Athens was now slipping into a period of decadence, of which comedy was one manifestation. The more decadent the age, the more sophisticated its comedies. The tragic hero suffered so others might have a better future. His wounds were springs of hope; his death, a reconciliation that brought about new harmony and understanding. Comedy was a retreat from the future, a concentration on immediate gratification, the product of a petty-minded age. Comic playwrights contributed to the present growth in decadence. They made buffoons of heroes, ridiculed the gods, attacked traditions, undermined morality. Denying the soul, they pandered to the body, titillating it with laughter. Aristophanes called Agathon a conservative. The artist was not a demigod who moved the world, but simply a mouthpiece for the times. This was a revolutionary age. The old order was breaking up, and comedy was perfectly suited to express this break-up. He agreed with Agathon that the future was uncertain, people were afraid; Athens wasn't the power it had been just fifty years ago. Tragedy had no place in a *time when the idea of the sacred had lost its relevance to the man in the Agora. The sacred had been replaced by the absurd, which found its true form in comedy. At this point, Xanthipes, I must have dozed off for a moment. When I woke with a start, Socrates was standing between Aristophanes, who was on the verge of sleep, and Agathon, who wasn't far behind. He was asking Aristophanes what he observed when inspecting a mask-maker's work for a new production. I must have dozed for longer than I thought, for I could tell from the way the question was worded that the crafty old goat had already put several questions to his companions. Comic faces, replied Aristophanes, eyes almost closed. Socrates then put the same question to Agathon. Tragic faces, he replied, bleary-eyed. Did the craftsman roll with laughter in making the comic mask? Of course not, replied Aristophanes, he concentrated all his skill on the matter at hand. Did he shed tears over his creation? He was neither mirthful nor melancholy, said Agathon. So, he could quite possibly make an excellent comic mask while in the throes of a personal crisis? Aristophanes agreed, his head sinking to the couch. And, conversely, he could make a tragic mask even though he had just won the first prize in the State Lottery? Agathon nodded. Then, said Socrates, straightening himself to the full height of his short stature and raising his hand as though about to play a trump card, just as the skilled craftsman could make excellent tragic and comic masks, so a skilled author could write great comedies and tragedies. Such a person had not emerged to date because we lived in an age of artistic specialisation, but the time would come, if not in our culture perhaps in a culture and language yet to be born, when a playwright would write both forms equally well. With that pronouncement, Xanthipes, it was as if the great sage vanquished his companions, for they were both fast asleep, open-mouthed, breathing in perfect rhythm. I followed Socrates outside. The sun had arisen and the shops were open. Socrates said he would take a bath in the Lyceum, before going to the Agora, where he would meet a few young friends who wanted to discuss the question of bravery. Lacking the sage's stamina, I went home and straight to bed.*

    – Thanks, Themachos. I'll pass it on to Polyxeros.
    – I trust he'll put it to good use.
    – He's got a big head on his shoulders. You'll see it on parchment soon enough. But let's get away from these cicadas, my friend. I'm in for another ear-bashing at home.

    Themachos picked up his vine-leaf cap and they stepped into the implacable light. Xanthipes hobbled, broken sandal flapping at each step. Behind the tree, the woman was embroidering a red line above the letters. A wisp of sacrificial smoke rose from the Acropolis and unwound in a black script across the sky. As they passed the mask-shop a breeze sprang up, as though from the sleeping owner's dark mouth. The masks hanging from the lintel kissed.

She is in this story, too – there is no mistake. The scar on the woman's knee matches her own: the legacy of a bike fall. The would-be thief is not the author: she could not possibly know about the scar. Someone is playing games with her: either a friend or a customer who has visited the shop in the summer months, for that is the last time she wore a short dress. The scar would have been visible as she sat cross-legged on the stool behind the counter. The author did not send the first dialogue inadvertently: this is also an original, more than likely the only copy. Why? She can do without these games. There is enough to think about. Business is bad, and getting worse. What does the author want? The writers she knows are eager to discuss their work, to receive comments, to be told how well they write. This one seems not to care. Why? And it is a good story. She enjoyed it a great deal and would gladly make time to meet the author and convey her thoughts. How many more dialogues will she receive before the author comes forward to claim them? The author's trust in her is astounding. She could do any one of a number of things with these dialogues: use the backs for calculations, toss them in the fire, or claim them as her own. Only someone who knows her well, or who has seen into her heart from a meeting or two, would have entrusted her with their precious work.

She peruses the manuscript, picking out the first word of each paragraph, hoping to extract some esoteric message embedded in the text. This was done in antiquity with the Sibylline Books, and with the Bible in the middle ages. They were opened at random, lines selected according to a cryptic code, and oracular readings given to those seeking enlightenment in matters of life, love and death.

the THIRD dialogue

Having priced a quantity of books bought last night from a deceased estate, Sonya leans on the counter, absent-mindedly scratching letters on the back of her hand with a twisted paper-clip. The first day of winter, and she senses a circle of darkness closing in on the city, the shop, her heart. Stuffed in fog all morning, the street now gleams with chilly brilliance. The maple tree in front of the bread shop clings stubbornly to a few large brown leaves, as though its very definition lay in their veined lines. Again Sonya chastises herself for her precipitous action: at a time when she ought to be curtailing her spending, she went out and purchased three large cartons of books belonging to a poet who died a few weeks ago. The young man's sudden death was discussed at the market yesterday morning. One of the stallkeepers mentioned that the poet's girlfriend was keen to dispose of his books, most of which were poetry titles. The stallkeeper was not interested, but if she, Sonya, wanted to follow it up he was more than happy to pass on the girlfriend's telephone number. Sonya hesitated, but only for a moment, long enough for the bearded stallkeeper to empty a box of books on the trestled table – and then that irrational compulsion began gnawing at her. In writing the number on a cigarette pack, beneath the caution that smoking was a health hazard, she warned herself that books could also ruin health. As the stallkeeper stomped in the dark and clapped books against each other as though waking them from their dreams, she reasoned there was no harm in having the number: it did not mean she would succumb to her weakness. Simkin, the recession, the mortgage on the house, the glut of books in the shop – what further deterrent did she need?

Gazing vacantly through the black roof-beams of PLAMEN'S GRILL, she follows the path of a skywriter. No bigger than the point of a pen, the aeroplane emits a sharp line of smoke on the blue sky. Advertising, she winces, scratching deeper with the clip. An immaculately blank sky used to sell toilet paper! The sky is to daydreamers what gardens are to strollers and nature lovers. In certain meditative moments, a clear blue sky reflects one's hopes, dreams, cherished ideas. It is to the thinker what linen canvas is to the artist, a sheet of paper to the mathematician, a mirror to those who simply muse, and whose musings might well be unrealised works of art. The skywriter is defiling precious public space! As it completes the first letter, B, Sonya's indignation grows. Advertisers have polluted the earth with junk mail, and now they pollute the sky, corrupt the alphabet, demean the miracle of reading by using it to sell their products. There should be two alphabets, she suddenly thinks. One for texts that enlighten; the other, for advertising. The point moves smoothly in describing the O. The depletion of the ozone layer? The greenhouse effect? Out of sight, out of mind. But she would angrily demonstrate against the graffiti on the sky and the corruption of the alphabet.

Yesterday morning she managed to exercise some restraint at the market, leaving with only half a suitcase of books. But her resolve was short-lived. Upon returning to the shop, she telephoned the poet's girlfriend and arranged to inspect what the unfortunate fellow had left behind. After another day of declining takings, she locked up and drove off to a suburb near the waterfront. The wipers screeched away the misty rain as the van, caught in stop–start traffic, stuttered through the heart of the city. A sense of growing foreboding seeped into her being. Simkin's lugubrious warning echoed from shops, showrooms, office buildings stripped of fittings and fixtures – all lit brightly with signs announcing FOR SALE OR LEASE.

Having completed the word BOOK, the skywriter is starting another. But the B and O are already losing their linearity: the crisp jet of smoke is spreading, thinning, diffusing in the sky. Today it is the impermanence of smoke, she thinks, tomorrow they will use laser beams to write on the sky, to scar it with permanent advertisements. And not just the blue sky, they will use coloured laser beams on the night sky. The awe and wonder evoked by the stars, the experience of seeing the human condition against the backdrop of eternity, every child's first encounter with the universe – all this will be obliterated, and the sky will become a screen for advertisements. Welcome to the third millennium, they will announce with seductive laser beams. They will promise immortality, while subtly enslaving us.

BOOK NOW, the message advises. For what? A concert? A circus? A comedy show? Yes, comedy is being performed in venues all over the city. Comedy on the streets, in restaurants, in theatres. Sonya is reminded of the second dialogue. The recession seems to be conducive to comedy. Perhaps Agathon – or the anonymous writer of the dialogue – is right: comedy thrives in a spiritually and morally bankrupt society. It appeals to the lowest common denominator – the sole of one's foot. Sonya bows close to the counter in order to see above the words, but her view is blocked by the verandah at the front of the shop. The letters of the first word are barely legible now. They have gone from capitals to cursive, to a scrawl, and finally to a cirrus script.

Bells rang, red lights flashed, a boom-gate fell like a sword of vengeance. Waiting at a railway crossing, she glanced in the rear vision mirror at the long line of headlights. A train clattered past: silver carriages gleamed with mist, foggy windows were crowded with dark forms. Despite the ravages of recession, a sharp decline in profit, Simkin's warnings and admonitions, she had managed to maintain a silent faith in second-hand books, as if they would see her through these difficult times. Waiting at that dismal railway crossing, however, she was struck, perhaps for the first time, by the thought that she might also fall victim to the recession.

The skywriter's message is now illegible, the letters having fused into a formless cloud. But why does the reverse never happen? Given a formless cloud, or a puff of cigarette smoke, what are the chances of a distinct letter emerging through the randomness of the particles? Could the word CLOUD ever emerge from a cloud. Order tends to chaos, proclaims a law of thermodynamics. What is now left of the message? A meaningless blur indistinguishable from a cloud. What is order anyway? Those shifting letters would mean nothing to a shepherd in Macedonia, while he could read much in the shape of a cloud.

As the van rattled along a tram-tracked street she noticed a crowd in front of a shabby cinema. People were sipping from steaming polystyrene cups. In the foyer a large poster boldly displayed: THE TEN COMMANDMENTS. She was reminded of the first dialogue. For countless people the face of Moses would be associated with Charlton Heston, and for them the Moses of Hollywood would be far more real than the Moses of the Book of Exodus. The word and the moving image, she thought. Was a picture worth a thousand words? Was the picture somehow more valid than the written word? And what of the Bible and icons? In the beginning was the Word. One of the ten commandments proscribed the making of graven images. Why? Images and pictures had a way of seducing the mind, of imposing themselves indelibly, of weakening the imagination. Perhaps the Byzantine iconoclasts were right: through the abolition of icons, people would be compelled to return to the divine authority of the Word, and be restored to God.

Across the street a man and woman were scraping the sign from the window of a vacant shop. All that remained of FINE FURNITURE was the ghostly outline of each letter, and this would soon be wiped away with a spray of ammonia. There were several large cardboard boxes on the floor and new shelves along the walls. Another second-hand bookshop? But no sooner did she feel a swell of resentment than it turned to reassurance: another bookshop was proof of the demand for used books, despite the recession and Simkin's warning. As she glanced aside for a better look in the shop, a man dashed out from a Greek cafe and ran in front of the van. She braked and swerved. The man leapt to the other side. A wire tray crashed against the back of the seat, spilling its books over her. The van slid on the wet tram-tracks, and it was only by sheer reflex that she was able to regain control. Looking back over his shoulder, the man smiled at her, and pursued a shadowy figure down a cobbled lane.

A sheep's skull had been mounted on a stake in the small front garden of a single-storey terrace house. Sonya pressed the doorbell. The poet's girlfriend answered and led her down a long corridor lined with computers, keyboards, monitors, printers, and boxes containing circuit boards and other hardware. In the living room at the end of the house, a child was rattling toys in a playpen. The girlfriend pointed to a few large boxes in the corner and invited Sonya to inspect them, saying she preferred to sell them as one lot, from deference to the poet, who would not have wanted his books sold off piecemeal. Sonya bowed to the contents. After examining the first box she felt her passion beginning to stir. Business might pick up, she told herself. The shop must not appear understocked, or customers would go elsewhere. She knew from her own experience: second-hand book buyers were attracted to shops bursting with books, seeking in such places titles that could not possibly be found in shops selling new books. By degrees she persuaded herself that, despite her financial uncertainty, these books were necessary for the continuation of her business.

While the girlfriend was in the kitchen making coffee, Sonya jingled her keys at the child, who was now gnawing a coloured letter made of plastic, crying in frustration at not being able to take a bite. Was the poor thing hungry? Or was it teething? It threw aside the letter and began biting the pen's wooden top rail. The girlfriend returned and they sat at a table covered with electronic components and a computer whose insides were exposed, like a patient on an operating table. Sonya stressed that books were not selling, and made an offer, which she was quite prepared to increase if the girlfriend had not so promptly accepted. There was no place in the house for them, she said. She respected her late boyfriend: he had been a fine poet, who appreciated the elements of nature in a city-scape. He died at his desk of a massive heart attack, working on a lengthy poem about a river coursing through the city. He always wrote freehand, using a fountain pen. She tried to introduce him to computers, but he remained unconvinced of their efficacy, especially with regard to poetry. He said that his thinking process was too intimately connected to the act of holding a pen and moving it across the page. She wanted to help him, create a web-page, put his poems on the Internet, make them accessible to a wider readership, but he refused. He preferred to see his poems collected in a book, even if such a collection were lucky to sell a few hundred copies, earning barely enough to pay for the child's nappies.

Piqued by something, the girlfriend drew a keyboard toward her and struck pointedly at the X several times. If only he had not spent so much time at his desk, writing unprofitable poems, he might not have had the heart attack. She urged him to exercise more, to enjoy the nature he was forever writing about, but it was always one more poem, one more book. Books have had their day, she scowled. They would soon be replaced by computers and CD-ROMs. Books were repositories of memory, nothing more. Memory would be stored more efficiently once digitised and compressed onto a disk. Books would be obsolete in the new millennium. Computers would become the size of a book, having a thousand gigabytes of memory, enough to store an entire library. One would open them like opening a book, the pages on the screen would turn like the pages of a book – they could be read in bed, on the beach, on the train to work. Precious space would be saved, forests spared, and there would be no more headaches in moving house. Whenever she spoke of these things to him, he would become gloomy and shut himself in his room for hours, staring at the books on his shelves. In many ways he was living in the past, still walking beside a river, while the world was flying at the speed of thought along the million-lane information super highway. As they loaded the boxes in Sonya's van, the child cried in the pen, biting the sharp edges of the letter M.

The girlfriend's words now echo in Sonya's ears, adding a chill to the darkness closing in on her. Are books on the verge of extinction? All these titles, words, thoughts, smells, everything reduced to a silicon-chip? The entire shop replaced by something smaller than a full-stop, the primal point from which a universe of texts explodes into being at the press of a key? But her life has always been inextricably bound to books; she has lived for them and through them as others live through the natural world; she has invested her future in them, and now she is confronted by the prospect of her future being obliterated, though not by the nuclear war she feared in her youth, but by a silent, invisible chip. A flutter of anxiety passes through her. In recollecting her past it is always in terms of the book she happened to be reading at the time. Among her first memories, at the age of three, the book looms large on her mother's lap. She recalls the page glistening in the sunlight and her hand reaching to grasp its own shadow. Thinking the large letters were also shadows, she would look around for the objects casting them. Even then there was something magical in those shadows: they would mellow her mother's voice, give it a sing-song quality it otherwise did not possess.

These intense memories, these defining moments in her life, are threatened by computers and the possible death of the book. Disturbed by this thought she reaches for Pepel's book and reads a short poem, her lips moving, as though silently nibbling each word. Why is it that the moment her eyes meet the text she feels in her element again. What is there in this mysterious act of reading that can allay her fears and uncertainties? Her eyes are drawn from left to right, letter by letter, but she is not conscious of each letter; they skim the line from word to word, without stopping at each word; they grasp the meaning of the poem as though the words were nothing more than stepping stones toward that meaning, or as though the meaning were somehow independent of the words. She recalls one of the famous paradoxes in modern physics: Heisenberg's Uncertainty Principle. If an electron's position is specified, its velocity cannot be determined; on the other hand, if its velocity is calculated, its position is indeterminate. Reading is like this: if one concentrates on the letter, meaning is lost; if one grasps the meaning, the individual letters are a blur.

The front door opens and the old woman with the shopping trolley enters. Sonya is quick to point out that she has no need of more books today. Whether slightly deaf or simply persistent, the old woman ignores Sonya's firm tone and shuffles to the counter. Been walking the streets all day, looking for odds and ends, she says. No more horses, though! Nothing but bad luck! She lifts the trolley's cover and, to her own surprise, takes out a large gold envelope with Sonya's name on it. What's this? she asks, holding it up, her face contracting in wrinkles. Must be losing my memory, she chuckles. It was not there when she left home. Was it slipped in without her knowledge? But why? Has someone mistaken her trolley? Used it for an illegal activity? It's meant for me, says Sonya, heart beating against her arms crossed on her chest. Suspicious, the old woman reflects a moment. How can she be sure? My name's on it, insists Sonya. It's all Greek to me, she counters, squinting in a way that suggests she has suddenly seen a possible advantage in the situation. Sonya offers to pay her for having been used as an inadvertent courier. She shakes her head, and the loose flesh under her chin trembles. No, she wants to examine the contents of the envelope first. It might be money from a drug deal. That sort of thing is always happening in this area. She tears open the envelope in a rough manner and takes out the sheets. What is it? she asks. A long letter, Sonya replies. A love letter! the woman snickers. Sonya nods, reaching for the sheets, but the old woman puts them behind her back. Must be very romantic. She might decide to keep it, even though she is unable to read these tiny words without her glasses. A love letter, she teases Sonya. Must be very interesting. She might be persuaded to part with it for the right sum. Sonya places a few notes on the counter. Look at all these sweet words, says the woman. Sonya doubles the amount. Pocketing the money in her long overcoat, she hands Sonya the sheets. Can she interest Sonya in books as well? Next time, Sonya replies sharply. The old woman thanks her and shuffles off, her trolley squealing at each turn of the wheels.

Sitting at the counter, Sonya lights a cigarette. It has been two weeks since the last dialogue, and she has read both many times in the hope of extracting a clue as to the author's identity. She is certain that they have been written especially for her. But why? Is there a way of reading them that will disclose their secret? A key, a code, that will spell out the personal message?

At times she feels there are two texts in what has been written: the heady dialogues between the protagonists, and all that lies unsaid – the spaces between words, the silent gestures and mannerisms. With each reading, the sense of there being a private message has become stronger. The anonymous writer has established a personal relationship with her. Perhaps the old woman is right: each dialogue is a kind of love letter. Her eyes and the writer's hand join in the private act of reading. The writer has given of himself (she can't help thinking of the author as male) in each word of the story, while she has accepted his offering, infusing it with her being. More than familiarity, she now feels a sense of intimacy toward the handwriting, as though the voice behind it were addressing her in a confidential tone. She considers putting the dialogue away until closing time, the better to savour the pleasure of reading, but the handwriting draws her with its irresistible charm.

The November night drifted in with the sea fog and settled over Marseilles. Ships loaded with cargo for Africa, buildings crowded with humanity, the hospital sighing with the sick and dying, everything dissolved like cubes of sugar in coffee. Pressing against the window with horizontal bars, the night breathed a chill into the room, found the patient's fingertips, stole into his lungs. He lay sleeping, in the bed diagonally across from the window. Three other beds were empty, their starchy sheets neatly folded back, waiting like brides for their grooms. On the wall above him a lamp cast a faint halo over his upper body. A pillow on each side propped him up a little, while a third supported his head. His hair, damp and matted, was brushed off his forehead, exposing an emaciated face which still bore traces of a dark tan. Despite the ravages of fever that had hollowed his temples and projected his cheekbones, there was still an arch to his fine eyebrows. Was it the last vestige of youth? Or perhaps a perverse inquisitiveness that was unafraid of death, just as it had been unafraid of all manner of love.

A nurse bustled into the room and sat on the edge of his bed. Resting his wrist on her thigh, she timed his pulse with a small watch pinned upside down to her white apron. Black hair springy under a cap, small mouth sealed tight, she looked down kindly on the sleeping man. The name on her identification tag read Agnes Oray. Nodding, she recorded the pulse rate on the chart hanging from the foot of the bed, adjusted the pillow under his head and left with a crisp step, her dress rustling like writing paper.

Muffled by the fog, a ship's horn moaned in the distance. Cutlery or surgical instruments clattered playfully in water. The patient stirred, wheezed a few times, then turned toward a bedside table. Carved from burnt wood an African demon or god leant against a vase full of white carnations, its solemn countenance like a sentinel over the sleeping man, warding off bad dreams. A jug of water distorted a silver crucifix and a few bottles of medicine.

A man appeared in the open doorway and stood there for a moment, as though deliberating whether to enter. He wore a shabby suit that reeked of smoke and wine, and carried a parcel under his arm. His stringy beard was neglected; his hair had receded at the front, exposing a broad forehead that hung low over his eyes. Perhaps no more than fifty, he walked toward the patient hesitantly, with a stoop, like a man who had aged before his time. Disturbing a chair and its shadow, he positioned it close to the bed and sat with arms crossed, biting his lower lip, looking painfully at the patient.

– Arthur, he whispered, in a voice like wind through dry grass.

Deeply immersed in a dream, or perhaps in the dreamlessness of morphine, Arthur didn't respond. Leaning forward, the visitor whispered his name a little louder and waited, wiping his upturned nose with the back of his hand. A few harsh breaths struggled from the patient's partly opened mouth. Plump as a toad, the visitor's hand tapped him on the shoulder.

– Arthur.

The effort of keeping his emotions under control cracked the visitor's voice. The patient's eyelids opened slowly, revealing a vacancy not unlike that of standing before the ocean on a starless night.

– Arthur, how are you, my friend?

Arthur turned his head slightly at the sound of his name, as though it now belonged to him by virtue of nothing more than a faint breath. He blinked a few times in releasing a sweet dream. Or was he perhaps released from morphine's purple embrace? His gaze strayed from the African idol, to the light above his head, and then rested on the visitor. His pupils were dilated, the whites of his eyes murky and yellow.

– Who are you? he asked, harshly breathing out each word.

– Don't you recognise me?

He blinked slowly in gazing at the visitor with a languid look that seemed too weak to take in anything. His gaze gradually focused, took in the visitor, drew him into its depths, and then gleamed with recognition.

– Paul, is it you?

Nodding, the visitor tugged on a full moustache drooping over his mouth, partially concealing a smile that accentuated the wrinkles around his eyes.

– God has brought us together, Arthur.
– Two sinners like us. Why?
– Don't be too harsh on yourself.
– Do we deserve mercy, Paul?
– I believe in redemption.
– Salvation through the teeth of death.
– Maybe it's a valley, Arthur, like in the Scriptures.
– You were always the Romantic.
– And you, the anarchist.
– Remember how we were going to change the world?
– It's all a blur now, Paul.
– Our revolutionary lyrics were going to free language from the constraints of a moribund Classicism. All great revolutions were inspired by the spirit of music, and our new poetry would express this spirit. It would touch a chord in all people – rich and poor, peasant and bourgeois – and excite a new sensibility, one that would realise the ideals of the Revolution.
– Did we believe in such things?
– Have you forgotten, Arthur?
– Music belongs to youth.
– No, it is the fountain of youth.
– And a hundred years from now there'll be another revolution, instigated by yet another rebellious generation, whose music would probably make you cringe. Forms change – the fire of youth remains constant.
– You were always the firebrand.
– And you the nightingale.

— You haven't forgotten, Paul smiled.

— Revolution through the purity of fire.

— Through the union of music and fire.

— A Season in Hell *was to be my New Testament. I wrote it in a fit, just after our terrible last meeting. I returned to Charleville disgusted by the debauched life we'd been leading and by the depravity to which we'd sunk. At nineteen my soul had passed through purgatory and, like Dante, I had witnessed a transcendent truth. I recorded my vision with a pen glowing white hot. It was to be my Book of Revelation: whoever read it would have their eyes seared, their soul branded by my vision. The conceit and arrogance of youth! The critics were harsh on the book: they found it incomprehensible. Devastated, I bought, borrowed, stole all the copies I could find and burnt them all in an empty water trough. Fire to fire, ash to ash. It was a wonderfully purifying experience, as though all the baseness in my heart were also burnt away. I arose like the Phoenix, and never wrote another poem again.*

— I heard you'd abandoned poetry, but couldn't believe it.

— When I was a child I spoke as a child ...

— You were a great poet.

— This is no time for nostalgia.

— No, my friend, A Season in Hell *is an inspired work.*

— In some ways you were its inspiration.

— By leading you to perdition?

— It was a long time ago, Paul. The young man who wrote that book overcame his anger and bitterness. Yes, he blamed you for his fall, but his sense of outrage passed and he soon enough forgot the profligacy of those years. Strange, this forgetting. I can't remember a single line from A Season in Hell, *as if the words went up in smoke with the paper.*

— I'll bring you my copy next time.

— No, Paul. Burn it.

— I could never do that, Arthur. You were right to compare it to Revelation. It went through my soul like lightning through a still night. I cried over it, Arthur. Hot tears fell on the pages and left permanent stains.

— Were they tears of remorse? Repentance for the shameful way we'd lived together? I've seen a lot in the past fifteen years, Paul, and yet I still shudder at the thought of our depravity. How did we allow it to happen? What drove us to it? Which demons possessed us?

— May I? asked Paul, holding up a shining cherry-wood pipe.

— Better the smell of tobacco than antiseptic and death.

He carefully filled the pipe from a green leather pouch, compressed the tobacco with a thumb whose nail was bitten down to the quick, and lit a match on a small stone. The flame snarled at his crumpled face. He puffed several times, until the strands of tobacco glowed.

— I should've known better, Paul said, exhaling a body of blue smoke together with a protracted sigh.

— We were both to blame.

— I was twenty-seven when we met, you were only seventeen.

— Seventeen, and the fire of hell in my heart.

— I wanted you from the moment we met. I melted in your fierce, proud look.

— Your infatuation stirred something in me, Paul. Awakened a magical power I never knew I possessed. I was no more than a boy and yet I had this terrible sway over a grown man. At first, of course, I was flattered by your attention. Together we were above bourgeois morality, above good and evil. Our relationship was an act of supreme revolt. The excesses of the flesh were all justified by the ideal. In time, however, new, dark feelings arose in my unbridled heart. I secretly wanted to dominate you, to humiliate you, to project my self-loathing onto you.

– If I had not corrupted you ... But you're right, Arthur. Weakness was my undoing. The stillness of prison was just what I needed after our tempestuous affair. The storm subsided and my frayed nerves got better. I found my faith again, Arthur. I served my sentence and was beginning to reassemble my life when I met Lucien Letinois, a young man with whom I experienced again some of our ideals. In his presence I forgot my faith and before long I'd seduced and corrupted him. His death at twenty-three devastated me. My grief soon turned to self-loathing, followed by prayers and penance. Now, Arthur, too ugly for youth, I vacillate between my faith in Christ and the company of old prostitutes, to whom I recite my verse. You know, sometimes I think I might even marry one of those sympathetic women, as a companion and comfort in my old age.

He closed his eyes and drew deeply. The ashy tobacco glowed. A patch of flaking paint on the ceiling reminded Arthur of the outline of Abyssinia. A woman's distressed voice called for assistance several times. The nurse's brisk footsteps clipped the tiles in the corridor.

– The fire of youth! said Arthur. Some are tempered by it, their will strengthened, their character prepared for life. Others are burnt and reduced to ash.

– Like the dead circle of yesterday's fire.

– A nice image, Paul.

– Words and images: the only currency I have.

– Are you still writing poetry?

— It's a way of life, Arthur.

— A way to poverty.

— Poverty isn't so terrible for one who lives alone. I don't need much — a pillow to dream on, a pipe to think with, and a pen to capture those states between dreaming and thinking.

— Poverty and poetry: seems they feed off each other.

— Poetry feeds on life — the misery, the squalor, the madness of the city — and transubstantiates it into music. It's nothing short of a miracle, Arthur. Like Christ's turning water into wine. When I'm under the influence of my muse, for want of a better word, I dwell in the world poetically — everything is a possible image or metaphor, everything becomes a possible symbol for the great order that is over and above us. I suppose it's what Baudelaire referred to as correspondences. Grasped poetically even banal things become echoes and reflections of angelic order.

— And does poetry make dying easier, Paul?

— Have faith, my friend.

— In poetry?

— Poetry, piety; sometimes I think they're the same.

A ship's horn sounded, low and long. Arthur started, as though summoned on a voyage beyond the equator. He struggled to push himself up with his elbows, but immediately grimaced in pain and slumped back into the pillow.

— You've done enough travelling, my friend.

— I need a fierce sun, Paul, not this European ghost that passes for the source of life. I need the sun of Egypt, Cyprus, Java, Abyssinia. I'd like to visit Australia, too, and feel its sun on my skin.

— Rest, Arthur, recuperate. There'll be time for Australia.

— There's one more journey to be made, Paul. My ship will call on a foggy night like this. Two sailors smelling of *wine and women will be waiting for me on the wet pier. They'll help me up the gangplank and take me to a cabin in the lower deck. It will happen just like that — I feel it in my bones.*

Arthur's eyes closed, his forehead creased. Paul's attention fell on a pair of crutches crossed beneath the bed.

— Fifteen years, Paul! One long feverish dream.
— When did you return to France?
— Five, six months ago.
— What do the doctors say?
— I'm a dead man, replied Arthur, forcing a smile.
— Medicine can work wonders these days.
— I've already lost a leg, and the gangrene's spreading.
— Don't give up, Arthur.
— Fate writes with one's blood, my friend.
— And faith transcends blood.
— How did you find me, Paul?
— I gave you up for dead four years ago, when my letter returned unanswered. Last spring word burgeoned like blossom that you were alive and convalescing at home. I went to Charleville, only to learn that you'd left on another overseas journey. I returned to Paris dejected. A chance encounter last week and hope fluttered in my heart. I was told that you were in Marseilles, ill in a hospital.
— I wanted to return to Abyssinia, convinced by a desperate hope that I'd be restored to health by the African sun. The spirit was willing but the flesh was too weak to undertake the arduous journey. I was brought here, instead. And here I spend my days gazing out the window, watching the feeble sunlight slipping from church steeples. Do you remember my little sister Isabelle? The poor girl has left home to look after her vagabond brother. She's gone to rest for a few hours, but she'll be back

soon and keep watch over me until morning. When the pain becomes too much, she pours me a dose of morphine.

For the first time, they looked at each other, probed the depth of each other's pupils, and connected in a way that stirred old feelings.

— And you, Paul? How has your life been?

— I'm trying to live decently, but ...

— What's become of your wife?

— She left me soon after you went away. I don't blame her though. The poor woman tried to raise me from my degradation, she tried to lead me to a better life, but all she got from me was abuse and misery.

— Our dissolute years would have exhausted the patience of an angel.

And once again they became silent and gazed at each other searchingly, looking for fragments of themselves in the vastness of each other's eyes. This wasn't the demonic look of former years, when one had sought to consume the other; it was marked now by resignation and a weary tenderness.

— Let's not be too harsh on ourselves for the past, my friend, said Paul, tapping his pipe on the second knuckle of his left hand, which was disfigured by arthritis. We've both suffered enough over our sins. But were those years all bad, Arthur? You know, as I get older I can't help looking back on them with ... a kind of fondness. Don't frown, Arthur. Hear me out. Look at me: a shadow with no future. The past is all that remains for me. Was it sordid? Was it perverse? Yes, and I've prayed for forgiveness. Let God be my judge. But until judgement day I must drag out this miserable life through the back streets of Paris. And when the good Christ slips from my heart, as so easily happens in the squalor and degradation of my surroundings, I turn to the past and make

poetry of it. Like your fire, Arthur, poetry can also purify. And like the philosopher's stone, it can turn the baseness of the world into pure gold. Do you remember the autumn we spent in London? And how we tried to live platonically. You worked on your Illuminations *and I on my* Ballads Without Words.

— *Your memory's good.*

— *Have you forgotten that sweet time?*

Removing his hand from under the blankets, Arthur extended it, palm up, toward Paul.

— *My thoughts stumble into this from time to time.*

Paul was spellbound by a small, craterous hole in Arthur's thin wrist. His face contorted with emotion. Placing the pipe on the table, he leant forward, clasped the outstretched hand and kissed the wound.

— *Forgive me, Arthur, he said. My thoughts and emotions were caught in a whirlwind at the time. I knew that you were sickened by my hypocrisy and shallow piety. Our relationship began to sour and we quarrelled badly on our second trip to England. I tried to hold onto you, but it was like holding a flame. You left for Charleville and I went to Brussels. I was miserable without you, Arthur. I would've killed myself if you hadn't answered my call. Those mad days in Brussels are burnt in my memory. I was obsessed with you, Mathilde was there, trying to rescue me, and all the time you were castigating me, saying how sickened you were by my drunkenness and grovelling. I can still see the look of contempt in your eyes, as though I were the lowest of the low. The stuff of French melodrama! But I was afraid, Arthur. Can you understand that? I'd abandoned my wife and child for your affections. I'd been ostracised by family and friends. I'd sold my soul for a life with you, and suddenly you were going to walk out.*

– I would've been spared this lingering death if you'd found your mark with that third shot.

– And the fourth would've found its bed in my brain.

– Forget the past, said Arthur, closing his eyes wearily.

– I've got my scars, too, Arthur! I paid dearly for that moment of madness. Eighteen months' imprisonment. Eighteen months of solitary confinement! And each day my forehead was branded deeper by the thought that I'd tried to kill you.

– They were insane years, Paul.

– Insane, but I've never again lived with such intensity. My feeling for you, our union of body and mind – I've never felt like that with anyone else, not even with Lucien. You were the meaning of my life. I would've followed you into hell, God forgive me. And now my life's nothing more than cold ash.

– It's nostalgia, nothing more.

– Are there no fond memories for you? he asked, rubbing the pipe's round head against his palm.

– I severed myself from that world fifteen years ago.

– Do you really mean that?

As though prodded by the question, Arthur raised himself a little. His dull eyes flashed for a moment, a note of anger sounded in his voice.

– Don't romanticise me, Paul. When all's said and done, I was nothing more than a spoilt, unruly child determined to smash all the laws. Nothing mattered, nothing was important. I was hell-bent on destruction to satisfy my own whims.

– And our friendship? Our freedom?

– I was wild and fatherless. Remember? You were ten years older than me. You should've been my guardian, encouraged me to lead a more disciplined life, guided me the way Socrates guided Alcibiades. Instead, you dragged me into the cesspit.

— *Guide you? You were a fierce flame, burning all who touched you. Besides, it was I who needed guidance. I'd fallen completely under your spell.*

— *What's the saying: blame's a beggar nobody wants.*

Scalp shining in the lamplight, Paul drew thoughtfully on the pipe. A blue sigh swirled over his face, drifted past the lamp, and dispersed into the darker regions of the room. Purple shadows filled Arthur's eyes as he gazed at the silver crucifix.

— *I took Communion yesterday,* he yawned.

The casual remark appeared involuntary, as though the idea had slipped past the threshold between thought and speech.

— *You've done well,* said Paul, leaning forward.

— *For Isabelle's sake.*

— *For a moment, I hoped . . .*

— *She prays over me day and night. The other day, tears shining in her gentle eyes, she implored me to see a priest. I couldn't hurt the poor girl's delicate feelings.*

— *Your spirit's still a flame, Arthur.*

— *A dying flame.*

— *A demonic flame.*

— *No, Paul, those demons have been exorcised.*

— *Then allow Christ into your heart, my friend.*

— *As He entered your heart,* he said sharply.

— *My faith's a daily struggle. I've been cast into a thornbush, and my salvation's the solitary rose that's just out of reach.*

— *Remember the last time we met?*

— *Stuttgart,* Paul nodded.

— *And you had just found Christ.*

— *Prison revived my faith.*

— *You came clicking a crimson rosary.*

— *Please, Arthur, don't shame me.*

— *That night you denied your Christ and started His ninety-eight wounds bleeding again.*

— *Your grip on me was delightful and diabolical.*

— *Christ won't approach me, Paul, even though I'm at death's door. Who knows, perhaps some souls are irredeemable. Yesterday, as the priest performed the rite and spoke the grave words, I felt nothing but death's garlic-tainted breath on my face.*

— *Christ meets us half-way, my friend.*

— *How far is half-way to heaven?*

— *No more than a step away.*

— *And how far is a step to a man with only a left leg?*

— *The space between two heart beats.*

— *Harar, in Abyssinia, was my spiritual home for years. There was a time when, in the furnace of a fever, I gave up all hope of living. My servant, companion and interpreter, Djami, brought in a tribal witch-doctor. Wrapped in a lion's skin and painted with blood, he grunted a few incantations, gesticulated, and rattled over my face a carved stick hung with amulets and bones. I swear to you, Paul, I drew more strength from that meaningless ritual than from the priest's tired words.*

— *Was this left by him?* asked Paul, picking up the crucifix and feeling its weight.

— *Isabelle brought it.*

Replacing the crucifix, he picked up the carved face.

— *What's this?*

Arthur grimaced with pain in turning on his side.

— *The face of Abyssinia.*

— *What does it represent?*

— *It's both a god and a devil, the cause of good and evil, the source of life and death. Christ and Satan reconciled at last.*

— *The natives worship such absurdities?*

— *It's no more absurd than worshipping the face of Christ painted on wood.*

Paul shook his head.

— *Their belief is wonderfully complete. It does away with the age-old problem of good and evil.*

After examining the face for a moment, Paul replaced it and, casually taking two white carnations from the vase, slipped their dripping stems into its gaping eyes.

— *Ten years in the abyss, Arthur. How did you endure it?*

— *Each day had its struggles and challenges.*

— *Is it true you were gun-running?*

Arthur nodded.

— *And slave-trading?*

— *That, too.*

— *Didn't it bother you?*

— *What do you mean?*

— *Dealing in slavery and death.*

— *Abyssinia isn't bourgeois Europe.*

— *You became a savage.*

— *We're all savages beneath the cosmetics of civilisation. The factories of your church-going capitalists are full of slaves forging weapons for the world market.*

A sudden spasm twisted Arthur's face.

— *Are you all right?*

— *Pass me one of those tablets.*

Pipe in mouth, Paul fumbled with the small bottle, rattled the jug against the glass, and watched solicitously as Arthur swallowed the tablet with a mouthful of water.

— *Is the pain bad?*

— *It'll pass,* he winced, handing back the trembling glass.

— *You wouldn't be like this if you'd remained in France. What on earth possessed you to squander so many years in that god-forsaken place?*

— *The need for a new life.*

— *A new life?*

— *It can arise only in a god-forsaken place.*

— *The prophet and the wilderness?*

— *No, Paul. I went there to become rich.*

Paul drew deeply, but the tobacco in the pipe didn't glow. He emptied the ash into his palm, cleaned the pipe with a deft index finger, and slipped it into his pocket.

— *You went there to make money?*

Arthur nodded.

— *Have you changed so much?* *Paul asked, shaking his head.*

— *A man's not a machine.*

— *And the ideals you once held?*

— *Ideals! After what you've called our inspired years, I set out on a kind of pilgrimage. I wandered around Europe in a desperate search for confirmation of those ideals. But everywhere I went, money's silver talons scratched my eyes. On my way to Russia, I was robbed in Vienna and left without a penny. At that stage, Paul, with my blood boiling, two courses of action were open to me: either a bullet through the brain, or throw myself into the pursuit of wealth, with the same passion as I'd pursued poetry. It was a winter's afternoon, and I was huddled in a doorway, when the shopkeeper came out and prodded me with a broom and a few barbed words in German. That scrawny broom decided my fate. I vowed there and then, as two men walked past discussing the price of coal, that when I returned to France it would be as a wealthy man. By the time I reached Abyssinia, I'd planned everything: I'd make a fortune, return home, get married, and have a son, whose education I'd supervise. Guiding him away from literature, I'd make sure he became an engineer or a mathematician. You see, Paul, I've learnt life's lesson, even though it has cost me dearly. Everything else is fantasy: the spawn of indolence, boredom, weakness.*

— Does that include poetry?

— More so than anything else.

— You believed it justified the world's existence.

— I should've studied something worthwhile, instead of wasting my youth on meaningless words. Mathematics, that's how I would've made a lasting contribution to the world.

He closed his eyes as though experiencing a vision of numbers. Paul scratched a spot of candlewax on the sleeve of his overcoat.

— Have you heard of Evariste Galois, Paul? he asked, rubbing his eyelids lined with dark-red veins. A firebrand, he burnt for mathematics the way I burnt for poetry. He made his discoveries at seventeen, then abandoned mathematics and threw himself into the turmoil of politics. At nineteen he was dead, shot in a duel. The similarity between us is remarkable, even though he refused Communion on his deathbed. His discoveries were in pure mathematics, but in time applications will be found for them in the physical sciences. Who knows, they may even contribute to a cure for syphilis, or some new contagion that spreads from illicit love. Mathematics, Paul — the ultimate ideal, the only way of improving mankind's lot.

— I know nothing about mathematics, Arthur, even though I live in rue Descartes.

— Mankind's salvation lies in it.

— Our new lyricism was going to save the world.

– Poetry changes nothing, my friend.
– We were such idealists.
– Dreamers in a drunken boat.
– But isn't the dream reality's seed?
– They're just literary words, Paul. I've outgrown those sweets. Abyssinia showed me the truth: the world is in the hands of science, not poetry. Ah, if I could live my life again...
– I've also learnt a few things, Arthur. Poetry isn't a tool or a weapon: it will never change the world as we believed in our youth. And yet through it we're better able to accept the contradictions of this world: the stars and the sewers, the rose and the thorn, life and death. If there is to be a change in human consciousness, it will occur only through a humble, open-hearted acceptance of the world.
– Have you learnt to accept the world, Paul?
– I haven't abandoned poetry.
– A martyr to life, he smiled.
– No, Arthur, simply a poet.
– It's the same thing.
– If anything, maybe I'm a martyr to my memories. Unlike most contemporary poets, whose aim is to spiritualise the material world, I live solely for my memories, striving to transform them into music.
– That's precisely why you'll never make an impression on the world. Memory, culture, the past – they don't matter any more. Science is sweeping us forward with bewildering speed, shattering our old beliefs. What's true and sacred today will be obsolete tomorrow. What will your poetry mean to the man of tomorrow? He'll refuse to be burdened by personal and racial memory. Living exclusively for the future, his goal will be the conquest of the stars. Yes, Paul, in the past I also lived solely for poetry, and thought we could change the world with

words. I still remember my belief: in the beginning was the word, and the world grew from the primal word. If I found this primal word, I'd have the key to the world. When I realised that my belief was nothing more than adolescent conceit, I wanted extinction. In a kind of desperate self-annihilation, I travelled without purpose or destination, but the past always sniffed me out like a bloodhound. I went to Java and joined the Dutch army in order to sever myself from the past, not just my personal past, but Europe's past as well. After a month I was on the move again. And then I found a remote corner of Abyssinia where the bloodhound lost my scent. In Harar there was no past, no memory, no excess baggage imposed by our European civilisation. There, Paul, I was no longer a poet — a self-proclaimed prophet whose utterances would transform the world. There I realised that the words that made poetry were no different from the sounds natives made by striking two dry, dead sticks.

His chest fell slightly, as though the rush of words had exhausted his breath, and his dilated pupils circumscribed his friend, the cross, the native face. Having crossed his legs one way then the other, and twisted a few strands of his beard to a point, Paul now gnawed at his arthritic knuckle.

– Did you find your freedom, Arthur?

– The Abyssinian sun purged my soul.

– And you haven't written a thing in all these years?

– I cured myself of that curse.

– You renounced your genius.

– And found the truth, Paul. The savage sun taught me that words are nothing but the shadow of the world.

Heavy with disappointment and sadness, Paul's gaze fell to the crutches under the bed and, beyond these, to a red Turkish slipper that was slightly misshapen and full of darkness.

— *You were both flame and hammer, Arthur. More nihilist than anarchist, you smashed and burnt the old morals, though you never offered anything in their place. I was more circumspect, even in those wild years. I never aspired to be a prophet, just a nightingale, hiding in the dark, compelled to sing by nothing more than instinct.*

— *Still the anguished poet.*

— *I can't be anything else.*

— *Are you writing much these days?*

— *Yes, but my best poetry is behind me. The muse's call is faint and I'm finding it more difficult to trace the outline of a memory and render it in music.*

— *Have you much to show for your efforts?*

— *A small circle of faithful readers.*

— *That was never my conception of a poet.*

— *You wanted to be both poet and prophet.*

— *And tragic hero,* he smiled weakly.

— *You wanted to live poetically.*

— *It's been years since I've thought of these things, Paul. You know, ever since my youth, when I broke away from home, I've been possessed by a demon with an insatiable appetite for new experiences. At first, it fed on poetry; later, it sought life for its appeasement. During the last few months the demon has loosened its grip, and only now have I come to feel the meaning of the words 'freedom' and 'peace'.*

His dry, cracked lips quivered in sustaining the faintest of smiles. Drawing his hands from under the sheets, he crossed his fingers on his sunken chest.

— *Why so silent, Paul?*

His question was answered by a lachrymose look.

— *Save your tears, my friend. I'm not afraid of death. I confronted it in Abyssinia — sickness, starvation, tribal wars.*

Life's a passing occurrence in nature, just like the fall of a leaf or the shape of a cloud. At this moment, Paul, I'm at peace with myself and this night.

– I must go, Paul said in a faltering voice.

– Isabelle will be here soon.

– I hope my visit hasn't distressed you.

– Can I have the ash?

Paul looked surprised, then opened his fist and emptied the ash from his moist palm into Arthur's cupped hand.

– Thank you for coming, said Arthur.

– I'll come again, just as soon as I'm able.

Paul stood then bent over and kissed him on each cheek.

– Forgive me, he whispered, swallowing his words.

– We're all victims of fate.

Wiping his eyes with a wrinkled handkerchief, Paul was about to straighten up when he took Arthur's closed hand and kissed the bullet hole in the wrist. He then turned abruptly, picked up his parcel from under the chair, and walked out, the worn heels of his shoes scraping the tiles at each step. Arthur struggled onto his back and sighed in a way that suddenly made him look smaller. His body became limp and his head sank deeper into the pillow. A ship's horn called from the depths of night. He stared at the flaking patch on the ceiling, until his thoughts were absorbed by the outline of Abyssinia.

A few minutes later the nurse came in with a book in her hand, her finger as a bookmark. She sniffed the air a few times before turning to the patient, whose eyes were lightly closed. Taking a carnation from the native face and using its stem as a page mark, she placed the book on the table, took the patient's fisted hand and felt his pulse. Concern flitted over her forehead. She took a small mirror from her apron and rubbed it on her breast. The ship's horn sounded again, this time fainter than before, as though it had set sail. She placed the mirror over his nose and mouth for a moment, then held it up to the lamp – not a trace of breath. As nothing more could be done, she took the opportunity to examine herself, smoothing the black line of her brows and pushing a recalcitrant curl back beneath the cap. Nodding, though it was impossible to say at what, she drew the crisp sheet over the patient's face, checked the time, took her book and left to make her report.

On the table, the crucifix appeared to quiver through the jug of water, while the native face kept watch over the bed, one eye a black hole, the other white with a carnation.

Streaming through the blackened window of PLAMEN'S GRILL, winter sunlight filters into the bookshop as well, glossing the displays in the front, brightening the spines on shelves, touching the last page of the manuscript, enhancing the contrast between the textured paper and the beautiful writing, and adding a gleam to the carefully written words, giving each letter a kind of holy glow. Sonya gathers the sheets and, in placing them to one side of the counter, uncovers her faint reflection in the glass top. She recognises herself in the nurse's features. Agnes Oroy – the name resonates with a note of familiarity. She writes it on the envelope, beneath her own name, and studies it a moment. Suddenly, in a flash, the letters rearrange themselves into Sonya Gore. Is it simply a coincidence? A case of reading too much into the text? No. This is his way of reaching out to her. And what if each dialogue is in fact an extended anagram? An alternative text existing in parallel with what is actually written, just as quantum physics postulates the existence of parallel universes?

She collects her thoughts and impressions while gazing at a punter outside the betting agency rolling a cigarette. The poignant story of the two poets is relevant. Change the names, the location, the nature of the illness to AIDS, and it could be a scene in a modern hospital. The poets could quite easily be one of many such couples who come into the shop, and whose conversations and whispers reach her from behind the shelves. But the content soon gives way to the physicality of the writing itself. Once again Sonya focuses on the text in an attempt to reconstruct the fingers, the shape of the hand, the body that lies behind the letters. If she were a graphologist she might read the words not just for their literal meaning but for their sensual disclosure – words as fingerprints on the page. The linearity of the writing, the uniform spaces between the words, the precision with which the *i* is dotted, the lovely curvature of the *s* – all this is also meant to be read, but how? Her pleasure comes as much from the look of the writing as from the content. But what vicarious pleasure is derived by the author in the absence of discussion and feedback? Or does he know that she is going through a difficult time? Are the dialogues a lifeline? Intended to rescue her from possible bankruptcy? But what is the place of philosophy, idealism, art in the depths of a recession that threatens to swallow all that she has worked so hard to establish? If only he would come forward. Perhaps he also has a deep feeling for books. He might be interested in becoming a partner in the business, in sharing the burden of providing shelter to all these books. At times she feels so alone, so helpless against an economic force of global proportions. The dialogues are high-minded, serious, not the sort of things from a person who would be simply playing mind games with her. She senses a message in them, some kind of hope, a way out of the impending doom. But how much longer will it be before the message comes through the text? Before hope appears from behind the words, and the face of her saviour shines from the letters?

the FOURTH dialogue

The bronze frog on the counter squats on the growing pile of bills. Several are second and third reminder notices in threatening red. Blowing on her cold fingertips, Sonya attempts to dispel the thoughts clouding her mind. Will the present recession lead to a depression? Who is promulgating these rumours? Is it the work of those in power? After all, if people are kept in a state of fear and anxiety, they can be more easily manipulated, made to accept the closure of businesses and loss of jobs without complaint, as though a depression were an act of God, like an earthquake. She was still teaching when the last recession gripped the country seven years ago. It had little effect on her, though she recalls the feeling of gloom among friends and acquaintances in business. Almost overnight wealth changed hands, entrepreneurs went broke or fled the country with fortunes, large companies changed their board of directors, middle managers became salesmen, salesmen became gardeners, work on construction sites was abandoned, and the corner shop near where she lives became a residence. But the storm passed, businesses were restructured, and people accepted their new circumstances, just like a colony of ants when their nest is disturbed. Fear and anxiety, she thinks, that is how people are managed and made to swallow the unpalatable. The Cold War used fear and anxiety to cower people into a state of subservience: nuclear war and the extinction of life could only be averted by massive amounts being spent on defence. And what happened? In time, the Cold War thawed, the black bulbous cloud of a nuclear explosion became a backyard mushroom, bullets turned into the blossom of the wild plum tree, and old enemies were embraced as allies. Work, an active mind – that is the best defence against fear and anxiety. If she would save her business from bankruptcy she must not succumb to the infectious gloom pervading the city.

With a feather duster she brushes the books displayed in the front window, the shelves, the tightly pressed spines of paperbacks. Here and there she stops to replace a book left on the tops of others, or to rearrange those put back without regard for alphabetical order. Moving between neatly arranged pine shelves marked according to subject, among authors and titles made familiar as much by letters as by colour and size, she feels less apprehensive concerning her struggle against the ubiquitous forces threatening her existence. These books are like a wall of defence: the two hardback volumes of *War and Peace* are a bulwark against the powers out there. She has handled every book in the shop, given them her tender touch, invested each with a small part of herself, set them in their rightful places, and, through this imposition of order, she has in turn imposed order on her life, defining herself in terms of her stock. Protectors of her identity, they now stand firmly against the disorder on the street, the uncertainty of the times, a world threatened by chaos.

If only she could lock the front door, keep out the intrusive world, shut herself in with her beloved books. She recalls the set of *Children's Encyclopedia* and the happy hours she spent with them in her room. The world in those red books was more real than the one beyond their borders. What she read and saw in them would always superimpose itself on the real world. She thinks now of her first encounter with fennel: a bright green stem with small clumps of yellow at the ends of smaller stems. A few years later when she found real fennel growing wild on the banks of a creek not far from her house, when she broke a sprig and rubbed it between her fingers, the sharp smell blended with the smell peculiar to that glossy page in the encyclopedia. To this day the smell of fennel contains a hint of that page. And then there were the colour plates of numbered butterflies from places she was unlikely ever to visit. At the bottom of the page there was a legend that matched the numbers with exotic Latin names she could barely pronounce. *Catagramma excelsissma* – the name has remained with her to this day. The game was to conceal the pictures and attempt to summon the shape and colour of the butterfly from the name alone, the unusual arrangement of common letters, as though the names had a wonderful innocence about them, never having moved lips and tongue, never having been corrupted by speech. In this she imagined they possessed magical qualities whereby the butterfly would flutter to the sound of its name, as though the name, the word, existed before all creation, and creation simply answered the call.

Memories swirling in the morning light, she thinks, going to the back. A bookcase seals the room's only window, making the dust in here less conspicuous. She quickly feathers the shelves and, keeping an ear on the front door, goes to the backyard and returns with a few logs from a pile delivered last week. The wood from a recently felled tree is still green, its eucalyptic smell reminiscent of the liniment she used as an adolescent, when a growth spurt caused her knees to swell painfully. She places a few logs in the hearth, rousing the slumbering fire. As the shop's only source of heat, the fireplace must be kept well stoked to warm the larger front room. In previous winters, when business was better, she would order deliveries of good red firewood which had been split into chunky wedges. This year, to save money, she has been on the lookout for demolition sites with signs inviting people to help themselves to free wood. With the downturn in construction around the city, however, building scraps have suddenly become scarce, and she was compelled to buy a truck-load of poorer quality wood, and even that was beyond her monthly budget. But she knew only too well that a cold shop was worse than a morgue, and that there was nothing like an open fireplace and the smell of burning wood to make customers feel comfortable and more inclined to browse and buy. The log begins to smoke, the tang of eucalyptus fills the room. Ideal firewood it is not, but the smoke will clear and warmth will spread through the shop. Who knows, the eucalyptus might permeate the books and add to their presence and character; it might remind buyers of their visit to the shop and save from oblivion the moment when they first set eyes on some book that has pride of place on their shelf.

At the sound of the door opening, Sonya returns to the front as two men enter. They accord her a nod and look around as though determining whether the shop is worth their while. Both are unusually gaunt, with short-cropped hair, thin necks protruding from loose-fitting collars, and wearing black jeans with silver-trimmed belts. The shorter of the two, whose hollow temples are lined with prominent veins, asks in a very precise manner, stressing each word, whether she has any books on French cooking. Sonya directs them to a shelf in the back corner and returns to the counter, where she is taken aback by the now familiar gold envelope. Who brought it in? The two men? No. The author must have been watching her movements from across the street, waiting for a moment to enter the shop unseen and leave the envelope. Perhaps he is watching from an upstairs window across the street, enjoying her reaction to the envelope. Is that someone peering from between the curtains? No, just the reflection of a passing cloud. She studies the people across the street. Nobody appears to be taking an interest in the shop. Punters are milling around the front of the betting shop, more interested in form guides and tickets than in playing a game of anonymous author. Two women are having coffee and croissants on a table outside the bread shop, but there is nothing suspicious about them, unless one reads intrigue in the vapour rising from their intense conversation. Who is that fellow outside the body piercing salon? He is wearing sunglasses and appears to be looking in her direction. Is he the author? She recognises him behind the sunglasses: he has visited the shop a few times in recent months, sometimes to browse, other times to buy, replying with a silent nod or shake of the head when asked whether he would like a bag for his purchase. Sonya starts. Was that a tentative wave? Or was he catching something in the air? Or perhaps shielding his eyes from the sun? But is she making too much of him? He might be looking elsewhere through his sunglasses. No. She feels that his presence is significant. Testing her intuition, she picks up the envelope and waves it. He smiles, turns, and enters the parlour. Was the smile for her? She is not certain. The mystery of the dialogues persists, even though the author may have taken the first hesitant step in disclosing himself. Perhaps tomorrow he will come and explain everything.

There might be a letter this time, she thinks, running the envelope's sharp edge across her lips. That smile, if it was intended for her, might be his way of making contact. She is about to open the envelope, when the conversation in the back corner suddenly drops, arousing her suspicion. Instinct tells her this is not the silence of reading. What are they doing back there? She wonders, annoyed at being kept from reading the manuscript. Not long ago, a young couple entered hand in hand and disappeared behind the shelves in that very corner. When their animated talk stopped, she went to check, and was stunned to find them in each other's arms, with the girl's back pressed hard against the shelves. It was just as well they are fixed to the wall, not free-standing, or they would have toppled, burying the rapturous bodies in books.

If the two men are doing something illegal or illicit she is determined to evict them at once. Pressing the envelope to her breast, she strides out from behind the counter, her steps sharp on the bare floorboards. One of the men is leaning forward, with hands on slightly bent knees, his back to the other, who is standing directly behind him in a position that would appear compromising, were it not for the pen in his hand. The man in front is serving as a writing table, supporting a heavy cookbook on his back, while the other, acting as the scribe, is hard against the table, busily copying a recipe on a sheet of paper. They do not notice Sonya, who, humoured by the sight, walks briskly to the back room. She removes the manuscript, flicks through the crisp pages, and looks inside the envelope – nothing. She is a little surprised and disappointed. She smells the pages: not a hint of aftershave. Checking her impatience to read, she prods the log in the fire and returns to the counter, where the men are waiting with a few selections, and a look of satisfaction at their find. Sonya is surprised: nothing on cooking. Commenting to themselves on how reasonable her prices are, they pay for their books, tuck them under their arms, and leave with a promise to return. In the doorway they deliberate for a moment about whether to go left or right. The pen prevails, takes the table by the arm, and they set off to the right.

There is something in the manuscript, in the fact that it has been written exclusively for her, that demands it be read in private, in one sitting, without interruption. Yes, private reading – the intimacy between reader and text. She recalls the first great event in her reading life, perhaps more exciting than reading her first chapter book. Upon turning eight she discovered that she could read in silence. Prior to that she had read aloud to teachers, parents, even to herself. Reading had been very much a public activity – words had to be sounded out to make sure they were being read and pronounced correctly. But the voice came between her and real involvement with a book, while the sound of a word diminished its authority by virtue of it being dissipated in breath. Through silent reading she was suddenly able to slip into the book as though it were a dream. She took in the word more immediately, and it, in turn, worked its magic on her more powerfully. A few years later, silent reading would allow her to read whatever she wanted. In class she would often conceal her illicit pleasure within the covers of a prescribed book.

She ought to wait until evening, but her desire to read the dialogue overcomes her sense of business. She locks the front door and turns a sign outward: BACK IN THIRTY MINUTES. In the back room, she studies the handwriting for a moment – not the meaning of the words, but the shape and slant of the letters. Does the author reveal himself in this? A girl with whom she shared a house in her university days was into palmistry and graphology. If the author does not make contact soon, she might visit her old housemate, out of curiosity if nothing else. A thud sounds from the funeral parlour, rattling the window behind the bookshelf. The fridge door, she thinks, as a chill goes down her spine. Reading, her lips move ever so slightly (a remnant of reading aloud never quite overcome), as though nibbling the sentences, tasting each word.

Here, my name is on this business card, shining in embossed black. Ah, but on second thoughts, it's best that I remain anonymous, for then you are free to invest me with whatever attributes you choose: gender, appearance, disposition, down to the size of my shoes. Let's think of each other as strangers: pedestrians driven into a doorway by a sudden burst of rain; patients in a doctor's surgery, suffering from high blood pressure; two minds drawn to a time and place by the gravity of ink. Besides, introductions are not needed – what matters for the purpose of this story is that I am an interpreter, not a translator. I make this distinction at the very outset because there is a world of difference between these two apparently similar professions. A full treatment comparing and contrasting the two would draw on such disciplines as philosophy, neuro-psychology, linguistics, semiotics and sociology, and would reward anyone contemplating a doctoral thesis. As I have neither the time nor the temperament to undertake such an exhaustive study, and as my interest is more that of a dilettante than an academic, I'll restrict myself to a few general remarks concerning the two, before relating an incident for which all this is a kind of foreword.

First, the translator is a man or woman of letters. Alone in his or her study, with the source material before him or her, the translator works patiently, in the manner of a ferryman, using eye and hand to ply his craft in conveying words from one silent shore to another. Ideally, then, the translator should not favour one language over the other, but stand midway between the two as a mirror stands exactly midway between object and image; in fact, he or she should possess the reflective equanimity of the mirror, taking in the object-word and reflecting it as faithfully as possible, without the distorting effects of subjectivity. This ideal is, of course, impossible to realise. The expressions 'one stone' and 'ein stein' are identical in a meta-linguistic sense; however, the latter translated for an American author from the upper-class suburb of Oak Park, Chicago, would convey a different meaning from the former translated for a German-writing, Czech–Jew born in, and bound to, Prague.

The interpreter, on the other hand, works with the spoken word, using mainly the ear and mouth. He or she does not dwell in the silence of paper and print, but in the original medium of language – flesh and sound. As the nature of their work involves a minimum of three people, good interpreters are inherently social beings whose particular skills are used to facilitate understanding and a feeling of communion between people in the present, not for the sake of enlightening an unknown reader in the future. This immediacy, this presence of other people, means interpreters can never be as detached from language as their counterparts. They do not prod still words with their pens or pick through the skeletons of dead languages: for them each word is alive, redolent of humanity, accompanied by emotion, gesture, facial expression, stress, intonation, and a host of other subtleties, all of which act on interpreters, colouring their judgement, influencing their choice of this word over that, affecting important decisions which often have to be made not in the leisure of solitude, but in the space between heartbeats.

I know all this from my long experience in acting on behalf of the judiciary, the medical profession, heads of state and businessmen. Try as I do to maintain a neutral position, I find that my emotions and sympathies sway from side to side. For example, I once acted as a court-interpreter in a case involving a young foreigner who had been charged with murder. An argument arose over a game of cards, and it was alleged that he pulled out a knife and stabbed one of the players. In conveying the prosecutor's words to the bewildered defendant, I found myself unwittingly affected by his manner: my questions acquired a sharp edge, my tone became slightly vindictive, my feelings inclined toward belief in the young man's guilt. Not only this, I must confess to experiencing a sense of authority at being directly responsible for the way the defendant's thin hands grasped the railing around the dock, for the tears brimming in his dark eyes, for the knot tightening in his heart. The prosecutor's words meant nothing to him, but when I looked him in the eyes and interpreted the severity of the charge I was the first to see the fear evoked by comprehension. Conversely, in relaying the words of the defendant to the prosecutor – words trembling, cracked, half-swallowed – I conveyed them with genuine pathos, with belief in his innocence, as though I were the accused. From this example alone, and there are countless others I could adduce, it should be evident that the demands placed on the interpreter are much greater than those on the translator.

Interpreting precedes translation by virtue of the fact that the spoken word precedes the written. I've often wondered about the role of interpreters in ancient cultures, before the use and spread of the alphabet. I imagine that they must have been viewed with a great deal of suspicion, particularly among barbaric people. I use the word 'barbaric' in its original sense, to denote a people for whom the sophistication of writing had not yet tempered the crude tongue. How are we to explain the diversity of languages if not as a deliberate attempt on the part of one tribe to safeguard and protect its innermost rituals and secrets from a neighbouring tribe? In other words, a language served the same function as a wall: it surrounded and safeguarded the tribe's songs and secrets, bestowed a sense of uniqueness, protected the inner sanctum. In short, language shaped a tribe's identity, and in this we have the beginnings of nationalism. The person fluent in two languages must have been considered a potential threat by both tribes. True, such individuals may have been held in esteem by their tribe for the fact that they could steal the innermost secrets of another tribe, but there was also a danger: they might run off with the secrets of their tribe and disclose them to the enemy. In all this, one can clearly see the precedents of the modern spy; in fact, the entire phenomenon of agents and counter-agents may well have its origins in the tribal interpreter.

As the tribe grew into a society, and societies became interdependent in matters of commerce, interpreters became more acceptable, though still regarded with ambivalence. Merchants and traders, by whom they were chiefly employed, were, and perhaps still are, ambivalent towards them: on the one hand they saw them as vital to concluding a successful business transaction; on the other, being suspicious by nature, they felt very uneasy about entrusting their material prosperity to people who often knew nothing about commerce and lacked business acumen.

Today, where the translator is accorded universal trust, the interpreter is still viewed with suspicion. A translation of, say, a poem by Novalis is read with an absolute faith in the veracity of the secondary author, which may have something to do with the power of the written word to inspire a sense verging on divine authority, which may in turn be due to the fact that writing was once the prerogative of the priestly caste. That translations are viewed as reverentially as the original work can be seen from the example of the Bible. Credence could never have been given to Holy Writ unless the act of translation itself were invested with sanctity. William Tyndale, perhaps the first martyr of translation, was burnt at the stake as a heretic in 1536 for translating the New Testament, the Pentateuch, and the Book of Jonah from 'the original tongues'. Now, more people read the New Testament in this new language than in the old.

In more secular spheres, it has been said of certain literary translations, such as Baudelaire's translation of Poe's poetry, that they surpass the beauty of the original. Other literary critics would argue that if a translation surpasses the original in all the attributes of good writing, then it is in fact a bad translation, in that the author had little respect for the source material. Despite the odd anomaly, translators are accorded far more honour and prestige than interpreters. Again this is due to the marketability of the printed word, not the essential value of their work. There is profit to be made from a book translated into fifteen languages. Still, we interpreters are not envious of our counterparts: we are the heirs of the ancient interpreters — those who read the future in dreams, leaves, smoke, the flight of birds. And if our names are never mentioned when heads of state meet, we take heart from the fact that our words decide the fate of the world.

I now come to the event which is responsible for this introduction to my profession. It occurred in Berlin a long time ago – 1923, if my memory is to be trusted. With the whitening of the temples memory becomes part fact, part fiction: the blanks, which seem to grow each year, are inevitably filled in by the imagination. It's more than likely that the entire memory of some people may in fact be the work of their imagination, even though they would swear to its reality.

I'd been sent to Berlin by the Foreign Ministry – no, not as a spy, but to act as interpreter for a trade delegation. Let's not disparage trade: it has often resulted in the exchange of ideas which have led to momentous developments in art, science, mathematics. Indeed, our alphabet and number system are directly attributable to trade. As I recall, we had concluded the morning session of formal introductions, during which I stood behind the head of our delegation and whispered into his crimson ear. Our programme allowed a few free hours before the afternoon session, so I set out on my own on a brief tour of the city.

Visiting several art galleries with exhibitions of modern art movements, I thought about the universality of art as opposed to the regionalism of language, and how these new movements were attempting to transcend cultural barriers by taking primacy from content and restoring it to colour.

I then wandered around the Bohemian quarter for a while, until I found myself in front of a crowded beer garden, where the thought of a refreshing ale proved irresistible. I jostled my way through to the back of the courtyard, to a small circular table occupied by a man bowed over a book. Pointing to one of the two vacant chairs, I asked whether I might share his table. He glanced up at me and replied with a sullen frown that expressed not so much objection as indifference. I interpreted the frown as saying: do as you please, only have the courtesy to leave me alone. He was about forty, though there was a gravity to his eyes that made him appear older. His pale features, in particular his ears, were accentuated by short-cropped black hair; in fact, his colouring had a tinge of yellow, as though he had spent the summer indoors, convalescing.

I sat down and gave my order to an overly polite girl who, judging from her circumspect manner, was probably studying to be a librarian and worked as a waitress over the summer. She placed her notepad on the table and wrote my order very precisely, as though practising calligraphy. I couldn't help noticing a white fleck in the shining nail of her index finger holding the pen. She then asked the other fellow if he wanted another drink, but he shook his head and pointed to an almost full glass of pitch-black beer whose froth had gone flat. The waitress slipped the pad into a breast pocket, picked up her tray and left. I accorded the fellow a smile in the hope of initiating a conversation, but it could have been a snarl for all the good it did: he scowled, opened the book on which his fingers had been tightly crossed, and began writing. The waitress promptly returned with my order. As she placed the mug on the table I noticed her right ear: there was no fold along its perimeter and it glowed as though full of hot coals. I handed her a note and, quick as a magician, she produced the change from the pouch around her slender waist. Others would have put on an act: rummaging in the pouch, pretending they couldn't find the right change, all with a view to the customer saying don't bother. Impressed by her honesty, I pushed back her hand with the change. She smiled and hurried to another table, leaving behind the scent of lilac.

Dismissing the fellow, I sipped my beer and wondered at the diversity of languages mingling amiably in the garden. From time to time I was able to pick up snatches of conversation in German, English, French, Italian, Slavic; for the most part, however, the languages fused into a meaningless Esperanto. Such diversity could never be found at home, I thought, relishing the linguistic excitement. The garden was a polyglot's paradise! My spirits rose as the level of frothy beer in the large mug fell. I glanced at the fellow: his attention was fixed to the book, as though the written word had far more significance than the speaking world. It was obvious he was in no mood for a conversation, so I opened my ears to the delightful sounds of this garden of Babel.

I was about to signal to the waitress for another beer, when a young man in his mid-twenties strode brashly into the courtyard. Glass in hand, he looked around for a vacant seat, then bustled his way through the crowd and came to our table. After looking down at us he stretched a broad grin and asked whether we objected. The writer didn't look up; I gestured to the vacant chair. An American, he was tanned, solidly built, sported a moustache of the type popular in Paris, and wore a loose floral shirt which revealed a hairy chest and bullish neck. After surveying the courtyard, he rattled the ice in a small glass smelling of peach schnapps, and turned his attention to the writer, who darted him a nervous glance.

– What are you writing? the American asked, cocking his head to one side in an attempt to read what was on the page.

Startled by the overt intrusion, the writer closed the book and, adopting a more upright posture, viewed the young man with an uneasy look, which reminded me of a defenceless creature seeking to escape a predator.

– People who write in public arouse my curiosity, continued the young man.

Each word seemed to act like a prod on the writer, who reacted by retreating from the table. Having observed that the fellow had been writing in German, I concluded that he didn't understand the American, so I took it upon myself to act as an unbidden interpreter.

– He wants to know what you're writing, I said in faultless German.

The writer turned suddenly toward me, as though he had been attacked from a totally unexpected quarter.

– It's youthful curiosity, I added, using all my experience to allay his suspicion.

Spreading his right hand flat on the book, as though taking an oath, he scrutinised the American for a moment, then spoke directly to him.

– I'm writing a short story, he said in a halting voice.

I interpreted this for the American, who drew his chair closer to the table. Quite unexpectedly, a conversation between them arose through me. Exercising all the skills of my profession, I was so unobtrusive that a distant observer would have taken them to be conversing directly.

– Are you a writer? asked the American.

– I'm more a worrier than a writer, he replied.

– What worries you?

– Sometimes it's a feeling of personal insignificance that reduces me to a state of zeroness; other times, it's a sense of guilt that gnaws at my being; and then, it's a

desperate need to be accepted that can't be fulfilled because of a crippling inability to reach out to another human.

– You need to get away for a while, muses the American, rotating the ice in the glass. A good dose of Spanish sun will dispel your worries.

– Does the Spanish sun cast shadows?

– Sharp as a tuxedo.

– Then it can't help me.

– Why are you Germans so ponderous?

– I'm a German-speaking Czech of Jewish descent.

– German, Czech, Jew – you Northern Europeans are too sombre for your own good.

– What are you?

– American, from Chicago.

– And are you also a writer?

– A reporter, but I hope to write fiction.

– Going from fact to fiction?

– Fiction should have its basis in fact, in the world.

– And the fiction which has its basis in fiction?

– Europeans! Always complicating matters! You should learn from us Americans to be more direct in your speech and thought. Tell it as it is.

– Tell it as it is, nods the writer. But the very act of telling changes what is. Words disclose, but also dissemble; they reveal and conceal at the same instant. Often I think that the true function of language isn't so much to communicate as to disguise thought and screen emotion.

– You're very suspicious of language.

– Yes, but I also place the utmost faith in it.

– There you go, confusing things again!

– Consider our present situation: you can't be certain that your English is being interpreted honestly, just as I

can't be certain in relation to my German. I accept the necessity of our interpreter — a necessity mingled with misgivings. It's the same with language: I mistrust it when I use it to convey my thoughts and emotions, but in the absence of anything else (the alternative is really silence) I'm compelled to place my trust in it. Consider also this: it's possible that our present conversation, logical and coherent as it may appear, is in fact entirely his creation. I mean, he might be misinterpreting our words to create a conversation different from the one we think we're having. What you've just heard in English may have nothing to do with what I've actually said in German. But, ignorant of each other's languages, we're compelled to place our trust in him.

I appreciated the writer's fine dialectic, but I assured them in their respective languages that I was an interpreter, not a fabricator.

— Your mind's like a ferret, said the American.

— More like a blind mole, added the writer, with a feeble smile that flickered and faded in the same instant.

— Always burrowing, always questioning. What are you looking for?

— Perhaps the very act of burrowing is the mind's ultimate end. Perhaps ...

A violent fit of coughing shook his whole body. His eyes dilated as he struggled to smother it with a wrinkled, bloodstained handkerchief. Having subdued it, he spat discreetly into the handkerchief and apologised.

— There's no need to interpret that, he said, looking embarrassed. A cough is a cough in all languages, just as a cry is a cry.

— Sounds like a problem with your lungs, the American said.

– *Have you studied medicine?*
– *No, but my father's a doctor and I know the sound of tuberculosis.*
– *You're very perceptive.*
– *Has it been diagnosed?*
– *Yes.*
– *You need to spend some time in a warm, dry climate.*
– *Spain?*
– *Yes.*
– *Is that where you got your tan?*
– *No, Asia Minor. I've been reporting the Greek–Turkish war for an American newspaper. Terrible casualties on both sides. Smyrna and dozens of other Greek-populated towns on the Asia Minor coast have been destroyed. Hundreds of thousands of refugees are still fleeing in carts and on foot.*
– *I wasn't aware of it,* said the writer in a preoccupied manner.
– *There were plenty of German war-correspondents.*
– *I seldom read newspapers.*
– *Aren't you interested in world affairs?*
– *What can my interest do for those refugees?*
– *It's a question of humanity.*
– *From a distance it's nothing more than curiosity.*
– *People are moved by what they read,* retorted the American, with youthful indignation.
– *War-correspondents,* said the writer, shaking his head. *You exploit the misery and suffering of others to satisfy your own vanity and sense of adventure. Your reports on the suffering of the Greeks in Asia Minor will be quickly consumed and forgotten, adding a little flavour to an American breakfast thousands of miles away. We're all hunters, only our weapons are different. The will that compels a soldier to aim his rifle*

at the enemy is the same as that which drives the correspondent to bayonet the soldier with his pen, or which dares the photographer to shoot him with a camera.

– There are readers who make donations to refugees and speak out against oppression wherever it's reported.

– No doubt, conceded the writer. It may just be my prejudice against journalism.

– What kind of writing do you appreciate?

– The kind where the battlefield is the writer's own heart.

– That's too literary for me.

– You Americans are still fascinated by war, as though it's something out of Homer. Having experienced enough real wars in our own backyards, we Europeans are not interested in reading about other people's wars.

– So you burrow into yourselves.

– Americans! Such confident people! With you there's never doubt, never uncertainty – the world's yours for the taking. And yet sometimes I envy that conceit: you're a young nation, unburdened by the weight of a past trailing behind like a cortège. Full of hope and possibility, you live predominantly for the future, which manifests itself in vigour and action. We Europeans are surrounded by the past: at times it's like a labyrinth from which there's no way to the future, other times a state of mind, a morass of thought, which makes action impossible.

– I suppose Europeans make thought an end in itself, while we use thought as a means to an end.

– A means? To what?

– To the world of course! The dominant beasts were those that developed and strengthened their teeth and claws through repeated use. It's no different with thought: it can only be strengthened through the act of devouring the world, otherwise it becomes subject to atrophy through self-reflection.

— *You say it with such confidence.*
— *I know what I want from life.*
— *And that is?*
— *To experience the world, devour it if need be, in order to transform it into literature. I want to write about men without women, men confronting their moment of death. I want to write of death not as the Romantics wrote, from a feeling of weakness and melancholy, but from a condition of strength and virility. I want to know death, not in an imaginative sense, nor from the safety of the study, but in terms of blood and bone. I want to see death in the screaming shrapnel-wound of the young soldier saying his 'Hail Mary'. I want to see death eye to eye, the way a matador sees it, who is dressed for the occasion as though for his own wedding, who stands proudly erect before the bull thundering at him, soles squarely planted in the blood-stained sand, and who doesn't plunge the sword into the beast's brain until he sees his own reflection in its pupils. I want to travel to Africa and confront death in its natural state, not the death sanitised by civilisation. I want to aim a rifle at a lion and hold off pulling the trigger until I've looked into its jaws yawning before me like a grave and felt its warm breath on my face. And only after having experienced such things would I consider sitting in a quiet study to write fiction.*

Fixing the writer with a challenging look, the American finished his drink and bit on a piece of ice, flexing his strong jaw-line. The writer flinched and lowered his eyes to the book. I was taken in by the young man's intensity, and this may have caused me to interpret his hopes in a slightly more lyrical manner than he had used. But I stress once again: interpreters are not bridges, serving all in a stony fashion; more like a conductive metal, they heat up when a current of conversation passes through them. The waitress came, her tray chattering with empty mugs and glasses. The American ordered another peach schnapps. I declined, saying I needed a sober head for what awaited me. The writer, who had not touched his glass since my arrival, was more interested in continuing the conversation.

— I admire your resolve, he said.

— It comes from having faith in yourself.

— I've never had that.

— Then you've had too much of the other faith.

— I've lacked that, too.

— And confidence?

— Confidence? he repeated with a sardonic smile. How old are you?

— Twenty-four.

— When did you leave home?

— I ran away a couple of times before making a final break at eighteen.

— Was it so effortless? So natural?

— Easy as a bird leaving its nest.

— And yet for me the simple business of leaving one's paternal home became a problem of metaphysical magnitude. I was thirty-two when, after a decade of ambivalence, I finally moved out. And even then it wasn't to experience the world, as you've done, but to take up residence in a boarding house a few blocks from my parents.

— You made a mountain out of a molehill.

— I simply wanted a corner of my own — a burrow where I could concentrate on my literary activities, of which my father vehemently disapproved and continues to disapprove. He is a strong and self-made man, for whom the world is a marketplace where only the quick-witted survive. He can't understand my preoccupation with the profitless business of *writing. Is it any wonder I have such self-doubt? He has always disparaged the only thing that ever gave me a sense of meaning and worth. As a younger man, I often saw myself as an insect crawling about in his shadow, and imagined that one day he would crush me with the soles of his smelly slippers. And then I wrote out of a sense of desperation, to avoid being crushed by producing something that would move him to accept me.*

— I went through that at sixteen, said the American, accepting his drink from the waitress and tipping her with a wink.

— Perhaps I've never really grown up, mused the writer. It seems I've never crawled out of my father's shadow. Who knows, if I'd moved out earlier I might now be married, with children of my own.

Both paused for a moment and turned a sidelong glance at me, as though I were the source of their conversation.

— Marriage, sighed the writer. That was my last hope — now even that's impossible.

Once again he was shaken by a fit of coughing, but this time he couldn't smother it with his handkerchief, and it lasted some time before subsiding, leaving him dazed and visibly paler.

— What was I saying? he asked, raising a hand that seemed incapable of holding anything heavier than a pen.

— You were talking about marriage.

— Are you married?

The young man spread his left hand on the table, revealing a wedding ring which cut into his thick fourth finger.

— Been married two years, he grinned.

— Marriage, he frowned, and the tips of his ears moved. For most people it's no more than going out to buy a bucket of coal, and yet for me it proved a nightmare. I was engaged for four years, during which I vacillated, examined, analysed, probed the depths of my being, and finally broke it off.

– Did you love the woman?

He seemed surprised by the question.

– I don't know, he added defensively.

– Is love a matter of knowing?

– I had to come to terms with it.

– Haven't you ever done anything spontaneously? Haven't you ever acted first and considered the consequences later?

– That requires confidence.

– It seems you killed the feeling of love by dissecting it with your too-precise thought.

– I've always feared other people, said the writer, and as a result I retreated further and further from the world. When I met Felice I'd already burrowed too far into my own private world – a world where fears were transformed to fiction, and existence was at least bearable. The mechanisms of my self-sufficiency, albeit of a negative nature, were so fragile and finely tuned that I couldn't risk it for anything in the world, not even for what may have been my salvation.

– This is too convoluted for me.

The American heaved a protracted sigh of exasperation and shook his head, which revealed the taut muscles along the sides of his bullish neck.

– I can't accept life based on fear, he added.

– What else is there? asked the writer in a pitiful voice. Yes, yes, you'll no doubt mention love, strength, joy. But they're fleeting emotions, nothing more than a spasm, a flash, a trickle. Over and above such things there's the ubiquitous fear which reduces the sensitive soul to an insect-like state.

– What exactly do you fear?

– If only I knew. Perhaps writing is a way of giving shape and form to the darkness at the core of my life; and even though it may ultimately prove futile, I think it makes

the darkness a little more human. Unlike your journalism, this kind of writing, this creation of images from one's private darkness, is more than a vocation – it becomes as vital as breathing. You see, in my system the world has been replaced by a private language.

– Are you happy with your work?
– It's not a question of happiness.
– Your writing leads to a dead end.
– And in this it mirrors life.
– No, the American said firmly (and I involuntarily conveyed his resolute tone), writing should affirm life, even when its subject is death. I want to write about the world and its wounds. I want to write novels that sell, that get translated, that serve as the means for new experiences and confrontations with death.
– You're a reporter at heart.
– To write is to communicate as clearly as possible, to the greatest number of people possible. The idea of writing for one's self, in order to purge the so-called demon from one's soul, sounds too much like psychiatric therapy.
– Perhaps great literature can only be written by those who aren't well, who don't feel at home in the world. The process is analogous to an oyster suffering the discomfort of an irritating speck of sand, which it coats with a secretion of its own being, making it smooth and round, producing a pearl from the very source of its pain.
– And literature written by the healthy and strong?
– It belongs to the world.
– I knew it wouldn't be long before the 'other world' entered the conversation – a realm which you, of course, reserve for writers such as yourself.
– The other world is none other than the world of the individual: the private world which may well have no relevance

to others; or, rather, the relevance others attribute to it may be totally different from that seen by the author. The value of the pearl is one thing to the oyster, quite another to the connoisseur.

My sympathies had now turned from the American to the writer. His weak voice, which strained under the weight of each word, together with the expression of his emaciated face, had subtly affected me, making me interpret with unintentional pathos.

– And what do you write about? asked the American.
– Myself.
– Autobiographically?
– Allegorically.
– I expected as much.
– Allegories and fables allow me both to express and con-ceal myself at the same time. Temperaments such as mine no sooner commit something to writing than they want to retract it. These forms allow me to hide behind the tone, the texture, the layers of possible meaning. In fact, the ultimate meaning of each story is as much its style and form as its content.

– Why are you deliberately difficult?

He involuntarily thumped the table with a fist like the head of a small battering-ram.

– Why aren't you plain and direct? continued the American. A clean short sentence strikes the reader like a fist in the eye.

– As I don't write about the so-called real world I have no need for your direct form of expression. My sentences are invariably long, convoluted, full of qualifying subordinate clauses and parentheses, which lead the reader into my inner world (at the same time as concealing me from him) – a world of corridors and burrows from which the reader emerges not with enlightenment, but with a sense of bewilderment, which is precisely what my writing seeks to evoke.

— And you expect readers to appreciate that?

— I expect nothing from the reader because I'm constantly ambivalent about my work. At times I'm revolted by everything I've written, as though this compulsion to write has cheated me of life. And then I feel like gathering my work in a pile, setting it alight, and immolating myself in the fire. But I'm too weak even for this. Still, it's a wonderfully ironic image, don't you think? One's funeral pyre stoked by the very paper that one had substituted for the world.

— Like a hunter turning the rifle on himself, mused the American.

— Or a judge becoming his own executioner.

— Are you working on a story?

— Yes, replied the writer.

Reflecting, he looked aside for a moment, his hands clasped tightly on the notebook, as though resolute in his determination not to read from the story.

— But it's not taking shape as I'd like, he continued. I'll most certainly tear it up tonight.

— And the title of your story?

— 'The Crevice in the Glacier.'

— What is it about?

At this point I glanced at my watch: the afternoon session of the conference would soon start. I apologised for the abrupt end to their conversation and left the table. As I brushed past her the waitress smiled and scratched a small mole on her left cheek. Before leaving the courtyard, I glanced over my shoulder: the two men stared uncomfortably at each other, separated by the gulf of silence that exists between languages.

Sonya feels her ear: there is a point and, to her surprise, the larger part of the perimeter does not have a fold. She scratches the mole on her left cheek. As for the white fleck in her fingernail – sheep, as her mother called them – it has almost grown through. But it was fully visible two months ago, and the author could only have seen it if he were in the shop at about that time. She runs her fingers lightly over the textured paper and feels the indentations of the words written by a fountain pen. If the author is the fellow who was standing outside the body piercing salon, he is about her age and must surely be computer literate. Why use a fountain pen? Why part with what is obviously the original copy? What does he expect from her? An opinion? But when will he make direct contact? She likes his writing, feels charmed by it. Reading this dialogue, and the previous three, she can almost feel the author's presence in the look of the writing. As for the content, she recognised Kafka and Hemingway, and was completely absorbed by their conversation. The author's style, the serious tone of his voice, his philosophical preoccupations, which many would consider unfashionable, strike a chord in her. Lately, she has started growing tired of the fiction written by people of her age. Most of it bludgeons the reader with its unmitigated bleakness. Who needs a slice-of-life novel when one can experience the bleakness just by taking a stroll up and down the street? They are all out there: those who spend their youth in bars and cafes; the drunks and addicts who huddle from wet nights in the doorways of shops; musicians who set up on the footpath at midnight and beat their rhythms to smiling pedestrians; young graffiti artists who prowl lanes and dark side streets, searching for blank walls on which to spray their messages of doom and despair, angst and anarchy, peace and perversion. Confronted by it every day, she does not want to read about her generation. The turgid river described by those angry young authors, one full of the flotsam and jetsam of humanity, flows along this very street and spills into her shop. Just the other morning she prodded a young man with her umbrella in order to open the front door. He was asleep, covered in sheets of newspaper. When he finally stirred, he gathered the sheets under his arms and set off in search of another shelter.

How different her response to these dialogues! For fifteen minutes the author transports her to a realm where characters live solely for ideas. For fifteen minutes he calms her with his steady, rhythmical tone, caresses her fears with his gentle handwriting, confides in her his innermost thoughts. For fifteen minutes she is not alone in her struggle against dark, implacable economic forces: the characters in the dialogues, names she has grown up with, are like friends who have come in her hour of need; their beliefs and ideas are like steadfast beacons; the world they inhabit is beyond material necessity. And now, with this dialogue on her lap, she senses in the author a kindred soul reaching out to her, offering his hand not just in a gesture of friendship but perhaps in . . .

the FIFTH *dialogue*

Unable to concentrate on pricing more books from a cardboard box labelled PET FOOD, Sonya gazes through the misty drizzle at a few workmen demolishing the black roof-beams in PLAMEN'S GRILL. The books were brought in late yesterday afternoon by a woman in her mid-twenties, with rings pierced through both nostrils and a larger one through her lower lip. Her hair was cropped close to the scalp, and she wore jeans that were slashed at the knees. She placed the box on the counter and invited Sonya to make an offer, saying she would accept anything that sounded reasonable. Despite having tightened her budget in recent weeks, to the extent of curtailing her visits to markets and fairs, Sonya was moved by the wide-eyed look of desperation. The girl was more than pleased with the deal and went on to say that she was through with literature. She had wanted to be a writer, but a few nights ago the Angel of the Word had appeared to her in what seemed like a revelation. It was an enlightening experience: she was now determined to enrol in a course of theology with a view to becoming ordained as a minister. Intrigued by the girl's vivacious manner (was she under the influence of a stimulant?) Sonya asked about the nature of her revelation. The girl needed no coaxing: she told her story fluently, as though it had been written and memorised, her eyes fixed unflinchingly on Sonya.

Three nights ago, on the winter solstice, she had been sitting before a blank computer screen, waiting for a thought to twitch the sinews of her fingers and set them springing happily over the keyboard, playful in the endless possibilities of the word processor. Unlike other such occasions, nothing happened this time. She sat there, staring at the cursor winking hypnotically, until a drowsiness pulled at her lashes. It was then that the Angel appeared, as though from the blue depths of cyberspace, and called her by name. The voice seemed to arise from the hum of the computer – a hum which sounded like countless languages blending into a hymn. The Angel asked whether she wanted to be a writer, and before she could reply they were soaring through cyberspace at a speed between that of sound and light. The Angel pointed to a domed building with a classical facade, surrounded by a colonnade surmounted with statues. She took it to be a temple or a shrine, until the Angel said in a sweet, sisterly voice that it was the World Library. The next instant, very much in the way events unfold in dreams, they were inside the library. Her spirit began to sink at the sight of countless books with gold and silver letters on their spines, in languages dead, living, and yet to move the human tongue, and all arranged according to some inscrutable system. She was led through a narrow doorway, to a musty labyrinth of corridors lined with texts and tomes whose titles and authors had faded, and which had not been opened in centuries. As light from a bare bulb struggled in a tangle of cobwebs, and silence settled on everything like dust, the Angel preened the iridescent feathers of her wings and asked if she still wanted to be a writer. Yes. The word fluttered like a moth in its death throes.

Another instant (or was it an eternity?) through cyberspace and they zoomed toward a fractal spot of light which suddenly exploded and became a constellation. As they sped toward what seemed a random bright point in this constellation, it also exploded, creating a nocturnal megalopolis. They approached a vast industrial complex adorned with strings of lights. A plume of steamy smoke rose from a chimney and spread into a cloud against the blank sky. They flew toward a compound where powerful arc lights shone on mounds of books. Pages crucified on barbed wire topping the surrounding fence rustled to life in the rush of air caused by the Angel's powerful wings. A mechanical beast appeared and groaned into the compound, its sinews gleaming with hydraulic oil. A massive jaw opened, bit into a mound of books, and dropped them into a shoot from which they fell onto a squealing conveyor belt. The yellow pages of a thin paperback novel rustled entreatingly at her feet, but the Angel gripped her by the right wrist and drew her away, to an elevated metal walkway overlooking a pulping room with a dozen large vats. Directly below them, a man was skimming the thick mixture with a sieve attached to a long rod. Authors, titles, text – everything was reduced to black sludge and separated from the pulp. Again the Angel turned and asked, in an even sweeter voice, almost verging on song, whether she wanted to be a writer. The stench was so overpowering, she held her breath and managed a nod. The Angel drew her away, through the swirling, steamy smoke: the ideas, thoughts, hopes, dreams, truths of countless authors whose work had been pulped.

They flew upward, toward a black disc the size of a pupil, which the Angel called the anti-sun. As they got closer, she heard what sounded like the twittering of morning birds, but which soon became the unmistakable cry of human voices. The disc turned out to be a pit full of humanity – men and women were fighting and struggling against each other in a desperate scramble to reach up and touch the Angel. They were the souls of writers, said the Angel, holding her hand in sisterly concern. A voice rose above the chorus of despair and cried out: the word eclipses the sun. A second: the letter stills the breath. And a third: love the word and suffer this. She wanted to reach out to those suffering shades, alleviate their misery if only for an instant, offer a gesture of consolation. But the Angel's grip tightened and held her back. Suddenly her eyes brimmed with tears, and she felt an overwhelming love for the world. She wanted to experience the earth again, commune with it, just as she had done as a child. And once again, this time in a voice that sang and appeared to soothe the souls in the pit, the Angel asked whether she still wanted to be a writer. Tears dripping from her cheeks fell into the pit, and countless souls flocked to each tear and drank from it as though it were a drop of life. She swallowed back a wave of emotion and whispered: no. The Angel plucked a coloured feather from the right wing, gave it to her, and vanished without a word.

According to the digital clock on her desk, the experience had lasted less than a minute. The computer was humming, the cursor on the blue screen winked from the same position. Outside, a bird was daring the darkness, announcing the sun with its fearless song.

Shoving the money into her jeans without bothering to count it, the girl left the shop with a beatific radiance on her ring-pierced face, as though her belief in the mystical vision had been strengthened and made more precious through communicating it. Sonya was impressed by the girl's fervour, and the melodious tone of her voice still echoes in her ears. Unlike her advanced ability to grasp and remember precise details through the act of reading, Sonya's retention of information acquired aurally is quite short-term. She usually forgets jokes and anecdotes the day after hearing them. The girl's story, however, is an exception. Is it because she can empathise with her feeling for books? But was her experience really a vision? Could it have been no more than a dream? An extended thought in a half-waking state? Virtual reality? Or had it been induced by an hallucinogen? Whatever the origin of the vision, the girl has taken it as a revelation: it has given her strength to embark on a new life.

Sonya thinks about her own Angel of the Word. It has been over a week since the fourth dialogue. Each day she has left home with a sense of expectation, endured the hours in the shop with thoughts of his imminent arrival, and closed at nightfall full of disappointment. Has she made a mistake? Is the author somebody other than the fellow outside the body piercing salon? Her former housemate, Caroline, the graphologist, has provided a good portrait of the author – one that accords with her own view of him. Sonya shared a house with her and two other girls during their student days. Of the three, she has kept in touch only with Caroline, who still lives in the house, while a dozen or more other tenants have come and gone. Sonya paid her a visit a few nights ago, taking the fourth dialogue.

Caroline occupied the same room: upstairs, its balcony trimmed with lace-work and overlooking a park, lined with massive elms. She abandoned a degree half-way through the final year, when she came across the work of Gödel, whose Incompleteness Theorems shattered her faith in mathematics as the key to the universe. From then on she sought a balance of mind and heart. Symbols still fascinated her, though mathematical symbols were now one part of the great universal alphabet. Working as a private tutor, she went through a period of assiduous study in alternative ways of reading. First there was numerology, and this was followed by gematria – the study of esoteric messages embedded in the number systems of ancient civilisations whose alphabets also served as numerals. After this there was the reading of dreams, Tarot cards, palmistry, and the protrusions on people's heads. At one time she befriended an elderly Greek woman, and through the woman's granddaughter, who acted as interpreter, she learnt to read coffee cups – stains formed when the thick black sediment is worked around the inside of the small cup, which is then turned upside down in the saucer and allowed to dry. This had presented her with problems: often the interpretations offered by the old woman involved letters from the Greek alphabet. How was she to translate these to non-Greeks? Was this way of fortune-telling culturally specific? Were there some arts that perhaps could never be translated? In the end, she overcame the difficulty by placing her faith in the primacy of the symbol, in this case the stains. As she explained to Sonya, the symbol could be equated to light, and just as light was broken into the spectrum of colours in passing through a prism, so symbols were broken into different languages by the prismatic mind, and each language had its own validity and truth.

But all this had been a preparation for what she believed to be her ultimate calling: graphology. From her first reading into the subject, she saw in it a true union of art and science, a coming together of the inner and outer, a manifestation of the invisible through the visible, the revelation of character through the act of writing. After years of dedicated study, she has developed her art–science (as she calls it) to such a level of professionalism that she uses it in consulting with clinical psychologists, forensic scientists, and in court cases involving forgeries and defalcation. Unlike other forms of reading, where subjects were often distant in relation to symbols, graphology was concerned with personal, intimate disclosures. The act of writing was an expression of the will, the life force, the logos, channelled through the intellect, transferred to the nervous system, and given form through bones and muscles as the written word. A graphologist could discern unfelt psychic tremors – precursors to events that would shake a person's very foundations. More personal than the revelation of character through painting and music, the word written by hand was the true fingerprint of the soul.

Caroline had been in the shower when Sonya arrived. Once Sonya explained the reason for her visit, Caroline sat down in the lotus position, and tucked the hem of her bathrobe between her legs. As she studied the first page, a faint smile played on her full lips, while her light-brown eyes were lively as winter sparrows. She asked Sonya for the ruler and large magnifying glass on a table, and proceeded to examine the writing in greater detail, taking measurements and making notes. Sonya had been ambivalent about visiting Caroline: she had come to consider the dialogues as private letters intended for her eyes alone; showing them to another person would not only diminish their intimacy, it would betray the author's confidence in her. Now, seeing the first page in Caroline's hands and the others resting on her bare knees, she felt possessive toward the manuscript, and regretted her hasty decision.

As Sonya chided herself for lacking discretion, Caroline looked up and, face glowing from her intense scrutiny of the work, announced her initial findings. She began by pointing out that the majority of graphologists failed to consider the occasion that prompted a piece of writing. A note intended as a self-reminder would be written in one script, a message to one's boss in another, while a letter to a lover in yet another. From what she could see this manuscript was written by a male who was evidently very fond of her, possibly in love with her. The small spacing between words indicated a need for proximity, for closeness – a desire to love and be loved. The absence of a pronounced slant showed a gentle person, one considerate in his views, who tended to avoid extremes. The print-precision of the words, together with the absence of loops and flourishes, revealed a person who was withdrawn from society, living in some form of isolation that may be self or socially imposed. And then there was the first person pronoun – the 'I' of the text. At this point Sonya interrupted her to say that of the four dialogues, this, the fourth, was the only one to use the first person. Caroline mused for a moment, running her finger along the bridge of a prominent, slightly upturned nose. Even though the dialogue was not autobiographical, the presence of the author came through in the 'I' of the narrator. The plain letter, lacking a top and bottom stroke, and only marginally bigger than its lower case equivalent, pointed to a lonely figure – a person with no firm hold on life and no great aspirations. There was in this single, unadorned letter, a person deeply in need of love, though he found it difficult to express his emotions, which could be attributed to a fear of rejection. Of course, she could analyse the writing more thoroughly, but this would only serve to add colour to the initial sketch. She felt it was only a matter of time before the author disclosed himself, and advised Sonya to be receptive, to broaden her emotional experience, to pull down the barriers she had set up around her life.

The conversation then turned to the demise of handwriting. The few authors Caroline knew used computers even for their first drafts. Initially they had found it difficult to break the link between the action of writing by hand and the movement of their thoughts and ideas. But they were soon enough writing with all ten fingers, and swore that not only had their writing become more polished but they were now more prolific. She pointed to the work of the anonymous author and admired his use of a fountain pen: in an age driven by productivity and profit, when authors wrote for mass readership, her faith in the human spirit was strengthened by works written by hand, addressed to an individual reader. In her gloomier moods, though, she feared the death of handwriting and graphology. The word was being digitised at an alarming rate. People were no longer writing letters because it was more efficient to send messages by digital phone or email; software was available that could scan handwriting and convert it to typed text, obliterating all trace of the original, the personal; signatures, the very symbols of identity, the signs that revealed most a person's character and disclosed secrets that were often unknown to the person in question – the crucial elements of graphology – were being replaced by barcodes. And though her background was in mathematics, she feared the digitisation of the word because it prefigured the digitisation of the world. Just as all handwriting would be reduced to uniform text, so the individual would be subsumed by the crowd, freedom by the common good of the ant colony, the soul by virtual reality, God by the ultimate computer.

A face cupped in two hands peers through the lower part of the B on the front window. Simkin. Absorbed by the dialogues and the author's identity, Sonya has forgotten that it is already the sixth of the month again. Before she can gather her thoughts and find an excuse for not having the rent, the landlord enters. If only he accepted cheques! She would have a few days' grace between the cheque being banked and its clearance. But he insisted on cash when Sonya signed the tenancy agreement. He said he was too old to be running back and forth between banks, chasing bouncing cheques. Sonya's gaze wanders from Simkin's protruding lower lip, to the snake and eagle on the window of the body piercing parlour, to the workmen struggling with a black beam in PLAMEN'S GRILL, to the butts in the ashtray. Her thoughts drift from what is being said, to Caroline's description of the author, to the warning given by the bank's Credit Officer. He telephoned about a week ago, saying, with an 'um' after each word, that certain problems had become evident to the Credit Department which required urgent attention. Next morning he was in the shop at precisely the appointed time. He was no more than thirty, with a rosy tinge to his cheeks from the cold, wearing a navy-blue suit, and carrying a leather satchel under his arm. His shoes, scuffed and badly in need of polish, were out of keeping with his otherwise neat dress. Smiling with boyish ingenuousness, he introduced himself by thrusting out his right hand in an awkward manner, as though making a conscious effort to overcome his diffidence. He looked around and sounded a protracted whistle at the number of books. Did she have many science fiction? A few shelves. He had been an avid reader of that genre in his school days. But that changed once he enrolled in an accounting degree. In the past ten years, it had been books of a different kind: books detailing debits and credits, profit and loss, success and failure. He was sorry to bring this up, but their records had revealed certain weaknesses in her business. The last two repayments on the loan were overdue and her overdraft had been in debit for some time. The country was going through difficult times, businesses were going bankrupt, and the bank was picking up the losses. His presence was not a threat of foreclosure; the bank's policy gave struggling businesses a chance to trade their way out of adverse circumstances. He was here to remind her of the terms and conditions of the loan agreement, and, more importantly, to offer whatever help and advice she might need. Crossing the second and third fingers on both hands, he hoped that she would be able to weather the recession. Sonya assured him that future repayments would be met on time and the overdraft balanced. He nodded, opened the satchel, and wrote a few things in a notebook, taking time with his thoughts and care with his words, occasionally biting the end of the pen while looking up at the pressed-metal ceiling.

When he closed the satchel his manner was suddenly less officious, though his cheeks still glowed like hot coals. He loosened his tie and top button. Did she know that almost seventy per cent of businesses closed within the first three years? The effort, the cost, the hopes – all ending in ruin and heartache. Why? It saddened him to see so many people starting out with such innocence, such belief in a system that promised to reward hard work, only to be reduced to despair. When this sadness got the better of him, he always recalled a novel he had read at school: *A Catcher* or *The Catcher in the Rye*. Just as the main character (whose name escaped him) had imagined being in a field of rye, catching children about to fall off a cliff, he also wanted to be a catcher in a field of dreams, saving people from the unseen abyss of business failure and all the suffering it entailed. He hoped (with crossed fingers) that his presence in the shop would serve to make Sonya wary of the pitfalls that lay ahead. He paused just long enough to glance up wistfully at the workmen in PLAMEN'S GRILL. There were times, he sighed, when he questioned his suitability for what he was doing; when he felt that his sensitivity was a hindrance in his aspirations to become a liquidator. He hoped (again with crossed fingers) that, through experience, he would overcome his sentimental nature and make his way in the world. Moved by his frankness, Sonya attempted to encourage him by pointing out that she was determined to avoid the abyss, that she was confident in the demand for second-hand books, and that, with his support, she would trade through this recession. His right hand flew out of his pocket and caught Sonya's. He would pay her another visit in a month: it was the bank's policy to keep an eye on ear-marked businesses.

Simkin takes a green receipt book from his coat and places it on the counter. Sonya apologises, struggling with her words. She has used the rent money to offset her overdraft. A bank officer came last week to discuss her situation. Liquidator? frowns Simkin, flicking the pages of the receipt book. No, Sonya assures him. He was a young man, very sympathetic. Banks, scowls Simkin. He avoids them like a plague. One should not be fooled: their sympathy is that of a vulture for a dying creature. He is sorry that Sonya has come under their scrutiny: more often than not such visits are signs of worse to come. As for the rent, he is a human being, not an institution: he will give her a little time. Of course he does not want the shop to be vacant in this difficult climate. On the other hand, he does not want a repeat of what happened with his previous tenant. If there are to be losses, he will minimise them by acting quickly this time. He is a fair man, not a fool: he will give her another month, by which time she must have both the arrears and the advance. Sonya thanks him, adding that she will tighten her operating expenses, work longer hours, and trade out of her predicament. He would be fair to her, but she must return the fairness. If things become worse, his debt must be settled first. After all, the bank could absorb losses far better than he. Sonya promises that, in the unlikely event of liquidation, she will come to some arrangement with him concerning outstanding rent and the remaining life on the lease.

Simkin ponders a moment, holding the ends of the tape, fists moving up and down as though weights on a pulley around his neck. A cyclist in black lycra stops abruptly outside the shop, leans his bike on the window, and rummages through a container fixed above the back wheel. Nodding, Simkin takes his receipt book and turns to go. Wearing a balaclava and sunglasses, the cyclist swings the door open and strides in, startling Simkin, who, clutching the measuring tape, raises both fists in the air. Drizzle dripping from his balaclava, glistening on his skin-tight lycra suit, the cyclist thrusts a large gold envelope at Sonya. She is about to open the wooden drawer containing a few notes and coins, when the man places the envelope on the counter, asks for a signature, and flies out. Before Sonya is able to collect her thoughts, the man leaps on the bike and speeds off through the drizzle, water spraying up from the back wheel.

Expect the worst in times like these, says Simkin, shaking his head. Sonya's heart throbs. His envelope! She turns it over: her name and address are in his fine handwriting, though a few raindrops have swollen the first three letters of her name, making them run into each other. Was he the cyclist? Pretending to be a courier? No. She recalls Caroline's description of his character. He is too serious for games like that. His reluctance to come forward is due to other reasons. Lacking confidence, perhaps he needs more time to establish a relationship through his dialogues before approaching her directly. Simkin looks at the envelope over the top of his glasses. He hopes it is not a bill or, worse still, a summons for unpaid bills. It is a letter from a friend, says Sonya. With the envelope in her hands she does not feel as despondent about the future: it has dispelled the cloud that has been gathering around her all morning. Banks, recession, rent, liquidation – now all this is not so overwhelming. By the way, Simkin says, smoothing the twisted tape. He has heard that the vacant property next door is going to house a brothel. The permit was approved before anyone could lodge an objection. It will be open for business in a matter of weeks. A funeral parlour on one side, a brothel on the other. Stiffs in one, stiffs in the other, he laughs wryly, and turns to the door, nodding as though before the Wailing Wall.

If she were not holding the envelope, news of the brothel would have come as yet another blow to her business. If people shied away from a shop next to a funeral parlour, they would be even more guarded and reticent about walking into one next to a brothel. But eager to open the envelope, she quickly dismisses these thoughts. There may be a note inside this time, perhaps a letter of introduction. Should she close the shop for half an hour? No. A customer lost means another nail in her coffin. Exhaling a plume of smoke up at the ceiling, she takes out the new dialogue and inspects the envelope.

Are you poor, oppressed, persecuted? Remember: your eyes are your wealth, your freedom, your strength in adversity. Look around, fortunate ones. God has blessed you with sight not only that you may read this, but that you may gaze in reverential awe at this wonderful building. The library is a regular octagonal prism surmounted by a dome with arched windows in the cupola. Rosewood bookcases sixteen shelves high, with a ladder attached to a rail running along the top shelf, span each side of the octagon. There are four balconies, one above the other, between the top of each bookcase and the dome's circular base. Their width decreasing in geometric ratio from bottom to top, these balconies contain rare books and manuscripts, accessible only to those with special permission, and then only for the purpose of research. The facility of access to each balcony is inversely proportional to the square of its width. The floor plan consists of eight concentric octagons of reading-tables, each with a small overhead lamp and a green top adjustable to the reader's angle of least neck strain. Like the spokes of a wheel, eight aisles converge at the hub, where a square-based mahogany rostrum, carved with fabulous figures, rises above the tables and imposes its authority upon the readers. Worn smooth by countless hands, an eagle's head stares fiercely from the four corners of the rostrum's balustrades, ready to swoop down on anyone who merely thinks of breaking the rule of silence.

You see, I know this library as well as I know the inside of my own skull. I have been a librarian here for fifty years, and in that time this edifice has come to be an extension of my being. Now, though almost totally blind, I can still locate any book as easily as I can locate the fourth finger of my left hand with my right index finger. But books are now of little use to me: a bibliophile, countless books at my fingertips, and I can't see a single word! The exquisite tricks that fate plays on us mortals!

At first, when my sight began to weaken, I felt irony's sharp point whenever I touched a book. The printed word has been my sustenance since the age of nine or ten. I still recall the disappointment of that child: when he would accidentally cut himself in games with sticks and stones he quite expected to see a trickle of ink instead of blood. As my sight dimmed, and ophthalmologists could do nothing to arrest the deterioration of my corneas, I began to feel the anguish that Eratosthenes must have felt. Not Eratosthenes the Greek—Egyptian mathematician, who calculated the distance to the sun using the lengths of shadows, and whose sight remained unimpaired, despite the fact that he studied something far more blinding than black words. I am referring to the other Eratosthenes – the octogenarian director of the great library of Alexandria. According to ancient sources which have found their way into Canetti's novel Auto Da Fe (also about books and bibliophiles), this Eratosthenes took his blindness very badly. He refused food and drink, despite the tender pleading of his many assistants, and remained adamant until the very end: if he could no longer read, he would no longer live. Intellectual food was, for him, more vital than bread. My reaction was similar to the great old man's: I, too, pined for the written word; and I, too, might have starved to death had it not been for the saving grace of my imagination.

Borges, I admonished myself at the onset of what would have been soul-destroying anguish, you are also a writer – avoid the folly of Eratosthenes the reader. Remember those other writers who endured their blindness, and who were rewarded with great insights. Homer, the father of Western literature, is said to have conceived his epics in blindness. His affliction must also have occurred late in life, for a person born blind, or blinded at a relatively young age, could not have described the paternal tears that fell from Priam's eyes. The truths that Homer saw in his blindness are still truths today. We no longer marvel at Greek cosmology, but we are still moved by the wrath of Achilles. What about Milton? The scope of Paradise Lost could never have been envisaged by anyone capable of seeing the sun. And I compared the wide-eyed Shakespeare to the squint-eyed Milton: the former grasped the passions of the flesh (he was a butcher before turning playwright), while the latter peered into the darkness and glimpsed the soul in its struggle to overcome the flesh. And in the twentieth century there is the case of the Russian Bulgakov, whose surrealistic vision in his novel The Master and Margarita was inspired no doubt by the cloud of impending blindness.

I considered Braille: replacing sight by touch. But, getting on in years, I was set in my ways. Reading the word through the medium of light had been a soaring experience, a journey through time and space at the speed of light. Reading through the medium of flesh, I would be like a mole groping in the dark. In the end, the thought of learning not only a new alphabet but a new way of reading proved too daunting to even attempt. A friend suggested I employ someone to read for me: hire a pair of bright young eyes the way others hired young men and women for other uses. The idea sounded interesting. Yes, it would be reading once removed from the word, the voice would not be my own (even in silent reading one is always conscious of one's voice), the pleasure would be vicarious; still I would not be restricted in my range of books. My first reader was a young woman – the daughter of Mother's third cousin. Her name was Sonya and she was fluent in Spanish, French and English. I asked her to describe the colour of her eyes, and I was immediately taken in by the shy quality of her voice and the charming manner in which she said 'green, verging on brown at the perimeter of the iris'. From this small detail I knew at once that, like most shy girls, she had spent many hours before the mirror. I then asked whether I might feel her eyes. She did not object, though she sounded apprehensive. Her eyebrows were arched, more of a line made by a crayon than a pencil, meeting lightly in a depression at the top of her nose. The lashes were long, with an upward curve. The lids were soft as rose-petals. I tested her on a poem by Lorca – if the poem sang in her voice as it had in my own, I would not hesitate in hiring her. Strange, as she read I was a child of four or five, being read to by Mother again, lulled by the same sweet rhythms. Sonya was my eyes for almost a year, until she became engaged, upon which her fiancé forbade her reading what he imagined pornographic literature to a dirty old man. Since then I have had many readers (always in a metaphysical sense), and though the experience has never approached the ethereal quality of private reading, I have not gone without a little of my former pleasure.

Taking heart from Sonya's readings and other blind writers, I overcame my anguish and began to intellectualise my condition, gradually developing the following theory, which I fervently still believe. Blindness has affected neither my memory nor my imagination – the 'third eye' of the poets. On the contrary, I now recall events from my past, not to mention characters and situations in books I have read, far more vividly than when I had my sight. My imagination, too, is now sharper and more inventive than before. Adaptation, you may well say. Perhaps. After all, when we step from the sunshine into a dim room, we cannot make out a thing until the pupils adapt and dilate. At first my blindness eclipsed both memory and imagination, but after a while the 'third eye' opened its lid, its pupil dilated and I began to perceive objects, the library, and people I had seen, characters I had read about (authors and their creations), and those I had created in my own stories. This new sight, or insight, helped make my condition bearable. I referred to it as willed sight: the projection onto the screen of my blindness of people and things that I will to see.

Instead of the physical world imposing itself on me through my eyes, I imposed my imaginative will onto the physical world.

Allow me to tell you something, and I make this almost as a confession: there are moments of such lucidity in my present condition that I would not relinquish them for my former sight. After all, I am an old man who has seen much and read voluminously. What new things can the world show me? What new truths can I discover from books? 'There is nothing new under the sun. To the making of books there is no end, and study is a weariness to the flesh.' So we read in the remarkable Book of Ecclesiastes. Perhaps it is preferable to imagine, to invent a world in which there is something new.

My position as Director of this library is now an honorary one. I do not have much to do with its administration or daily operations. Because of my literary reputation and my years of service, I have been set up as a kind of figurehead, a national icon – a status I accept with a degree of self-deprecation, and then only for the fact that I am allowed to remain in my beloved library. When not meeting with public figures and foreign visitors, l am left relatively undisturbed to work on my short stories and poems. But when everyone has left, I derive great satisfaction from walking along the shelves and running my hand over the spines of books. At such times, when the intensity of feeling induced by the books is especially strong, I use my willed sight to summon the ghosts which inhabit this place, just as Ulysses was said to have summoned the shades of the underworld to the pool of blood.

It is late on Christmas night and the library has been closed all day. I imagine the moment: here and there a few pale lamps peer into the vast space, their weak sight strug-

gling to reach the upper shelves. To someone looking down from the windows of the cupola, the floor-plan must appear like a spider's web, with the spider weaving its intrigue from the rostrum. The conditions are ideal for writing: no readers, no pages turning, not even the murmur of the air-conditioner. Having been at my desk since midday, I now stand and stretch, eager for a little conversation after so much silence. The thought of being alone with so many books sends a charge of excitement between my shoulderblades and ripples through my body. I place my right index finger on the spine of Don Quixote, concentrate all my will, and whisper: Miguel de Cervantes, come forth. Miraculously (blindness has its miracles which sight would never believe), the author steps from the darkness, circumspectly at first, then with a little less hesitancy, until he stops beside a reading lamp.

— Welcome, Miguel, I greet him.

As he orientates himself to his surroundings, I notice that this is not Cervantes the soldier of fortune, the person for whom the sword was still the equal of words, but an old man worn out by a hard life.

— I am pleased to see you, I say, keeping my finger on the X embossed in gold on the spine.

He nods and rubs the lamp's green cover with a withered left hand.

— Are you all right, compatriot?

I want very much to approach him, reach out to him with both hands, but I am keenly aware of the fact that I must not take my finger from the book, for it would cause the moment to vanish. Yes, physical contact is a necessary condition for this metaphysical moment. I am reminded of the Greek myth in which not only the strength but the very existence of the giant Antaeus depended on contact with the *earth, and how, once lifted off the ground, he was vanquished by Hercules.*

— Old age is a bitter experience, Jorge, he replies, placing the claw-like hand under the light, so that a large deformed shadow falls on the table.

— The poet said: 'Old age hath yet its honour and its toil'.

— And poets often lie.

— They are redeemed by the beauty of their lies.

— Can a lie be beautiful?

— Beauty is the greatest lie.

— Because it does not exist?

— Because we cannot help believing in it.

— I stopped believing in it a long time ago, Jorge.

— What do you believe in now?

— Nothing.

— Another lie.

— No, the truth.

— Then you believe in something.

— You are playing with words, Jorge.

— I am sorry, Miguel. Words sometimes get the better of me, as if they had a life of their own.

— There is no life in words.

— If that were the case, we would not be here.

— Here? In this graveyard of words?

— You wrote a million words, Miguel. You gave your flesh and blood so they would rise to life. Surely you have felt the mystic quality inherent in words — a quality that comes from the fact that even a simple word like 'night' has had life breathed into it by countless generations. Surely you have felt your own insignificance beside the word 'night', which in many ways has a greater claim to life than either you or I.

– *Words have never quickened my heart, Jorge.*
– *And your imagination?*
– *I am not a book man, Jorge. With me, imagination has never arisen from reading and thinking. I always preferred unsheathing a sword to scratching a page with a feather. Quixote arose from an abundance of life, not from an abundance of thought.*
– *And yet Quixote is so profound.*
– *Profound? The poor man went mad from too many books.*
– *That is precisely where his profundity lies.*
– *In his madness?*
– *His imagination.*
– *Your age, Jorge, reads too much into the unfortunate Quixote. In fact, there seems to be a plethora of readings into the life of the Don. Critics, writers, and readers as nothing more than readers – they appropriate aspects of his life for their own purpose. The first for academic advancement, the second for a literary work, the third for nothing more than a few laughs.*
– *Just as the physical world alters consciousness and is in turn altered by it, so the stationary word in print moves the eye, quickens the heart, and expands the mind in a way that alters subsequent readings of the same word. You see, Miguel, each generation reads the literature of the past through the lens of the present. We see more in Quixote than you could possibly have imagined.*
– *Is there no rest for the poor knight?*
– *He moves with the times.*
– *Even though he died?*
– *He is resurrected whenever the front cover of the book is opened.*

Miguel shakes his head and smiles, revealing a few isolated yellow teeth.

— Do you mind if we sit, Jorge? I suffer from rheumatism in the legs. The years of soldiering and seafaring have taken their toll.

As I am unable to sit without taking my finger from the spine, I invite him to make himself comfortable. Wincing, he slowly lowers himself onto a rotating chair, raises the desk's reclinable top to its steepest angle, and, turning his back to the reading lamp, rests his head on the padded top. He sighs and rubs his knees. I notice that his boots are spattered with red mud.

— I haven't walked so far in a long time.

— Exercise, Miguel — it helps against rheumatism.

— Why did you summon me from my dark corner?

— You are an historical figure.

— Am I to have no peace?

— Very little.

— You modern writers are insatiable.

— We want to fathom Quixote.

Shaking his head, he leans further back and gazes up at the dark dome. A prominent Adam's apple protrudes from his long thin neck.

— We are also fond of using authors in our works of fiction, and not only authors from the past. I, for example, a writer of modest achievement compared to you, have already been placed between the covers of a novel. The Italian, Eco, has turned me into a medieval monk who murders so that others will not discover the secret of the monastery's labyrinthine library.

— Who knows what you will make of me!

— Such are the times, Miguel.

— The book seems to have taken the place of life.

— It is conceivable that a great epic or a monumental novel may be written by someone who spends a lifetime in a library, without ever venturing into the so-called real world.

— It would be a sterile work.

— Literary tastes have changed.

He sits a little more upright, tugs at his stringy beard, and casts a wondering look around the library.

— How long have you spent in this place, Jorge?

— A lifetime.

— Among all these books?

— They have been my sustenance.

— Can books really nourish life?

— In Ancient Greek, bios *means life, and* biblios *means book. Is it simply orthographic coincidence that* bios *is contained in* biblios*?*

— Words.

— Words must have some relation to reality, especially ancient words, which were coined at a time when man had a clearer view of objective reality.

— You are a metaphysician through and through.

— Nothing will cure me of that, Miguel.

— This place is like a prison.

— It is a prism.

— No, I said 'prison'. The smell reminds me of the time I was locked up in a cell.

— So you were, but I've forgotten why.

— Misappropriating official funds. I borrowed a few réals *to help me through a difficult time.*

— You conceived Quixote in prison.

— In solitary confinement.

— *Just think of it, Miguel, had it not been for those réals, your imagination might never have found its wings.*

— *It was a crushing experience.*

— *But you found liberation in Quixote.*

— *Yes.*

— *In the written word.*

His chuckle flutters blindly through the library, reminding me of a dark moth that suddenly springs to life from the spine of a book, where it has spent the night embracing a gold letter, investing it with dreams, incubating an I *or an* O *in the warmth of its furry, outspread wings.*

— *You would have been a great sophist, Jorge.*

— *My point, Miguel, is this: there is liberation in books. In fact, the Latin for liberty is* libertas, *and for book,* liber. *If we saw things as clearly as the ancients, we might conclude that life is liberated from physical necessity whenever it is transformed into a book.*

— *Can you be certain of that, Jorge?*

— *There is no certainty in life.*

— *Except death.*

— *Even that cannot be ascertained.*

— *Spiritually speaking?*

— *Are you a spirit, Miguel?*

— *I am a bag of bones.*

— *But according to the calendar we are separated by almost four hundred years.*

— *Then I should be dead.*

— *Or a ghost arisen from the dead.*

— *But I feel very much alive, Jorge. How else can I explain this pain in my knees?*

— *How do you explain your presence here?*

He looks down thoughtfully for a moment, scratching a spot of mud from his boot.

– Perhaps you are a magician.

– A magician? It is the first time I have been called that. Magician? Well put, Miguel. No, I would not call myself a magician – I see myself more as an imagician.

– First you play with words, now you make them up.

– Imagician: a person who uses pure imagination for effect. Imagination can work miracles, Miguel. It can span time and contract space; it can fill a man's palm with a galaxy of stars; it has brought us together. But my imagination is limited by what I have seen and read. There is, however, a mind with an unbounded imagination: the library. This skull-like building contains every significant thought in the history of civilisation; it is the mind of the world, and the closest approximation to the mind of the Creator. If this library became a living mind, if it started thinking and imagining, it would create a new, ideal universe based on the written word. Such a mind is more than just fantasy, Miguel: we have invented a form of artificial intelligence which cannot only perform a million binary operations in a second, but which can think at a rudimentary level. It is foreseeable that once the written word is stored in this dynamic intelligence, imaginative possibilities would be unlimited.

– Do you look forward to such a time?

– I look forward to the transformation of man to pure idea.

– Have you ever seen this place as a sepulchre, Jorge? Have you ever considered that you might be spending your life among the dead?

– Thoughts are more alive than the living.

— Don't you want to step out and feel the sun?

— I prefer to imagine the sun.

— Wouldn't you rather inhale the fragrance of a rose, than the autumnal smell of yellow pages?

— I experience the rose in the name itself.

— Have you discarded everything outside these walls?

— The world is chaos and uncertainty, Miguel. Intelligence and imagination conjoin within these walls to produce harmony and order.

— How do your contemporaries see you?

— I live for ideas, not for my contemporaries.

— Your immersion in books and ideas reminds me of Quixote before he set out on his exploits.

— That's what I want to discuss.

— Quixote's exploits?

— His books, Miguel! Quixote has always fascinated me, and not so much because of his ideals and exploits, but because he is the first recorded figure to have come under the magic spell of books. I would go further even than this: Quixote, your knight of the sad countenance, who rides out to right the wrongs of the world and present his victories to Dulcinea Del Toboso — this tragi-comical figure represents the first incidence in all literature, and perhaps in the history of mankind, of a person's identity being overwhelmed by books and a new identity arising solely from the written word. You created a human type, Miguel, and your creation was four hundred years ahead of its time. Your Quixote is no fool — about this I am emphatic. Yes, he may have appeared foolish to your generation because books were then a relatively new phenomenon, and no one, not even you, understood their magical nature and their power over the human personality. But I assure you, Miguel, the prolif-

eration of books since your time has made the Quixote-type quite common. In fact, as we become more technological, the human personality will become more fragile, and the Quixote-type will become more prevalent.

Having sat for some time with his left hand in his right armpit, as though trying to keep it warm, Miguel now strokes the withered fingers resting on the buckle of his broad belt. A smile, or perhaps a twitch, flits through his unkempt moustache.

– My poor Quixote has come a long way.

– He is no longer yours, Miguel.

– Because an author's copyright expires after fifty years?

– No, because he belongs to the present.

– I will always see him as he was four hundred years ago: wide-eyed and emaciated from reading instead of eating.

– We see him as a metaphysical problem.

– You may be right, Jorge: there might well be as many Quixotes as people who have read him. Even in my time, money-hungry scribblers were writing their own versions of Quixote before I had finished the second part. Untalented hacks were embroiling him in spurious adventures so that they could cash in on his popularity. I was furious with those opportunists, but could do nothing to stop them appropriating my intellectual property.

– I have always considered that part of the book to be one of your masterstrokes, Miguel. In particular, the scene where Quixote comes across a spurious version of Quixote – it contains a wealth of metaphysics.

– My intention was simply to denounce those false Quixotes.

– *Great literature has a life of its own, one that transcends not only the author's time and place but his very intentions.*

As Miguel yawns up at the dome, his jaws cracking, I consider telling him about my short story, 'Pierre Menard, Author of the Quixote'. But could a sixteenth-century mind follow the tortuous reasoning of the twentieth century? Would he understand that, composed without knowledge of the original, and after a lifetime of countless revisions, all of which were destroyed, Menard's fragments of Quixote, though identical to the original, were infinitely more difficult to write because of the very fact that an original existed?

– *Next, Jorge, you will tell me that Sancho Panza is more than just a simple peasant.*

– Some have seen the proverb-loving Panza as the book's real protagonist. A certain Kafka, for instance, in his fragment 'The Truth about Sancho Panza' has argued that Quixote was in fact Panza's demon, whom the latter was able to exorcise by feeding him tales of chivalry; and that this demon set off on his mad exploits, while Panza tagged along, perhaps from a sense of responsibility or perhaps out of the need for entertainment.

Miguel's laughter reverberates in the dome.

– *If this continues, Jorge, some future writer will see the book from an asinine point of view, proclaiming Dapple, Panza's donkey, to be the real protagonist, and quite possibly drawing a connection between Dapple and the Golden Ass of Apuleius.*

– Such are our preoccupations, Miguel.

– *If I were to write another book it would not have an audience in your age.*

– As I said, Miguel, consciousness has changed in four hundred years.

– It appears to me that your age is too preoccupied with the image of life instead of its reality.

– Light brings to life both the image and the object.

– 'And God said, Let there be light.'

– Your age was founded on a rock of faith, Miguel; ours, on an electron of uncertainty. In such an age it is not surprising that some have made literature their faith.

– It is a dangerous thing to live by literature.

– More dangerous than living by hope?

– Look at what it did to Quixote – it drove him mad.

– We see his madness as the imagination's attempt to assert itself against the phenomenal world. Quixote is now a symbol: the struggle for imaginative freedom.

– Then my Quixote has left me a long way behind, he sighs. *He lives and breathes, while I remain a shadow.*

– The creature has outgrown its creator.

– Cervantes was because Quixote is.

– The word as life.

– Sometimes I feel very bitter about this, Jorge.

– The parent must make way for the child.

– That is little consolation.

– Take comfort in the knowledge that you have contributed something to this library. Our perception of God and the universe has changed greatly in the last four hundred years. Philosophers have declared that God is dead, while astronomers have proposed that the universe originated from a mighty explosion which scattered matter away from the centre. I imagine that God's death occurred at the instant of this explosion, and that God was scattered in fragments of matter and phenomena. In my cosmology,

Miguel, man is a manifestation of God's brain cells; every human being is an independent brain cell containing one essential idea, and all these essential ideas formed the original mind of God. This library contains many of those ideas; in time, when all the ideas have been collected in this skull-like receptacle, God's mind will be reassembled, and God Himself will be recreated.

— An interesting theory, Jorge, but I'm afraid it gives me little comfort.

— It is my faith, Miguel.

— In my age you would have faced the Grand Inquisitor for such faith.

— We have had our Auto Da Fe, *too.*

— It seems each generation has its madness.

— Ah, you've just reminded me of something.

— The burning of Quixote's books by the priest and the barber?

— No, although not so long ago books blazed in the stony squares of Berlin. It has to do with the last few pages of your book, where people gather around the dying Quixote to hear his last will and testament, and where he appears to regain his sanity and denounce his former exploits. Quixote's words seem to have a hollow ring to them. Did Quixote really overcome his so-called madness, or was he simply feigning sanity, knowing full well that one's last will and testament is not recognised when made by someone considered insane?

— There you go again, you and your modern mind! Remember, Jorge, we had none of your sophistication, nor your predilection for images and symbols; as for metaphysics, we left that to philosophers and theologians. Our straightforward narrative contains, at most, elements of satire,

small doses of allegory, a little mythology, and the occasional pastoral romance. All in all, our aim was to entertain, not to examine. Now, concerning Quixote's sanity, if you knew the impact he had on the reading public of his day, you would understand at once that he had to be reconciled to his audience. The laws of aesthetics, as well as public expectations, demanded that he regain his sanity. In tragedy, aesthetics demand the death of the protagonist; in comedy, and my book is essentially comedy, the protagonist must learn from his experiences, and thus attain a state of greater self-awareness. Quixote regained his sanity, he denounced his exploits and everything related to knight-errantry, he made his will, confessed, and left this world as befitting a gentleman. He had to regain his sanity, Jorge, if not for the reasons I have just given, then most certainly for poor Sancho. Can you imagine how he would have felt if Quixote had died in madness? He would have pined all his life for the governorship of the island that Quixote had promised him. Quixote's sanity saved Sancho a great deal of heartache, and possibly from a madness that would have driven the poor man on a desperate, lifelong quest for that promised island. As it turned out, he was not left out of the will, and the trials he had endured in his squireship provided him with stories for his grandchildren.

— His sanity is not convincing, Miguel.

— Perhaps your age is too predisposed to insanity.

— You had hidden intentions in restoring his sanity.

— Hidden intentions?

— Subterfuge — of which even you may not have been aware.

— Subterfuge? On his deathbed? In the presence of a priest?

— *What better occasion for the most subtle subterfuge?*
— *Your thinking is too labyrinthine, Jorge.*
— *Allow me to explain. What did Quixote cherish most of all?*
— *Dulcinea Del Toboso.*
— *Who was this Dulcinea?*
— *A figment of his imagination.*
— *Nothing more, Miguel?*
— *I don't think so, Jorge, though it has been a long time since I last read the book.*
— *Dulcinea was more than a figment of Quixote's imagination; she represents the creative, imaginative force capable of transforming windmills into belligerent knights, sheep into soldiers, and a barber's bowl into Membrino's golden helmet. In striving to win her admiration through his arduous exploits, Quixote sought the very core of that creative force capable of transforming him permanently into the knight of his own imagination. At the end of his adventures, when he was brought home bruised and battered, I can't believe that reality had succeeded in knocking out the image of Dulcinea. Once a person has experienced this creative force, it is not something that is denounced after a few knocks on the head. Why, then, did Quixote denounce everything relating to knight-errantry? Why, as I maintain, did he feign sanity? So that his will could be executed? Hardly! Quixote could be a crafty old devil, as is evident from certain incidents in his adventures. I can see him suppressing a devilish smile while denouncing his exploits. Why? To keep the rabble from embarking on the quest for Dulcinea. He feigned sanity, at least the sanity of those around him, so that the rabble would more readily believe that he was formerly mad, and thus dismiss Dulcinea as the nonsense of a madman. If*

you recall, Miguel, Quixote himself encountered one or two worthless characters who, having read the first part of his adventures, had put on some cheap armour and set out for Dulcinea. Quixote had to put a stop to this kind of thing, and so he resorted to his exquisitely cunning subterfuge.

Head supported by his right hand, Miguel has been gazing wistfully into my eyes. His bony Adam's apple moves almost audibly as he swallows back a swell of emotion.

– You may be right, Jorge.

– In four hundred years from now, when you meet another librarian, he will expound a totally different truth about Quixote, and it will be the truth, Miguel.

A shadow, perhaps a sadness, passes over Miguel's sharp-featured countenance, and suddenly, for a fleeting instant, I see clearer than ever before the face of Quixote and the truth of all Quixotes, of all times.

– May I go, Jorge? he says, raising his head from the inclined top. I tire very easily these days.

He stands, looks me in the eyes for a moment, and walks somewhat painfully away from the lamp, in the direction from which he came. I remove my finger from the spine of the book: as though pulling the plug on a computer-screen displaying virtual reality, darkness engulfs the library. I go to the reading desk and feel with my fingertips: warm, the seat of the rotating chair; hot, the lamp-cover; distinct, the impression of a head in the inclined top's soft covering.

Sonya's heart beats against the edge of the counter, and the last page trembles in her hands, as though she has been reading a lengthy love letter. Perhaps because of its setting, she finds the present dialogue more intimate than the others. The author must have a passion for books and reading or he could not have invested the 'I' of Jorge Borges with such thoughts and feelings. She can almost hear his voice through the words of Jorge, and feel his fingertips in the way the blind man caressed the eyes of his hired reader. If only she could summon him to the shop as Cervantes was summoned to the library. Now, more than ever, she needs a kindred spirit, a lover of books, a lover of her body. As relentless forces begin to close in on her ordered world, she needs to confide in him, to draw some strength from his idealism, which is so distant from the pragmatic rationalism that moves the world. She glances outside. Is that him? Yes! He is watching her from the steps of the body piercing salon! How long has he been there? Is it a form of voyeurism? A perverse pleasure in watching as one's thoughts are being read and devoured? No. The content of the dialogues intimates a loftier mind. Should she wave, signal for him to come to the shop? But before she can do a thing, he smiles, skips down the steps, and runs up the street through the light drizzle.

the SIXTH dialogue

As winter's bite deepens, the recession spreads like an influenza virus, crippling businesses large and small; closing factories, offices, shops; leaving its blight not just on windows covered in lease signs but on the face of that Old Testament prophet – that scab-browed Jeremiah of the street – who harangues pedestrians for a coin or cigarette, and whose weathered hands cupping the lighted match are translucent magnolia petals around the stamen.

As winter's bite deepens, the country's once-strong currency is being devalued daily: bankers dealing in foreign exchange are photographed in newspapers with arms crossed defensively, ties knotted tightly the night before, lips sealed by a dry silence that increases the price of Spanish olive oil, forcing the old Greek woman to buy a cheaper oil – sunflower – which, being thinner, is consumed more quickly by the still flame in the corner icon-chalice.

As winter's bite deepens, young anarchists in army coats distribute leaflets at stations, shopping malls, universities, that warn of secret societies with occult connections and individuals with palindromic names, whose agenda today is to privatise public utilities, hospitals, education; tomorrow, entire nations under the pretext of a more peaceful world; and the day after, to appropriate the name of God.

As winter's bite deepens, the rumour permeates conversations like the smell of lamb chops frying on a chilly night: this is not a seven-year-cycle recession, but a new strain, virulent, resistant to economists and fiscal policy, one that may spread to global proportions, causing the collapse of the present order and the fulfilment of a new order, the one announced yesterday by the watery-eyed millennialist swaying outside the corner hotel.

Sonya shakes out two aspirin into the hollow of her palm. Half an hour ago, at the first appearance of those small white circles floating across her vision, she placed the aspirin-bottle on the counter, as though its very presence would dispel these starry precursors of migraine. But they have proliferated and, even though they are not yet sparks from a migraine's chisel, she knows better than to wait too long. She swallows the tablets with a mouthful of coffee and turns to the window. It is almost noon. The ceiling of concrete-grey cloud that has covered the city for days is now starting to crack. Moments of sunlight brighten the street. People are gathered outside the funeral parlour, talking quietly, hands hidden in pockets, perhaps against the chill, perhaps as a measure against too much animation, perhaps from not knowing what to do with them on such an occasion. Standing apart from the knot of mourners, a woman in a dark overcoat and sunglasses is talking into a mobile phone, prodding the air with a red fingernail. Full of flowers, the hearse is steaming, sparkling with drops of water from a recent wash, waiting like a sleek panther. The driver, whose rosy complexion makes him look barely old enough to drive, is cleaning the side mirror with a yellow cloth. At one point, after looking around to ensure that nobody is watching, he squats beside the mirror, inspects his teeth, and quickly squeezes what must be a pimple on his forehead. In front of PLAMEN'S GRILL, a man with snowy hair removes a floral tie from around his neck, folds it carefully, and puts it in the pocket of his navy-blue jacket. From the other pocket, he pulls out a black tie, knots it, and runs across the street, where he shakes hands with a few of the mourners.

In a short burst of sunlight the eagle and snake on the window of the body piercing salon spring to life. For the first time, Sonya is struck by several details in the vivid painting. The snake's crimson tongue resembles a flicker of lightning, with the end forked like the letter Y. The eagle's right talon is raised, clutching what appears to be a quill, a pen, and an instrument for tattooing – the three arranged in the shape of an X with a vertical line through the centre. There has been no sign of the author since she received the last dialogue more than two weeks ago. She has often considered going across the street and inquiring about him. Is he a tenant in the building? Does he live in the rooms above the salon? Does he operate a business from there? Suddenly she is struck by another possibility. What if he works downstairs? What if he is a tattooist? The precision of his writing and the fact that he uses a fountain pen intimate a careful hand, one that knows the significance of each point. No! He is not a tattooist: she senses this as much from the content of the dialogues as from the glimpses she has had of him. But is this simply a reaction to her prejudice against tattoos? She has always considered them a violation of the body, a kind of self-destruction by the very symbols that people hold most dear. He is not a tattooist: the hand that wrote the dialogues cannot possibly pierce the flesh.

The sun finds a crack in the clouds just as the coffin is carried out by four men, employees of the funeral parlour, all in grey suits. The knot of mourners tightens. Splinters of light dart from the coffin's silver trimmings, the ornate handles, a silver cross attached to the lid. For a moment the street is reflected in the polished rosewood: perhaps the short bearer at the back is surprised by how old he appears; perhaps the woman twisting her gloves regrets having worn that scarf; the young driver straightens his cap; a pedestrian, a youth in a hurry, stops abruptly before his startled image; traffic glides past along the dark grain as though on glass; peeping between clouds, the sun glimpses itself in the lid. Suddenly, as though frightened by what it has seen, the sun disappears, and the rosewood loses its reflective quality. Strain showing on their faces, the bearers carry the coffin to the hearse and slide it between the colourful wreaths.

A bearded derelict eating a French stick, gazing at the hearse setting off, triggers a vivid dream Sonya had last night. Hunger in a land of plenty. Hunger gnawing at her bones. Hunger afflicting her very soul. She measures the circumference of her left wrist with a strand of hair: she is wasting away, yet cannot stomach food. If only she could eat the printed word or a body of text. She is in a stonemason's workshop: a short, elderly man limps to a slab of marble and begins chiselling. The letter S appears. Hopeful of finding sustenance, she reaches out, runs her finger along the engraving and tastes the fine powder – it is sharper than salt. Pursued by the workman's laughter, she runs from the workshop, to a dazzling courtyard with a massive mulberry tree heavy with fruit. She has been here before. When? In another dream? A story? The tree of knowledge, the thought flashes to mind. She picks up a large leaf and studies the veined lines. The next instant the leaf is covered in writing. She recognises individual words: *Man is ohm*. What does it mean? The leaf's fragrance allays her growing exasperation. Could this be it, a leaf from the tree of knowledge? At first she nibbles its serrated fringe, then takes large bites, finally stuffs it into her mouth. But the words suddenly become bitter-green, revolting. Disappointed, she spits out the leaf and looks around the courtyard for another tree, certain there must be one with more agreeable leaves. Nothing. Is she doomed never to find her sustenance? Hurrying from the courtyard, she soon finds herself on the side of a gentle hill, covered in spring grass. A young shepherd appears on the crown of the hill, whistling, his outspread arms resting on the crook across the back of his neck. He scolds her in a friendly manner. She should count her lucky books his dogs did not get wind of her. The garden has made her oblivious of danger, she says. But she is hungry. He smiles and leads her to a sheep-fold on the other side of the hill. Three hundred lambs, he says proudly, pointing with the crook. All shorn on the first of the month. At twilight they must be sacrificed to the Book of Life. He invites her to stay and partake of as much meat as she can eat. Tonight the smell of roasting lamb shall fill the countryside. Meat? No. It is too heavy for her constitution. Three hundred lambs, muses the shepherd. Hear them bleating in joy, praising the Word? Nine men in striped aprons will strop their knives on their tongues and slaughter the flock for their skins. Seven girls, all eleven, will gather the wool with the swallow's song. On five Sundays, working between matins and vespers, they will spin the wool into a single thread on which souls will climb to paradise. The hide will be salted, dried in the sun, and pressed into parchment, just enough for both books of the Bible. Suddenly, she has a craving for the Bible – the Book of Numbers. She is running toward a large sandstone church. People are gathered on the steps leading to the wide entrance. A bride and groom emerge, greeted by a shower of rice and confetti. She picks a few grains from the bride's veil and places them in her mouth, together with bits of confetti, each with a different letter. On biting the rice, she chips a tooth and spits at the feet of the groom, who takes it as a sign of good fortune. The organ's last note is still groaning in the empty church. She is at the altar, struggling to open the clasp on the Bible's jewel-encrusted cover. Her sustenance is inside, but there is no sign of a key to unlock the eagle's claw. Wearing one shoe, a small girl dressed in white as though for a confirmation skips to the altar, takes a small cross from around her neck, and uses it to unlock the clasp. She then runs off to play hop-scotch on the tiles, oblivious of the blood trickling from her bare foot. The parchment crackles like a fire, and in the crackling she can hear the cries of three hundred lambs. If only she could devour the book. She opens it at random: the page is covered in colourful calligraphy, and each paragraph begins with an ornate capital letter surrounded by a pastoral scene. A shepherd tends his flock beside the letter X. She remembers her hunger, and at once it starts to gnaw at her again. The Book of Life. She tears out a page and begins eating: the parchment is crisp, while the words vary from salty to spicy, from sweet to sour. She eats a second page, then a third. Suddenly her mouth fills with unbearable bitterness. What evil word is responsible for such a vile taste? Unable to hold it back, she turns away and vomits all she ate. Will she never find the food she seeks? Tears streaming down her face, she goes behind an altar and finds herself in an old-fashioned kitchen. An old woman is at a thick wooden table, vigorously kneading dough. From the large fleshy mass she extracts thirteen smaller bodies, shapes them into spheres, and presses each with a different wooden disc, each disc inscribed with its own test. Using a flat board, she shovels out round loaves from the oven at the back of the kitchen, and shovels in the bodies on the table. Thirteen loaves glow on the table, each stamped with text. The old woman picks up a loaf with her apron and extends it to Sonya.

She accepts it, but has nothing to give her by way of gratitude. Offering a smile, she sits on a three-legged stool and places the hot loaf on her knees. On the golden crust she reads: *This bread is my body*. She breaks off pieces and eats greedily, feeling the letters with her tongue, careful not to allow a single crumb to fall on the floor by collecting them in the lap of her outspread dress, whose hem her mother has forgotten to take up.

Would she have remembered the dream if not for the fortuitous presence of the gaunt derelict? Strange. The dream would more than likely never have arisen to consciousness, eventually fading like the print on parchment kept in centuries of darkness, until it disappeared as though it had never been. But even if the derelict had not triggered her dream, if it never rose to consciousness, would it have left a subliminal resonance in her? Would it have affected her in some way? Who knows, perhaps people's inexplicable impulses, their irrational actions, may have their source not in repressed memories of actual experiences but in these ungrasped dreams, these images that never see the light of day. A young woman enters the bookshop. She nods and asks in a heavy Slavic accent for Dostoyevsky's *Netochka Nezvanova*. The novel has been in the shop for months: it was in a box of books Sonya bought at a church fete last summer. Directing her to the shelf, Sonya is intrigued as much by her appearance as by the fact that she should be looking for that particular book. The woman is about twenty-five, tall, attractive, with a full figure. She is wearing a green woollen overcoat buttoned to the neck, a matching belt around the waist, and a pair of knee-high boots.

Returning with the book, she places it on the counter and takes out her purse. In doing so, the overcoat opens a little, revealing a white knee. It is Dostoyevsky's least-known work, says Sonya, hoping to engage her in conversation. The woman nods. She read it in Russian ten years ago and now wants to read it in English, to improve her vocabulary. Is she a recent arrival to this country? In accepting her change, the woman studies Sonya for a moment, as though deliberating whether to answer. Her eyes are blue, sharp as glass. Two years, she says, placing the book in the overcoat's wide pocket. Was she a casualty of the collapse of communism? No – a victim of the rise of capitalism. She left her small town on the outskirts of St Petersburg because, at the time, she felt there was no future in her country for young people. Her generation was brought up with the idea of the state as heaven and Marx as God, but when the state collapsed and statues of Marx were pulled down, they were left without direction, without a sense of right or wrong, without belief in Christ.

Pausing, she closes her eyes and crosses herself slowly three times with the first three fingers of her right hand. Sonya is moved by her display of piety, even though she senses something incongruous in those long, bright red fingernails coming together to touch the forehead, the navel, the right shoulder, the left. The woman then takes out a small wooden cross on a black chord around her neck, kisses it lightly with full lips glistening pink, then slips it back into her coat.

Her family has always been religious, she says, even under communism. They lived their faith in secret, underground, persecuted like the early Christians in the catacombs. The atheists did not succeed in crushing their belief; if anything their candles glowed more brightly in those years of darkness. They greeted with joy the collapse of communism. At last they could worship freely, under the dome of the Russian sky, and Russia would become holy once again. But holiness is brought about only through suffering. The time has not yet come for Mother Russia to step out into the light; she is still in her dark corner, bowed, head covered in black, praying for her wayward children. As the Revolution of 1917 unleashed satanic forces which, in the name of the state, desecrated churches and monasteries, and murdered the tzar and millions of Christians, so the turn to capitalism has spawned the Russian mafia. Like the characters in Dostoyevsky's *The Devils*, those drawn to this mafia are mainly young, cynical and, raised in the spiritual void of communism, have elevated money in place of the state. Driven by satanic greed, they have no morals and will resort to anything, including murder, to satisfy their lust for money and power.

Her opportunity to leave Russia came through a marriage agency in St Petersburg. She was given some information and a photograph of a forty-five-year-old Russian businessman who lived overseas. He was keen to make contact with a woman whose description she closely matched – with a view to marriage. The agency sent him her photograph, a correspondence began, and four months later he came to Russia and they were married. A few days later she boarded a plane bound for a new life. But her marriage did not last long. He was possessive, jealous, with an explosive temper.

Having rescued her from the chaos of Russia at great expense, as he often said, he acted as if he had exclusive rights to her body and soul. Alone, in a strange country, not knowing the language, she tolerated the situation, having been brow-beaten into feeling obligated to him. But when he became even more overbearing, stopping her from attending church, she packed her suitcase and left him.

Swallowing the last few words with a swell of emotion, she considers Sonya for a moment, her eyes darting from side to side. Sonya is uncertain of how to interpret this look. Has she come to the end of her story? Is she now waiting for a comment from Sonya, a word of sisterly encouragement? Is she trying to determine whether Sonya has listened out of genuine interest or simply politeness? Or is she ascertaining whether to continue? But the front door swings open at this moment, just as a fire engine blazes past, its siren screaming, red and blue lights twisting. Sonya is momentarily stunned: the author! He places the gold envelope on the counter, flutters a shy smile, and leaves without a word. It happens quickly and by the time Sonya overcomes her surprise and hurries to the door, there is no sign of him. Anything wrong? asks the woman. Preoccupied with the lost opportunity, she returns to the counter without answering. His figure is still clearly before her, like the sudden and unexpected glimpse of the sun whose image flashes at each blink. He is about thirty, tall and lean, with a self-effacing manner. She sees again how he averts his eyes in approaching the counter, as if his very presence in the shop is an act of temerity. She observes his boyish smile, though she cannot be sure whether it is a smile or simply the natural curve of his lips. She is captivated by his right hand: thin, pale, with a band-aid around the tip of the index finger, and prominent blue veins describing the characters of a strange alphabet. How reticently it extended the envelope, as though going beyond the bounds of propriety. Certain that he watched her from across the street before deciding to act, Sonya is perplexed by the timing of his appearance. Why choose a moment when she is with a customer? Could he not have come earlier, when she was alone, as she is for most of the day? Or was this initial contact made somehow easier in the presence of a customer?

Sonya apologises for the interruption, saying she has been expecting this envelope for some weeks, though not in the manner it arrived. Nodding, the woman checks her watch: she must be on the other side of town at twelve. Sonya invites her to come for a chat whenever she pleases, without feeling obligated to buy a book. Business has been very slow these past months, and she could do with a little company from time to time. The woman thanks her, adding that she likes to read between clients and appointments, and as her base is next door she will be a regular visitor to the shop. Does she work in the funeral parlour? Reaching for her cross, the woman says she works on the other side, indicating with a slight tilt of her head. Sonya is flustered, uncertain of what to say. Sensing her awkwardness, the woman thanks her for listening. She is running late. During the day she works a broken shift as a topless waitress in a hotel near the docks. In the hours between, she likes to sit in the back room and read. She is already at the door before Sonya can fully gather her thoughts, and then just manages to ask for her name. Her real name? Or the one given by the agency? She was baptised Xenia. The agency has rebaptised her in perfume: she is now Maroussia. Waving *Netochka Nezvanova* in the air, Xenia stops a passing cab. As she gets inside, her coat parts at the knee, revealing a bare thigh.

Expecting something more in this envelope, Sonya pulls the flap, which opens smoothly, as though sealed just before its delivery. For an instant, she is tempted to lick the flap still moist from his tongue. His confidence must be growing, she thinks. He is working himself up to make a meaningful contact. Who knows, he may have primed himself for the visit, left his room with a resolute step, crossed the street determined to speak to Sonya, only to falter and lapse into silence at the sight of Xenia. She tips the contents onto the counter: nine or ten sheets held together by a paperclip, nothing more. Her disappointment is short-lived, dispelled by the sight of his lovely handwriting. Is he watching from across the street? Three men in overalls are arguing outside the betting agency. She would like to close for half an hour, to read the story in private, savour his writing, surrender herself to his intimacy without thought of interruption. She rubs her temples. Closing will not pay the bills, appease Simkin, keep the bank from her door. She flicks through the pages: the writing breathes, springs to life. The movement of his hand comes through in the flowing text: that gentle hand will banish the demons pressing against the inside of her temples, sharpening their instruments of torture.

Constructed solidly on the crown of a grassy hill, in an architectural style popular in the nineteenth century – at a time when Romantic excess was breaking through Classical restraint – the hospital's administration building overlooks numerous compounds and annexes partitioned from each other by fences with computerised surveillance equipment. The bluestone used in the building was hewn from a nearby quarry, which may explain the strange sounds reported by inmates of the hospital, among them the echo of chisels ringing angelically. From the circular window in the clock-tower (the clock was removed when it gave up the ghost) one could, if permitted up there, see a river snaking past on one side of the hospital and a ten-lane freeway speeding past on the other.

As the sun sets crimson behind the administration building, casting a cool shadow over the eastern side of the hospital grounds, a man and a woman present their identification cards to a guard who, showing little interest in security, opens the gate to a well-treed compound with numerous cottages, each skirted by a colourful flower bed.

– I've kept the most interesting for last, comments the man.

According to his identification card, he is a lecturer in the hospital's Teaching Unit, though the morose, ashen face in the photograph bears little resemblance to the thirty-year-old smiling at his companion.

– The afternoon has been very informative, replies the woman in a lively voice.

Her card is stamped: VISITING STUDENT. *She is in her early twenties, with an alert look and small pouting lips. The top of a gold envelope protrudes from a folder pressed to her chest.*

– The inmates in this section have been diagnosed with a condition specific to our times.

– A new disorder?

– It seems so, he replies, pushing back his glasses, which have slipped down the bridge of his nose.

The student opens the folder, places the envelope under a writing pad, and makes a note with a red pen.

– In our last lecture we were told that both the incidence and variety of mental disorders is decreasing.

– Yes, your associate professor is right. Imaging technology has enabled us to produce a detailed map of the brain and to locate areas of the cortex responsible for a range of human activities. The brain is like a new continent. It awaits explorers and cartographers – those who will lead humanity to a happier, healthier place. The old maps internalised the physical world; the new maps will externalise the psychic world. Everything from the passive act of reading a book to the passion of falling in love has its source in the cortex. And if, for example, we probe the area which controls the act of loving, we find sub-areas which determine one's sexual orientation; and these areas in turn contain smaller areas that predispose us to our future partner's height, facial features, the very colour of their eyes. How do these areas form? Why are some active and others dormant in varying degrees? DNA. The codes stored in a microscopic quantity of acid, the bewildering combinations of the genetic alphabet – that's what moves life forward, just as the computer program humming quietly in a basement drives the life of a city. And so the phrase 'my genes' will eventually take the place of 'my fate', and 'what fate has written' will be replaced by 'what's encoded in my genes'. It's possible the cortex plays a significant role not *only in physical matters but in metaphysics. A recent paper postulates an area that makes people receptive to the idea of God, and that the degree of faith or belief is directly proportional to the amount of electrical energy in this part of the cortex. If experiments prove this postulate, then one could argue that atheists are people whose metaphysical area is dormant or insufficiently active, and that this could be overcome not by abstruse theological arguments about the existence of God, but through appropriate electrical stimulation of that area of the cortex. Of course, psychopharmacology, in conjunction with brain mapping, has enabled us to develop drugs which have eliminated many types of neuroses and psychoses. Nevertheless, each generation seems to provide an environment for the emergence of new disorders. So, too, with mental conditions: we've eliminated many disorders which afflicted great numbers in the past, but we have opened the door to this new condition, which seems to be spreading at an exponential rate.*

The student scribbles as they proceed along a brick-paved path leading to a cluster of cottages. An evening breeze redolent of freshly cut grass stirs a willow's overflowing branches, which have been neatly trimmed to a horizontal plane a child's height above the ground.

— And the name of this new disorder? she asks.

— We haven't agreed on one as yet, though most here refer to it as Literary Identification.

— Literary Identification, she repeats, recording the name.

— Yes, patients adopt the identity of literary figures.

— Are such disorders new?

— In the form we're witnessing today, yes.

— How do they differ from cases a hundred years ago?

– Firstly, the identification is so complete, all trace of the patient's former identity is expunged; secondly, we're not talking about a few isolated cases here and there, but of such numbers as were afflicted by Saint Vitus' Day dance in the Middle Ages, when thousands left their homes and wandered the countryside in a state of frenzied hysteria.

– It's like a form of Quixotism, remarks the student.

– Keep in mind that Quixote is a creation who adopted his identity from books – that is, that of other creations. As such he is an image of an image, or twice removed from reality. The patients here are real – at least to the extent that flesh and blood are real – and they've adopted the thoughts and manners of real people.

Nodding, the student acknowledges the distinction and notes this as a significant fact, underlining it twice.

– Furthermore, continues the lecturer, warming to his subject, the patients aren't driven to pursue Quixotic fantasies and adventures; on the contrary, they seem content to spend their time writing and discussing their works and ideas – or, I should say, the works and ideas of the writer whose identity they have appropriated. Not only can they write from memory the entire works of their chosen author, they can also write original material which could easily pass for the work of the author; in fact, some of this original material has confounded even specialist scholars, who've conceded that if the patient's identity had not been disclosed they would have attributed the work to the famous writer in question.

– Is it a case of doppelganger? asks the student, biting the end of the pen.

– Judge for yourself.

He stops abruptly at a junction of several paths and points to a sprawling oak tree in full leaf. An elderly fellow *with a mane of white hair is sitting on a bench beneath the canopy of branches. At that instant, another man appears on the scene, walking briskly across the lawn in the direction of the seated figure. He is about thirty, robust, with short reddish hair cut in a high fringe.*

— You're in luck, the lecturer beams. Follow me.

— Where are we going? inquires the student, taken aback by the sudden development.

He takes her by the elbow and, describing a wide arc, they proceed to a bench situated on the other side of the oak tree's wide trunk, behind which the two men have just met.

— Listen carefully, he whispers.

— To what?

— Their conversation, he replies, and raises a band-aided index finger to his lips.

The student opens her folder and, crossing her legs, rests it on her knee, where her jeans are worn almost white. Head tilted back and cocked to one side, she listens intently, pen poised to spear anything significant.

— Good evening, Herr Goethe. May I sit down?

His voice is high-pitched; his words, edgy; his tone, uncertain, yet urgent.

— As you please, Herr Kleist.

His voice is deep; his words, smooth; his tone, relaxed, though more through experience and acceptance of life than through resignation.

— Examining leaves again? asks Kleist.

— There's enough in this solitary oak leaf to occupy a curious mind for a lifetime. It's all a question of seeing. One person sees the outline of the tree itself in the veins of the leaf; another, the perfect communion and transformation

of sun and earth; while for another, the leaf absorbs sunlight, utilises those colours of the spectrum essential to its nature, and emits the rest as this particular shade of green. Light, Herr Kleist, above all else one must have light. Colour is the universe's fourth dimension, the expression of inanimate matter. Those who would know the secrets of creation should seek it in the mystic language of light, whose alphabet is colour.

– Wonder can be unappeasable, Herr Goethe.

– Democritus said that he would rather know the cause of one thing than be lord of all Asia. I understand what he meant: if I knew the primal cause of this leaf, I would be omniscient – a state far more desirable than the lordship of Asia, for omniscience subsumes not only the lordship of Asia, but the lordship of the universe. You see, Herr Kleist, the beautiful subtlety of the Classical mind.

– Greek thought has done much to shape the German mind.

– For our betterment, Herr Kleist. The Classical archetype has done much to contain our wild Teutonic temper.

There's a pause as both men consider the leaf twirled by Goethe's long fingers with nails cut back almost to the quick. The lecturer and student exchange looks.

– Have you read either? he whispers.

– Goethe, a little. I haven't heard of the other.

– Nor I prior to his admittance.

– Classical wonder! says Goethe. It keeps the mind eternally young. The pre-Socratic philosophers were moved by wonder, and their oracular words continue to stir those who approach them with a childlike mind. Read the fragments of Heraclitus the Obscure, and you will see that he was *deliberately dark so that his words might be like lightning. Consider Thales, and you will believe the story that says he died by falling down a well while walking along, wondering at the night sky. Study Pythagoras, and you will appreciate that he who has mathematics has religion, and he who does not have it better have religion. Look at Empedocles, and you grasp not only the closeness of science and poetry, for he wrote his cosmological works in verse, but that overpowering love of creation which drove him to plunge into Etna's lava in order to fuse his being with the primal elements. Their philosophy arose from wonder, Herr Kleist. They were moved by leaves as much as by stars, which is more than can be said of philosophy today. It arises from pessimism, despair, irrationality – from the very swamps of subjectivity.*

– A certain temperament is required for such wonder, Herr Goethe. I suspect the student of nature must consider himself above nature, or at least its equal, if he's to approach it objectively. I've never been able to view nature from such a lofty Olympian standpoint. On the contrary, I've always considered it threatening, unpredictable, intractable, with the power to reduce me to insignificance. When you look up there, Herr Goethe, at that crimson sunset, what do you see?

– Refraction of light by the earth's atmosphere.
– The equanimity of light!
– There's nothing else.
– And yet I see terrible apocalyptic visions.
– You must constrain your imagination, Herr Kleist.
– With Classical restraint?
– Yes.
– The Classical mould is cracking, Herr Goethe. The

great Enlightenment hasn't delivered its promises. Yes, I was imbued with its ideals: humanity could be perfected. I believed in its Utopia: if this wasn't the best of all possible worlds, then it was only a question of time before heaven would be realised on earth. I studied its mathematics: it was the foundation of science, and science alone would alleviate human suffering and bring universal happiness. But all that changed, almost overnight, when I read Kant. Suddenly, truth was a category that couldn't be apprehended. Our knowledge, far from probing the essence of things, could never penetrate their appearance. And reason, the very God of the Enlightenment, was a product of the world, and ultimately limited to understanding nothing more than appearances. This was a profound shock for me, Herr Goethe. My soul was thrown into confusion. And now, as if rubbing salt into my soul, Bonaparte has swept away the Enlightenment and reduced Europe to a state of chaos.

— Harmony, order, form — these are the foundations of society, the unfolding of nature, the spirit of art, which is really an extension of nature. As literary men, we must never lose sight of this trinity, Herr Kleist.

— Having travelled through Europe and seen the chaos, I need forms that will contain my grief-stricken soul, rhythms that will resonate the terror of the age.

— In good time, Herr Kleist. You're too impatient. New forms will unfold in the fullness of time. It seems you want to push everything forward, including the process of evolution.

— I feel threatened, Herr Goethe.

— Threatened? By what?

— The madness storming over Europe.

— Bonaparte is a passing phenomenon, though I was impressed by his wit when we met a few years ago. Anyone *who maintains that the wellbeing of a nation is determined by the state of its mathematics cannot be an agent solely of chaos.*

— You possess an historical perspective on life, Herr Goethe. I can't see beyond the present.

— Stop projecting your emotional state onto the world. Clarity requires reflection and a distancing from oneself. Remember, Herr Kleist, the unexamined life is not worth living.

— Reflect? There's no time, Herr Goethe. I'm compelled to act by the bewildering state of the world. I say this as to a confessor: there are moments when I'm driven to act from fear of going mad or doing away with myself. And then I run from myself and my obsessive thoughts, and throw myself into action — spontaneous, unpremeditated action, divorced from reason, morality, social conventions. Recently this need to act impelled me to Paris, where I made inquiries about joining Bonaparte's army on his intended invasion of England. I wanted to lose myself in the whirlwind of chaos and destruction. Needless to say, I suffered a breakdown and was escorted back to Germany by friends. After a short period of convalescence, the restlessness started again: wandering from city to city, desultory work, projects and plans that would never be realised.

— Enough, Herr Kleist! Enough! That's all I hear these days. Only last week I was visited by another young man who poured out his anguish. You may have heard of him — Hölderlin. A very high-strung person: intense, serious, with the presence of the martyr-to-be. He brought some of his poems; he spoke of them as though they were revelations. He considered himself an instrument, recording the utterances

of some higher being. And what poetry, Herr Kleist! Formless, cryptic, full of ellipses and inversions, dispensing with traditional grammar and syntax. I'm sure his intentions and aspirations were noble, but his composition lacked clarity and structure. In this he typifies much of today's youth, who believe that truth lies in extreme emotion, in raw energy, in sound and fury signifying nothing.

— And are we wrong in that belief? You are a child of the Enlightenment; I, of doubt and uncertainty. You have faith in rationalism; I, in nothing. In your youth you cherished the future; I have no future, and dread the present. This extreme emotion is all I possess, Herr Goethe. Without it I would have ...

— Herr Kleist, enough!

Passing through the tree like a shiver, a light breeze rustles the leaves on the upper branches, causing a few to flutter to the ground. A crow swoops down and struts awkwardly before the men. It is an old bird, with wing feathers hanging low, touching the grass, and eyes red as the sunset. Kleist picks up a twig and snaps it in two. He tosses one part away and begins scratching the back of his hand with the pointed end of the other. Face set in concentration, Goethe stares at the silhouette of the administration building.

— Goethe's upset, the lecturer whispers, leaning close to the student, their shoulders and thighs touching.

— Why?

— Perhaps he's afraid.

— Of what?

— Sh ... Listen.

— Ah, Herr Kleist, Herr Kleist ...

He reflects a moment, hands flat together in front of his mouth, in an attitude of prayer. From the depths of the oak, as though defying the gathering dark, a small bird, perhaps a finch, embroiders the evening with its silvery song.

— I must also make a confession, he continues, with a slight falter. We all have a skeleton, not just in the closet either. Madness, uncertainty, desperation — at your age I felt the claws of those demons, too.

Where his voice has been smooth, untroubled, like a deep river's imperceptible flow, suddenly it crackles like a rocky creek.

— Those demons tormented me, Herr Kleist. I struggled with them for years before subduing them to a point where life could be more balanced, ordered, relaxed. Two courses of action are open to those who look into the abyss of the human condition: succumb to a kind of vertigo and plunge into the abyss, or overcome it through order and discipline. Consider the pre-Socratic philosophers: they discarded the veils of religion and superstition, and confronted the abyss in all its starkness. But, instead of succumbing to horror, which was no doubt exacerbated by the devastating Persian invasion, just as Europe is presently being ravaged by Bonaparte, they overcame it by a force of will that transformed dread into wonder, chaos into order, and the transience of human life into immortal art.

— And you've followed their example, Herr Goethe?

— It's the only way to vanquish the abyss.

— The only way?

Goethe opens his palms as though a book and studies them for a moment. A flutter of feathers sounds from the tree. Kleist has scratched either the letter S or an elongated integration symbol on the back of his hand.

— The only way, says Goethe, stressing each word.

— No, Herr Goethe, we must explore the other way, too. It's time we turned away from the path set by the ancient

Greeks. Each generation must discover its own way, even if it leads to ...

— It's madness, Herr Kleist!

— It must be explored.

— Hubris, the sin of pride, was punished by death in antiquity, today it's punished by madness.

— The irrational must be explored if we're to set limits on the rational.

— No! Evolution will see to its elimination.

— Evolution? Ideal forms? The perfectibility of man? But you forget the Persians, Bonaparte, the advent of new tyrannies that will plunge the world into apocalyptic wars. We can't ignore the irrational.

— It has no place in the light of consciousness.

— I'd rather it were in the light, where it can be seen, than in the shadow, where it poses a greater threat.

— You're too impetuous, Herr Kleist! A good writer is master of his emotions, not mastered by them.

— Have you read my new play?

— I finished it yesterday.

— What do you think?

— I prefer The Broken Jug. We Germans take ourselves far too seriously, Herr Kleist. Our stage needs more comedies such as yours. I enjoyed directing it.

— Your production misrepresented my play, Herr Goethe. You directed it as though it were a farce. You didn't bring out the irony, the satire, the opposition of appearance and reality, the thread of tragedy that runs through the work.

— I'm afraid I saw it principally as a good laugh. The other elements were a little irrelevant — the lapses of a young writer. You have considerable talent, but you must avoid ambivalence.

– *Life is ambivalent.*
– *The writer should stand some distance from life.*
– *That's not always possible.*
– *Discipline and patience, Herr Kleist.*

Called by a flock circling the administration building, the crow beaks the twig tossed aside by Kleist and flaps off heavily in that direction.

– *And* Penthesilea? *asks Kleist. Will you consider staging it at Weimar?*
– *That's out of the question.*
– *The play's relevant to our times.*
– *Relevant? Perhaps, as a study in chaos. Your characters seem to have got the better of you: they run riotously through far too many scenes, always raving, emotional states vacillating from one extreme to another, never shrinking from violence and destruction. In your excesses, you have abandoned all the elements of good stage craft. And the end, dogs on the stage! If the critics were unkind to* The Broken Jug, *they'll tear this one to shreds.*
– *Critics belong in kennels, not in theatres.*
– *The public won't accept it.*
– *You'd have me serve them porridge?*
– *A dramatist isn't a lyric poet, Herr Kleist. Avoid that voluptuous self-abandon which makes swampish so much of the writing of our younger authors. Be objective, mindful to stand midway between the poet and the journalist.*
– *And the writer's freedom?*
– *Freedom? To do what? A licence to indulge in meaningless subjectivity? I'd rather a writer who wears a heavy yoke and produces something pedestrian but meaningful, to a writer who soars with borrowed wings, producing material that has relevance only to himself.*

– *What about your early works, Herr Goethe? Your Werther and Tasso? Aren't they full of excess?*

– *I regret having written them.*

– *Nevertheless, they were very popular, especially Werther. It's said the book was found in the pockets of many suicides.*

– *The very reason I now abhor excessive sentiment.*

– *And now you always write according to a rule?*

– *Yes.*

– *The fire must conform to brick?*

– *Art arises from order – that's the law of nature.*

– *I write in response to life, to my emotional state, to the chaos of my dreams. Writing is an experience of the body and mind. My characters are not shadows, they are as real as you. I suffer with them and feel their fleeting joys. There are times, Herr Goethe, when my identity fades in the stronger light of my creations, and then I, as it were, create myself anew in them. Just as I'm unable to distance myself from life, so I'm unable to distance myself from my work. And just as life and action precede thinking, so, too, creation must precede theory. I create first, Herr Goethe, and then, if time permits, I theorise.*

– *Your creations are monstrous.*

– *Perhaps, but they are born of freedom.*

– *So are the ravings of madmen.*

– *Freedom has its price.*

– *And its pitfalls.*

– *Where then would you have me turn, Herr Goethe? Religion? Tradition? Reason? The revolution has crushed the old certainties. No. There's only one thing that can't be doubted – the individual. I can doubt that your leaf has a finite perimeter, but I will never doubt that I suffer and do not know why. And where the sense of I is acute, one becomes a creator, a critic, even an executioner.*

— *You impose terrible burdens on the individual.*
— *Freedom is terrible.*
— *Madness even more so.*
— *Perhaps because it's the greatest freedom.*

Kleist stands.

— *Good evening, Herr Goethe. I must pack.*
— *Pack? Where are you going?*
— *I'm leaving for Paris in the morning.*
— *What will you do there?*
— *I'll leave that to circumstance. They say Bonaparte's looking to mount a new offensive. It wouldn't be such a bad thing to fall in battle, as history was being made. What could be nobler than to sacrifice one's life to an historical event? A true fusion of the individual and the anonymous spirit of history. But I never commit myself to a particular course of action, Herr Goethe. Who knows, once in Paris I may decide to board a ship for South America. It's said there are plenty of opportunities in a place like Chile.*
— *It's notorious for earthquakes.*
— *Well, if I don't fall in a history-making battle, I may as well fall to the shattering wrath of Mother Earth, just like your Empedocles.*
— *You're hell-bent on destroying yourself, Herr Kleist.*
— *Nothing's certain, Herr Goethe. Who knows, I may wake in the morning and decide to remain in bed all day.*

Goethe watches with a sombre expression as Kleist walks off, twigs snapping under his boots. Sunset has subsided to a soft, dull glow. The shadow cast by the administration building is colder. A breeze struggles in the grip of the oak tree. Raising his collar, Goethe examines the leaf in the fading light for a moment, then stands and goes the way of Kleist.

— *What do you think of our inmates?* inquires the

lecturer, extending his left arm onto the back-rest behind the student.

— Fascinating.

— Their number has doubled over the past year.

— And they're locked in their present identity?

— To the annihilation of their former.

— How do such things happen?

— We don't know, though a theory has been proposed which maintains that the thoughts of authors have somehow come to exist as entities in themselves, and that they possess a person with a weak identity, in the manner that a parasite or virus possesses its host body.

The student scribbles this in her book.

— Can anything be done for them?

— Nothing, apart from providing a comfortable environment.

— Who was the young man?

— We don't know anything about him.

— And Kleist?

— A contemporary of Goethe's, who committed suicide after killing a woman in a bizarre death-pact.

— Is this Kleist likely to meet the same end?

— It's possible.

— That's terrible, says the student, with a slight shiver.

The lecturer places his arm around her. She closes her folder and presses against him. From the darkness gathering in the tree, the small bird sounds again: a song more ardent than that with which it greets the morning sun. She takes his right hand and examines the band-aid around his index finger. He is about to kiss her, but the folder falls and opens, revealing the gold envelope.

— Let's go, he says, taking her by the hand.

And without another word, they set off briskly for the administration building, whose presence appears to grow in the greying light.

In reading this dialogue, Sonya senses that she is being watched by the author – no, more than being watched, being read by him, just as she was reading him through his words. She glanced across the street several times, but there was nobody who resembled him, nobody peering from behind a newspaper, nobody in the body piercing parlour's doorway, nobody mingling unobtrusively among the motley bunch outside the betting agency. Now, having read the intimate story several times, she is in no doubt about his intentions: he is out there somewhere, savouring the moment, though not voyeuristically, but as someone lacking the confidence to approach her directly. She caresses the first page of the dialogue, feels his presence in the script. The light blue ink is remarkably similar to the colour of the veins on the back of his hand. Having taken the first step in making contact will he come again soon? Or must she wait another two or three weeks for the next dialogue? If the recession continues, she may not be here in three weeks' time. Simkin, the bank – they may insist she cut her losses and close the business. Written especially for her, these dialogues are a refuge amid so much uncertainty, providing a protective wall of words between her and a hostile world, a place to which she can retreat for half an hour, and which nobody, apart from the author, has ever visited. But these heart-fluttering musings are short-lived, lasting only while she reads; for in putting down the manuscript, the world asserts itself again and closes in around her shop. In such moments, when a feeling of hopelessness threatens to overwhelm her, he suddenly appears like a watermark beneath the text, and then he is her confidant, her helper, perhaps even her lover ...

the SEVENTH *dialogue*

In years past, Sonya would feel a sense of relief at having seen out another winter. A stirring of apprehensive joy mingled with cautious expectation made her receptive to the early signs of spring: the distinctive pitch of a yellow-beaked bird swaying on a strand of barbed wire, or a shrub crouching in a corner of a front garden, ambushing the unsuspecting with its scent. This year, burdened with crushing problems, she has not responded to spring's tentative approach. To make matters worse, rain of one form or another has been falling continuously for three days: from hail the size of camphor-balls bouncing madly on the bitumen and concrete, to misty sun showers almost too fine to be felt.

A thread of smoke unwinds from the cigarette in her extended fingers, spirals past her face, curves to a symbol resembling a G-clef, and drifts away like a gentle melody. She left home earlier than usual this morning, not to go to the market (she has not been there in more than a month), nor to attend to urgent work in the shop, but because she was unable to sleep. In recent weeks she has been subject to an increasing number of anxiety attacks when at home: irrational fears for the safety of her books in the shop. At 5.17 this morning (as though branded in her memory, she can still see the red numbers of the digital clock), she was woken by the sound of windswept rain hammering on the tin roof, lashing her windows. What if there were a leak in the shop? The thought struck her palpably, sending a surge of blood ringing to her ears. She had a fleeting vision of a deluge sweeping through the shop. Her books were drowning, as humanity must have drowned in Noah's flood, but she could do nothing to rescue them. What sins had her books committed to warrant this terrible fate? If water was 'a sore decayer of your whoreson dead body', its effect on healthy books was even more deleterious. It blurred the text, soaked the page, bloated the body, warped the spine, and made the book heavy as lead. Better a book destroyed by fire, its fine ash scattered by the wind, vanishing without trace, than one disfigured, saturated, rendered unreadable, reduced to rubbish that is not so easily disposed of.

She threw aside the blankets, dressed hurriedly, and sped through darkness and rain, the window-wipers squealing, though to little effect. Parking in front of the funeral parlour, she threw a jacket over her head and just managed to leap over the water streaming brightly in the gutter. A pink, cursive QUEEN OF HEARTS flashed intermittently across the brothel's front window. Sonya wondered about Xenia: she had not seen her since her first visit. Had she finished *Netochka Nezvanova*? Was she in there at the moment?

Her anxiety was allayed the instant she opened the front door: apart from the faint smell of dampness, there was not a drop of the deluge she had feared. Without switching on the lights, she walked around the shop, running her fingers along the spines, feeling closer to them not only through having envisioned their destruction in the flood, but because of the way in which, dripping with rain, the orange streetlight angled dimly into the shop. The books were safe and dry, and in their wellbeing she sensed that there was still hope to trade her way out of this recession. Strange. The more the recession filled her with a sense of helplessness, threatening to reduce her to nothing more than a silverfish in the dark, the more she turned to her books for meaning and strength. Their order and equanimity empowered her, engendering a confidence that enabled her to continue to struggle.

It was only six o'clock, still three hours before opening. Sonya went to the back room, scraped the ash and remnants of wood from the hearth, put in a few logs, and lit a white cube which gave off the smell of kerosene. As the logs spat and hissed, she sat with the dialogues on her lap, hands folded on them, eyes closed. Rain spluttered in the downpipe just outside the window. Sharp footsteps, as though stilettos on bare floorboards, sounded from the brothel. Purring sonorously, the fire caressed her hands and face, while the smell of books loosened the knot of anxiety in her stomach, gradually restoring her to herself. She must have dozed a moment, for her head shot up and her body shook at the sound of a coin or a key pecking at the front window. In an instant her thoughts ricocheted from the author to Xenia to someone with sinister intentions. Had the caller seen her enter the shop? Was the light from the back room door visible from the street? Was it simply a derelict using the doorway as shelter from the rain? She waited, but the pecking started again, louder, insistent. She turned off the light. The rain trickled in the downpipe. The pecking continued. Opening the back room door a little, she could discern the figure of a man, his forehead pressed against the glass. Her heart pounded. Was it him? Had he seen her enter the shop from his nearby upstairs window? Did he have another dialogue for her? She slipped into the front room and crept forward behind the shelves, peering between rows of books.

Lou Cape, the short-story writer! She deliberated a moment, then stepped out and opened for him. He had seen her enter the shop from his car, he said, pointing to a grey, dinted sedan parked in front of the brothel. After more than an hour of vacillating between yes and no, during which a thousand and one thoughts fogged the windows of the car, he had finally decided to step out and visit the premises next door, but was checkmated by her unexpected, though welcome, appearance. He paused and swept back his thinning hair. Moved by his forlorn look, Sonya invited him inside, but immediately regretted her action. He followed her to the back room, where they sat in front of the fire. The wife's treachery had turned his life upside down, thrown his thoughts into chaos, he said. He had decided to give up writing, despite some progress on his comic novel. Last night, after a few beers, he put the current work in progress on the barbecue (the hotplate still had bits of burnt meat from last summer, when he had a family) and set it alight. No more writing, he had vowed, as the sheets curled and the print was absorbed by a stronger black. Perhaps his obsessive drive to write had contributed to his wife's treachery. Yes, in his relentless pursuit of the word he had perhaps neglected his precious world of wife and family. And for what? Three collections of short stories which have all sunk without trace. In fact, he came across one of his books in the shop a few months ago: battered, dog-eared, covered in graffiti. On the title page a disgruntled reader had written: *there should be a money-back guarantee on unpalatable books*. And maybe the reader was right. After all, he or she had paid dearly for the book. Converted into time, they had to work an hour or two to pay for it, and then spend another three or four hours reading it. Six hours of precious life, and all for what? A product whose substance was more in the bright packaging than in the contents. Like a carton of Corn Flakes, most books were full of promise when seen, half-empty when opened, of little nutritional value when consumed. Yes, writers should be more accountable to their readers. Who knows, in this time and age of litigation, it was foreseeable that a reader might take a publisher to court on the grounds of false advertising, while the author might be accused of fraud and deception, though a little fraud and deception had always been part of the trade of writing fiction. Three collections, and what did he have to show for it? A broken marriage and an empty bank book. He would have made more standing on a street corner, pretending he were blind, extending a can at passers-by. Besides, books would become redundant, obsolete, anachronistic space-consumers. Yes, he knew that her livelihood depended on books, and he loved them too, but a new reality had to be faced, and those who did not come to terms with it would be left behind in its wake, perhaps buried in the mountains of books that would arise on the outskirts of cities, circled by screeching seagulls searching for food. He apologised for sounding so pessimistic. Of course he would continue reading books; in fact, now that he had given up writing and no longer had a family, he would return to his first true love – reading. But as a reader, he had no preference for the material on which the word was presented: papyrus, parchment, paper, computer screen – they were all one in the presence of an engaging text.

He stopped at the sound of voices and footsteps coming from next door. The idea of the book's decline and death disturbed Sonya. What if he were right? What if the recession were only a precursor to more doom? The fellow from the bank would be visiting her again today. Business had deteriorated since his first visit. How much longer would it be before the bank decided to pull the plug? They would sell her house, recover their debt, and she would be left with a crippling loss.

The image of her books as a mountain of refuse flashed vividly to mind, and for an instant she was transported to an arid landscape, a wasteland after a cataclysmic event. The great revolution, the new enlightenment, that was to have been brought about by the computer did not eventuate. On the contrary, when mankind had become dependent on the computer and every aspect of life was regulated by it, a virus began spreading through the integrated network, destroying systems, spreading panic and hysteria. The virus was another Black Plague, infecting computers with malfunction, and their users with suspicion and fear. Panicking, people made a run on the banks, but their savings were inaccessible, and wages and pensions were frozen in cyberspace. Business ground to a halt; transport was in chaos; economies collapsed; governments resigned. Riots broke out, with looting and destruction of entire cities; anarchy was unleashed throughout the world. Armageddon was not to be the nuclear war she had feared in her childhood, nor the devastating effects of global warming; its spawn lay in the silicon chip, the very thing that had promised to deliver a heaven on earth.

In this fleeting vision, Sonya found herself beside a mountain of smouldering books. Smoke rose from the city in the distance, while the smell of rubber thickened the air. Suddenly, an unmanned bulldozer appeared from the shimmering horizon, groaned toward the books, and began pushing them into an enormous pit. The grave of the book, she thought, looking to save from burial those which had not been damaged. Evening descended, bringing with it a chill. Raucous jackdaws circled overhead. Small ragged children, faces blackened by smoke, began appearing from all sides of the mountain, gathering armfuls of books and using them for fires against the piercing cold. The moon appeared, full and icy, though providing sufficient light by which to read. She continued fossicking, reading a line here, a paragraph there, until the cold became unbearable. She could not bring herself to sit by a fire and watch as books were devoured, so she burrowed into the mountain. Buried in books, curled in a foetal position, she gradually began to warm up, to feel a stirring of joy, as though she were safe and in her element. And then she was a child again, reading in the warmth under the blankets, feeling safe while outside the stormy night raged.

Lou Cape stood and thanked her for her timely arrival. Looking shyly at the flames, he said that he would more than likely have entered the brothel if he had not seen her. He had never been to one before, and that was why he deliberated in the car for so long. She had saved him not only from the certain self-loathing that would have followed, but from throwing away a good deal of money he could little afford. He would show more restraint in future, and remember how providence had sent her at the crucial moment. And now would she mind if he browsed for a little while? Sonya turned on the front lights and as she busied herself tidying shelves, Cape selected an armful of books and placed them on the counter. Bookshops should be open all night, he said, taking out his wallet. Just like brothels and convenience stores. For some people books were more necessary than sex or food. Sonya nodded, feeling the need for a cigarette. He gathered the pile under his arm, but appeared preoccupied, as though he had left something unsaid. Taking a few steps toward the door, he turned abruptly and asked if she would consider having dinner with him, not right away, of course, but perhaps in a few weeks' time, once she has had a chance to think about his invitation. Careful not to hurt his feelings, Sonya replied that she was seeing someone. He was a writer, too, and had written a number of beautiful short stories especially for her. Cape looked outside, in the direction of the body piercing salon. Yes, he understood and hoped that she did not have the wrong idea about him.

A woman, a regular customer, entered the shop. Roused from her morning reflection, Sonya stubs her cigarette and disperses the smoke with a wave of her hand. The woman leaves a dripping umbrella beside the front door. Sonya removes the ashtray from the counter. About fifty, with a large girth and no neck, the woman shakes a small round head with a bob haircut, which appears as though it is attached directly to her broad shoulders. The street is flooded, she complains. Governments spend billions on space research and nothing on clearing leaves that clog gutters and drains. She comes in several times a month and buys as many as a dozen bulky novels on each visit. And you must give up those vile cigarettes, she continues. In walking to the counter, she reminds Sonya of a walrus struggling among boulders. She has often expressed her disapproval of Sonya's smoking. It not only damages the lungs, which is of course entirely a private matter, but the smoke contaminates the books, which are very much goods for public consumption. Her sense of smell is as acute as her sight: there is nothing worse than opening the covers of a long-sought book only to be confronted by the loathsome stench of cigarette smoke permeating the pages. It was like opening the glossy gates of paradise only to find a stinking sewer. She has often fumigated a book with her strongest perfume before sitting to read it. Sonya apologises. She has tried to quit but has found it difficult. Willpower, says the woman, her shining black eyes darting about the shop. We can discipline ourselves to do anything. And in Sonya's case she ought to make a concerted effort or run the risk of losing customers.

The warning comes as another blow to Sonya. Is everything to be bad news? And the fellow from the bank who is due shortly? What will he bring? It seems that implacable forces are working toward driving her from the shop. The recession from one direction, computers from another, and social attitudes toward smoking from a third. And is it such a terrible thing if books smell of cigarette smoke? If they have the odd stain here, or spot of blood there? After all, they are second-hand: books read as lived experiences; books with a history independent of their content, a history which at times may be a little sordid; books as objects of life, not art. If the woman wants something pristine she should buy them brand new, in a state where, still smelling of the press, ten thousand books feel and look identical.

As on previous occasions, the woman does not spend hours browsing: knowing precisely what she wants, she goes to the shelves on the back wall, places her selection of historical novels in a plastic bag, and returns to the counter. Time is precious for those who live to devour books, she huffs, walking awkwardly, flat masculine shoes splayed because of her bulk. She was a slow reader years ago. At two hundred words per minute, it would take her two minutes to read a page, which translated to a thousand minutes, or close enough to seventeen hours, to read a five-hundred page historical novel. If she allowed six hours a day for reading, that meant about one book in every three days, or approximately one hundred and twenty-three books a year. She was forty when she questioned her efficiency. Taking the average life span of a woman to be about seventy-eight, it meant she had thirty-eight years of reading life left, or, converted to books, four thousand, six hundred and seventy-four. The figure had jolted her. Twenty-five good reading years had passed plodding through a book in three days – nothing could now be done about that wasted time. But she could do something about the next thirty-eight years. She would discipline herself, undertake a course in speed reading, increase her consumption of words per minute. And after six months of breaking lazy and inefficient reading habits, of training her eyes to glide over the page, to take in entire paragraphs at a glance, she managed to double her rate. Reading word by word was a remnant of childhood, it was like crawling over the page. Having outgrown this, she could now fly through books, and her life was immeasurably enriched. In time, she increased her rate three-fold, then four. Eight hundred words per minute – the equivalent of one hundred metres in ten seconds. Yes, she has always been a large person, never good at sport, and these days even walking can be an ordeal, but when it comes to reading she can proudly and honestly say that she has met nobody swifter. Training and discipline, she says, eyes darting from side to side as though Sonya were a text.

Sonya has listened with rising interest to the account of the woman's appetite for books, wishing that she could consume them at the same rate. But her heart suddenly sinks when the fellow from the bank enters the shop. He waits near the door as the woman takes her plastic bag and manoeuvres to leave. Just before she reaches the door, the author dashes into the shop, places the envelope on the counter, and dashes out, brushing past the woman, who vents her anger at his rudeness, her body quivering with indignation. Flicking open his briefcase, the fellow from the bank searches for something among the papers. Before Sonya can react to the speed of events, the author is already out of sight. She hurries from the counter and squeezes past the woman who almost fills the doorway. The footpath is busy with lunchtime pedestrians. No sign of his black jacket. She can still see herself in the reflection of his sunglasses. A thief? asks the woman, poking at the door with the point of her umbrella. A friend, replies Sonya. You should teach him a few manners, she huffs, and sets off down the street, the books stretching the plastic bag to transparency.

The fellow from the bank has set his case on the counter, over the envelope. Everything all right? he asks. Sonya nods. Faltering a little, he points out that she has not reduced her overdraft in recent weeks – in fact, it has marginally increased. She had an unforeseen bill at home: the hot-water service needed replacing. The situation is urgent, he says, with a troubled look.

Her loan is under review. He has been instructed by the manager of his department to impress upon her the need for tighter control of expenditure. The bank is suffering enormous losses through bad debts, and it has started foreclosing risky loans to avert further losses. In view of its performance in recent months, her business has been placed in a high-risk category. It was not his decision, he says, almost apologetically. On the contrary, he spoke in her favour at the last meeting with the manager. He admires her commitment to the shop. His cheeks begin to flush, and he tugs at the knot of his tie, which appears to be drawn too tightly. He is impressed by the number of books the last customer bought. It might be a sign of better things to come, he says, crossing his fingers. If only he could assist her in some way. Perhaps banks are to blame: in the past they lent too readily, without thorough screening. And now people like Sonya are paying the price for bad banking practices. If only he could offer her a lifeline: some way of saving her from the abyss into which so many well-meaning people have fallen and continue to fall. The situation will be assessed in another month, he says, making a note in a diary. If the arrears on the loan are not repaid, then ... He clicks the briefcase shut.

Does she have a copy of *The Catcher in the Rye*? He needs to read it again. It will help him retain his humanity in these ruthless times, perhaps give him strength to intercede on behalf of honest clients, people such as Sonya. She goes to a side shelf and pulls out a silver paperback with a cigarette burn on the front cover. In opening his wallet, a photograph of an attractive, middle-aged woman falls onto the counter. My mother, he smiles, slipping it back in its clear plastic holder. She died a year ago. After an instant's reflection, he shakes his head, flicks out a note, and extends it to Sonya. The book has been on the shelf for over a year, she says, declining the money. But she is in no position to be giving books away; besides, there is also a matter of propriety: it is not right that he accept anything which might be construed as a bribe. Sonya takes the money, while he smiles and places the book in his coat pocket. By the way, is her insurance policy current and fully paid? Sonya thinks for a moment, surprised by the question. Strange things happen in an economic climate like this, he frowns. Zeus's lightning strikes unexpectedly and places go up in flames, like the property across the street. They both turn to PLAMEN'S GRILL. The corrugated metal sheets have been removed from the front windows, exposing a black interior with a pile of charred beams knocked down from the roof. One can't be too careful, he says. He wishes Sonya good luck in the coming month and, crossing his fingers, hopes that he is not her messenger of doom.

Like a burst of sunshine, the golden envelope dispels a sense of foreboding. Suddenly she is not alone in her struggle to survive: the dialogues are like markers in these turbulent times, leading her forward to their author, and a place where the word, not economics, moves the world. On opening the envelope, she is again disappointed by the absence of a note. Why is he holding back? He has made his feelings clear in the previous dialogue. Or has she read too much in that intimate moment between the lecturer and the student? No. She has read that passage many times, and always with a strong sense of being there on the bench, under the tree at twilight, his arm around her. No. She has not misread that scene: she is the student, and he the lecturer. Having removed the paper-clip from the sheets and bent it into the shape of an L, she is now absent-mindedly scratching the outline of a circle on the back of her hand. The rain has become heavy again, falling obliquely in the grip of a driving wind. The punters have crowded into the betting agency, steaming the windows. Protected by only a small verandah, the window of the body piercing salon is lashed by rain. The eagle and snake quiver in their life and death struggle. In the bread shop – is that him? It is hard to tell through the rain. The black jacket looks the same. He is eating at a counter against the front window, looking in her direction. Sonya waves the manuscript in an attempt to catch his attention. No response. Heart pounding, she is about to dash across the street, when he stands and goes to the door: a young woman steps out of the shop, protecting a loaf under her coat. Sonya lights a cigarette and succumbs to the flowing handwriting.

Not restricted by blindness (though the blind aren't as handicapped in the narrow night, as in the broad light of day), Homer managed to find his way into the dreams of several ancient figures. One famous visitation is recorded by the generally reliable Plutarch. After his conquest of Egypt, and upon his return from the Oracle at Siwah, where the priests had greeted him as the son of the god

Ammon, Alexander of Macedon was anxious to found a city that would bear his name and grow to be the centre of his vast empire. Having conferred with his engineers, he settled on a favourable site and intended to issue orders the following day for marking and measuring. That night, however, he dreamt of a grey-haired man of venerable appearance standing at his bedside, reciting lines from the Odyssey. The figure, whom Alexander later swore was none other than Homer, advised him in hexameters to construct the city elsewhere, giving precise details of a location near the island of Pharos. Alexander visited the site and was impressed by its natural advantage over the one he had chosen. He praised Homer for his perspicuity and instructed his engineers to design a city which would conform with the geography of the new location.

That Homer should have appeared to Alexander in a dream is quite plausible; after all, a number of ancient historians mention the fact that the young conqueror kept a copy of the Iliad under his pillow. His reason for this was probably more inspirational than rational. Religious by nature, he no doubt believed in the divine origin of dreams, and would have had several soothsayers on his campaign. In those days soothsayers not only interpreted dreams they also instructed people in what must be done to determine the content of a dream – a practice that involved placing natural objects under pillows. A laurel leaf, for example, was said to promote auspicious dreams. Always inventive when it came to customs (his handling of the Gordian knot attests to this), Alexander extended the scope of what could be placed under pillows, and was probably the first to sleep on the written word. Perhaps it is unfortunate that our modern soothsayers (psychiatrists) *have concentrated only on dream interpretation, abandoning completely the more subtle craft of dream determination.*

Alexandria arose, and became great not so much through its maritime and commercial importance (though it rivalled Piraeus, Carthage and Syracuse), as through its academic activity, which saw it replace Athens as the centre of scholarship in the Hellenic world. The city which sprang from a few verses in a dream represented a kind of intellectual Utopia. When the famous library was constructed and stocked with the treasures of the human mind, Homer's works must have occupied pride of place. Here, far from his native Chios, Homer was enshrined in the city which he had helped found. A cynic could well question the old poet's motives in appearing before Alexander. Who knows, he may have used the impetuous conqueror for his own glorification.

More circumspect than Alexander, Plato did not set much store in a vivid dream he had one night not long after returning to Athens from an arduous voyage to Syracuse. He most certainly remembered the dream in writing his **Republic,** *but he never related it to anyone, for it was never mentioned by ancient writers, not even Aristotle, who was the link between Plato and Alexander. In this dream Plato finds himself in his ideal Republic. Recently elected monarch (sole ruler) by the assembly of Guardians, in recognition of the fact that he is the architect of the Republic, he now stands on the Acropolis surveying his masterwork with a swell of pride. It is an immaculate spring day: the light breeze is scented with camomile, swallows thread the sky, there is not a trace of smoke from the sacrificial fires. Below, in the white-washed houses, the clean streets, the well-stocked marketplaces, all is as he envisaged. Each citizen lives in perfect harmony of body and mind, in harmony with their* *neighbours, in harmony with the law and the gods. Yes, everything is just as he planned. Each citizen has willingly abrogated a little individual freedom and imposed a degree of restraint on their emotions for a common good that vouchsafes peace of mind. This restraint is still a source of discomfort to a few citizens, which is to be expected in the first generation of Republicans, but with education and training Plato is certain that subsequent generations will accept the restraint more readily, as the ox becomes accustomed to the yoke, or the stallion to the chariot, or the soul to the pull of the body. Yes, everything around him moves according to a divine harmony, just like the motion of the heavenly bodies. With a philosopher as head of state, the irrational, the excessive, the primitive has been eliminated from public life, producing greater sobriety and reason in private life. Citizens venerate the city-state with a reverence that was formerly reserved for religious institutions. The state and religion are inseparable in the new order: the state prescribes and enforces religious law with the same stringency as its civil code, while religion promotes the wellbeing of the state, which the state reciprocates by constructing impressive temples and condemning heretics. The respect which citizens accord the state permeates all areas of life, manifesting itself in better relations between man and god, soldier and general, son and father, pupil and teacher. Yes, everything in the Republic is in order. The citizens are content (as for happiness, it was forfeited on the elimination of suffering); they go about their work willingly, satisfied with their position in the state's hierarchical structure; their lives are no longer governed by the promise of the politician, nor the pursuits of the poet, nor the prayers of the prophet, but according to the purpose of the philosopher, whose wisdom and insight distinguishes fact from fiction, truth from imitation, the ideal from mere appearance.*

As Plato admires his creation from a height reserved for shrines and temples, the head gatekeeper springs up a flight of steps and informs him of a stranger at the main gate — an elderly fellow who is seeking residence in the city. Though he has appointed capable men to oversee many areas of government, Plato has retained for himself the sole authority to decide resident status of supplicants such as the fellow at the gate. Through a process of subtle interrogation learnt from Socrates, he has developed a sixth sense for reading a stranger's soul and determining whether they would benefit or threaten the Republic. His acumen is especially penetrating whenever he suspects the latter. He knows only too well that a solitary stranger can be a greater threat to the new order than open attack by a belligerent army. The Republic is fortified to withstand the strongest aggressor. Walls have been built to protect the road linking the city to its harbour, a vital lifeline in the event of a protracted campaign. The young men and women in the army are drilled and disciplined, and would not hesitate to sacrifice their lives. The strong sense of national pride engendered in the people allays his fears concerning the physical defence of the city, but the more insidious threat from subversive and hostile ideas still troubles him. He knows that, as an ideal, the Republic is most susceptible to ideas, and that an idea could potentially destroy the harmony of his state, just as the plague had ravaged Athens and made her vulnerable to enemies. And so Plato draws on his extensive knowledge of philosophy, psychology and physiognomy to screen all prospective residents for subversive ideas.

A grey-haired tramp and a young girl stand on the

side of the dusty road leading to the bronze-armoured main gate. When Plato signals for them to come forward, the girl takes the old man by the hand and they slowly make their way to the shadow cast by the wall surrounding the Republic. Plato studies them carefully. The girl is about fifteen, with a long thin neck and a shy look. A wreath made of camomile and daisies sits lightly on her black curly hair; similar bracelets adorn her wrists and ankles. Despite the warm day, the old man is wrapped in a dark cloak made from coarse wool. He walks with a shuffle: his steps short, tentative, his thick sandals always in contact with the earth. At Plato's approach, the girl lowers her eyes to her dusty shadow, while the old man gazes unflinchingly at the wide entrance. Even when Plato cuts across his line of vision and stands directly before him, the old man does not blink, as though the philosopher's body is transparent. Plato's broad shoulders fall a little.

— Who are you? he asks.

— An old man in need of a place to rest, he replies in a remarkably clear voice.

— And you? he turns to the girl.

Flustered by the question, she drops the old man's hand, which falls like a dead bird, and picks at the daisies around her wrist.

— She was born mute, says the old man, with a glistening smile. We adopted each other on the island of Lesbos last summer, and now we're inseparable. I give her my croaking voice and she gives me her innocent eyes.

Plato focuses on the old man's pupils: they are the size of olives.

— Where have you come from?

— Wandering the length and breadth of the land.

— *A beggar?* Plato asks in a sterner tone.
— *A beggar, a beginner, a begetter.*
— *Begetter? Of what?*
— *Heroes.*
The philosopher is momentarily stunned.
— *Are you ...?*
— *I am,* replies the old man.
Plato passes his hand in front of the fellow's face.
— *Homer,* he whispers.
— *People are always disappointed,* chuckles the old man. *They expect me to be taller, or better dressed, or more dignified. As if appearance matters to an old man, and one blind at that.*
— *Have you come a long way?*
— *How can I answer? Time and distance are measured by the sun, which doesn't exist for the blind and the dreaming.*
— *Let's sit for a while.*

Plato takes him by one arm, the girl by the other, and they go to a bench beside the entrance. They sit close together, with Homer in the middle, their backs against the wall warmed by the late-afternoon sun. The philosopher examines the poet. His sandals are battered from collisions with stones, toes yellow as the claws of an old tortoise, feet covered in a network of small purple veins. A leather band around his head is almost lost in a tangle of hair. His eyes, reduced to black and white, make it impossible to tell what colour his irises may have been. As for his body odour, it is so acrid Plato has to overcome a feeling of revulsion in order to sit next to him.

— *Why have you come to our city, Homer?*
— *I've heard it's clean and peaceful.*
— *You wish to live here?*
— *An old man needs peace and cleanliness.*

– *I am the sole judge in these matters.*

– *Then I'm speaking to the right person.*

– *There are certain restrictions.*

– *A corner would be sufficient*, Homer smiles, revealing the remnants of a few isolated teeth. *I wouldn't be in anyone's way. When not reciting my work I'll be as silent as a snail.*

– *And the girl?*

– *She'll be even more silent.*

Plato casts a glance over his shoulder in the direction of the entrance.

– *I admire your work very much*, he says in a voice that suddenly loses its authority.

– *Then you must have read it, for I've never recited in your city.*

– *Yes, many times*, Plato whispers.

– *My work should be recited from memory, not read from a dry piece of parchment. The thought of my words on skins flayed from animals fills me with sadness. This business of reading! Where will it lead? Even as recently as my grandfather's time, from whom I learnt the techniques of oral poetry, there was no such thing as an alphabet. The eye wasn't needed in our art – and it is an art, just like music. The alphabet has corrupted the younger generation of poets: they no longer bother to memorise their work. Writing and reading is a curse: it will usurp the role of memory and lead to its eventual atrophy. Some of these younger poets sat me down one day and wrote down my epics, which have had an oral tradition going back generations. A profound change came over the nature of my work as a result of that experience. Where formerly the epics had been inseparable from me, suddenly they existed independently of me, which meant they could be read and recited by anyone, at any time. The poems that I* had perfected through oral tradition, and which had existed only in my memory, were now public property — objects independent of their source. The written word has been a double blow to me: it has not only deprived me of my authority, it also rubs the salt of irony into my eyes in that I'll never be able to read it. One young fellow wrote the alphabet in clay, baked it in an oven and gave it to me so that I could feel its shape. Needless to say I couldn't make out a thing. It reminded me of the scattered skeleton of a small bird. I resent the alphabet not so much because it has rendered the oral tradition obsolete and weakened memory, for perhaps this is simply the natural progress of communication, but for the fact that people now choose to read my work in silence.

Despite missing teeth, his speech is well-modulated, his voice strong and clear. Plato overcomes his aversion to the smell of onion on the old man's breath and hangs onto every word. In fact, if he were a blind listener, he would have taken the voice to be that of a virile young man.

— The ability to read in silence has been one of our greatest advances, says Plato, with a note of pride. Before the creation of the Republic, people read aloud because the written word was still very strongly associated with the ear. We've taught our citizens to dispense with the mouth and ear, which rely on air for propagating and grasping the word. As an organ of light, the most ethereal of all substances, the eye is especially suited to grasping the essence of the word — the logos. Through the miracle of silent reading, people don't need private spaces in order to avoid the babble of other readers. The skull becomes the most private of places. One vast reading room will take the place of hundreds of smaller rooms. Not only this, silent reading promotes harmony, enabling people to be together while reading: a man and a woman can read while sharing the same bed. Yes, some of our citizens still whisper as they read, others still move their lips — these are minor things which time and discipline will correct. Who knows, just as the suppression of the voice in reading opens the way to a true apprehension of the logos, so perhaps the suppression of conscious thought in contemplating beauty may lead to the apprehension of ideal forms.

— You set great store in reading, muses Homer.

— Our city is built on the written word, says Plato. Writing frees the mind of the need to memorise, liberates it from the past, and allows it to create the future.

— You must have a fine city.

— We're proud of our achievement.

— A place to live out one's life.

Plato is about to reply when two crows call from a nearby olive grove. Homer turns his head by degrees to the source of the sound. His eyes are wide open, as though enticing the birds to roost in his pupils.

— A small corner, that's all I need.

— I understand, replies Plato somewhat awkwardly. But the world has changed from when you first recited your epic to illiterate listeners.

— It has changed, echoes Homer, his sigh smelling of onion.

— Utopia exists behind this wall.

— It must be like no place on earth.

— No place.

— That's why I've come.

Plato looks searchingly at the weathered old man, at first with a kind of reverence, but then, as though chastising himself for this moment of affection, he cracks the knuckles of his little fingers, sits more upright, and straightens his broad shoulders.

— We can't accommodate you, Homer.

— There must be a corner, he pleads.

— It's not a question of space.

— I don't understand.

— You don't belong here, says Plato, stressing each word.

— Don't belong?

— Our constitution forbids poets.

He says the words as though expelling something that has caught in his throat. Homer adjusts the sweat-stained leather headband.

— First the alphabet, now this. Why?

— You're a threat to our city, Homer.

— I'm an old man.

— You're a poet.

— Has poetry become an offence?

— Its very essence is subversive.

— And what of my work in the written form?

— Not a single copy exists.

Homer shakes his head and turns to the girl, who, oblivious of the conversation, amuses herself by scribbling in the dust with a forked twig.

— You were still widely read when we started realising the Republic, but once it was established the Guardians were relentless in their endeavour to track down all copies of your work. They resorted to coercion and threats of expulsion against those unwilling to give up their scrolls. It was all for the good of the state, just as the threat of the rod produces better pupils. In the end the copies were burnt and the ashes thrown to the wind. Your work lingers in the memory of the older generation, but if we're strict in our vigil the next generation will know neither your work nor your name.

Plato appears a little disconcerted by the vacancy of

Homer's gaze, as though standing before a deep well.

– What does it all mean? the poet asks.

– It's a new order, replies Plato in a firm voice. A world you couldn't possibly imagine.

– A world without poetry?

– We've extirpated poetry from the hearts and minds of our citizens, and they're grateful to us, Homer. We see it in their faces, in their attitude toward each other, in their respect for the state.

– You've impoverished them, and they're grateful?

– Eternally grateful, my friend.

– It seems I've come to the wrong place.

– Your tragic poetry served its purpose at a transitional phase of human development. It helped wean us from primitive excesses and prepared us for a more civilised society. Your shattering account of the Trojan War stirred our senses and appeased our blood-lust through a vicarious experience of war. Your poetry awakened our imagination, so that our aggression was expended on the poetic word. But all this was generations ago, Homer. Your poetry has now outlived its use. Our citizens aren't swayed by the emotional excesses of the past. Allowed into our city, you would only stir up old emotions better left forgotten. We've elevated our citizens to a higher level of consciousness. We've taught them to bear misfortune with equanimity, to do away with dirges and lamentations, to overcome suffering through understanding. In short, Homer, we've given our citizens contentment. Your presence would expose them to the very things we've laboured so hard to eliminate from our city. You, Homer, pose the greatest threat to the stability of our state and the wellbeing of our citizens.

– Has it come to this? frowns the old man.

— *It has, Plato replies pointedly.*
— *The poet: an enemy of the people?*
— *An enemy of order and sobriety.*
— *Poets were once awarded the highest public honours. Now you deny them residence in your city. Tomorrow you'll set your dogs on them.*
— *Their importance has always been exaggerated, even when revered as instruments of the gods. After all, they're nothing more than artists, crafty imitators occupying a place between the exalted loftiness of the musician and the earthiness of the potter. Seduced by the phenomenal world, they are blind to that which lies behind phenomena — the ideal. I won't deny that poets have helped raise our consciousness to a state where we can appreciate the beauty of the natural world, but that's not the end of our development. We're now living in the age of the philosopher: a time when human consciousness will be raised to a higher plane, from where humanity will grasp the ideal. We're succeeding, Homer, and our city is proof of that success. The Guardians and I have uprooted fear from the hearts of our citizens and locked it in the vaults of our minds, allowing them to pursue the ideal. When we die, their fear will be buried with us, and they'll inherit the Republic.*
— *Life without poetry is a body without a soul.*
— *Poets! Always quick with metaphors.*
— *Have you banned metaphors, too?*
— *A new society needs a pure language.*
— *Metaphors are the very yeast of language.*
— *Our language serves to promote the ideal.*
— *And freedom?*
— *That word's almost obsolete, Homer. A remnant of times when class oppression forced many into servitude. As all*

our citizens are content with their position in society, the concept of freedom is meaningless.

— Language dies without metaphors.

— You sound like a prophet.

— Poet, prophet — they're almost alike.

— Is that why both you and Teiresias are blind?

— We're not deceived by appearances.

— And you always grasp the truth?

— Perhaps.

— A truth nobler than the philosopher's?

— Nobler? No. Slightly different, that's all.

— Are there forms of truth? Plato asks, with a deprecating smile, as though addressing a child.

— The prophet's truth arises from interpreting dreams; the poet's, from recording them.

— And the philosopher's, from dismissing them.

— Dreams and metaphors spring from the same source — man's longing for freedom. Language is a prison in the absence of metaphor, just as life is unbearable in the absence of dreams. Freedom in language promotes freedom in body and mind. When poets speak of 'the wine-dark sea' they transmute the physical world and create in an instant what an eternity of evolution could never do. Through metaphors poets rise above a fatalistic world and stand on the threshold of endless possibility.

— Poets! Forever praising yourselves! All right, let's talk about your 'wine-dark sea'. How long have you been blind, Homer?

— I was born blind.

— As 'wine-dark sea' is a visual metaphor, how can you use it with authority?

— Blindness has its blessings, says Homer, opening his mouth in a curious manner.

Struck by the pattern of lines on the old man's slightly protruding tongue, Plato is reminded of a grave he once stumbled across, which, though foul-smelling, had provided him with ideas on the immortality of the soul.

— Hearing is my dominant sense, continues Homer. Blind from birth, immersed in the oral tradition since childhood, I've lived exclusively for sound, which is the very soul of the physical world. Gazing at the sea, you're compelled by your sense of sight to view it according to the laws of nature. Sight fixes, sometimes for life, one's perception of the world. When I stand on the shore and listen to the windy wave shattering boulders, my image of the sea isn't circumscribed by my pupils. Blindness has a scope that sight cannot imagine. Sounds, without the visual constraint of the object producing them, offer the possibility of creations unable to be apprehended by poets with sight. Through this deeper appreciation of sound, the blind poet has a greater affinity with words and language. For me, therefore, language is the world in a way it can never be for you. I live more in language than in the physical world. In saying 'wine-dark sea' I use language in its purest form, free of physical necessity, in what you would call an ideal sense.

Perhaps bored by their conversation, the girl leaves the bench and, careful to step over the wall's sharp shadow-line, makes her way to a dusty clearing, where she reaches up to smell the white blossom of a solitary almond tree humming with bees.

— What you say may be true, says Plato. I see an analogy between you and the mathematician. Just as your blindness frees the word from its object, enabling you to use the word not so much for the purpose of communication, which was its original use, but for aesthetic ends, so the mathematician frees numbers from counting and commerce, frees lines and

shapes from objects, and uses them to create wonderful axioms and theorems which are just as aesthetic as your poetry.

— Are mathematicians allowed in your city?

— The Guardians hold them in highest esteem.

— And deny the poet a corner?

— The mathematician, perhaps more so than the philosopher, comes closest to apprehending the ideal that permeates the natural world. The poet, on the other hand, is once removed from the ideal because he cannot see beyond the world; while the blind poet is twice removed because he cannot hear beyond the word.

— Do the citizens of your Republic esteem mathematicians?

— They will, in time.

— And honour them as poets were honoured?

— It's a question of education.

— No, mathematicians will never sing to your citizens as the tragic poets sang to the Athenians. For all their truth the propositions of Euclid will never assuage the heart in its hour of need; they'll never address the problem of love and death; they'll never make dying easier.

— We're educating our citizens, Homer. In time, through a process of enlightenment, we'll raise their consciousness to a level where death will hold no fear, where it will be welcomed as the liberator of the soul. Religion has been trying to do that for ages, you'll say. But what are the results? Mankind is still terrified by that dark encounter. And the reason? Religion has never attempted to overcome the irrational; on the contrary, it has exploited it to further its own ends. We'll assist our citizens in understanding the irrational, by reducing it to a set of axioms and propositions. Through understanding and enlightenment they will overcome their fear of death and have no need of tragic poetry.

— Do you really believe this?
— The mind's capable of everything.
— And nothing is beyond the mind?
— Our citizens will know the truth.
— I should feel happy for them, but ...
— They don't need happiness.
— No, only certainty: life without suffering and happiness.
— Was mankind's welfare your concern when you recited your hexameters? Have you ever considered the motivation behind your poetry? Why are you a poet, Homer? Because your metaphors make a difference to mankind, or because they make life more bearable for you? Was it ever your intention to liberate people from their fears, as we'll succeed in doing? No, Homer, mankind's welfare has never been your aim. Vanity — that's what motivates poets. Your verse lacks humanity, my friend. It has no ethics, no morality, no sense of justice. It's full of death and cold-blooded brutality. Your scenes don't inspire a feeling of humanity in the listener or reader; on the contrary, the obscene cruelty of your gods and mortals fills people with uncertainty, suspicion, misanthropy. We abhor horror in life, why should we admire it in your work?

Casting a glance at the entrance, Plato leans closer to Homer, feeling with his bare shoulder the coarse wool of the old man's cloak. Dark brown wax clogs the opening of Homer's hairy ear, as though the residue of a lifetime of hiving words.

— I must confess, whispers Plato, *I'm still a great admirer of your work.*

But he straightens up immediately and continues in his didactic tone.

— We'll put an end to such contradictions by abolishing the glorification of the tragic. Our educated citizens will

denounce violence in both life and art. And a new art will arise, one that is instructive, exemplary, setting before its audience noble actions and praiseworthy individuals.

– And my Achilles? Homer asks plaintively. Isn't he an exemplary figure? A model of friendship and bravery?

– Achilles! says Plato, pointing skyward with a long index finger. Your Achilles is a spoilt, selfish, sulking child. He represents the excesses we want to eradicate.

– But as a work of art he embodies my highest achievement. He's the sun of my blindness, the youth of my old age, the beauty of my stinking body.

– There can be no real beauty in brutality, no matter how skilful and seductive the artist is with words or marble. Beauty resides in essence, not in outward forms.

– He comes to me, friend.

– Comes to you?

– Whenever I prepare to recite the Iliad.

Both men are thoughtful for a moment, their gaze on the girl: Plato's, fixed to a sprig of blossom in her hand; Homer's, on the darkness between the earth and her footsteps. Stopping beside a ring of stones containing the corpse of a full-bodied fire, she plucks the blossom from the sprig, sprinkles the petals over the ashes, and picks up a stick of charcoal, which she weighs on a flat palm.

– Achilles comes to me quietly, says Homer. I feel him like a shadow on my hands. Go, outstare the sun, I reprove him gently. Prepare yourself for battle as though for your wedding day. Go, clash with the Trojans and light this darkness with the sparks of your sword. He goes, and through him I experience the world.

The shadow-line has climbed up the olive trees which now cling to their crown of light. A breeze stirs the new grass bristling on the side of the road. The wall around the Republic is losing warmth. Feeling a chill across his broad shoulders, Plato leans forward.

– In time, he says in a softer tone, perhaps several generations from now, when the Republic is well established, we may consider permitting your work into our city. At the moment, however, I must oppose it on the grounds that it arouses primitive instincts and emotions – conditions which could easily destroy the harmony of our state.

– Your Republic seems very vulnerable.

– No, as an idea it's inviolate. If there is vulnerability it lies in the hearts of our citizens, not in a system based on mathematical laws.

– And you're certain they'll embrace these laws?

– Yes, and be cured of the need for poetry.

– You speak of it as an illness, an addiction.

– It is, like wine, which we also strictly prohibit. In fact, both poetry and wine are equally detrimental to our state. Both unsettle the mind, stir excessive emotion, and promote that primitive Dionysian throb – the impulse we're trying to overcome.

– Both offer freedom.

– Offer freedom! But even then it is an illusory freedom; more precisely, diversion and escape from fears that threaten humanity. Ours is the true freedom, Homer. Freedom based on honesty and clarity of mind, not on deceptions created by poets.

– It's time I went, he says, standing.

The girl, who has been scribbling on a section of wall near the gate, throws the charcoal aside and runs to him. Before taking his hand, she wipes her palm, blackening the side of her tunic.

– *You're more precious than sight, my child*, he says, lightly patting her head.

– *Where will you go?* Plato asks.

– *We'll find a place, won't we?*

The girl nods, the curls of her black hair springing. Plato watches pensively as they set off.

– *Wait!* he calls, going after them.

– *What is it, friend?*

He stands on one side of the ring of stones, they on the other. Homer sniffs the air.

– *You're both welcome to stay, on the condition that you never recite your verse.*

Wide-eyed, Homer stares down into the ring, the way children stare at each other to see who'll blink first.

– *Consider it carefully*, Plato continues. *You're old, blind, near the end of your life. We'll provide you with food, shelter, and a peaceful environment for the remainder of your days. And when your time comes we'll bury you as befitting a noble man.*

– *I'm too old to change my ways*, he smiles.

Plato probes the world in the old man's dilated pupils: the evening sky, the city walls, the thoughtful philosopher.

– *Homer*, he says in an uncertain voice, then casts a glance over his shoulder at the gates. *Would you recite Priam's visit to Achilles?*

– *You want to hear Priam's grief?*

– *For the last time.*

Releasing the girl's hand, Homer steps into the ring of stones. Black branches and fragments of bone crackle under his feet. He recites in a voice that has no resemblance to his speaking voice, that seems to come not from within his ageing body, but from some external source, from logos and language, *which use the old poet as their mouthpiece. Eyes closed, Plato is transported to that sorrowful night. He is in the tent, witnessing the meeting between the grieving old king and the proud young man. How long does the recital last? Has the shadow-line moved a hair's breadth or a foot's length? He can't say, but when the poet finishes Plato's eyes are brimming with tears, and the walls of the Republic dissolve before him.*

— Go, says Plato, wiping his eyes. There's no place for you in our Utopia. Go, and never come this way again.

The girl takes the old man by the hand and leads him toward the darkness gathering in the olive grove, where a narrow path winds between the twisted trunks. Plato watches them until his tears dry and the world becomes rock solid once again. In turning to go, he notices Homer's footprint in the scrappy ash. Should he disperse it? On further reflection, he steps over the ring and strides to the gate, where the girl's writing on the wall catches his attention. Black and bold, the unusual combination of familiar letters appear to be one word, but he is unable to decipher it. He studies it intently, tries to find a point of entry into the cryptic word, a narrow space between two letters, but the strain begins to sting his eyes. His frustration turns to anxiety. Why can't he read this Attic script? Why has the playfulness of a mute girl reduced him to this state? The more he concentrates, the more painfully intractable the letters become, until he is forced to close his eyes. Suddenly, this nonsense is a threat to the harmony of the Republic: a source of madness and chaos that will overwhelm his creation. He must act, save the Republic, but he can't open his eyes. Desperate, he reaches out and begins scrubbing the smooth, cold blocks with his fingertips, palms, clenched fists. The next instant he feels something crawling over his hands: the letters have become ants. In the flit of an eyelash, he is outside the walls of Troy, fighting with the Myrmidons, swept along by the implacable wrath of Achilles.

It was from the girl's incomprehensible scribble that, upon waking, Plato was able to reconstruct the details of his dream. Like countless others, this dream was never recorded by ancient sources, though it may have been related to students in Plato's Academy, and from there may well have travelled by word of mouth to Alexandria, where it echoed in the famous library.

Once again sensing that she is being observed (and more than a case of the author looking at her through the text's two-way mirror), Sonya raises the manuscript in a gesture intended to elicit some response. She examines the shops across the street, the doorways, the upstairs windows – nothing. Flicking her cigarette lighter, she brings the blue flame close to the corner of the manuscript, maintaining her threat for several minutes – nothing. Why is he teasing her? She has neither the time nor the inclination for cat and mouse games. If only he knew that her future, her very life, is on the line! He would have come long ago and offered his help. Together they would ... She checks her thoughts. Why has she become like this: believing that a man, a complete stranger, would somehow solve her problems? Why is she behaving like a schoolgirl? What has become of her once strong convictions? When her friends married several years ago, she remained true to those convictions: she would make it on her own, succeed in life, become financially independent, and only then contemplate marriage – a union of equals in all respects. But now, at the first sign of real adversity, she wilts. Why has she placed him on a pedestal? Made him her saviour and sun? She chastises herself for dwelling on fantasies and foolish hopes. No, just as Homer did not relinquish his convictions for a place in the Republic, so she must remain steadfast and overcome the present crisis on her own. In her blind desperation, she has never stopped to consider the type of person the author might be. Yes, he writes well, he has a poetic sensibility, his characters are serious, their preoccupations are lofty. But does all that say anything about the man? He may be a voyeur, watching from his window as she reads his work; or a stalker, infatuated by a female second-hand bookshop owner; perhaps a rapist, teasing her with his charm, tormenting her with his silence, waiting for the ...

Charging into the shop, a man in oil-stained overalls and a fishnet stocking over his face thrusts a gun at Sonya. Stunned, she presses the envelope and manuscript to her breast. Money, he demands in a garbled voice, and with a powerful swipe sends a row of books crashing to the floor. Sonya freezes. Money, he growls, or I'll splatter your brains over the books. Bouncing on his toes, pointing the gun at Sonya, he pulls out a small sack from his overalls and throws it on the counter. Fill it, he demands, tapping the counter with the gun's barrel. Placing the manuscript under her arm, Sonya opens the drawer and empties the contents of a grey box into the sack. And the envelope, he shouts, barely able to pronounce the word with his lips distorted by the stocking. Sonya's first instinct is to defend the manuscript, tell him that it is a work of fiction, but her throat tightens. Now, he shouts, as his bounce becomes more agitated. He snatches the material from her, flicks through the sheets, and throws them in the air. Finding nothing in the envelope, he crumples it into a ball and kicks it away. Not a word, he warns, pressing the gun against Sonya's left temple. He turns abruptly and, picking up a book from the floor, rushes out, slamming the door behind him.

Sonya presses her hands between her closed eyes, as though in an attitude of prayer. Sobbing quietly, she stays like this for some time, until her hands open like the covers of a book and she buries her face in them. Five minutes later, gathering the manuscript scattered on the floor, she is still crying.

the EIGHTH *dialogue*

When, wakened by morning light streaking grimly through a gap in the curtains, her first thought is to burrow under the blankets; when she finds fault with the world, and cringes at a customer's cough, cursing inwardly that she is unable to lock the shop for the day; when, returning home after a day full of browsers but few buyers, she shoves her indolent cat from the doorstep with a brusque foot as though its contentment were the cause of her spiritual doubt; when she rustles indifferently through the evening newspaper, too drained to be moved by the death of 200,000 people, which she reduces to nothing more than a number with five zeros; when, as though in spite of hunger, she stubbornly refuses to cook and even bread has lost its taste; when the vast night seeps into her thoughts, displacing her hopes, plans, the future, leaving her brimful of darkness; when a sense of detachment unsteadies her, so that she is not the Sonya Gore belonging to the green dressing gown hanging crookedly from a hook on the door, not the woman clinging to the mirror like a leaf in a puddle, not the owner of a bookshop, but simply a creature with arms and legs that bend at sharp angles – then, more than any other time, she feels the need to crawl into bed, click on the small bedside lamp whose switch is held together by black tape, prop herself on two pillows, and pick up the book which has been waiting for her like a faithful lover. Then, more intimately than any other time, she is taken by the hand and led from the world into the word, as though into a mosque, a temple, a basilica; then, caressed and assuaged by the rhythm of each line, she surrenders to the lightness of being induced by bed and book; then, transported from pain and disappointment, she finds herself in a state where dream and text merge and become indistinguishable; then she is filled by the text as though by the Holy Spirit, and the text is fulfilled in her, becoming the most intense and private of experiences – a dream.

It has been one of those days, but Sonya knows only too well that her beloved book will not come to her rescue as it has in the past. No, the world has suddenly become too demanding: its calculating grip tightens daily, preventing her from succumbing to the word. She knows that just as the sleeper must be a certain distance from consciousness in order to dream, so as a reader she must distance herself from the world in order to enter the spirit of the word. But the world now demands its pound of flesh before it will liberate the imagination, and because of this she has been in no mood to read in recent months, apart from the dialogues and the occasional poem. Yes, she can still enter the word in the dialogues, but the experience, though intense, is short-lived. If only he were not so reticent. If only he would come to her, discuss his work, offer his friendship. Through him she might find the strength to withstand the encroaching world. But what of her determination to succeed on her own? Her pride, at times verging on arrogance, that she could overcome any obstacle? What will her feminist acquaintances say? Accuse her of weakness? Scorn her for needing a man in difficult times? What of it? Besides, she has scarcely seen them since opening the shop. Her life has moved in a different direction. They know nothing about the cut-throat world of business. Secure in the sheltered world of teaching or the public service, their lives are given meaning through dissecting each other's relationships and spouting ideals over cappuccinos. Not one of them has entered the jungle, not one has known real fear, not one has faced the prospect of losing everything.

Sonya stands from kneeling beside a carton of books marked DISCOUNTED. Placing her hands behind her head, she pushes forward: the small bones at the top of her spine crack like a hardback that is opened for the first time. She has been slowly culling titles from the shelves all morning, filling cartons to be placed on a trestled table outside the front window. The process has been difficult, even painful, like selecting victims for execution. Pulling out a book that has not been touched since it entered the shop, she would consider it for a moment, recall her first contact with it, perhaps read a paragraph or two, and deliberate over its fate. She would often place a book in the carton only to take it out again, consider it a second time, and slip it back on the shelf. And so what should have been an hour's work to fill three cartons has taken half the day, and she has not managed to fill the first carton. She borrowed the idea of the trestled table from the bookshop up the street: the bearded fellow has been doing it for some time. Observing his trade last week, she was impressed by how readily the discounted books on the footpath drew customers into his messy shop. She noticed also that the fellow had set up a computer system to scan books as they were bought and sold, so that all his titles were a keystroke away. Not only this, a new service was advertised on his window: he could order any book in print through the Internet. She returned to the shop dejected. How could she compete with him? Computer illiterate, she felt threatened by this new technology. Should she enrol in a computer course? Invest capital in a system? But where would she find the money? She was already in debt to Simkin, and the bank would never consider a further loan, even if she could prove that the new technology would rescue the business. As she recalled the fellow's fingers skipping happily over the keyboard, her spirits sank even further. A feeling of hopelessness began to envelop her, and might have been overwhelming, if not for the presence of her books. As though making contact with her source of strength and being, she reached out and, fingers stretched, placed both hands on the spines of a row of hardbacks. Eyes closed, she remained like this until the hopelessness dissipated, when she felt strong enough to open her eyes and confront the street.

At the sound of the front door, she pushes aside the carton and goes to the counter. Sonya, how are you? Mark Zitta greets her with a broad, dimpled grin. He shakes her hand and, in Italian fashion, kisses her on each cheek. More acquaintances than friends, they were at high school together, then went on to study at the same university. Even in those days Zitta was a flamboyant character with a penchant for wheeling and dealing. Intelligent, though not studious, he would use his insinuating charm to persuade good students to allow him to copy their assignments and sit behind them in examinations, often obtaining better grades than those considered to be the brightest. Tall and imposing, though never a bully, he would often be seen doing the rounds of the schoolyard collecting money from students on the basis of it being a loan, though few ever had their loans returned. In the later years he introduced a notorious pyramid selling scheme to the school: not only students, teachers also were duped by the lure of large returns for small outlays. When the pyramid collapsed Zitta pulled back his broad grin, opened his arms, and invited the disgruntled to search his pockets, saying that he was as much victim as they. Everyone was stunned when Zitta passed his final year with an exceptional score – one that admitted him to study Law. Rumours were rife. He had infiltrated the Education Department's security, discovered where the examination papers were stored, and made copies without anyone suspecting a thing. Others maintained that he had bribed the examiners responsible for marking his papers.

Zitta thrived at university, becoming even more colourful and flamboyant, charming his way into the confidence of lecturers, tutors and fellow students, both male and female. It was not long before he was strutting about as though he were king of the campus. In fact, he became president of the Italian Club, but only after stacking the general meeting with a number of Greek students, whose appearance qualified them as honorary Italians. He defended his action and silenced his opponents by arguing that Greeks and Italians were a case of *una faccia, una razza*. Under his presidency, the club organised wildly extravagant parties, ski trips, gambling nights. Of course it was only a matter of time before money went missing. When members finally accused him of misappropriating funds, he was so outraged that he resigned without a word, promptly joining the Debating Club, which was known to have students from upper-class backgrounds, who might be useful in his aim to climb the social ladder.

Sonya neither saw nor heard anything of him for five or six years after university, when she began reading about him in the papers. His trial, which lasted months, was reported in great detail. Successfully practising as a solicitor, he soon outgrew the law and aspired to higher things. The judge sitting on the case described him as an megalomaniac who showed nothing but contempt for the law. It was reported that Zitta, of Sicilian background, had become so besotted by the role of Don Corleone in the film *The Godfather* that he set out to emulate the deeds of his hero. He wanted to be the local Godfather. Lording it over a group of shady characters who had come under the influence of his domineering nature, he set about trying to build an empire. His legal office serving as a perfect front, he masterminded, among other things, the operation of illegal gambling machines and brothels, cultivation of marijuana crops, schemes for defrauding insurance companies. At his trial the judge commented on how, despite his numerous criminal activities, Zitta still managed to attend to the affairs of old pensioners who knew neither the law nor the language of the land.

It was a failed insurance scam that proved his undoing and exposed the extent of his involvement with the underworld. In this, working with an insurance assessor who had five children and was desperate to give them all a costly private school education, Zitta had approached a number of second-rate artists to paint works ranging from landscapes to abstract. Grateful for the commission, the artists worked frenziedly night and day for weeks, producing hundreds of canvases which were classified as highly original works by several of the country's most important contemporary artists. Zitta had them insured for fifty times the amount paid for them, engaging the services of an expert art dealer, who, for an envelope under the table, signed the requisite statutory declaration attesting to their artistic originality and excellence. The paintings were packed into containers and shipped off to Italy, where they were to be exhibited and sold by an important dealer in Bologna. The assessor took care of the technical details and the policy was accepted by his insurance company. Meanwhile, Zitta set the wheels in motion for the paintings to be burnt while they were still in a warehouse in Genoa. The conflagration was reported in the Italian newspapers. Unfortunately for

Zitta, the arsonist was caught, he confessed and implicated others abroad. Interrogated by the local police, the assessor panicked and offered information for a reduced sentence. Zitta's empire crashed around him. Where others would have crumbled under the sheer weight and gravity of the charges, Zitta was shown on television escorted from a police van, handcuffed, flashing an indomitable smile at reporters and cameramen. Undaunted by the evidence against him, he dismissed his expensive counsel and defended himself, hitting back at the police force, accusing it of conspiring in his downfall because he would not be coerced into offering bribes to certain senior officers. The judge was unimpressed by Zitta's haughty attitude, which at times verged on contempt, and, in the absence of mitigating circumstances, he sentenced him to eight years, with a minimum of six, to be served in a new, privately operated, medium security prison.

And now here he is: still imposing, robust, smartly dressed, greeting Sonya with a smile that is as ingratiating as his arm over her shoulder. After telling her how well she looks, he asks whether she is married. Why not? Other priorities. Excuses, he laughs. The country needs children. Populate or perish. He has three and would love a dozen, but his wife has other ideas. He recalls with what seems genuine affection a few teachers and students from their high school days. Though in no mood for laughter, Sonya is drawn in by his comical impersonation of a teacher who struck fear into the hearts of students. How is business? he asks. Slow. He has opened an office just down the street. Another legal practice? No. His certificate was cancelled for life. He now works as a business consultant and adviser. He has been meaning to pay her a visit since learning from another old school friend that her business was nearby.

Looking around the shop, he smiles and nods in what appears a deliberately ambiguous manner. Prison has not crushed his exuberant spirit, thinks Sonya. There is still much of the schoolboy in him, especially in those dimples. But what should she make of his visit? Given his notoriety, she is flattered that he has looked her up after so many years. Together with this, there is also a curious mingling of fascination and apprehension, as though his having challenged the law and spent time in prison has given him a negative mystique, a dark halo around his head. Quite a collection, he remarks. Sonya nods. Is she making any money? Things could be better. Has the bank moved in yet? he asks, smiling. The question jolts her. Times are tough, he says. More businesses have closed in the last six months than in the previous five years. And things will get worse, especially in the retail sector. He looks around again and shakes his head. It would be a shame to see such a lovely bookshop fall victim to the recession. She has worked hard to set it up, right? She has put her soul into it, right? If it goes down she will lose the lot, right? But every cloud has a silver lining, he winks. He is in the business of helping struggling businesses. Does she want to hear more? Despite her growing apprehension, Sonya cannot keep herself from being drawn in by his smooth, congenial talk. What kind of business exactly are you in? she asks, lighting a cigarette. He takes one from her pack and uses her lighter, holding the flame in front of his face for a moment. Unlike Sonya, who issues a line of smoke between compressed lips, he yawns out a cloud. I free people from their debts, he says. In the past year he has advised many people who faced financial ruin. Last month he was approached by a couple who had put all their savings into a material shop. They had paid an enormous amount for the goodwill. When the recession hit and interest rates went up, they were unable to make repayments. The bank moved in and prepared documents to sell off their home. With two young children and nowhere to go, they came to him in tears. He could still see the haunting look of insomnia in their eyes as they sat in front of him, holding each other's hands, fingers knotted, as though being forced to jump off a cliff.

A mobile phone twitters in his pocket. Excuse me, he says, and turns his back to Sonya. Yes, Joe. Pause. That's not what I want to hear, mate. Pause. What the friggin' hell do you mean he won't pay? Pause. I need the money, Joe. Understand? Lean on him, sit on him, jump on him if you must. Tell him if he doesn't cough up we'll make him shit it out. Business, he smiles, turning back to Sonya. Sometimes a little strong language is the only way to get things done. Where was I? Yes – they were desperate when they came to him. Had nowhere else to turn. He saved them, though. No money up front, no questions asked. Payment on completion of the job. He pauses, as though waiting for her to take the bait. What sort of job? she asks, guardedly, almost regretting the question. He leans over the counter confidentially. It'll be done by a real pro, Sonya. A master of the game. He knows fire the way I know the law, the way you know these books. Neither the police nor the insurance assessors will suspect a thing. Once it's done, you'll collect on the insurance, I'll get my cut, and everything will be sweet. Set fire to my books? Sonya asks, barely able to bring out the words. Fire's your only hope, he replies, straightening up to his full height. Sonya shakes her head. The man's an artist. No. The very idea sends a shudder through her body. He swears (making the sign of the cross) that not another soul will ever know. She would rather lose everything than allow her books to be burnt. Yes, he can understand her fondness for the business: so much of her has gone into it, but she must realise that the bank has no sentiment. Her business is a liability that must be liquidated. I'll survive, she says, butting her cigarette. Don't be a fool, Sonya. Idealism and business don't mix. I'm giving you a chance to save your skin. Thanks for your advice, but I've got work to do. Look, he says, with an edge to his voice. Why don't you meet this guy? Have a chat with him? Sound him out. If after that you don't want to go through with it – fine. No obligation. I'll take my services elsewhere. She is annoyed by his persistence, and his presumption that she would even contemplate such a course of action. His smile has set into a thin line, his voice has become sharper, his index finger taps the counter. Sonya recalls his overbearing manner at school, when he went about coercing students to join his pyramid scheme. She must not allow herself to be talked into anything. If only she had the strength to say: take your services and go to hell.

A face peers through the window, haloed by the letter O. A gold envelope is tucked under the person's arm. Sonya starts. Fate could not have brought him at a better time! She signals for him to come in. Who's he? asks Zitta. A friend. I've been expecting him for some time. Zitta points out that, in her own best interest, she should keep their discussion quiet. The author of the dialogues enters the shop diffidently, looking from Sonya to Zitta. I must be off, says Zitta, extending a black business card whose red letters are raised from the surface. Give me a call, he smiles. We promise you peace of mind and a lifetime guarantee on the quality of our work. The mobile phone twitters again. Zitta taps the writer on the shoulder and steps outside, where, facing PLAMEN'S GRILL, he presses the phone to one ear and plugs the other with a little finger.

Heart racing, thoughts scattering, Sonya manages an awkward greeting. The author darts a glance at her, nods, and extends the envelope. Sensing that he might once again take flight without a word, Sonya walks around the counter, saying how much she has enjoyed his stories. He studies her for an instant, as though ascertaining whether she is just being polite. Encouraged as much by his evident reticence as by his plain clothes, Sonya assures him that the stories are as good as anything she has read in recent times. In fact, his writing has made a deep impression on her. In an age when most younger authors are writing dull slice-of-life stories about sex and various kinds of relationships, his metaphysical themes have struck a chord in her. Count me one of your loyal fans, she smiles, rubbing Zitta's card between her fingers, feeling the pimply letters. Looking up slowly from the envelope, the author extends his hand. A tremor passes through Sonya at the touch of his cold palm, his wrinkled knuckles, the slender fingers that wrote the careful script. He is exactly as Caroline described. An intimation of a smile flits across his clean-shaven face, and then he becomes pensive again. Sonya glances over his shoulder: Zitta is still on the mobile outside, gesticulating wildly.

Is that another dialogue? Sonya asks. His thoughtfulness suddenly disperses, revealing an intense face set in resolve. Placing the envelope on the counter, he makes a few deft signs with his hands and utters several incomprehensible grunts. Are you ...? she begins, so taken aback that she is unable to finish her question. He nods. I'm ... sorry, she falters. Her thoughts are in turmoil: she has invested him with the attributes of both saviour and lover, someone to whom she could give herself in a relationship that would lead to the ultimate union of reader and writer. But these fanciful expectations borne of desperation have suddenly turned to disappointment: his muteness is a disability, like being lame or having a hunchback, but worse still – a form of impotence. Those grotesque sounds fill her with revulsion: she feels sorry for him, she might be his friend, but she could never love him, despite her initial attraction. What's your name? she asks, feeling uneasy in the protracted silence. He begins to use sign language again, then drops his almost effeminate hands and turns to the counter. Sonya gives him a notepad. *Theo Besson*, he writes, in that cursive script with which she has become so intimate. And in the instant it takes to read his name, her attitude toward him changes.

Does it matter that he cannot talk? Is speechlessness really a handicap? Could it be that his wonderful dialogues are due to his inability to speak? Who knows, perhaps if he had the power of speech he would not have written them and Sonya would not have been privileged to read them. Maybe it is a form of compensation: nature at her ironical best – depriving him of speech yet giving him the talent to write. She sees a kind of purity in this: the word untainted by the sin of speech; in fact, the word spoken by the bestial tongue is purified by his silence and presented on the page in primal innocence. She recalls those opera singers of the eighteenth century who were castrated as boys in order to preserve their alto tone: they were young martyrs, whose flesh was sacrificed for the sake of art. He is no different from those youthful martyrs, she thinks. Indeed, his sacrifice is greater even than theirs, his state of purity more sublime: he has sacrificed his voice, the organ of music, in order to live exclusively for the divine word. He is a martyr, too: having relinquished his voice, he is one with the word. In his silence he has risen above the spoken word, as though he is the incarnation of the written word. Her revulsion subsides as quickly as it arose, and she is once again attracted to him, though more strongly than before, for the very fact that he is mute, that he has suffered, and through suffering has been elevated to a higher plane of existence.

There's so much I want to ask about the dialogues, she says. I've read each one many times and feel that I've lived them. He writes on the notepad: I hoped you'd like them. I close the shop at six, says Sonya.

Would you like to discuss them over a coffee? He signals with his hands and nods. And by then I will have read the new one, Sonya adds, her words crackling with excitement. They stare tenderly at each other for a moment. He extends his delicate hand with its fine blue veins. Sonya reaches out: the tremor through her body is stronger than before. He nods and walks out, past Zitta, who is now raging on the phone, and across the street to the body piercing salon. Sonya returns to the counter elated, buoyant, in love. She opens the envelope and removes the sheets, but her heart is like a wild bird in a cage. Lighting a cigarette with a quivering flame, she draws deeply and closes her eyes for a moment, not only to calm herself in preparation for the dialogue, but to prolong the feeling of heightened anticipation.

Zitta has gone, taking with him the prospects of an inferno worse than Dante's. Having dispersed the morning clouds, the sun shines on the street in a manner characteristic of the first days of spring: with a light that casts warmer shadows and draws people outdoors, that peels off coats and extends the lunch hour, that caresses the flesh of the young and stirs them with vague longing. Rising above her concerns for the business, Sonya locks the door, and takes the manuscript to the back room. Now, more than ever, she must be alone with his work, become intimate with him through his writing.

It had become his daily ritual (for both his ageing body and his ageless mind) to set out for a brisk walk in that no-time between darkness and dawn, when the world is still an idea with barely an outline, and the cat, straying like a shadow, is all eyes. Striking the cobbled square, his steel-tipped cane led resolutely toward the alpine mountain rising steeply above the town. Lately, his solitary walks had become progressively longer, more pensive, facilitating a state of expansiveness best described as detachment not only from his surroundings and acquaintances, but from his own once firmly centred sense of self. The crisp alpine air had added a visionary quality to his morning meditations, a reality that now distanced him from both the church and the university (his fiery ideas could not be contained by institutions), from the townspeople (tomorrow he would dispense with even the baker), from his own skull (he no longer cowered in a dark corner, waiting for the night to offer him scraps of dreams, like a prisoner fed through a narrow slit, but took his dreams in broad daylight, making them as he willed, face to face with the world).

Stopping before the fountain in the square, he raised his cane and addressed the arching water.

— In my youth I yearned for your cool body; in my manhood I envied your soaring splendour; now I desire nothing but your poise in the instant before you fall.

He continued, footsteps keeping pace with his impatient heart. Turning off the main road, he followed a path winding through a coniferous forest that skirted the mountain. The tangy air burnt his lungs; the layer of needles shuffled under his shoes; here and there an open pine cone caught his attention and reminded him of his childhood. Breathing heavily, he rested at a crossing of two paths: one hand on the crusty trunk of a spruce, the other on the cane pressing into the soft earth. Suddenly, as though stung, he straightened up, looked around, then closed his eyes as though listening for something. Barely audible, a bird tested the silence with a daring note. A shiver *passed down his spine. Satisfied with the first note, the bird sounded again: a trill that overflowed with joy, that stirred the forest, and made the surroundings perceptibly lighter.*

– Harbinger! he exclaimed, emotion rising to his throat. Prophet of the only sun! It's said of John the Baptist, no greater man was born of woman. I say, yours is the greatest voice born of Mother Earth. Oh, you pure voice! Extoller of light!

The bird's song was taken up by another, then by a third, and soon a discordant chorus filled the forest, consisting of baritone crows, tenor magpies, soprano finches.

– Sunrise is at hand, he said, and set off at a quicker pace.

Emerging from the forest, he was soon looking down on the pointed tops of the trees. In the open now, the path was steeper, rockier, with hoof-prints and goat-droppings from the numerous herds that grazed the higher regions of the mountain. Dawn was somewhere between grey and blue. Without stopping, he glanced over his shoulder at the narrow valley below: the fields were a patchwork, the town a collection of pebbles in a child's palm. He marched on, despite the pain in his legs, determined to greet the sunrise from his favourite spot. At one point he stumbled, dislodging a few rocks which crackled down the mountainside and echoed in the valley.

– Only those who know the heights can look into the abyss. Only those who fall without fear experience the joy of gravity. The falling rock moves the mountain to the sea. Praised be the falling rock!

At another point further up, his footsteps disturbed a snake coiled in sleep. Springing to life, it slithered across his path and disappeared into the dewy grass.

— The time has come to throw away our old symbols, he announced, tapping a mossy rock with his cane. We have long burdened the snake with the sin of our making. Let us cast off the snake's artificial skin. There is no more good and evil, only the snake — earth's closest companion. Poets and preachers have been too prodigious with their symbols. It is time to strip our language of its old symbols and meet the snake eye to eye. It is time for truth.

The sky was becoming blue and the world was reclaiming its colours. In spite of the path's steepness, his stride lengthened, became stronger, and the pain in his thighs eased until he was barely conscious of his body's weight. Thoughts sparked from his spinning mind in the rarer atmosphere of that altitude. His senses were sharpened, and he became receptive to details he would not have noticed down below. At a glance he took in the number of petals of a small yellow flower, and was pleased it was prime. Water trickled underground like crystal glasses breaking. The smell of goat-droppings mingled with the pungency of sap on his palm from leaning on the spruce tree.

Exultant, he reached the snow-line and picked his way up a rocky escarpment patched with white. At the top, where the mountain levelled out before another almost sheer ascent to the summit, he stopped beside a body of snow surrounded by spiky grass.

— Immaculate conception, he said, catching his breath. Where is the selfless poet who would write a masterpiece on this sheet of snow, knowing it would never be read by humanity, only by a wind that has no memory?

Reaching out with his cane, he wrote on the crispy surface: first a large S, followed by a circle around it.

— So! It's time for a new alphabet. Tomorrow I'll cut my own characters, symbols that will more faithfully, more personally, express my love.

He set off again, and without another stop climbed to his place of meditation: a spur jutting out from the side of the mountain. Filling his lungs with icy air, he extended his arms at right angles to his body and remained like that for some time.

— Yes!

It was a triumphant sound: the victory of the spirit over matter, the culmination of humanity's struggle, the very meaning of existence. Evolution had found its ultimate fulfilment in that instant of transcendent joy. The extinction of countless species, the murder of Abel, the rise and fall of civilisations — everything was redeemed by that cry, everything gathered in that resounding syllable.

— Praised be the mountain! he shouted, his words echoing in the valley like thunder. *Praised be Olympus and Valhalla. Praised be the mountains of Abraham and Moses, the mountain of Christ, the mountain of Mohammed, the mountain of the Lamas. And praised be this — the mountain of mountains. Denying life, many have climbed mountains for the sake of heaven. But few have climbed them for the sake of earth, in affirmation of life. Give me a lever and I will move the earth, Archimedes claimed. My spirit is that lever, this mountain my pivot. The time has come to catapult the earth above all mountains, to make of it a new heaven, and ourselves worthy of paradise.*

The sun appeared above the horizon at the far end of the valley: snow-covered peaks gleamed, small daisies opened their eyes like maidens-in-waiting, and the walker's forehead glowed.

– Behold! The meaning of life! he exclaimed, ecstatically. Father Sun, Mother Earth, and midway between them, Man. Sun: the highest expression of the will to create, will as power, will as light. Earth: patient recipient and transformer of this will. Man: part sun, part earth; part light, part dark; part life, part death. Man: a striving to pure light, to what the ancients called divinity.

Suddenly, as though unsteadied by vertigo, he stepped back from the edge of the spur and sat on a boulder. His breathing wheezed through a ponderous moustache that spilled from his nostrils and concealed his lips. Resting his chin on the cane, he focused on a small flower growing from a crack in the boulder.

– The will to light, he mused, bending closer to the flower. This violet has overcome the darkness of rock by yearning for the sun. Man, too, must strive upward, to overcome hope.

As though summoned by the word 'hope', a figure straight out of a Byzantine icon appeared from behind the boulder. Bald, bearded, wearing a dark-blue robe, he stepped forward pressing a book under his left arm.

– Good morning, Friedrich, he said in a solemn tone.

Alarmed, Friedrich sprang to his feet and considered him for a moment.

– Get thee behind me, he warned, raising the cane, whose tip flashed in the sunlight.

– I'm not ...

– Get thee behind me, you spirit from the grave.

– I've come to talk.

– You've come to poison my joy.

– I've come because you've summoned me.

– No!

— *Like memory, will can also span millennia.*
— *I didn't will you here.*
— *Your will has depths of which you're hardly conscious.*
Friedrich lowered the cane and stepped toward him.
— *Who are you?* he asked, scowling.

A sorrowful look darkened the stranger's face, creased his brow with its bony plate protruding through the thin covering of skin. Suddenly Friedrich became aware of the robe, the book, the smell of the ocean.
— *Is it you?* he asked in a low voice.

Having stepped onto the boulder, the stranger stood against the blank sky like a figure painted without perspective, beyond time and space, against the background of eternity.
— *Yes,* replied the stranger.
— *I thought I'd left you down there.*
— *You take me with you wherever you go.*
— *What do you want?*
— *You know.*
Friedrich nodded as though resigned to the inevitable.
— *You want to talk.*
— *And so do you, Friedrich.*
— *I was on top of the world before you appeared.*
— *One can imagine anything up here.*
— *I come to this spur each morning to observe the sun rise and colour the earth. The moment fills me with profound joy. And now you creep up behind me like a thief, intent on stealing my joy with your sleight of tongue. Very well, let's talk.*
— *You've eluded me for a long time.*
— *And now that you've caught me?*
— *We haven't much time.*
— *For polemics?*

– For salvation.

– Is my soul in mortal danger? Friedrich chuckled through his moustache.

– You shouldn't joke about such things.

– Laughter is a tonic to the soul.

– The soul is above laughter.

– Yes, the soul that can't laugh belongs in heaven.

– Be serious, please.

– Serious, yes, by all means. Serious as a man with a fatal illness. But how shall I address you? Saul? Paul? Apostle? Saint?

– By my chosen name. Paul.

– How shall we commence?

– Like friends who haven't seen each other for years.

– We're not friends, and never will be. As for discussing our ideas amicably, that's impossible! I'm not an armchair philosopher, and you're not a Sunday theologian. My ideas aren't mathematical propositions: I live them as others live an intense experience. When people attack my ideas, they attack the essence of me, and I retaliate as though against a mortal enemy.

– Am I your enemy?

– As much as I am yours.

– No, Friedrich. You're a person who has lived too long within himself. It's time you reached out to others, time you learnt how to love.

– Spare me your pity! he snarled, teeth gleaming through his moustache. I don't need that sanctimonious soup you dish out to the poor, the suffering, the ignorant. If we're going to talk, it must be as equals, like two stags locking antlers in a contest of strength.

– I know your thoughts on pity.

— *It's a parasite that cripples the strong.*
— *Why are you so belligerent?*
— *We're here as antagonists, Paul.*
— *I'm here to . . .*
— *Weaken my will to power: a force that raises the sun, opens a flower, creates works of art.*
— *Your will to power arises from fear not strength: the fear that makes a creature burrow into the dark until its paws harden, calcify, become sharp claws. But fear and death have been vanquished, Friedrich. Christ has brought a new force into the world: the will to love.*
— *Love's for the sick at heart.*
— *It made a cross of the Roman sword.*
— *Rome fell through decadence.*
— *Constantine was transformed through the will to love. His vision of the cross was a revelation of that love, and he acted on it by proclaiming Christianity the state religion.*
— *It was political expediency, Paul. The cross in place of the sword. Constantine wasn't a pyromaniac like Nero: he saw in Christianity an instrument of power. People could be made docile through the promise of heavenly rewards! Not only this, he was shrewd enough to realise that ultimate subjugation lay not in whipping the vanquished, but in placing the whip in their own hands and persuading them to use it on themselves, in the name of freedom and salvation. Renounce the body, deny the world: this precept quickly rendered everything unto Caesar. There's never been a more subtle, more insidious weapon of tyranny. Rome appropriated and used this strange religion, and still uses it today, because it appealed instinctively to the poor, the sick, the hungry, the oppressed, and all those in whom the will to power had been crushed. It's no coincidence that Christianity became a world religion under Rome. From*

its thorny beginnings in the desert of Judea, it soon became an abundant vine that spread because it appealed to the oppressed. Pride and strength were condemned, replaced with pity and humility. Nothing of the sort had ever been said before. It found converts because it preached in the dialect of the slave: blessed is your poverty, your weakness, your suffering, indeed, your very death.

Paul attempted to interrupt on a number of occasions, but Friedrich's words flowed as irresistibly as lava. His delivery rose to such a pitch that saliva clung to his moustache and the whites of his eyes were fully visible.

– The new state religion was remarkably efficacious: the oppressed sensed hope, and through it a feeling of the long-denied will to power. They were happy to render unto Caesar, for they now saw themselves as heirs to a vaster kingdom – note the cunning choice of words – one that belonged exclusively to the poor, the sick, the oppressed. Unable to pass through the gates of heaven which are smaller than the eye of a needle, the rich and powerful would be hurled into eternal damnation for the sin of exercising the will to power on earth. It was a masterstroke of diabolical genius that transferred the seat of power from earth to heaven; that replaced the importance of the body with the transcendence of the soul; that made weakness and humility the strongest of virtues; that placed the meaning of life on the other side of the grave.

– And what of Christ? Paul asked.

Friedrich bowed his head, as though catching his breath. Straightening up, he placed the cane behind his neck, across his shoulders, and gripped each end.

– My quarrel's not with Christ, he said in a restrained voice. If we dispense with the question of his dubious divinity, then Christ was simply a product of his environment: a poor

Nazarene, essentially Jewish in temper and outlook, perhaps influenced by the Essenes, a sect with Messianic beliefs. If not for you, Paul, Christ's popularity would have been restricted to a few local towns and villages, and he would have eventually gone the way of that other Jesus, the son of Baruch, who is also said to have attracted quite a following as a reformer. No, my quarrel isn't with Christ. He spoke to the people he knew and loved; his intentions were ingenuous; he would never have taken his message to Athens and Rome. Naive — I use the word to mean the opposite of intellectual cunning — he believed in his simple words, believed them as one who doesn't know of other cultures and other truths. In all this, I don't object to your Christ; on the contrary, and I confide this to you, I've used aspects of him in realising my Zarathustra. My quarrel, Paul, is with you.

— *I know your Zarathustra, Friedrich.*
— *What's your opinion of it?*
— *Excessive, hyperbolic, rhetorical.*
— *I didn't write that work, I forged it with a hammer.*
— *Using the fire of hell.*
— *Your humour surprises me.*
— *I'm deadly serious.*
— *You consider it a diabolical work?*
— *For several reasons.*
— *Theologically speaking?*
— *Teleologically speaking.*
— *Well, let's hear your arguments.*
— *Firstly, your creation owes more to Christ than you've intimated. I'd go further: Zarathustra has emerged because of your envy of Christ.*
— *Envy!*

The word echoed through the valley.

– *Yes, Friedrich, your condescending attitude toward Christ betrays a passionate envy of him and his teaching. Your creation, modelled on Christ, is an attempt to surpass him. You see your Zarathustra, and through him, yourself, as the true Messiah. And yet you know only too well that Zarathustra is doomed to dwell between the covers of a book, with ink in his veins and paper for his skin.*

– *Let's not drag Christ into what's between us.*

– *He is the heart of the matter.*

– *My quarrel's with you.*

– *Then it's also with Christ, for I am nothing without him.*

– *I'm not the crowd, Paul. There's no need to proselytise. Put aside the otherworldly rhetoric for which you've become famous. Speak plainly, honestly. Apart from envy, which I strongly deny, what other faults do you find in me or my creation?*

– *Your use of the word.*

– *I'm a philologist by profession.*

– *You exploit the word's ability to seduce and deceive.*

– *As you know, the letter killeth.*

– *Yes, when written by a hand driven by vanity and pride.*

– *Will you condemn me for my artistry?*

– *There's a demonic aspect to art that few realise.*

– *And by that you imply I'm evil?*

– *It's not for me to place you on the scales of good and evil. Though I marvel at your mastery of language, and your prose imbued with music, I'm still fearful of its effect on the young.*

– *Your appreciation of music surprises me.*

– *I know the world.*

— *You aren't as naive as Christ, are you?*

— *I admit your genius for words, nevertheless I denounce your works because they are nothing more than perverse thoughts and emotions poeticised by your wizardry. Your writing is like the siren's song: both delightful and destructive to the unwary reader. I'm convinced that some future generation, moved by the goose-stepping march of your prose, will take up your ideas and use them to incite people to war.*

— *As the Inquisition misused Christianity?*

— *They interpreted it in their own way.*

— *All allegorical works are open to interpretation, mine no less than your gospels.*

— *All right, Friedrich, let's speak plainly. What's the nature of your quarrel with me?*

— *Look out there, Paul.*

With an outward sweep of both arms Friedrich took in the unhurried sun, the linen sky, the bristling mountain, the singing forest, the quilted valley, the pebbled town. Paul looked out impassively, shielding his eyes with the book whose cover was studded with coloured gems.

— *What do you see?* asked Friedrich.

— *A weary world waking for another day of toil.*

— *There!* snapped Friedrich, pointing his cane accusingly. *That's precisely where my quarrel lies. You're so obsessed with the Son, you've lost sight of the sun. I don't know what happened on the road to Damascus, but I'm sure you never fully recovered from the temporary blindness that struck you down on that fateful day. How else does one explain the absence of the natural world in your writings? Blinded by the Son, you see the sun, the world, nature, 'through a glass darkly', to use your phrase. But it's not only vision, your other senses were also affected by the life-denying experience.*

Your sight shrinks from the light, preferring the night or the darkness of the sepulchre; your hearing is deaf to everything, including music and song, except for the unspoken word of God; having acquired a taste for bitterness, you spit out the fleshy fig; your smell recoils from the lily, but rejoices in the body's corruption; your touch, accustomed to stone, dismisses the dove's feather. I find quarrel with you, Paul, because your preaching denies the world and makes man ashamed of himself. I find quarrel with you, Paul, because you burdened man with a conscience. I find quarrel with you, Paul, because you destroyed man's joyful nature, sowed guilt's thornbush in his heart, and turned him against himself and the world. I find quarrel with you, Paul, because you took man's smile and replaced it with a brooding frown, took his certainty and gave him hope, promised light but delivered shadow. I find quarrel with you, Paul, because you frightened playful man – Greeks and Romans, not Jews, who have never been a playful race and over whom you had no influence – and made him introspective. You and that snub-nosed babbler Socrates have done more harm to the human race than all the wars put together. Socrates!

He spat out the name in disgust.

– He was given that hemlock far too late. The damage had been done: he had corrupted the Athenian mind with his pernicious talk. He, more than anyone or anything else, killed the Dionysian spirit. Beauty, bravery, friendship: the ideals of Athenian life, which gave us unsurpassed artistic achievements, were destroyed by that babbler. It was no longer sufficient to respond aesthetically to a thing of beauty, Socrates, the ugly one, insisted that people must question their response. Bravery could no longer be an unpremeditated expression of confidence, strength, joy: it had to be scrutinised, intellectualised, examined

to its eventual detriment. If emotions couldn't be put in words and reduced to a system of syllogisms based on questions which always led to more questions, they were considered trivial. 'The unexamined life wasn't worth living', that was his pronouncement, and it fell on Athenian life like a pall. The useless babbler! If he had been a cobbler who used his mouth for holding tacks, or a pumpkin-seed vendor who shouted his wares in the Agora, he wouldn't have corrupted the young minds around him. His idleness spawned the contagion of rational discourse and introspection, and it spread through Athens more disastrously than the plague which ravaged the city. And yet, despite his speech before the Areopagus, and his refusal to live in exile, I'm convinced the old babbler saw the error of his ways just before his death. He didn't recant, at least not in so many words, but it was either Plato or Xenophon who mentions the curious fact that Socrates asked for a lyre in the last days of his life. This gratuitous detail is worth a textbook of psychology. It indicates his disenchantment with logos – the word, reason, questioning. Faced with death people turn to what they most fervently believe, they reach for whatever has been the mainstay of their life. Socrates, though, didn't want to talk, or to intellectualise his experience, he simply wanted to play the lyre. Death transcended through melody not logos. All that he'd babbled in his lifetime was swept away like autumn leaves, and he turned to the spirit of music for comfort and consolation.

– Perhaps he was under the influence of his daemon: that spirit which is said to have gripped him from time to time and held him in a trance for days on end.

– His daemon has become my demon, is that it? Are you comparing me to the old babbler?

– No, Friedrich.

— *His ears were bigger than an ass's, but they couldn't carry a note. He didn't have a musical bone in his body.*

— *And your body quivers with music, Friedrich.*

— *Dissolves in it, as yours dissolves in Christ.*

— *You know as well as I that music has the power to seduce the young and lead them to ...*

— *The jaws of hell?* he retorts.

A frown accentuated the three parallel furrows across Paul's brow. Erect against the Byzantine-blue sky, book pressed under his left arm, he raised his right hand as though in the manner of a secret salute: thumb and fourth finger enclosing a circle, the other fingers raised and slightly bent.

— *You're too high-strung,* said Paul.

— *The tightest bow projects the furthest arrow.*

— *And your soul's troubled.*

— *Better troubled than put to sleep with sermons.*

— *A vein in your left temple swells as you speak, as if it's about to burst.*

— *It proves there's no hypocrisy in what I say.*

— *What does it matter to the salvation of your soul whether or not Socrates played the lyre in his last days?*

— *Do you know anything about that man?*

— *What I learnt in the Greek academy in Tarsus. And then what I heard about him during my stay in Athens.*

— *Are you aware that he, and not John the Baptist, is the true forerunner of Christianity?*

— *An age that asserts God is dead is capable of proposing anything.*

— *How was your stay in Athens?*

— *It was crowded, unclean, full of loud merchants and shopkeepers, and idle layabouts ever eager to hear something new from abroad. I much preferred Thessalonika.*

— And the Parthenon?
— I saw it from a distance.
— The statues of Phidias?
— The place is littered with idols.
— Did you go to the theatre?
— I wasn't there for diversions, Friedrich.
— Yes, yes, you were there to preach. I've read your sermon on the Hill of Ares. Standing there, just as the old babbler had done in defending himself, you announced your new religion. The magnificent achievements of Athens made no impression on you; instead of the splendours which attest to man's highest genius, you saw nothing but an empty altar with the inscription: TO THE GOD UNKNOWN.

— The pantheon had already been long buried when I spoke to the Athenians about Christ.

— Just as the death of your god has inspired me to announce Zarathustra to the Europeans.

— Zarathustra is a work of art, nothing more.

— And you, of course, dismiss all art.

— I dismiss those who assert that art and religion have a common source. Art is anthropocentric: it begins and ends with the human ego. Though it may sometimes aspire to higher truths, it will always be retarded by the imperfections of the artist. Religion, on the other hand, is theocentric: it's a constant beginning, with God as the creator, not the created, as you would have it.

— Your Jewish temperament precludes you from appreciating art. A person raised in Jerusalem will never grasp the spirit of Athens.

— But many Athenians have grasped the spirit of Jerusalem.

— Which says more for an Athenian than a Jew.

— Or less, depending on how you view things.

— But there's this similarity between the two: just as your Old Testament prophets had visions of the New Jerusalem, so the Greek prophet, Plato, envisaged the New Athens, which he called Utopia.

— And this essential difference: our prophets start from God and come down to man, whereas Plato starts from man and ...

— That's the greatness of the artistic temperament, beamed Friedrich, now standing dangerously close to the edge of the spur. The artist starts from man, from the only certainty he possesses, and strives to overcome man by pulling himself up by his own hair. There's joy in this struggle because nothing is imposed on the artist from without: he creates in complete freedom, acting as both judge and executioner. The religious temperament starts from an unknown god, the x in the equation, and constructs a theology around an unverifiable premise. It belittles man's worth and denigrates his senses, insisting the I, the kernel of consciousness, must be expunged for the sake of the unknown. As men of the city, preachers — and you, Paul, are essentially a preacher, unlike Christ, who was a prophet, and a man of the wilderness — are communicators, the public face of the solitary prophet, performers who wrap the spirit in reason.

— Art can't transcend the human condition, just as human beings can't raise themselves by their own hair. Such a feat requires a force over and above man, and that force is Christ. Grace is the opposite of gravity, the overcoming of the ego's self-centredness, a lightness of being brought about by faith.

— Faith! sneered Friedrich. To live with a bad conscience! To live like an invalid! To resent the strong, and make a virtue of this resentment! To say no to life! No to the sun!

Never, Paul! I'll live artistically, aesthetically, in the full flower of my emotions, in the greatest gratitude to the earth and sun.

– I have concerns for your wellbeing, Friedrich.

– You fear wellbeing, so you promote weakness.

– You live too much for your ideas of life, and not enough for life itself. The ship needs buoyancy, but it must also have ballast. Your mind, Friedrich, has all buoyancy and no ballast – that can only lead to disaster.

– There's a note of pity in your voice, the stench of the grave in your breath.

– You spend too much time up here: solitude is only for eagles.

– And gods.

– Man finds God through the humanity of Christ.

– Get thee behind me!

Friedrich turned his back to Paul and stepped to the edge of the spur.

– Your art will always be its own obstacle to truth. Marble will always conceal the ideal; the human breath will always taint the word; the instrument will always retard music. In short, art will never overcome the physical world.

– Get thee behind me! shouted Friedrich.

– He who has faith has the ideal, but without need of marble; speaks the truth, without using a word; hears the perfect melody, without instruments, or perhaps from instruments never to be crafted.

– Get thee behind me! he whispered sharply.

Stones crackled behind him, skipped onto the spur, chuckled boisterously down the steep mountainside. A black spot appeared in the distance, as though from the sun, and in no time assumed the shape of a golden eagle with a snake writhing in its beak. He watched it glide toward him and circle overhead on rigidly extended wings. On the third circle, it dropped the snake, which twisted in the air, falling with a thud at Friedrich's feet. Its silver scales were iridescent in the morning light. In poking it with the cane he noticed his reflection in the green slits of its eyes. Friedrich picked up the dead snake. Toes over the edge of the spur, arms perpendicular to his upright body, snake in his right hand and cane in his left, he sang a hymn to the sun.

Sonya closes her eyes, savouring the dialogue's rhythm, feeling it reverberate through her. Will he continue to write them now that he has made contact? Is he expecting them back? Does he want them published? Or are they meant solely for her, like love letters? Or like letters written in snow for a wind without memory? She regrets having suggested going to a cafe. It might prove awkward for them. How is he going to communicate with her? A notepad? She should have been more circumspect. It would be embarrassing for both to have their first meeting in a public place. He nodded from shyness. Better to meet in the shop after closing time, where she could read his answers to her questions without being made to feel self-conscious by prying looks, and tell him without reticence how much she likes the dialogues and what they have meant to her in these difficult times. A flutter goes through her body. She would get to know him through the written word, just as she has always come to know the world. Strange: unlike first dates with other men, she is not apprehensive about meeting with him. Is this due to the fact that she would be reading his words instead of looking him in the eyes? Perhaps, at last, she would be in her element with a man.

How long has this elderly fellow been standing in the doorway, inspecting the shop? Nodding to himself as though in approval, he takes off a black beret and enters. Tall and robust, he sways his bulk from side to side, each step almost a stomp. Despite being in his seventies, his hair, cropped close to his scalp, is still ginger and the sleeves of a checked shirt are rolled up to his fleshy biceps. Sonya just manages to gather the manuscript as he swings a bulging plastic shopping bag onto the counter. He greets her in a gravelled voice heavy with an accent. Arms crossed over the manuscript, Sonya braces herself to withstand the stranger's sales pitch. She is certain to be interested in his very special collection, he says. Smiling broadly, he takes out five leather-bound books held together by two leather straps. German Gothic letters gleam on their spines and covers. They have been his most cherished possessions since childhood. He does not want to part with them, but has no choice: his eyesight is failing, reading gives him headaches, and the pension will not go far in these difficult times. She does not deal in foreign language books. They are not ordinary books, he says, raising his voice. He unbuckles the straps, picks one up and flicks through it close to Sonya's face: the smell of leather mingles with the autumnal pages. Make an offer, he says. She can have them at a very reasonable price and re-sell them to a rare book specialist at a good profit. He would have done it himself, but is too old to go chasing rare book buyers. Raising a large hand, he swears that she is the first person he has approached. He lives in a boarding house not far from here.

Undeterred by Sonya's shaking head, he opens the front cover and points to the year of publication. They are old and valuable, he says. And what are they about? Sonya asks, trying to decipher the Gothic letters, but she immediately chastises herself: he is now certain to become even more insistent. Folktales of the Ashkenazi: the Jews of Germany and Eastern Europe. These books have been with him almost seventy years. The night they came his way is branded in his memory: the 10th of May, 1933. He was nine and living in Berlin. It was a clear spring day, very much like today, he says, turning to the window with a squint. The willows in the sandy schoolyard were just beginning to sprout their light-green leaves. There was an excited chatter in the yard that day, not unlike the twitter of swallows darting over their heads. The older boys were discussing a bonfire that was to take place that evening, in a square not far from school. Books were going to be burnt, they smiled. A pile of books would go up in the biggest fire they were ever likely to see. Bring your textbooks, they advised the younger boys. Mathematics, Geography, History: they would all be needed for the fire. As of tomorrow there would be no more school. No more long divisions, no more borders between the countries of Europe, no more remembering the succession of Roman emperors. It would be the beginning of a new age, they said. The Third Reich would begin that evening, and with it the third millennium. He went home not knowing what to make of the situation. At nightfall he left for the square, without his textbooks.

He suspected the older boys of trying to deceive the younger ones and land them in trouble. Besides, he did not want to burn them: he enjoyed school and was good at his lessons.

The square was crowded with more people than he had ever seen. Pushing between suits, dresses and uniforms, he made his way toward the centre, where occasionally a tongue of flame rose above the surrounding crowd and licked the night, sending up a flight of sparks. A truck whose tray was raised at a steep angle had spilt a load of books onto the cobbles. He crawled under the truck and watched from the front tyre as young men in white shirts and others in uniform went back and forth, scooping up books and throwing them into the inferno that whirred like a giant bird struggling to take flight. In the meantime, a thin man in a uniform was addressing the crowd, urging the young men to destroy the evil books and prepare the way for a new age. The crowd cheered and roared as flocks of books flew through the dark and fell into the flames. Huddled under the truck, he watched with growing disbelief and fear as crimson faces delighted in stoking the fire. Why was this being done to these harmless books? he wondered, and his heart tightened into a painful knot. He was moved by the terrible plight of those defenceless things. The poor books were surrounded by hostile faces; they were without a friend to raise a word of protest, or extend a hand of mercy. Suddenly he saw himself as their saviour. Swelling with indignation, he noticed near the back tyre a set of books tied with straps. This was his chance to prove himself. On hands and knees, he crawled over the oily cobbles, pulled in the books, covered them in his jacket and returned to the front tyre. Embracing the poor victims of persecution, heart beating against their covers, fearing the truck's driver returning, he waited until the speeches were over, the last book had been condemned, the crowd dispersed to cafes and beer gardens, and the weary fire left to children. With the bundle under his arm and his jacket badly oil-stained, he crept out and made for the nearest lane.

His large hand splayed flat, almost concealing the uppermost cover, the fellow examines Sonya for a moment, as though assessing the effect of his story. She is deeply moved by the thought of the boy risking his life to save these books, but she knows not to show her feelings, for the fellow is sure to persist at the slightest hint of encouragement. To strengthen her resolve she reminds herself that she is a victim of a chaotic present, just as much as those books were victims of a frenzied past. The books were like homeless pups, he continues, stroking the cover. He was responsible for their welfare, and for the next seven years he concealed them from his parents, moving them about the house from basement to attic. He became their safeguard and confidant, and they in turn confirmed his bravery. When war finally broke out and Jews and Jewish sympathisers were being persecuted, he realised how dangerous they were to his family. He could burn them secretly and avoid any damaging implication, but the years had endeared them to him, and they in turn had defined his adolescence. His view of himself as a young man of worth and substance was reflected in them. He found better hiding places, yet the thought of soldiers storming into the house and locating his books terrified him. In the end he struck on the idea of changing their title. Just as Jews were obtaining false passports to flee the country, he decided to provide a new identity for his beloved books. He designed a wrap-around jacket for each book and had them produced by an old printer who specialised in calendars. The transformation was complete. The Jewish folk-tales were dressed in new clothes and christened *The Economics of Coal-Mining in the Ruhr*. He had spent some time on the new title: it had to deflect the inquisitive eye and allay the suspicious mind. Confident in his choice of disguise, he no longer moved the books from place to place. Throughout the war years they remained on a shelf in his room, untouched by family members. Friends who had joined Nazi youth organisations would often visit the house. In his room, after discussing the new order and the master race, and trying unsuccessfully to win him over to their cause, they would browse through his extensive collection with a view to borrowing something. His heart had never throbbed as much as when their fingers passed over the spines of his disguised books. Emboldened, he would take one of the books and read it in public, holding it up in full view of Gestapo officers. Such reading! He has never experienced the intensity of it since. He was not in a position to save Jews from the extermination camps, but he risked his life to save these books from a holocaust. After the war he packed the books into a small suitcase, with whatever else he could fit around them, and left Germany. Within days of setting foot in this country, he removed the jackets from the books, and set them on the mantelpiece of his room in the boarding house, where they have had pride of place for more than fifty years.

But life is about learning to let go, he says, running his hand over his bristling hair. Circumstances now demanded that he part with them. She can have them at a real bargain, not because he is desperate to get rid of them, but because he senses that she is fond of books and will provide a good home for them, or else see to it that they find their way into a good home. Well? he asks, stroking the cover as though it were a cat. Sonya knows that if she avoids his eyes and utters an emphatic no, the fellow will take his books and leave. Instead she meets his entreating look, and in that instant her resolve gives way. She nods and makes an opening offer which, to her surprise, he promptly accepts, pushing the books toward her. Counting the money onto his extended palm, she thinks of Simkin, her debts, bankruptcy. The fellow thanks her, glances affectionately at the books, and leaves. Sonya lights a cigarette and scolds herself for the purchase. She is no better than a gambler who, having vowed never to bet again, succumbs to that ruinous passion. The fellow crosses the street and enters the betting agency. She is momentarily stunned. Has she been conned? Was it all nothing more than a story concocted to evoke sympathy from a bibliophile? And the fact that the books are old and of some worth? Yes, but it was primarily the story's charm that persuaded her to buy them. She ought to be cross with herself, yet she accepts the likely deception calmly, looking forward to her meeting with the author of the dialogues.

the

NINTH

dialogue

Sonya has seen Theo on four occasions since their first meeting ten days ago, each time in the shop's back room after locking the front door at the end of the day. At that first meeting he seemed pleased by the suggestion that they have coffee in the shop rather than go to a cafe. It was a mild evening: the last customer, a young woman barefooted in leather sandals, placed her purchase in a backpack containing a loaf of bread, mounted her bicycle and set off with a smile for the world; like new leaves a flock of sparrows fluttered boisterously in the bare maple tree across the street; twilight gradually unfurled its banner until it blazed over the city, announcing the advent of warmer weather. She forgot the foolish purchase from the old man the moment Theo entered the shop. He was nervous, self-conscious, and kept flicking his fingernails. Taking a notepad, Sonya led him to the back and invited him to browse. In the small kitchen, she scrubbed the stains from two chipped mugs, made coffee, and returned to find him in the sunken armchair, face concealed by a large hardback: *A New Model of the Universe*. He placed the book on his lap and accepted the mug. Sonya sat at right angles to him, feet tucked under her. She wanted a cigarette, but held back in deference to him, biting her thumbnail instead. I'm pleased you came, she smiled. Darting a sidelong glance, he nodded. His dialogues were wonderful. Written with feeling and intelligence. She was drawn into their world and into the heads of the characters. Had he considered having them published? A young female editor who works for a large publishing company visits the shop regularly. Sonya could pass on the manuscript if he wanted. His gaze fell to the fireplace, where a few black scraps lay on a bed of fine ash. He shook his head slowly. Why? She knew books. His work was good. After a moment's reflection, he took up the notepad, unscrewed the top of a fountain pen, and wrote slowly, in a script that looked almost calligraphic. Sonya observed his slender fingers holding the pen as though it were a religious object, and writing an act of faith. She felt a strong desire to be caressed by the writing hand; to feel it move over her body as it moved across the paper; to burgeon under its gentleness, as those words were burgeoning in blue, like irises. He extended the notepad. The familiar writing caused a shiver to pass through her body. She read his reply slowly, her lips moving over each word, tasting each syllable. His dialogues were nothing more than a preparation for a work of far greater significance, he wrote. As for their publication, he was strongly opposed to the idea. Writers should venerate the word, for in the beginning was the Word and the Word was God. The word should not be exploited and corrupted through the process of commercial publication. Each text should be original and unique, just as an original painting was unique. Publication cheapened the text, in the way that a reproduction of a painting was cheaper than the original. His aim was to live for the word, to be faithful to it, to feel it in a way that few had done. He was not driven by a desire for money and fame – that was all vanity. As ascetic monks shunned the world in order to live in communion with God, so he sought to renounce the world in order to live more purely in communion with the word. These days how many writers would shed so much as a drop of blood for their work? The book had been reduced to a supermarket item: to be quickly consumed during the commercials on television and just as quickly forgotten, so that another could be bought tomorrow. Books as profit, diversion, entertainment, seldom as what the spirit of the word demanded: enlightenment. No, he did not want to be published. He wrote for himself, and for her, not for the public's consumption.

He sipped his coffee with a faint inward whistle as Sonya read the careful writing with its precise spacing, rolling curves and slightly forward inclination that drew her along as though she were in a boat rowed by sure hands. A tremor of excitement passed through her, induced as much by the script as by the fact that his eyes were on her, perhaps reading her face as she read his words. But what was she to make of his ideas? Did his condemnation of books imply condemnation of bookselling? Did he see her as profiteering at the expense of the spirit of the word? She hoped not, for it had been a long time since she felt this way about a man. As yet she was unable to say with certainty whether he felt anything toward her, though his disclosure about having written the dialogues for her seemed full of intimation. Those words made her heart beat with joyful expectation, something she had not experienced in a long time, perhaps since setting up the shop. Yes, he appeared aloof, preoccupied, but she attributed this more to diffidence than disinterest. He had, after all, chosen her as his confidante and guardian of the dialogues. Are there other copies of the dialogues? she asked. He shook his head. She felt privileged to be entrusted with his work. But why had he chosen her? And why send the originals, not copies? He took the notepad from her, laid it on the hardback and began writing again.

Sonya followed the silver nib as it curved and looped, stroked and dotted its way across the sheet. She was fascinated by the point and the scratching sound it made in its contact with the sheet. An anecdote from medieval theology came to mind: it was thought that an infinite number of angels could be accommodated on the tip of a pin. She imagined that an infinite number of words could be contained on the point of a nib. As he wrote, taking care with each word, a door closed with a heavy thud in the funeral parlour, rattling the window, perhaps resulting in a slight tremor in his writing hand. And it occurred to Sonya that a line of handwriting was like a seismic graph, recording a person's emotional state as well as their thoughts.

He handed her the notepad and for the first time looked her fully in the eyes. Sonya's heart quickened. He had been to the shop a few times before commencing the dialogues. On each occasion she had impressed him with her serious manner and obvious devotion to books. He had watched her furtively and noted that she read at every opportunity. In particular, he had been struck by the intensity of her reading: her total surrender to the word. It appeared to him that, in an ideal world, she would have been a full-time reader. Sonya smiled, nodded, blushed. When he started the dialogues, he had already decided that she should have them, not because he needed feedback or approval – that meant nothing to him – but because he felt that she was a kindred spirit. As for not making copies, he placed no worth on the dialogues. If it were not for her, he might have burnt each one after writing it. He had been greatly moved and impressed by two Buddhist monks who sat cross-legged in the city's art gallery for days, creating a calligraphic work using coloured sand. Grain by grain, they painstakingly produced a stunning replica of a page from the Tibetan *Book of the Dead*. He went to see their progress on a few occasions, and was there as the last grains were being put in place. No sooner had they laid down their slender glass straws, which they filled with sand by gently breathing in, than they filled their lungs and, in unison, blew fiercely on the work, instantly reducing it to the chaos from which it had arisen. His conception of art and life was deeply influenced by that moment. He placed no value on the dialogues themselves; in fact, their worth lay in the process of writing, and in that they were a preparation for his devotion to the word. He had distanced himself from each dialogue once it was completed, and they were now hers, to do with them as she wished. Sonya vowed to look after them. Who knows, he might have a change of heart about publishing them. Eyes closed, he shook his head. Would he write more of them? she asked. He raised three fingers. And then? My preparation will be complete, he wrote.

As the lunchtime crowd makes the most of a fine day, Simkin enters the shop solemnly, his lower lip more ponderous than ever. Sonya has been bracing herself for his visit all morning, and now she stands back from the counter, her arms tingling with pins and needles. As usual he is neatly dressed: the measuring tape, a striped tie, white shirt rolled to his elbows, and a vest with a receipt book in one pocket and a piece of tailor's marking soap in the other. What is the world coming to? he frowns. Not ten minutes ago a young man walked into his shop and took out a new pair of jeans. Naturally enough Simkin asked how much he wanted them shortened. No, replied the young man. Could he have a few holes cut into them? Holes? A clean rip across both knees and one across the right buttock. Why did he want to destroy a new pair of jeans? He was not destroying them, he was making a statement. A statement! He should open his mouth if he wanted a hole that would make a statement. The young man became angry. Would he make the holes or not? No, replied Simkin. His trade had taught him to mend holes not make them. All his life he had repaired clothes, respected them, and he now refused to violate an innocent pair of jeans that had yet to experience life. The young man snatched them from him and stormed out. What next? he asks, twisting the measuring tape. One should expect anything at the end of the millennium. These windy-headed young people may see fit to come in with the emperor's clothes, spread them on his work-bench, and insist that he stitch the braiding on the cape, using golden thread of course.

As he speaks his eyes are not still for an instant: peering over the top of his semi-circle glasses, he darts glances here and there, ensuring his premises are not being abused. Well, Sonya, he says, lowering his voice. Has business improved? The last month was bad, the worst she has experienced. And the rent? She is doing her best. Her best? Two months in arrears! Most of her earnings are going to the bank. At my expense, he frowns. Sonya appeals to his humanity. Having lived through hard times, surely he understands her predicament, and that she could not have foreseen this recession. No, Sonya, he says, raising both palms toward her. He was burnt by the accountant, he will not be burnt a second time. If the overdue rent was not paid by the end of the week, he would be forced to hand the matter over to his nephew, a very capable lawyer, who would take steps to have an eviction notice served. Sonya is stunned by Simkin's hard line. Could he give her a little more time? She would do her best to make up the arrears. The end of the week! In desperation she reaches up to the shelf behind the counter, takes out the five-volume set of *Jewish Folk Stories* and offers them to Simkin. German? he scowls. He does not know the language, and even if he did the print is too small to read. His sight is fading. Even with glasses he has trouble with the numbers on his tape. No! He has no time for reading. What little strength remains in his eyes will be spent on the sewing machine. Besides ... But they are old and valuable, Sonya interrupts him. He could get a month's rent for them, if not more. She knows a rare book dealer but has been too busy to take them to him. If he could give her another two weeks, she would sell them and a few personal belongings to meet the arrears. He has given her one month, he has given her two months. No more extensions. Sonya walks him to the front door, trying to assure him that the recession will not last forever, and that business will pick up. Look at that, he says, indicating the burnt building across the street. He turns to Sonya with a searching look that creases his forehead. People resort to desperate measures in bad times. Prodded by the insinuation, Sonya is about to retaliate that she esteems books too highly to even think of such desecration, no matter how bad business was. But she swallows her words as a young woman steps out of the brothel and hurries past them. You don't see brothels going up in flames, says Simkin, shaking his head. He knows the owner of the building: a Greek who ran it as a butcher's shop for years. The place is smaller than Simkin's, but earning twice the rent. There's more business in bodies than in books, he grimaces, pulling at the ends of the tape. And to think, the owner of the brothel offered him first bite of the apple. His principles would not allow him to accept the offer, and now he faces the prospect of a building that might be vacant for months. The end of the week, he sighs, shuffling out into the warm sunlight.

Returning the books to the shelf, Sonya lights a cigarette and draws deeply, holding her breath before exhaling. Simkin's deadline adds to an anxiety gnawing at her since her meeting with the fellow from the bank yesterday. He came with a spring in his step and a flush on his cheeks, explaining that, on his way here, he could not resist going for a jog through the nearby gardens. Placing his briefcase on the counter, he flicked it open and took out *The Catcher in the Rye*. He never goes anywhere without it, he said. The book had restored his youthful idealism. It was a pity the author had retreated into seclusion, surrounding himself in a wall of silence. He was now considering giving up the bank and going back to study. The recession was worse than he feared, with the rate of foreclosures doubling in recent months. As he could not save people in business from falling off the edge, he had decided to get into naturopathy. The idea had come to him out of the blue, while waking from an afternoon nap. It was not quite a conscious thought, nor a dream, but a strange combination of the two. He would study herbal medicine and help people who had lost faith in the medical profession. He thanked her: if not for the fortuitous encounter with the book, he would not have been receptive to that flash of inspiration. Suddenly his boyish enthusiasm subsided. He put the book down, shuffled through a few files, and produced a manila folder with the name of the bookshop in black texta. I'm afraid things look bad, he said, wincing, as though there were a sharp pain in his wisdom teeth. He had pointed out her energy and commitment to the manager, but in the end the figures did all the talking. The manager had wanted to foreclose immediately, but he interceded, and was able to obtain an extension of another month, perhaps two if there was some sign of improvement. What could she do in a month? Advertise a weekend sale with fifty per cent off all stock, that might attract customers and provide the flagging business with much needed momentum. There was marginal profit on books as things stood – at fifty per cent discount she would be giving them away. He shrugged his shoulders. And in the event of foreclosure? she asked. A receiver would be appointed at her expense, and they were not cheap, who would come in and value the business's assets. If the bank could not recoup its loan from the sale of assets, it would sell her home to make up the difference. Sonya fought back a swell of emotion that surfaced in her eyes. I'm sorry, he said, clicking the case shut. He hoped that foreclosure would somehow be averted. Meanwhile, though, he would keep his fingers crossed for her sake.

Struggling with a feeling of helplessness, Sonya gazes at her books. For some reason, she imagined that Simkin would be more understanding. She even considered asking him for a loan, to keep the bank from the door. But his manner was so abrupt, his tone so unbending, she could not bring herself to ask him. And now, for the first time, she is struck by the thought of losing the shop. The receiver will come to the shop, value her books, and have them carted away and sold. Her books, the very things that gave her life order and meaning, would be scattered throughout the city. Shuddering at the thought of the shop stripped and empty, she suddenly feels just as empty. And if the receiver should find a large deficit, she would also lose her house.

An old woman dressed in black struggles into the shop. Speaking with an accent, she says that she has come from the funeral parlour next door, where her husband lies in a coffin, waiting to be buried in a few hours. He loved books, at times perhaps more than her, and she would like to buy a few to place in his coffin, for the other world. Though bemused, Sonya manages to express a little sympathy. Pulling out a damp handkerchief from the sleeve of her cardigan, the woman wipes her eyes and smothers what sounds like a few pious words in her native tongue. What kind of books? asks Sonya, catching her reflection in the woman's shining black handbag. The woman ponders a moment, then asks whether those in heaven really need books. Sonya is taken aback: she has never considered the existence of books in heaven. Suddenly the thought of heaven saddens her. How can there be paradise without books? Consoling the woman, and perhaps also trying to persuade herself, Sonya replies that the way to heaven may be through books. In ancient times the souls of the dead gave the ferryman a silver coin for their passage to paradise, today perhaps only those souls reach heaven that carry their passport – the book that left its mark on the soul. Thank you, says the woman, clasping Sonya's hand in her two. As she does not have a knowledge of books, could Sonya please choose three for him. But I don't know what he liked to read, she replies. He read anything he could get his hands on. Please, insists the woman, kissing Sonya's hand. Three good books that would serve as a triple passport for his poor soul. Surely it would be more fitting for the books to come from his collection at home. Yes, but she thought of the idea in passing the bookshop, and it is now too late to go home. Averse to the idea of her books being buried with the deceased, Sonya is nevertheless moved by the woman's plaintive look. Freeing herself from the woman's grip, she takes a brown paper bag, goes to a shelf containing black-backed classics, closes her eyes, selects three at random and places them in the bag. I can't thank you enough, says the woman, fumbling in her purse. How much are they? Sonya cannot bring herself to accept money for three books that she is sending to the grave. My gift to a fellow reader, she says. Tucking the paper bag under her arm, the woman thanks her and walks out awkwardly, as though it has been a long time since she has worn high heels.

Gazing through her faint reflection in the front window, Sonya knows that she ought to be doing something constructive to rescue her business from receivership, but a sense of futility has undermined her will, making her incapable of lifting a finger. In a month's time, a new signwriter will come along and scrape BIBLIO-PHILE off with a blade, and, dispensing with brush and paint, spread an adhesive sign across the window, one produced in a flash by computer and laser printer.

She springs up from the counter. Is that Theo walking briskly past PLAMEN'S GRILL? Is he on his way here? No. She is beginning to see him in other people. He is on her mind continually, like a melody whose resonance vacillates above and below the surface of consciousness. In serving customers, in counting out their change, in replacing books, even in reading, she recalls their meetings in minute detail: his diffidence, those furtive glances as she reads his responses, his gesture and manner of writing. And when not dwelling on their meetings she waits with gnawing expectation for his next visit. In analysing her tumultuous feelings, she wonders whether this is the beginning of a relationship, or nothing more than her way of coping with the impending doom.

From their meetings Sonya has managed to extract bits and pieces of his own story, despite his reluctance, or perhaps reticence, to divulge his past. For the last five years, since the unfortunate incident that permanently deprived him of speech, he has been working part-time here and there. When she questioned him about the exact nature of the incident, he became evasive, writing that she would find out in due time. Before his misfortune, however, he worked as a tutor in Literary Studies at the university, and was completing a PhD on the role of confessions in the novels of Dostoyevsky. He was half-way through the thesis when he was forced to abandon it. Will you return to it? she asked. The incident had taken his voice but opened his eyes to many things, he wrote. No, he would never go back to the thesis, though even now, having destroyed what he had written, he still believed that confession was crucial in the redemption of so many of Dostoyevsky's characters. He no longer needed a PhD.

Having been certified an invalid, he was entitled to a pension for life. In the first year of his disability, cut off from society, unable to engage with those around him, he had retreated into his speechlessness. Initially this isolation had been harrowing: the will and the spoken word were so closely linked that the very reflex to speak caused a sharp pain in his larynx. In time, however, when the injury healed and the pain subsided, he experienced what he referred to as virtual speech: the sensation of speaking, of hearing his thoughts. He compared this to the experience of amputees who often felt the presence of phantom limbs. He was like a pianist who had lost his fingers in an accident, sitting at the keyboard, playing a virtual *Moonlight Sonata*. Family and friends encouraged him to undergo rehabilitation. At first he refused, remaining stubbornly aloof, like a creature nursing its wound, until their solicitude became too overbearing, and he joined a group that met weekly. Gradually, as his health and outlook improved, he started learning sign language as a means of direct and spontaneous expression. He mastered it in a matter of months, to a degree where he was able to engage in lengthy conversations with his instructors. Sign language was useful in communicating within the small circle of people who taught and worked with the speech-impaired, but it was still very much an unknown language in the wider community. A few family members and friends made an effort to learn this new alphabet; they started with a genuine desire to make life easier for him, but it was not long before they became frustrated by the finger signs, their enthusiasm flagged, and their hands reached out for the pen, as smokers reach for a cigarette.

Retreating into his speechlessness once again, he discovered books as though for the first time. Perhaps in compensation for the fact that he would never be able to utter a syllable of text, familiar words suddenly appeared in a new light: they were quieter, more intimate, their meaning enhanced by their purely visual presence. It was at this time that he began writing fiction, at first as a kind of therapy, then as an obsession. He never showed his first fruits to anyone: they were the work of his apprenticeship, short stories with an autobiographical touch, which eventually met with the same fate as his thesis. Despite his dissatisfaction with these early works, he sensed that, given his handicap, writing might provide him with a meaningful place in society. The printed word did not need a tongue, and the page was a level playing field for both the speaker and the mute. In time he became certain that writing was his only salvation, but he had yet to find his voice, as it were. A chance visit to her bookshop about a year ago gave him the idea of writing the dialogues. Since then he has found that just being in the shop fired his imagination. He has enjoyed the challenge of writing the dialogues, of engaging with philosophical and religious ideas. The exercise has disciplined him in objectivity: in overcoming the gravity of the personal, the autobiographical, which he dislikes in so much contemporary fiction. Lately, though, he has sensed that the dialogues were coming to an end. There might be another two or three left in him. And then? she asked, feeling a touch of apprehension. He did not know, although he was certain that the process of writing them was an inner preparation for something else, something important for his development, perhaps a state of consciousness where ideas were very much lived experiences. Did he see himself turning to religion? He wrote that he wanted to live an idea the way martyrs lived and died for their faith.

Zitta's cheerful entrance fills Sonya with foreboding. He strides in with his coat slung over one shoulder, the sunlight over the other. She stubs her cigarette and empties the ashtray into a metal bin beneath the counter. It's about time, he says, indicating outside with a broad sweep of his arm, revealing a patch of perspiration on his white shirt. Spring has finally stirred him. Does she remember their university days? He used to feel spring right here (slapping his solar plexus), sometimes weeks before it arrived. What has happened to that feeling? Was he getting old? Or has the greenhouse effect weakened spring's intensity? Wary of being drawn in by his smooth talk, Sonya busies herself with a few books on the counter. He looks around, pulls out a book from the shelf, and nods slowly. Remember the library at high school? he asks, his wry smile ending in two dimples. A great place for dreaming. It was there he discovered Machiavelli's *The Prince*. That slim book changed him forever. A boy when he reached for it out of curiosity, he was a new being when he finished reading it, and the world was suddenly bigger than the schoolyard. Have your dreams come true, Sonya? he asks. Are your books selling? His nostalgic evocation of the library puts Sonya off her guard. The bank is circling her shop like a vulture around a wounded creature, she says, lighting a cigarette. Zitta takes her packet and spins it. Not looking good, Sonya, he says.

He has had experience with banks: once they sense their loan is in danger they show no mercy. How long have they given her? A month, maybe two. Can she inject funds into the business? No. Then she is certain to lose it. Sonya draws deeply and holds her breath. I can help you, he says, spinning the packet so rapidly that it is impossible to read the brand name. Can you lend me some money? she asks, her words mingling with smoke. He can do one better than that: if she places her trust in him, he will see to it that she does not lose a thing. Two weeks ago Sonya would not have dared to ask how he could avert the inevitable; now, with the inevitable almost upon her, she takes the hook he dangles before her. What does he have in mind? He looks around and leans over the counter. This must remain between us, Sonya, he says in a grim manner. Understood? She nods helplessly. His friend would not be too pleased if word got out. Alarmed, she is on the verge of saying that she is not interested in his assistance when his mobile phone twitters. He turns his back to her. The caller informs him that some gambling machines are being removed from a club by their owner for lack of payment. Zitta fires a volley of swear words at the owner, threatening to fix him good if he so much as touches the machines. Tell him what I said, Joe. Got it? I don't want to hear any more. The caller protests, to which Zitta responds by pressing the phone's off button. When he turns back to Sonya, his cheeks are tinged red, jaw set like a trap about to spring. Dead heads everywhere, he snaps. Heads for nothing more than wearing a cap. His agitation is now directed at Sonya. Listen to me, he says peremptorily. I'm your only way out of this mess. Listen! And not a word to anyone! He can arrange for the shop to be destroyed by fire. Listen! His 'torch' has done several jobs for him, and the insurance company has come to the party on each occasion. Anything could happen in a bookshop: a cigarette butt thrown in a rubbish bin, the fire in the back room, an electrical overload. The investigators would not find a thing. She must act quickly, though, for he has been in great demand in recent months. Sonya's thoughts and emotions are swirling. Set fire to her books? No! And yet what is the alternative? Remain faithful to her books and lose everything! I know what you're thinking, says Zitta, loosening his tie. There was nothing to worry about. He would arrange everything. She need not lift a finger. It would be payment on completion, when the insurance company settles her claim and hands her a crisp cheque. Sonya, listen to me, he continues sternly, anger crackling in his voice. You're in deep trouble and I'm throwing you a lifeline. If only she could tell him in clear terms that she rejects his criminal idea, refuses even to contemplate it, but she feels trapped, intimidated by his aggressive manner. Her silence makes him more insistent. He will arrange for the 'torch' to pay her a visit. Have a chat with him, he says, leaning over the counter. Sound him out, judge for yourself the sort of person he is. If she was not impressed by his knowledge and attention to detail, she could call off the proposal. Agreed? Anxious to get rid of him, Sonya finds herself nodding, slowly, in time with his pronounced nod.

Vulnerable, sensing her world slipping away, Sonya spends the next few hours rearranging misplaced books.

She knows the exercise is futile, that she would be better off preparing for the receiver, but the titles on the spines, the feel of the covers, a sentence here and a paragraph there, the very proximity to her books allays her anxiety. Why is it that when alone with them she feels at home, sure of herself, ready to meet any challenge, but when the world intrudes, she is reduced to a moth shuddering on a title, desperate for the golden letter it will never embrace? And now, with the receiver certain to intrude, she feels especially close to her books. In a month they will be taken from her and sold off by people with no feeling for them. And the alternative? Better to die than be sold off into slavery. Zitta has no feeling for books either, but his proposal has this merit: her books would be consumed in a great conflagration and saved from the ignominy of being sold into slavery. Perhaps her books would become martyrs for her: she has given so much of herself and her time for them, now it was their turn to die so that she might live. The idea begins to take hold of her. But, as martyrs, their death would also be a resurrection: they would be redeemed by the flame, the word restored to a pure state.

    She recalls having read somewhere of an ancient Chinese emperor who had amassed a vast library of rare books, in which he took more delight than in his many concubines. In time, though, insurgents arose, rebelled against his authority, which was probably more trying than tyrannical, and marched to the palace gates. Seeing the inevitable end, the emperor took the flame from the holy shrine and set fire to the library. She has often wondered about the emperor's action. So many explanations are possible. He burnt them in order to keep them from enemy hands, for books were not only a symbol of power and authority, but their very source. He burnt them as an act of immolation: as they were his most precious possessions, he was in a sense burning himself. Perhaps he burnt them from a feeling of immense disappointment: all his life he had believed in the supremacy of the book, but that supremacy could not save his empire. Or perhaps ...

Theo enters, hesitant as usual, but just in time, for there is no telling where the thought of books as martyrs might lead. I'm glad you've come, she says. It's been a horrible day. He holds up the golden envelope. Sonya's heart throbs in anticipation, dispersing her foreboding. I've had enough for one day, she sighs, locking the front door and leading the way to the back room. I'm going to lose the shop, she says, and draws her armchair closer to his, their toes almost touching. She has done her best, but has been unable to appease the bank. He takes out a small notepad from a loose-fitting shirt buttoned to his neck and, resting it on the faded knee of his jeans, writes, Can I help in any way? Would you like to become a silent partner? she asks, and, in the next breath, apologises for her tactlessness. A smile lights his face, while a hoarse, grotesque sound, as though he were choking, issues from the back of his throat. I'm beyond help, she says. Have faith, he writes. Faith? In what? They look into each other's eyes fully, steadily, giving of themselves without reservation, as though reading each other. I'm afraid, she says, voice cracking, eyes welling with tears. I might lose everything. He bows over the pad, writes for some time, then hands it to Sonya. Life is about letting go, she reads. Sometimes our salvation comes from sacrificing our dearest possession. When Abraham heard the call from God he took his only child Isaac and set off for Mount Moriah. On the way, gripped by fear and trembling, he must have glanced into the boy's wondering eyes, but he didn't waver. And even on the mountain, having gathered kindling for the fire and bound his son like a lamb, he didn't falter. I'm no Abraham, says Sonya. She relates Zitta's proposal. What would he do in her situation? Follow it through, though not because he sees banks and insurance companies as evil, but because it would be a way of severing attachment to the world, thereby leading a freer life. Just as there is gluttony of the body, so there is gluttony of the mind through books. Too many books are being published, and most are nothing more than sweets, delicacies, trifles, providing little or no nourishment. If there is a way of extricating herself from the curse of consumerism, saving her soul from a slow death under the weight of materialism, then she is compelled to act, even though it may mean breaking the law. After all, matters of the soul come under the jurisdiction of a higher authority, one that transcends temporal laws. Looking up from the pad, Sonya meets his light-blue eyes fixed on her, as though reading her face. His reply startles her with its daring, makes her heart race, sends a surge of excitement through her body. Though barely able to admit it to herself, perhaps this is what she really wanted to hear. In him she has found a confidant, a kindred soul, and, dare she think it, a lover. Suddenly she is not alone in whatever is to happen: he will help her through this difficult time, lighten her burden, and together they will embark on a new life. But she checks these impulsive thoughts at once. No. If she takes up Zitta's proposal it must be for the right reasons. She must be certain of her motives, certain that she is not simply rationalising her fears.

Theo extends the envelope, with a note saying that he would very much like to watch her read his work. Aloud? Sonya asks, taking out the sheets. No. He is intrigued by silent reading: a state of outward passivity, yet inward engagement. He likes to study people on public transport. As the train moves forward through time and space along a straight line, the mind of the seated reader travels in the opposite direction, or in curves and warps, twists and loops, parabolas and asymptotes. I'd like to watch you read, he concludes, and extends the pad with a nervous smile. Sonya nods bashfully, having already taken in his words, upside down, as he was writing them.

The piazza you are about to enter from the comfort of your private space is one of those out-of-the-way places which has never found its way onto a glossy tourist map. It is the kind of place that a visitor to this illusory city (also justly famous for its deceptions and intrigues) might encounter after hours of nocturnal wandering through narrow, tortuous lanes, over numerous hump-backed bridges (or perhaps a few bridges crossed and re-crossed many times), and past sixteenth-century buildings whose basements have long since been reclaimed by the murmuring sea. And just as the visitor might begin to feel hopelessly lost, despairing of ever finding his small hotel, he turns yet another corner, and there it is: this precious space which almost takes his breath away.

An equestrian statue, appearing like an alloy of bronze and darkness, dominates the piazza lit by pale lamps at regular intervals along the perimeter. Balancing a hooded falcon in one hand, an open book in the other, the mounted prince or duke gazes from under a stern brow in the direction of the clock-tower. Suddenly, the clock's hands come together in an attitude of midnight prayer, while the large bell pulsates like a heart, each throb reverberating in the stony enclosure, adding to the frenzy of the odd bat tumbling and twisting in flight. The obligatory church is opposite the tower: its wide doors padlocked, windows lifeless, facade decorated with forms devilish and divine. Like angels with tightly folded wings, two ancient cypresses stand solemnly beside the steps leading to the front doors whose bronze panels depict scenes from the Pentateuch. One side of the piazza is bordered by a brick wall belonging perhaps to a convent or school. Clusters of wisteria hang from strands of barbed wire along the top of the wall. On the opposite side a row of arches and thick columns forms a covered walkway for small shops which, during the day, deal in leather goods. Leaning against a column, in the oblique shadow cast by an insipid lamp, two lovers are locked in an embrace. Above the walkway the windows on all four storeys have their louvred shutters drawn, not permitting a slice of light to escape. The sky is clear, bristling with stars, while the bluish ghost of the new moon peers from behind the sharp roofline.

At the bell's ninth throb, the shutters of a third-storey window spring open, revealing a young man with a fountain pen raised to his lips, gazing down onto the piazza as though deep in thought. Ceiling-high bookcases cover the wall behind him. Dangling from a twisted chord, like an eye from its optic nerve, a naked bulb casts a prism of light across the piazza. The young man's shadow also stretches to the far side, where the outline of his head encloses two men sitting on a flight of steps leading up to a bricked-in doorway. From a distance of the young man's window they could quite easily be mistaken for schoolboys, so slightly are they built. Their heads are disproportionately large for their sloping shoulders, and both are leaning forward, the man on the left because of a prominent hump between his shoulders, the other, because of a deformed spine. Wearing circular glasses with thick black rims, the one on the right squints at the church; the other stares wistfully at the moon, his elbows propped on knees, chin supported by both hands.

– I never expected to find myself in Venice, muses the man with the glasses. No, not even in my wildest dreams.

– These third millennium writers seem to overcome all obstacles, says the other in a toneless voice.

– One instant I'm in Copenhagen, the next ...

He removes his glasses, rubs the lenses on his vest's felt lapel, then raises them at arm's length toward the young man in the window. Shaking his head, as though in bewilderment, he secures the glasses over his crumpled ears and turns slightly, to take in what the other is saying.

– Being thought, one travels at the speed of thought.
– A thought?
– Flesh and blood can't transcend time and space.
– And yet I am here.
– In thought only, my friend. It may well be that thought is of a similar essence to time and space, in which case they would constitute the holy trinity of the universe.

— Whose thought am I? asks the one with the glasses, fixing the other with a sharp look.

Without lifting his head from his hands, he indicates the open window with a barely perceptible nod.

— God's?

— Not that far up.

— Whose?

— Our silent friend in that window.

— I'm myopic, says the other, eyes narrowing to slits.

— We're whirring in his mind faster than subatomic particles in an accelerator.

— Are we energy?

— Thought-energy.

— Like light?

— Faster and more illuminating than light.

Straightening up as far as his disability allows, the man with the glasses focuses his attention on the window.

— Who is he? he asks, in a thoughtful tone.

— Could be any one of a thousand foreign writers struggling for recognition, searching for that elusive inspiration. He's probably American, though he might just as easily be British, or Canadian.

— How can you tell?

— What's our language of discourse?

— You're right, he exclaims, tapping his forehead at the surreal nature of the situation. I'm thinking in Danish and speaking ...

— Language is no obstacle to writers of the third millennium.

— But why has he brought us together?

— Perhaps as an exercise, a preparation.

— For what?

– *The new millennium.*
– *Hey, you up there!*
His words flutter and fall to the stony stillness.
– *Save your breath,* smiles the hunchback. *He won't answer.*
He leans back slowly, painfully, as though the weight of the world were on his back. The other squints up at the window, his spine bent into a question mark.
– *You're Kierkegaard, aren't you?*
– *It sounds more melancholy than a bell tolling in a country churchyard. I'd prefer you call me Søren. And you're Leopardi?*
– *Yes, but I possess neither the grace nor the vigour of the spotted feline. Please, call me Giacomo.*
– *Remarkable, don't you think it? Here we are chatting like old friends, and yet this is our first meeting.*
Nodding, Giacomo picks up a sprig of wisteria from the step, and considers it for a moment before raising it to his nose. Søren removes a broad-brimmed hat and wipes the inside.
– *What time is it, Giacomo?*
– *According to that clock, exactly midnight.*
– *And the year?*
– *We're light years from our respective dates of birth.*
– *How can you tell?*
– *The light in the young man's room.*
– *You're very observant, Giacomo.*
– *Objective as a man of science.*
– *The physical world hardly exists for me.*
Søren tucks his left foot under his right leg and rests both elbows on the step behind him. In this more comfortable position he studies the young man for some time.
– *Why is he staring at us?* he whispers, tilting his head confidentially toward the other.

— *There's no need to whisper*, smiles Giacomo. *You can be sure that he knows everything we're saying. In fact, he even knows what we're going to say. It's probably to our advantage to ignore him, and concentrate on becoming better acquainted.*

— *Where do we start?*

— *With what we have in common.*

— *We're both writers.*

— *Both confirmed bachelors.*

— *Both geniuses.*

— *And both deformed.*

— *Such is the cross we carry, Giacomo.*

— *A cross for one person is a roof-beam over which another throws a noose. My hump is irrefutable, Søren. Sometimes it feels heavier than the load Atlas was condemned to carry.*

— *Are you an atheist?* asks Søren, pulling at his shoelace tied with what appears an inextricable knot.

— *What does the negation of God entail? A supposition that God once was but is no more? A condition of Godlessness? A return to a multiplicity of gods? A state of humanity where man becomes God? I don't know, Søren. I am an artist, a poet, a human being who communes with the world aesthetically. I've always struggled for harmony and perfection, and I expect no less from a just and poetic God. Are we works of art, Søren? A divine Creator wouldn't allow deformed creatures like us to see the light of day, just as I wouldn't permit the publication of a bad poem. From which it follows that we are not the children of God, but offsprings of Chaos fathered on blind Chance.*

As though too heavy for his slender neck, Giacomo's head sinks forward into his cupped hands. Noticing the lovers against *the column, Søren lowers the brim of his hat, casting a shadow over his eyes and affording them a little privacy.*

– Have you ever asked yourself, Giacomo, why your prodigious intellect is coupled to such a feeble body?

– For the reason that many beautiful bodies lack brains.

– A matter of chance?

– What else?

– I see it like this, says Søren, trying to untie the knot. Attracted to the earth by the very nature of physicality, a strong body is compelled to use intellect as a tool in gaining further advantage over the material world. I need only adduce Alexander the Great to illustrate my point. Genius in a deformed body, on the other hand, is less likely to be attracted by the material world and dissipated in contending with it for the trappings of fame, riches, power. Such intellects are perfectly – I was almost going to say ideally – suited to dwelling exclusively in the numinous world of thought, to working with ideas as a mason works with stone, to extending the frontiers of human knowledge. Who knows, in the not too distant future there may be a case of an incredible intellect sinewed to a body so feeble, so incapacitated, as to be permanently restricted to a wheelchair, and even then requiring assistance with everything from mobility to speech. Though unable to will even his tongue to move, he might nevertheless have such a powerful intellect, one so swift in the realm of ideas, that he may make advances in pure mathematics, proposing theorems and offering proofs which few can comprehend; or, through his grasp of theoretical physics, he may discover new laws, a model for unifying the forces of nature, a theory which must wait a hundred years before it's experimentally verified.

– Intellect can also lead to doubt and despair, says Giacomo, plucking at the wisteria.

– Yes, intellect can lead to the abyss, though not necessarily to despair.

– The two are inseparable.

Søren smiles and taps the sole of his left shoe.

– Intellect, even that of genius, can't overcome the abyss. But if something within us, something more essential even than intellect, were to defy the abyss, if this something were suddenly to impel us to take a flying leap ...

– Into the abyss, Søren?

– A leap of faith, Giacomo. A happy spring over the dreaded abyss, over time and the human condition.

Giacomo looks up at the sky. The faint circle of the moon is poised above the cross fixed to the church's bell-tower. The stars are like points in a children's game which must be connected sequentially for the correct pattern to emerge.

– And that? he indicates with a nod.

– What do you mean? Søren asks.

– Can your leap of faith overcome the night sky?

Giacomo's words are heavy with resignation; his question full of that irony which expresses itself in the faintest of smiles. Tilting his head to one side, Søren grimaces in looking up.

– I can't make out a thing, he sighs.

– Not even the constellation of Orion?

– Books have worn out my feeble sight.

– They've made you short-sighted.

– Where is it?

– There, just to the right of the cross.

– I see the cross ... nothing else.

– Then for you, Søren, it's as if the stars don't exist?

– Does it matter whether or not they exist?

– It matters, Giacomo replies firmly.

– What would be different in the absence of stars?

— *The Magi would never have found Christ.*

— *Perhaps, but each generation must discover Christ anew; in our age without a guiding star, perhaps through blind faith.*

— *Stars highlight the infinite.*

— *So does mathematics.*

— *Mathematics grew from the awesome wonder of the night sky.*

— *Wonder? It makes me feel cold, indifferent, wanting to hurry back to my study.*

As though the strain of trying to see Orion is too much, Søren rubs the corner of each eye with the back of his thumb.

— *This is where we differ, Søren. Your abyss is a metaphor that describes a certain state of being, or perhaps non-being. Stones and stars have no effect on you.*

— *Sticks and stones can break my bones, but stars will never harm me.*

— *Unless you were struck by a shooting star.*

— *Yes, because they're flying stones.*

— *My abyss is there,* says Giacomo, gazing up. *Stars, space, infinity: we're no more than fireflies against that backdrop. At times, in moments of heightened lucidity, I fear that it will annihilate my flickering consciousness.*

— *And there's nothing beyond this objective universe?*

— *Nothing, Søren.*

— *Your pessimism is dreadful.*

— *I live with it, just as I live with this hump.*

— *Our friend up there was reading in silence from your poetry just before we met: the lyrics didn't strike me as the work of such a pessimist. In fact, a ray of light gleamed through the most melancholy poems. Am I mistaken?*

— *You're not the first to make that comment. Yet I*

assure you it's only an illusion, what I call the illusion of art. When dark emotions are cast in artistic form they sometimes emit an aesthetic light which is often mistaken for an affirmation of life. This light, which is another name for beauty, is really an illusion, just like a rainbow, and the sense of affirmation it evokes is without foundation. No, Søren, this ray of light you detect in my work has nothing to do with your Christian hope.

— What do you know of my hope, Giacomo?

— I followed our friend's lips as he read from one of your books. The maze of subordinate clauses in each sentence mirrors perfectly the labyrinthine nature of your hope.

— You spoke of your pessimism, Giacomo. Well, let me tell you, my hope isn't exactly a Sunday picnic.

— But it supports your crooked spine.

— Friend, you haven't understood my hope.

— It's a source of strength.

— Strength? It's more dreadful than your pessimism.

— What kind of hope is that, Søren?

Fingers crossed tightly under his sharp chin, he reflects a moment, peering at the mounted figure circled erratically by a bat.

— My hope, Giacomo, isn't the sort you find at a Sunday-morning service. It's not a reward for the suffering endured in life, nor a light glowing from the promise of paradise. My simple hope arises from a faith that accepts miracles and reconciles the absurd — that is, from Christ's word in relation to the world. True faith follows intellect to impossible heights, then goes one step further: it dares to look down into the abyss and hope.

— Your faith resembles my despair.

Søren's doleful gaze finds its way back to the lovers.

– Faith requires sacrifice, and often grows from despair, he says in a low voice, as though thinking aloud. The spirit can only arise when the body is crucified on the cross of this world.

– You're fond of paradoxes, Søren.

– Faith's paradox is this: to sacrifice all hope of ever attaining earthly happiness, and, at the same time, to believe that one's ultimate happiness lies in this very sacrifice.

– And have you sacrificed much?

– The greatest earthly happiness: love.

– A woman?

– I was engaged to be married, Giacomo. I loved the girl, and she loved me, twisted spine and all. Everything was arranged, the wedding-date was set, but ...

A swell of emotion, and his words falter, catch painfully, making him clear his thin throat with a grunt. Giacomo taps him on the back until he regains his composure.

– Sounds as if it ended unhappily.

– Have you ever been in love? asks Søren, picking earnestly at the knot.

– I came close to marriage once, too.

– What kept you from it?

– Ah, you've turned the table on me in true Socratic fashion. All right, I'll answer first. In mentioning our superior intellect, you failed to add that it's also a two-edged sword: both a blessing and a curse. Lesser minds are swayed by instinct and emotion. In our case, the reverse is true. Our intellect is insatiable, Søren; it dissects and examines everything, even the emotions. I questioned love and happiness, wanting to know what lay at the heart of both. I wanted to understand them, as I understood Euclidean geometry. In the end, I concluded that they were nothing more than mechanisms for

human survival, adjuncts to consciousness, whose primary function is to shield humanity from too much reality. My intellect saw through the illusion of love, so I left the woman and never saw her again.

– Your outlook is bleaker than I imagined, Giacomo.

– No bleaker than life, he replies, looking up from the cobblestones.

– Without hope, existence is a living death.

– That's the curse of too much intellect.

– It needn't be, my friend.

– Every thought leads to the abyss.

– But the abyss can be overcome.

– Your flying leap of faith again, Søren?

– A faith that grows stronger in the face of despair.

– Now you sound like a minister.

– Theology's in my blood.

– You should have entered the Church.

– Or the Theban desert. In another time and place I might have been an ascetic monk, like Saint Anthony. There, in the harsh wilderness, I would have won my faith by vanquishing all manner of temptations.

– You'd make a good minister, Søren.

– I considered it in my youth, he says, gazing up at the still figure in the window. In my enthusiasm I dreamt that I'd stir people with my words, open their hearts to the truth of Christ, like roses opening to summer. But the more I saw, the more I understood: Christ's truth is a searing flame which few can confront, let alone embrace. The Church does not challenge, it does not take a stand against materialism, it does not teach renunciation of the world; on the contrary, it makes a pillow of Christ's parables and lulls people to sleep. In its quest to please parishioners, to keep backsides on pews,

the Church has made Christianity comfortable. Who knows, if this continues, the time will come when the Church will declare: we can minister to parishioners without the need of Christ, whose precepts are too thorny. And so the humanisation, or should I say socialisation, of Christ will result in the withering of the human soul.

Søren blinks a few times in focusing on the clock in the tower: the black hands are still clasped in a vertical position. Sitting a little to one side because of his hump, Giacomo hangs his head in contemplation.

– Look at them, says Søren, indicating the lovers. Young and oblivious to everything.

– They've overcome the curse of consciousness.

– The laws of necessity.

– The dread of the infinite.

– For them language has become a probing tongue.

– And the world has contracted to each other's pupils.

– Do you envy them, Giacomo?

– Envy, Søren? No, I pity them. Smothered in each other's love, they can't see that life will inevitably cheat them, as it cheats us all.

– Is your outlook really so hopeless, my friend?

– And how real is your hope, Søren? Why didn't you marry?

Søren grimaces, his face creases, becomes an inscrutable hieroglyph, and his gaze turns from the lovers to the shadow of the book in the hand of the mounted figure.

– Why? Because of my hope.

– Another absurdity?

– Hope is the greatest absurdity.

– A fine aphorism.

– Very well, Giacomo. I walked out on Regina, not

because I'd stopped loving her – in fact, my love grew stronger each day – but because I felt that my love was becoming an obstacle to a religious way of life.

– Were you happy with Regina?

– As much as is earthly possible.

– And you turned your back on her?

– Are you being facetious?

– It was unintentional, Søren, he smiles, raising his right hand in a frail gesture of apology. What I meant was, you renounced certain happiness for ...

– A life in Christ.

– For what may be an empty promise?

– Hope is not an empty promise, Giacomo. It arises from the faith of Abraham: a faith that moves a person to renounce his most cherished possession, to sacrifice his dearest love, all in the name of a higher love, one that will not only assuage the faithful in his dreadful act but restore fully the poor victim of his sacrifice.

– And the girl? How did she feel?

– She was hurt, of course.

– Was that a Christian act on your part, Søren? To propose marriage to the poor girl one day, only to walk out on her the next?

– I've wrestled with that question hard and long, Giacomo. I believe there are situations when, teleologically speaking, religion must take precedence over ethics and morality. This is perfectly illustrated in the case of Abraham and Isaac. From a human perspective we find it abhorrent that Abraham should have raised his knife to sacrifice his only son. But at that terrible moment Abraham had transcended the human and remained steadfast in his relation to God. He was justified in his obedience to God, for he was reunited with his beloved son and earnt the honour of being called the Father of Faith.

– Who knows, perhaps God spoke to men in those days, and they were moved to act through the power of His Word. But we live in different times, Søren. God no longer moves among us, no longer speaks directly to us; in fact, He may have forgotten our language altogether. So how is one to be sure that, if one hears the call, it stems from God and not from one's own ego, or, worse still, from the Evil One, who can't be eliminated from religious considerations? That's the problem with your intense subjectivity, Søren: there are no external signposts. Faith is your only guide, and many courses of action, including atrocities, can be argued on the basis of faith.

– You sound like a rationalist, Giacomo.

– Perhaps because I choose to live without illusions. I expect no compensation, no rewards. My only consolation is my poetry: a vein of lightning which flickers intermittently through my darkness. I ask for nothing more, Søren.

– Poetry is uplifting, my friend, but it's only one of the stages in life's way, perhaps the first. In our youth we're close to the earth, one with it, and our relationship to the world and our fellow man is essentially aesthetic. In time, as we confront right and wrong, good and evil, this relationship assumes an ethical character. Finally, in becoming a real individual, and perhaps there are only a few in each generation, one rises above even good and evil, and lives religiously.

– You categorise life too neatly.

– Life is a problem that must be solved.

– Does it have a solution?

– One's soul.

– Listen!

Both men turn their head slightly to the right, toward the sound of a bird trilling from the cypress on the left of the steps leading to the church.

– A nightingale, whispers Giacomo, smiling.

Søren is about to say something, but Giacomo silences him with a reproving forefinger. The clear notes echo in the piazza like a tap trickling in the dead of night. They listen intently until the song recedes. Giacomo wipes his eyes.

– You're closer to nature than I thought, says Søren.
– Weren't you moved?
– I recalled my troubled youth.
– Some of us never leave our first stage of life.
– For you there's only the nightingale?

Giacomo shrugs his shoulders, causing the hump to move in the manner of something independent of his body.

– The paradox of faith sustains my life, says Søren.
– Mine's sustained by nothing more than a bird's fleeting song at sunset, the fragrance of a nameless herb after a storm, the sight of an old shepherd leading his flock from the hills, the affirmation of the flowering broom in a desolate landscape.
– Between my faith, Giacomo, and your poetic imagery there's ...
– The abyss.
– Or at times a mere sigh: as much breath as is needed to sustain the word 'hope'.
– At times ...

In the lighted window the man yawns, stretches, and reaches for the church with his left hand, the fountain pen in his right. The piazza echoes with the bell's ninth throb. Suddenly, as though prodded by something, he draws the shutters toward him, obliterating the two shadowy figures in inky blackness just as Søren managed to untie his shoelace.

The bell throbs a tenth time, followed by another, and the last sound quivers over the piazza before dying away. Scented with wisteria, a blind breeze stirs the cypresses. The lovers bow in walking past the church. Alone in the piazza, shadowless, the horseman is half-way between the bird and the book. The new moon rests on the cross, cradled in a silver crescent.

Feeling his dark eyelashes almost caressing her as she read the dialogue, Sonya resisted the urge to look up. Now, heart beating, she meets his steady gaze and tells him how much she enjoyed the story and how evocatively he writes. She has not come across Leopardi, but would like to read his poetry. He has a collection of his poems and prose pieces at home, he writes. She would be more than welcome to it. He adds that he enjoyed watching her read. Her lovely eyebrows rose and fell with the text, her face radiated a gentle glow, her lips moved, as though tasting each word. She laughs bashfully. Yes, her lips move involuntarily when she comes across something really engaging. Sonya taps the sheets on her thighs and extends them to him. He gestures that he has written it for her. She thanks him and promises to keep it with the others in a safe place. As though leaping into the abyss, Sonya reaches for his right hand. Will he teach her to read sign language? She would like to communicate with him more directly, looking into his eyes in the instant of expression. He smiles faintly and nods. His friendship will help her through this difficult time, she says, firming her hold. He reciprocates. She promises to be a good student and learn the new language quickly. In looking deeply into his eyes, Sonya finds a refuge, a retreat from the encroaching chaos, the bed she climbed into with her books as an adolescent. Raising his hand to her lips, she lightly kisses each finger, tasting an inky spot on his thumb. They approach each other slowly, with the reticence of people who have led insular lives, exploring with eyes timid in their probing, with hands hesitant in their touch, with lips modest in their desire, until their tongues, emboldened by each other's pointed tip, engage in a silent dialogue.

the TENTH *dialogue*

Three weeks since her first lesson in sign language, Sonya is making rapid progress in reading his lovely hands. Excited by his presence, by the hands she kisses and which hold her tenderly, she memorised the new alphabet easily, as though her mind were soft dough in which his fingers had left their impressions. By the third lesson she was already able to make out words and short sentences. There is an intensity in reading the graceful movement of his hands that she has not experienced in the printed word: a letter shaped by flesh and bone conveys stronger meaning than the same letter struck by print. His delicate hands, in particular the hand that writes the dialogues, seem to give more body to the text. Letters are shaped by the full dexterity of his fingers working in harmony, each joint playing its part; words, moulded like clay in a potter's hands, are immediate and sensual; the message is so replete with sub-text, she is unable to separate the meaning from the man. Reading his fingers, she has often found herself wanting to be caressed by them, not only for intimacy but to be given meaning through a kind of laying of hands, and then she has impulsively caught them in a sudden full stop and kissed them playfully.

Despite an obvious growing attraction to each other, their intimacy has not advanced beyond the probing tongue. Is he coy by nature, despite his impediment? Perhaps he has never made love. Or, given the content of the dialogues, is it because of a religious belief? Just as they become passionate, he will suddenly pull back and indicate that the time for going further is not yet right. She has invited him to her house for a meal several times, but he has declined, without explanation. At their last meeting when she pressed him about this, he communicated by a combination of pen and sign language that he was expecting something important to happen soon: an event that required his utmost concentration. He became thoughtful, prodding the back of his hand with the pen's gleaming nib, describing a cross within a circle. She did not pursue the matter, except to remind him that he could rely on her for help.

Yesterday Theo came in just as she was closing. It had been a bad day, another nail in the coffin of her business. Earlier she had been visited by Zitta, who was in his usual buoyant mood. How glad he was not to be practising law! A desk covered in dull files, constant phone calls about minor car accidents, petty-minded clients who wanted everything done on the spot, and, worst of all, the Law Association hovering over him like a vulture. He much preferred the freedom on the other side of the fence: mixing with interesting characters, wheeling and dealing, helping people out of tough times. Had she heard from the bank since his last visit? She hesitated a moment: perhaps the Chinese emperor was right in burning his books when the enemy was at the gate, perhaps Zitta was her only hope of salvaging something from the inevitable. Yes, she replied, and felt as though she were leaping into a volcano. How did things stand? A receiver appointed by the bank was only a matter of weeks away. Zitta's dimples disappeared, his brows fell, jaw set in a firm line. There was no time to waste, he said, standing almost over her as she leant on the counter. The job had to be done before the receiver set foot in the place, otherwise the whole thing might look suspicious. Zitta would endeavour to expedite matters. The 'torch' had been out of town for a few weeks. His work was in demand all over the country. When Zitta spoke to him about Sonya's problem a few nights ago his face lit up with enthusiasm. Not having done a bookshop before, he was looking forward to the opportunity. The 'torch' was a very private person, at times inaccessible, but Zitta would do his best to arrange a meeting between them as soon as possible. You'll like him, Zitta smiled. He was a real character, a wide reader, well travelled and full of stories. There was nothing to fear. If only I'd known him years ago, Zitta sighed, as though talking to himself. He would have sent him to Italy to do a proper job on that damned shipment of paintings. If things had worked out, if he had not done time in that stinking prison, he would by now be running his own empire. But Zitta shrugged off this regret almost at once. No use crying over scattered ashes, he beamed.

The 'torch' would do a perfect job on her place, with payment upon satisfactory completion.

Theo was edgy, preoccupied. She invited him for a coffee in the back room, but he declined, signalling something with his hands very quickly. Unable to read the message, Sonya asked him to repeat it, at which he snatched the notepad from the counter and wrote that he did not have time to give her a lesson today. He was a page away from completing another dialogue and must return to it before his ideas slipped away. Tomorrow, he would most certainly bring it tomorrow. Is anything the matter? Sonya asked. He paced in front of the counter for a moment, then stopped abruptly and wrote: he had made notes for a new dialogue, and it might well be the last. The preparation was almost over, and he sensed in the depths of his being that his moment of truth was imminent. Just as his body responded to the advent of spring, so his soul now sensed the coming of the fifth season. The new millennium was now only a month away. What were her views on it? She had been too caught up in the problems of the shop to think about anything else. For the first time since his arrival, he looked Sonya directly in the eyes. Slowly, with the sort of solemnity reserved for benedictions, he signalled that they must prepare for the new millennium. Sonya pointed out that she was going to lose the shop very soon, and that she would then have plenty of time to prepare for a new life in the new millennium. They would prepare together, he indicated. The world would be a frightening place. The computer had already digitised the Holy Word, which was the reason he chose to write by hand. In time the human soul would also be digitised and made compatible with the designs of the Evil One, who would rule the next thousand years. Sonya was surprised by his apocalyptic warning. Though she shared his apprehension about computers, the thought that he might belong to a millenarian sect made her feel uneasy. She loved him and his writing, and did not want to share him with anyone. As though catching a pair of pigeons, she clasped his hands and kissed them. The tension in his body relaxed and he looked at Sonya affectionately. She was frightened and needed to discuss something with him. Did he have a little time? He must return to the dialogue. It would take only a few minutes, she said, kissing his right hand.

In the back room he leant against the door frame, she against the shelves on the wall. She told him that Zitta had paid her another visit. Should she go through with his proposal? What would he do in her situation? He crossed his fingers, cracked his knuckles by pushing them outward, then signalled that he would act in a way that freed him from material necessity. My freedom lies in Zitta's offer, she said, barely able to utter the words. Then she should act accordingly. Yes, Zitta might save her from financial bankruptcy, but she would be plunged into moral and ethical bankruptcy. How would she live with her conscience? He reminded her of Kierkegaard, the Søren in his recent dialogue. The Danish Christian existentialist (no, that was not a contradiction in terms) believed in the teleological suspension of the ethical, by which he meant that the individual moved by faith had the right to transgress temporal laws in the name of a higher law. Did she believe in freeing herself from the seductions of materialism? Did she believe in her responsibility toward her soul? If so, she must accept Zitta's proposal. I need help to believe in my freedom, she said, reaching out for him. He went to her and took her hands. I love you, Theo, she whispered. They embraced and kissed tenderly. As she caressed his hands, he signalled that he would never forget the moment he had fallen in love with her. It was in the bookshop, on a sultry afternoon last summer, not long after he had moved into the area. Browsing through a much-used, and sometimes abused, paperback edition of Augustine's *Confessions*, he sneaked glances at her between the shelves. He was attracted by her at once: she was sitting cross-legged behind the counter, wearing a knee-high skirt with a blue floral print, reading intently, her lips moving sensually at each word. Why had he waited so long to show his feeling? He thought she would be put off by his impediment, so he proceeded to make himself attractive to her through his writing. You're very attractive, she said, kissing his hands. In time she would become more fluent in reading sign language, and then his lack of speech would be no impediment to their relationship. He looked into her eyes for a moment, as though deliberating a course of action, then conveyed with slow movements that his misfortune had occurred because of a woman. Sonya was taken aback, but managed to say that there was no need to explain if it was all still too painful. He shook his head. His hands were in front of his face, and Sonya could read and see his expression at the same time.

It happened five years ago. He should have known

better, but could not help it: he fell in love with a student in his tutorial group, a shy girl with long pitch-black hair and olive eyes. Detaining her to make a few comments on her essay, he learnt that she preferred writing poetry to essays on poetry. He asked if he might read some of her work, and they met often in his small windowless office. She was of Italian descent, the only child of a wealthy Calabrian stonemason: a proud self-made man who had come to this country with nothing and succeeded in acquiring a number of shops, apartments and factories. They lived in a spacious house surrounded by a two-metre brick wall with surveillance cameras at each corner. At first, afraid of what her father would say, she concealed things from him, but as they saw more of each other and their relationship became serious, she summoned the courage to tell him. He became furious, demanded that she stop seeing him, threatened to terminate her studies, swore that he would take the matter to the university board and have him expelled for using his position to take advantage of his daughter. She had shamed the family. What would relatives say? He was ten years older than her, and not Catholic. Raging, he then directed his anger at his wife: he had wanted his daughter to handle the administration of the business, but she insisted that a university education would make the girl a better person. University! It had ruined her and the family name. Theo became concerned when she did not attend the following tutorial. That afternoon two burly men in mud-splattered overalls and gum-boots came to his office and introduced themselves as her cousins. They apologised for their appearance, saying they had been working on a new mausoleum at the cemetery. Standing over him sitting at his desk, they took it in turns, a sentence each, to point out that he should stay away from their cousin. One of them passed a massive concrete-coloured hand over the books on the shelves, pulled out a hardback text on Post-Modernism, and suggested he take their advice, otherwise his skull might be cracked by the text's spine. Just like a walnut, added the other. And his brain might find its way between the pages. Just like egg yolk, added the other. The stockier of the two took out a spirit level from the side pocket of his overalls and struck it against his thick thigh. Their cousin was not for him, he said. If he did not get the message, he might find himself in the foundations of the new mausoleum. The other added: a custom in their part of the world had it that if a body were buried in the foundations the building would stand forever. He stood and, almost chest to chest with them in the cramped quarters, thanked them for their advice. This was a free country, he reminded them. He loved their cousin and, with all respects to her father, he wished to marry her. They turned to each other, pulled a long face with raised eyebrows, and left making several threatening gestures, leaving him to wipe with sheets of paper the yellow clay left on the carpet.

When he saw her a few days later, she was pale, red-eyed from tears and lack of sleep. Her father would never relent, and she feared the worst. He would speak to him, try to make a good impression, convince him of his love for his daughter, and then he might be less hostile. No, she said, alarmed. They must stop seeing each other. Did that mean she no longer loved him?

he asked, taken aback. It meant she was afraid of what her love would do to him and her father. She wanted to protect him from possible harm, and spare her father the heartache she had caused him. And what about their love? It was a mistake, she said, with a bluntness that stunned him. She had already taken steps to defer her studies until next year; in the meantime, she would go overseas for a few months, to visit relatives in Italy and clear her head and heart. A dark pit opened in his being, into which his thoughts and emotions plunged.

She possessed him like a fixed idea. He saw her features everywhere: in coffee stains, the shape of clouds, his absent-minded scribbles. Unable to concentrate on his PhD, which was almost ready to be sent out to examiners for assessment, he took time off work, and for days neither ate nor slept. He had to see her again, speak to her father, point out to him that he had no right to tyrannise his daughter. Certain that she still loved him, he would not allow her to be a sacrificial victim on the altar of her father's outdated traditions. One evening, dishevelled, unshaven, having consumed several glasses of red wine, he went to her house and pressed the button beside the remote-controlled steel gates. Nothing. The camera was trained on him, its red light winking teasingly. Shouting at the lens, he demanded to be let in. They had no right to refuse him access to the girl he loved. He insisted on meeting the father, on being given a chance to be heard. Nothing. His frustration aggravated by the mocking red light, he climbed onto a strip of metal half-way up the gates and shook them violently. He knew that he was behaving like a drunken fool, but he could not control his emotions. Reaching up to the camera, he cried to be allowed inside. He was a human being, not a dog. And if he were reduced to whining and howling like a dog, it was the fault of others. Suddenly, the intercom speaker beside the gate beeped. He jumped down and put his ear to it. Go, before the police come, said a man's voice coarse with accent and anger. He replied that he would not leave until he spoke with his daughter, whom he loved more than anything in the world. She wanted nothing more to do with him, replied the voice. That was a lie, he shouted. He was a possessive, small-minded tyrant. How dare he send his thugs to intimidate him. That showed what a backward peasant he was. She loved him and they had spoken of marriage. The intercom crackled for a moment, and then she spoke, calling him by name in a voice made harsher by the sound system. There was nothing between them. Could he please leave her and the family alone. If he persisted in this disgraceful behaviour she would personally call the police. Her words cut him to the bone, sapped his strength, left him feeling null and void. He gazed dumbly up at the camera, at the winking light, knowing that they were watching him and thinking how ridiculous he looked.

He returned to his apartment in a daze, drained of emotion, her words rasping in his head. Why had he spoken like that to her father? If he had not offended him, she would not have dismissed him in that cutting manner. Perhaps if he had shown more restraint, if he had held his tongue, the father may not necessarily have opened the gate, but he would have left with at least a semblance of hope, even if it were only self-deception. That would have been better than this state of nothingness. Slumped in an armchair he felt himself being drawn to a gaping pit, from which the red light winked hypnotically. He got up and went to the kitchen. On the sink, among the unwashed cups and dishes, there was a container of caustic soda, which he had used a few days earlier to clear the clogged S-bend. An evil eye, the red light summoned him. He half-filled a glass with water, poured in a small quantity of glittering flakes, and stirred with a knife until the mixture turned milky. Raising the glass as though proposing a toast, he clicked with his haggard reflection in the window. To love, he smiled, and drank the mixture. In an instant he was overwhelmed by darkness, and the red light became a bright coal burning through him. Alarmed by the coughing and choking and retching, a neighbour forced the door open and called an ambulance. I was lucky, he signalled, with a wry smile. If the neighbour had been less attentive and if the mixture were more concentrated, he would have lost more than his speech.

His hands fell to his sides, like wings that suddenly lost their ability to fly, and he looked plaintively at Sonya, as though trying to determine her reaction to his confession. Would she condemn him for his action? Would she be repulsed by the thought of kissing a mouth that had swallowed that horrible mixture? Would she end their relationship? Sonya knew what he was thinking. Taking his hands, she kissed each palm tenderly. Tears welled in his blue eyes as he wrapped her in his arms. She caressed his face, smoothed his unkempt eyebrows, and kissed his lips. He pressed her against the spines of the books. Probing with her tongue, she wanted to explore his speechlessness, fathom the darkness at the root of his tongue, assuage his damaged larynx and withered vocal chords, taste his very soul and bring it to light and sound.

The old woman shuffles into the shop, still wearing her overcoat despite the warmer weather, and pushing her trolley squealing for a little oil. Sonya leaves the shelves along the wall neighbouring the funeral parlour and returns to the counter with a cardboard box full of books. After her talk with Theo yesterday, she resigned herself to Zitta's proposal, but a restless night, during which nightmares of books being sacrificed in the flames alternated with visions of her own salvation, filled her with such anguish, that she left for the shop at the crack of dawn and went directly to the shelves. She felt compelled to spare as many books as possible from the inferno, and yet, after hours of what has seemed like judicial deliberation, she has only managed to reprieve one boxful of books. At times during the morning she could not help seeing herself as the Grand Inquisitor: holding up a book for judgement, she could almost hear its plea for clemency. And how can you justify yourself? she would ask. What have you done to deserve being spared the flame? Some books answered that they had provided entertainment, a screen between the reader and the harsh reality of the world; others, knowledge that enabled mankind to overcome the pain and uncertainty of physical existence; while others, consolation for the inevitable suffering of being human. Sonya struggled with the role of Inquisitor, and had on more than one occasion imagined sacrificing herself to save those plaintive voices.

Thank heaven for summer, remarks the old woman, removing her sunglasses. It is her favourite time of year, despite the fact that she no longer follows the horses. Winter rains made the race tracks heavy and unpredictable, and picking a winner was a matter of luck. In summer though, when the tracks are firm and fast, she used to pick winners from the very sound of a horse's name. She will never forget that summer just before the war, when she was seventeen and in love. She did not have arthritis then. My hips could dance and carry on all night in those days, she chuckles, covering her mouth with a hand laced with wrinkles and veins. She went with her boyfriend to lots of races. As she could barely read her own name, newspapers and form guides were useless, so they would stand near the starting gate as the horses were taking their positions. She would study the look of a horse and if its name matched its appearance, she would place a bet on it. They had such fun together that last summer. She picked so many winners. They went to theatres, restaurants, dances. It was heaven. But her boyfriend was conscripted into the army, and she never saw him again. He died somewhere in Europe.

Raising the trolley's cover, the old woman takes out a few paperbacks from the collection thrown carelessly inside. They are smelly, warped, bloated. She found the lot of them a few days ago in a back lane around the corner. It was pouring, and she was hurrying home when she came across a box ready to fall apart and spill its contents. Young people, she says, slapping the books together with a dull thud. Back in her days nobody would have dreamt of throwing them out: paper was scarce, and the pages of a book would have been used in the toilet, if nowhere else. These books were wet and soggy and weighed a ton. Drenched, she threw them in the trolley and set off down the lane's uneven cobbles, holding her breath in case the wheels fell off. At home she lit the heater and arranged the books on the floor, turning them this way and that. On others she used a hair-dryer, blowing warm breath on each page, until they regained some of their crispy rustle. They're not perfect, she says, extending them to Sonya, but they're still readable. She would sell them cheaply, despite the time and effort she put into them. Sonya thanks her, and apologises that she has neither the space nor the money for more books. Besides, they are really worthless in their present condition. I've nursed them back to life, the old woman insists. People will not read, let alone buy, badly soiled books, Sonya says. But the words are clear as daylight, the woman retorts, flicking a book's pages in Sonya's face. And of course, a little imagination can always be used to fill in the odd word that can't be made out. Sonya closes her eyes, shakes her head. What shall I do with them? the woman asks, dropping them into the trolley. Sonya shrugs her shoulders. But surely they must have some use in this day and age. The other bookshop owners in the area will tell her the same thing. She would be better off disposing of them in a paper recycling bin. I was hoping to get something for my trouble, she says. Moved by the woman's efforts in rescuing the books from the rain, Sonya picks up her box of selections on the counter and tips them into the trolley. Take them up the street, she advises the startled woman. Not only would she get a good price, but her good deed would save them from the flames. Perplexed, the woman stares at Sonya for a moment, then puts on her sunglasses and manoeuvres the crying trolley like a new mother pushing a pram. Signalling to the traffic which parts like the Red Sea, she crosses the busy street and shuffles off in the direction of the other second-hand bookshop. Two men in shirts with short sleeves are standing in the empty shell of PLAMEN'S GRILL, unscrolling construction plans. With the burnt roof-beams pulled down and the corrugated sheets removed, light streams into the front of the building, cutting sharply across the smoke-stained brick walls at the back. The old woman stops before the body piercing salon and adjusts her glasses against the reflection of light from the front window. Almost too vivid to behold, the eagle and snake appear as though about to turn their ferocity on her. Undaunted, she goes to the window, reaches up on tip-toe, and just manages to touch the snake's crimson tongue with her index finger.

As a sense of futility seeps into her, Sonya dismisses the idea of filling another box with books fortunate enough to escape the flames. Instead, she lights a cigarette, closes her eyes, and for a moment feels her troubled self dissolving in the warm sunlight. And now, in the absence of Sonya Gore, there is only the smell of smoke mingling with books, a fly simmering for summer on the front window, a solitary heart beating neither for life nor love, but for the great silence beyond the last word, the absolute stillness beyond the last number. Suddenly, jolted by the thought of losing her centre of gravity and dispersing like a sound or smell, she opens her eyes and, in a kind of panic, stares at her name above the doorway in small red print. Sufficiently centred, she draws deeply on her cigarette and feels the sunlight slanting languorously into the shop. Its warm touch on her left cheek evokes a midspring morning when she was at university, approaching the end of her first year. Uncomfortable among the throng of students in the cafeteria and main library, she was drawn to a small library discovered by chance in one of the university's resident colleges. This soon became her favourite place: a refuge conducive to reading, reflecting, meditating, and daydreaming – all of which, at times, flowed into one another. This was the essence of true reading – a state in which the printed word interacted with ideas, hopes and dreams.

That morning she responded to spring's eruption with an excitement she had never before experienced. Walking past the cemetery on her way to the university, glancing through the barred fence to read a faded name or a golden death-date, she had often been filled with a dark melancholy which only the library could dispel. Today, however, the cemetery was a frenzied artist's palette: bright flowers bought from the vendor's stand led the living forward; weeds with yellow stars pushed through fissures in the granite; butterflies played tag among the headstones; small birds quarrelled in the pine trees, hopped about with bits of twigs in their beaks, splattered black crosses with white droppings; a tap left running sounded its happy song. All this aroused in her a sense of expectation, though of what precisely she was unable to say.

It was a Friday, and the mid-morning sun streamed into the quiet library as though it would justify its existence by highlighting the titles of books, love-hearts scratched on the desk, her small hands, whose shape she grasped as though for the first time. Bowed over her book, she suddenly sensed that someone was watching her. At the table in the centre of the room, sitting low in the chair, almost reclining, a boy stared over the top of a large physics textbook resting vertically on the table. Their eyes impinged and deflected. He slid lower in the chair and hid behind the covers of his book. Heart beating, she was unable to concentrate on her novel. It was an idle look, she told herself. It signified nothing. Perhaps he was pondering something, attempting to come to terms with a difficult problem. Spring, she rebuked herself, trying to focus on the page, yet unable to overcome that look. Suddenly (and she dared not look across) his chair scraped back and his footsteps hurried out, just as the bell in the clock-tower struck eleven, each toll sounding a blow of disappointment. Had she misread his look? Perhaps it was nothing more than her own sense of wishful expectation. In fact he may have been so absorbed by the wonderful possibilities of quantum physics that he forgot his next lecture until reminded by the clock.

On Monday she set out again for university. The morning was crisp and clear, but her thoughts were vague and confused. As though going to her execution, she climbed the stairs to the library, her legs almost giving way at each step. She hesitated before her reflection in the plaque, took a deep breath, and entered. A slender hope snapped, and her heart was a dead weight in free-fall. From the desk she gazed out on the cemetery until the clock in the tower sounded noon. Numb with disappointment, she was about to leave when the door opened. A rush of blood rang in her ears. Acknowledging her with a faint smile, he occupied the same place as last week. They darted glances at each other: she, looking up from her novel; he, over the top of his physics textbook. Occasionally their glances engaged, and each pretended to be deep in thought, as though not seeing the other person. After an hour of eyelashes fluttering like butterflies, he closed his book with a thump, came to her desk, and, in a quivering voice, asked if she would like to join him for a walk.

They met for lunch every day for the remainder of the week. Suddenly the university was less daunting; the cafeteria, less intimidating. The following week, they held hands, while strolling through a nearby park. Stretched out on the freshly-cut grass, in the shade of a sprawling fig tree with massive, intertwining limbs, they discussed their courses, the coming vacation, career prospects. As she lay on her back, hands behind her head, looking up at the leaves shaped like tongues, he moves closer, until their bodies touched. Time and place slipped away as she was drawn into his eyes. She gave herself to him as she had to the printed word. Embracing, they screened each other from the prying world, and soon their awkward, tender kisses become more knowing, their hands more adventurous, their tongues bolder.

The next week they were alone in the college library. The afternoon was overcast, sultry, and now the sun found a crack in the clouds and filled the room with golden light. They took advantage of the privacy in an alcove at the back of the reading room. At first she was uneasy, not because the librarian might suddenly return, but at being watched by these old books with their gleaming titles. She felt she was betraying them, abandoning them and all that they have given her, for this moment of pleasure, this warm person in her arms.

Another Friday, the last day of lectures before the examinations. They strolled through the cemetery. Arms around each other's waist, they commented on names, subtracted years, read dedications of undying love. The broad, blue day felt like summer. Cicadas creaked in the trees as though unable to strike the correct pitch. Finding themselves in the shade of a row of pines, they sat on the foot of a grave. Black and smooth, the horizontal slab had been inscribed in gold with an outline of an open book, and on the book a poem of eternal memory. They caressed each other's eyebrows, the line of their lips. Succumbing to his whispers, assured that they are well concealed by the surrounding headstones, she deftly removed her shirt and bra and reclined on the cool slab. They took their pleasure quickly. He pressed down on her, and she felt the outline of the book, the words of the poem, the mirror image of LOVE. As she turned from him to slip into her bra, he caressed her back and spine, where the poem was impressed on her skin.

Sonya is snatched from the past by Theo, who strides into the shop looking agitated, as though pursued by someone. She crushes her almost full cigarette and waves away the smoke. Pale, unshaven, with dark rings under his eyes, he frowns at the ashtray brimful with butts. On several occasions already he has reproved her for smoking. One must endeavour to live with less, avoid material dependence, overcome the world, be self-sufficient, all through strength of will. Nodding, Sonya promises to give up once her business affairs have been settled. He could help her though, she says. If they saw more of each other, instead of the stolen hour here and there, she might find the strength not only to quit smoking but to accept the reality of losing the shop. They will spend more time together, he assures her with sunlit hands, but the circumstances are not quite right. Things are stirring in him. He has a feeling – no, a premonition – that something is about to occur that will change his life forever. The third millennium is at hand. Yes, they will consummate their relationship on the eve of the third millennium and enter the new age one in body and spirit. He places the envelope on the counter and caresses her face. She grasps his hands, but he pulls away and signals that he must return to the next dialogue, which is proving troublesome. He is now certain that it will be the last. Has she heard of Savanarola? No. He was... Dropping his hands, he leans over the counter, kisses her and leaves.

Perplexed, at times perturbed, by his erratic behaviour, Sonya questions their relationship. Does he really love her? Or is he simply using her as his personal reader? But to what end? No. It is clear that his view of a relationship is coloured by a religious sensibility. And his agitation? Is it a sign of instability? A personality disorder that drove him to take the caustic soda? No. He is overwrought, preoccupied, perhaps a little obsessed by work, nothing more. A case of a writer desperate to finish one project in order to undertake another. As though just sealed the envelope's flap peels back easily. She removes the sheets and, before reading, tastes the moist flap, gliding her tongue from one end to the other.

Having struck a dead end in the play he has been struggling with for several months, Henrik Ibsen turns from his desk and, preening his side-whiskers, once again contemplates the portrait on the wall. This time though, instead of resuming work, elbowing the desk with greater concentration, he gets up and stands before a man with hair combed in a wave, brushed-up eyebrows, and a moustache waxed to a provocative point. But it is the elusive, changing expression in the man's feline eyes that continues to intrigue him almost a year after acquiring the work. Just as the eyes of certain portraits appear to follow the observer, the eyes before him seem to alter their colour and expression. They are strikingly those of a cat, but a cat which has been cornered, and which sometimes seems to be on the point of flight, other times set to fight, and occasionally resigned to its fate. Unable to determine which of these states the eyes now express, Ibsen decides to go out for a stroll, hoping the night air might clear his mind and bring his characters into sharper focus. For him clarity of characterisation is crucial to his art; in fact, he never writes a word of dialogue unless he sees the character who speaks it. The word must come from flesh and blood. He must know that the servant's fingernails are in need of cutting, or that the heroine has bought a new dress since last he saw her.

It is just after one in the morning when he pulls the heavy door behind him and steps out into a blaze of twilight. The cobblestones are still warm from the long summer's day. Children are playing with hoops and balls, shouting in games of hide and seek, hopping on numbers chalked on the pavement. Sitting on a doorstep, two women are complaining about the cost of carrots. The youths in front of the funeral parlour are discussing the new century. At one point he slows his brisk walk to overhear the conversation between a man and a woman.

– I'm happy to stand here all night, snaps the woman.
– Well, what do you want to do? asks the man.
– It's your turn to decide.
– I'm sick to death of making decisions!

He would like to hear more of this little quarrel, it might be useful in a future play, but the woman darts a castigating glance at him. He quickens his step, crosses a junction of streets converging to a circular flower bed, and enters a well-treed park. A brass band is playing in a gazebo covered in blossoms. Here, as on the streets, people appear relaxed, unconcerned by their usual cares and worries. The winter has been unusually long and bleak, so now everyone is enjoying to the full the longest day of the year. Walking along a path flanked by bushes bursting with roses, he is suddenly chilled by a sense of being watched. He turns abruptly: a young couple is strolling arm in arm in the opposite direction. Edginess, he thinks, attributing the sensation to the stress and strain of work. He dismisses it and continues along the sandy path with gritty steps. Tired of trying to grasp misty characters, of digging deep within himself to find sustenance for ghostly figures, of expending mind and matter to provide them with flesh and blood, he slackens his concentration and slips into a receptive mood, where impressions enter his consciousness of their own accord. Picking a blueberry from a small shrub, he bites it and at once tastes the colour spreading over his tongue, filling his mouth. A mouth full of colour, he thinks. Does colour have taste? The thought that each colour might have its own taste is a welcome change from the dull taste of words. He has lived with words too long, they are becoming stale. Perhaps he should devote more time to colour. He liked art, and painted a great deal as a youth, when he worked as an apothecary's assistant. He could easily have devoted himself to painting if he had not become a playwright. How did that happen? Why did he turn from colour to words? From fact to fiction?

Preoccupied by these and other thoughts, he now finds himself standing on the edge of a pond in the centre of the park. Children are launching paper boats on the dark surface tinged with twilight. He sits on a double-sided bench and gazes at the small island in the middle of the pond. The black cypresses and the large mossy boulders on the banks of the island remind him of Böcklin's painting Isle of the Dead. He follows a white vessel as it glides over the smooth surface and comes to rest against a boulder. Someone sits on the bench directly behind him, so that their backs touch. He is about to slide a little to one side when a man's high-pitched voice asks, almost commands, him not to move. Startled, Ibsen turns slightly, but is stopped by the man's sharp tone.

– *No, Henrik. You mustn't.*
– *Who are you?*
– *My name's not important, he says.*
– *What do you want?*

— *A talk, Henrik. A little chat. Ten minutes of your time. Nothing more.*

— *I've had a most difficult day.*

— *Yes, I understand. You'd prefer to be alone. I understand perfectly. You see, I'm ... Yes, you're no doubt working on a new play. It's certain to be a success, another wonderful example of contemporary theatre, a masterpiece, to be sure. I won't keep you long, Henrik. Ten minutes, and then you can return to your characters. What's ten minutes in this timeless evening?*

— *Well, what is it?* Ibsen asks pointedly.

— *A little tête-à-tête,* giggles the man as the back of their heads touch.

— *Did you follow me here?*

— *With so many people still out and about I hoped to avoid your attention. I didn't mean to alarm you, Henrik, certainly not. But the truth of the matter is ...*

— *Well, get on with it,* Ibsen grumbles. *What is it you want to talk about?*

— *I ... er ... don't know where to start.*

— *Begin by telling me who you are.*

— *I'm ... er ... I ... er ... Have you ever listened to the sound of the word 'I', Henrik? Yes, of course you have. As a great playwright you weigh each word with as much care as an apothecary weighs his potions and powders. We use the word too casually, don't you think? We say it hundreds of times a day, but we never really stop to listen to its sound because we're always in too much of a hurry to proceed to the verb. 'I hope to be famous', or 'I need a rest', or 'I will be a father'. We say it without thought, as though referring to an article of clothing or an old shoe. That word has a terrible sound for me, Henrik. A leaden*

object falling on the floor-boards of an empty room.
    — Stop this bookish babble! Who are you?
    — But that's just it: I don't know who or what I really am. Please, don't turn around, Henrik. Not just yet. To put it another way, my personality doesn't have a centre of gravity. I am whatever comes to mind. Yesterday I was Edgar Allan Poe, today I am Emanuel Swedenborg, tomorrow I may be that fellow Strindberg.
    — Strindberg! Ibsen echoes, craning his neck.
    — Don't, Henrik. I'll run away if you turn around.
    — So it's you?
    — It's me, you can be sure, it's me, he chuckles childishly.
    — I read that you'd been . . .
    — Confined to an asylum? I'm over all that, Henrik. I assure you. I'm the cat that survives the inferno with only superficial burns. I'm now ready to live again, to work again, to write again.
    — I sensed your eyes following me, remarks Ibsen, staring at the fleet of white boats stranded beside the boulders.
    — Sensed?
    — I've been long-acquainted with your eyes.
    — Is my portrait really in your study!
    — Above my desk.
    — I feel honoured, to be sure. But why, Henrik?
    — When Caesar returned triumphantly to the flower-strewn streets of Rome, to the adoring citizens who greeted him like a god, it's said a slave rode with him in his chariot, whispering that all glory is fleeting.
    — Is that a riddle, Henrik? Are you testing me?
    — Your portrait's very expressive. And yet, at any given moment, I'm never sure what exactly it expresses. At times it's a subtle madness, nothing more than a wayward breeze playing

among shimmering leaves; other times, it's a demonic force that can uproot a tree. You see, your portrait keeps me on my guard.

— You're Caesar and I'm the slave, is that it?

Ibsen follows another boat on its way to the boulders.

— Do you think I'm mad, Henrik?

— Your actions speak for themselves.

— And my dramas?

— Chaotic.

— But life's capricious, Henrik, at times malicious. It's a constant struggle for survival, not only between species but within a species, between man and woman.

— I thought you'd bring that up.

— You don't like my play The Father, *do you?*

— As much as you dislike my Doll's House.

— Feminists use it as a weapon against us.

— Us?

— Men!

— That's your misogyny speaking.

— Misogyny, to be sure! Our struggle's not against the dark forces and unseen principalities of religion. Let's call a spade a spade. We're in a life and death struggle against modern Amazons: feminists, free-thinking lesbians, women who've renounced not only their womanhood but their sacred maternity. I object to your play's heroine. She's morally bankrupt. There's nothing more sacred than the bond between a mother and child, and any woman who walks out on her children transgresses the holy of holies. Your heroine's a contemptible creature, Henrik. The feminists who praise your play and applaud Nora's actions lack the essence of womanhood: the maternal instinct. There's nothing more loathsome than a woman who'd abandon her children in order to pursue a romantic, self-indulgent notion of freedom. Don't be deceived by that word, Henrik. More often than

not it's nothing more than a fine sentiment, a rationalisation for all sorts of baseness and profligacy.

— You've over-reacted to my play, August. It's not an apology for feminism or the women's movement. Fundamentally it's an exploration of human freedom within the institution of marriage and the circle of the family.

— Yes, to be sure, your themes are most relevant. You're very clever, Henrik, or should I say opportunistic. Give the public what's in the air and they'll flock to your plays. Yes, forget the idealistic verse plays of your youth. Socially relevant drama, based on the principle of demand and supply.

— I've depicted a woman who walks out on her husband . . .

— And her children.

— Because she suddenly realises that her loving husband, that pillar of respectability, has reduced her to a nonentity.

— So she abandons her children and sets out to discover her real self.

— Nora doesn't abandon her children. Yes, she walks out on Torvil, but only temporarily, as an act of protest, defiance, to show that she isn't merely a doll in his house. The Nora I had in mind returns to her children, though not before Torvil realises that marriage, unlike motherhood, isn't based on blood, but on mutual respect and equality.

— Equality exists only in mathematics, Henrik. Marriage is a struggle for control of the house and children.

— Your views are blatantly obvious in The Father.

— Why are you so critical of my play?

— Because it's wild and improbable. Your Captain's nothing more than a caricature. You've endeavoured to portray him as a tragic hero, but in fact he comes across as nothing more than a raving clown. What was your purpose in reducing him to madness? To show the weakness of man, or the strength

of woman? You know, August, I really think your play supports the feminist cause far more than mine.

— Nonsense! Strindberg retorts, spitting out the word.

— Look at the facts, replies Ibsen in a calm tone. Your hero succumbs to baseless suspicion concerning the paternity of his child, a suspicion that undermines his reason and has him strapped in a straitjacket. A person lacking commonsense deserves to be led by the nose.

— He was manipulated! Can't you see that?

— He's a weak character, one who allows himself to be manipulated. Your heroic Captain wants to be dominated. His raving rhetoric is nothing more than the cry of a sulking child.

— You're blind! Blind!

He springs to his feet. Ibsen concentrates on the twilight fading from the water's surface.

— You know nothing of women, he continues, steps crunching the sand in pacing back and forth. A woman's first real authority is over her children. Carried away she soon enough attempts to extend this authority over her husband. She uses cunning and subterfuge in order to reduce the husband to a childlike state so that she can dominate him, too. How many husbands have been driven to insanity by a woman's deceit!

— Including you?

Ibsen feels the pressure of Strindberg's back as the latter sits down with a sigh.

— Yes, including me.

— It has always struck me as remarkable that the most fervent misogynists are men least able to live without women.

— Misogyny isn't a philosophical proposition, Henrik. It's a condition arising from the hell of sexual warfare. To be sure, my marriage bed was worse than a trench in the front lines.

– *I read that it ended badly.*

– *I gave her everything. Took her from a boring old husband she no longer loved. Encouraged her to act. Put her on the stage. Offered her the kind of life she'd always dreamt of having. And then her treachery started. She began associating with free-thinkers. Brought lesbians into the family home! She became deceitful, espoused emancipated ideas, made me doubt the paternity of my own child. I couldn't endure it, Henrik. The woman was a harpy. She fed off my heart, played on my suspicions, persecuted me. I doubted everything, refused to eat because I feared she was poisoning the food. The marriage crumbled. My nerves were shattered, my mind became an inferno.*

– *Plenty of inspiration for* The Father, *says Ibsen, and for the first time a note of humour creeps into his voice.*

– *I've lived and suffered every word of it.*

– *That's too confessional for me.*

– *Yes, you keep your personal life under lock and key.*

– *Writers need an overview of life.*

– *An ivory tower built from the proceeds of pandering to public tastes?*

– *Archimedes calculated that he could move the earth, given a fulcrum some distance away from the earth. The tower provides a position away from the world, from which life can be observed more clearly.*

– *You talk like a scientist, Henrik. In your zeal to observe and study the behaviour of tadpoles in a pond, you overlook the existence of your own reflection.*

– *Writers should learn from the scientific method. In fact, if more of them applied Ockham's razor to their work we wouldn't be overwhelmed by the deluge of drivel pouring out of our presses.*

– I respect the scientific method, Henrik, possibly more than you. But human life can't be put under a microscope. Human actions aren't based on laws and principles which can be deduced from observation and experiment. Life's too chaotic and ephemeral to be reduced to a formula. This is where I disagree with your method and craft: you place your characters in a crucible, an unreal situation, and proceed to study their dynamics in the way a scientist would study chemical reactions. Your plays have an artificial quality precisely because you've transformed the stage into a laboratory. You commence with a hypothesis, apply the laws of dramaturgy, observe the results, and conclude by proving your hypothesis. QED! Everything as it should be.

After fidgeting with the beetle-backed buttons on his tight vest, as though securing them from flying off, Ibsen now takes out a fob-watch, studies it intently, then puts it to his ear. Twilight's crimson hue has begun turning ash-grey. Called away by a woman, the boy who has been launching the paper boats leaves the edge of the pond reluctantly. The brass band stops with an abrupt clash of cymbals, which quivers through the garden for some time. The long day is finally waning.

– I work according to my temperament, Ibsen remarks.
He clicks the fob-watch and slips it into his pocket.
– You should have become a scientist.
– In my youth I was apprenticed to an apothecary.
– It might explain your approach to drama.
– Nothing without order.
– You went from mixing chemicals to mixing characters.
– They have their similarities. Two elements combine to form a compound, something quite different from its constituents; likewise, two people join together in marriage, friendship, or

some other relationship, and a new entity is formed, different from either of them.

— I know that better than most, Henrik! A man and woman meet, fall passionately in love, and marry as befits the ideals of human bondage, bringing to the union their highest hopes and deepest dreams. At first they see heaven in each other's eyes, call each other darling and angel, and finally consummate their union by having children. It's precisely the advent of the first child that marks the change in a wife's attitude to her husband. From this point on she begins to seek the upper hand in the marriage, upsetting the fine equilibrium. Of course a reaction occurs, becomes volatile, and soon life is hell for the husband. You see, Henrik, life is far more unpredictable than chemistry. And I should know: I went from characters to chemistry. Having sought goodness and harmony in people, but finding only evil and chaos, I turned to chemistry in the fervent belief that it contained all that humanity lacked. I gave up the theatre and went to Paris, where the university kindly provided a small laboratory. My aim was nothing short of the alchemist's dream: to convert base metals into pure gold. Immersed in research, I tested and experimented, pursuing with monomaniacal passion the elusive combination. One evening a couple of months ago, I was working feverishly along the lines suggested by the Jewish Cabbalist Yizhak ben Baruch Almosnino, who lived in Salonika in the sixteenth century, and wrote in Spanish. I was on the verge of what seemed a promising combination when the laboratory exploded in flames. I escaped with bad burns to my face and hands, from which I'm still recovering.

Ibsen is taken aback by a pair of white-gloved hands appearing over his head. He attempts to stand, but is kept in place by bony elbows pressing down on his shoulders.

— Please, Henrik, you mustn't see me in this condition. My hands suffered third-degree burns, and the doctors say I may never have full use of them again. They're still very sore. I carry them chest-high all the time, as though about to sound a loud clap.

Snickering, he removes his elbows from Ibsen's shoulders and sits down again.

— You're fortunate to have escaped with your life, remarks Ibsen in a guarded tone.

— Fortunate? Who's to say I would not have been better off burning in the laboratory? The leaden 'I' transformed into angelic light. What splendid irony! As it is, God has spared me simply to torment me longer. You know, Henrik, I've sought God in one form or another since my childhood, and the outcome's always the same: instead of finding heaven I fall into hell.

— You're too passionate in your pursuits.

— Perhaps, muses Strindberg.

— What will you do now?

— I don't know. Rest, recover, settle my nerves. I might even resume writing once I'm able to hold a pen. There's enough raw material in the past five or six years for a dozen dramas, not to mention novels and short stories. With a little composure and order in my life, I might transmute these chaotic years into art. I didn't succeed with the base metals, I might with the base matter of my life.

— You can't get away from yourself, August.

— Who can?

— Everything's autobiographical with you.

— I know myself better than anything else.

— And you're the hero of all your works.

— I give myself to my characters.

— But they fail to convince me, August. Your voice comes through in all your heroes, and always in justification of yourself. Look around: the world's much bigger than August Strindberg.

— Henrik, you're out of touch with modern sensibility. You'd have me look at human life objectively, make a commentary on it, as you do. But it's not the writer's purpose to study humanity. That's for the psychologist, the physician, the sociologist, the philosopher. A writer, in particular a dramatist, must deal with the experience of being human, not as abstraction but as existence. Writing which doesn't have its basis in personal experience is necessarily false, contrived, hypocritical. A writer's authority comes from his clashes and confrontations with the world, not from contemplating ideas, ethics and moralities. Integrity lies in personal experiences, everything else is interpretation and artifice. Shakespeare, for instance, didn't experience the jealousy which tormented the hapless Othello, and so his work strikes me as flawed and false. Treating the same theme, I write with an authority that gives my work vitality and validity, even though my language and technique may be inferior to Shakespeare's. I've felt the flame, therefore I'm qualified to describe the sensation of being burnt. We're on the threshold of a new century, Henrik. Writers of the future will be even more subjective, for they will have been driven further and further inward by advances in science and technology. They will be like barometers: recording the pressure of an increasingly complex world, though not through second-hand conceptions, but by direct experience.

— You're too self-centred, August. Writers must overcome egoism if they are to produce work that stands the test of time. We should follow the example of those mystics who sought God through self-annihilation. In order to empathise with characters and predicaments of which he has no personal experience, a writer should negate the gravitational force of his own identity. To extend the scientific metaphor: the strength and vitality of his creation is inversely proportional to the square of his sense of 'I'.

— If the feminists heard you, Strindberg chuckles, they'd chastise you for that 'his'.

— You mentioned Shakespeare, Ibsen continues calmly, leaning forward to avoid contact with his back. His personal life does not enter his plays; in fact, his genius lies in his self-transcendence, his ability to step out of his own skin and into that of his characters. How else can one explain his breadth of vision and diversity of characters? If one accepts that a writer must have personal experience of what he writes, one is compelled to denounce most of the classics as false. The ancient tragedians would be invalidated because they weren't tragic heroes themselves. No, August, life and literature would be impoverished by such a restriction.

— You refuse to leave your ivory tower.
— I want to see the world, not wallow in self-indulgence.
— Detachment, is that it?
— Clear-sightedness.
— Still playing the role of the Old Testament prophet.
— I'm interested in the times.
— The great sage, the voice of Europe, the northern light.
— I write for others.
— And I, my dear Henrik, write primarily for myself.
— That's where we differ.
— Yes, my work reflects my personal struggle with existence. It's a statement of my fleeting insights, a cry of my deep-rooted fears, a whisper of my flickering hopes, a confession of my infinite despair.

– A confession, or glorification?
– I write in order to make sense of my life.
– And how does that benefit others?
– Benefit others? I'm not a physician, Henrik. My work prods people, makes them squirm, challenges them to question their most cherished hopes and confront their darkest fears. In aspiring to enlightenment we must first sound our emotional depths, using one's heart on the end of the plumbline.
– Your characters are turgid, August. At times neurotic. They cause unnecessary agitation, confusion, doubt, particularly in young people.
– Still the apothecary of your youth, Henrik. You'd rather dispense morals and ethics than have people feel the intensity of existence.
– Great drama takes a moral stand.
– You would have made an excellent priest.
– We're living in times of bewildering change, an epoch where people, cultures, moralities are mixing as never before. Writers should endeavour to grasp some permanence from this confusion, some absolute from all this pluralism.
– Absolutes! Universal truths! I'm sick and tired of those empty words, Henrik. There's only one truth: the experience of a living, feeling, suffering human being.

Ibsen stares intently at the five or six paper boats stranded on the mossy boulders. The garden has become still, even the whisper that stirred the upper branches of the trees has stopped. The crimson blaze in the clouds has turned to ash. He stands, walks to the edge of the pond, and ponders his reflection in the dark-green water. At that moment a black swan with a ring around its S-shaped neck appears from behind the boulders and glides over his reflection, fragmenting it into ripples.

— Ideas, muses Ibsen. What's my life, or yours, August, if not a vessel for universal truths? Great drama is never the outcome of self-expression. After all, what truth can one expect from a creature full of fears and imperfections? No, it's our task to overcome self-indulgence and become a mouthpiece for the eternal idea. In the end, personality is irrelevant, just as Shakespeare's character is irrelevant to an appreciation of his work. I recall the words of a mathematics teacher from my youth: a steel ring can be bent, hammered out of shape, or melted to be poured into another shape, but the circle remains intact.

Ibsen casually turns around, but the bench is empty. Bemused, he peers into the greyness.

— Is this a game, August?

His words sink with the weight of resignation.

— Are you behind that tree?

A leaf flutters to its fate.

— Have I imagined you?

Flowing past, a cat holds him in its luminous eyes.

— I must get rid of that portrait.

As a shudder raises the hairs on the back of his head, he hurries off, shoes crunching the sandy path.

Sonya passes her fingertips lightly over the last sentence, feeling the indentations caused by the fountain pen in the textured paper, investing with fuller meaning each curve and loop, line and stroke, comma and point.

the ELEVENTH dialogue

The fireplace has been dormant over two months, and only now has Sonya managed to summon a little enthusiasm in order to remove a few scraps of charred timber and, clattering an L-shaped poker, to scrape out the crispy ash and wrap it in the classified pages of last week's newspaper. But in clapping the soot from her hands, she feels again that futility seeping into her being, as darkness steals into a house. In the past, when things were going well, she would spring out of bed at five each morning and set out eagerly for the markets and the shop. Now she wakes with difficulty, her head a swamp of murky dreams and forebodings. She has not been to a market in weeks, and it is only by sheer effort that she goes through the motions of running the business. In fact, there are moments when she feels like locking the door and walking away from the shop, leaving her beloved books to their fate, but a recent visit from the Credit Officer, followed by another from

Zitta, prod her to continue what she now considers a doomed struggle. The officer came on a hot afternoon a week before Christmas. He was thoughtful, troubled, and the usual peachy red was missing from his cheeks. He had tried his best, he said, unable to look Sonya in the eyes, and apologised for having to be the bearer of bad news at what should be a time of joy and celebration. The head of the department had been adamant: he wanted the loan called in and a receiver appointed to wind down the business. There was nothing more he could do, he said, wiping the fine drops of perspiration from his forehead. He had given her life – he corrected himself – her file, to a receiver. The person would be in touch without delay. Loosening his tie, he wished her the best for Christmas and the new millennium, adding that, having been accepted in a Naturopathy course, he had given the bank his notice of resignation. Hope I've made the right decision, he said, crossing fingers on both hands.

Zitta arrived a few hours later and apologised for the fact that the 'torch' had yet to pay her a visit. His thorough preparation for a job, the attention to detail, meant that his services were in great demand. But Zitta had managed to track him down that morning and had been assured that Sonya was at the top of his list. Given the nature of his work, he could not specify a time, though he would most definitely drop in before Christmas. In the meantime, the 'torch' had a few instructions for Sonya: stay calm; run the business as usual; appear industrious. At this stage, the appearance of her trying to keep the shop afloat was imperative to the success of his work. She must not appear careless or negligent, and must not convey to customers a sense of having lost heart in the business. If she carried out his instructions to the letter, and he well appreciated the great effort it required, all would end well and she could look forward to a bright future.

The receiver came early the following morning. Not much older than Sonya, she wore a dark suit that highlighted a blaze of orange hair. She spent a few hours asking questions, scrutinising the business's books, walking around making an inventory and assessing the stock's worth. In the end, she pointed out that selling off assets piecemeal would not recoup the bank's loan, and would necessitate the sale of her house to make up the shortfall. In her opinion, to optimise the value of the assets, the business should be sold as a going concern. Yes, she was aware that the books were not in good shape and that the business had been running at a loss in recent months, but that was not always the negative it appeared. There was scope to introduce new systems into the shop, bring it up to date with the latest computer facilities, which might well transform the shop and make a success of it, in much the same way as the fellow had done up the street. Throughout the woman's visit, Sonya felt flushes of anger and resentment at the thought of having to pay for her presence. Pay to be sold off, she kept telling herself, her anger exacerbated by the woman's diamond ring flashing as she wrote her report. Before leaving, the woman neatly put away her notes, and urged Sonya not to lose heart. She should continue to run her business with the same dedication as before. Above all, she should keep it tidy and clean. She would recommend to the bank that the business be sold as a going concern. In the coming weeks a real estate agent would be appointed to show prospective buyers through the shop. The price offered would largely depend on perceptions. There was no doubt that Sonya had not spared expenses in fitting out the shop, and this would prove to be a strong selling point for the business. The rest, she said, was very much determined by market forces.

As for Simkin, he now comes to the shop every Friday, curses the banks for instigating the recession, reminds her of their contract, threatens her with eviction, and leaves ten minutes later, giving her yet another extension to get her house in order. Not long ago, making a concerted effort to cut back on expenses and live more frugally, Sonya managed to put together a month's rent, which he accepted with a mixture of surprise and caution, wrapping the notes around the fingers of one hand and flicking each with a moist thumb. She was still two months in arrears, he pointed out. His nephew, eager to establish himself, was waiting for instructions to commence proceedings. She should not mistake or underestimate his resolve. He was accepting the present payment only on condition that the outstanding amount be paid in full on the following Friday. Combining a nod and a shake, Sonya rolled her head and assured him that she would do her best. He left unconvinced, sawing the measuring tape around his neck, knowing full well that he was caught between a dubious tenant and the prospect of an empty shop.

After considering her blackened palms, Sonya reacts almost by reflex in pulling out the nearest hardback, opening to the fly leaf and, fingers spread, stamping it with her print. Why? she asks herself closing the book, stunned by her own action. In the past her concern for books was such that she would wash her hands if there was the least likelihood of soiling them; in fact, at times she entertained the whimsical notion of conducting a small ritual of cleansing and purification upon first entering the shop, as though to prepare the flesh and make it worthy of the book – the receptacle of the pure idea. And now, to her own bewilderment, here she is blackening the object of her reverence. Why? The mind plays strange games in times of desperation! And she is anxious, vulnerable, desperate, caused as much by the imminent collapse of her business, as the fact that she has not seen Theo in more than two weeks. Christmas has come and gone, and not so much as a greeting from him. Has he walked out on her, too? Or is the present dialogue proving intractable? Given his obsessive nature, has he immersed himself in the work to a degree where everything else has lost its relevance, including Christmas and their relationship? If only she had his address, but he has kept it from her, indicating that he is renting a room in a friend's house, and that he is embarrassed to have her visit because of the owner's disregard for tidiness, and the fact that the house is being renovated, a process which has been going on for the past four years. She has asked Theo for his telephone number, in case of emergency. They could devise a system, a form of morse code, whereby he could communicate by tapping on the receiver. He signalled that there is one in the house, but, having never used it, he has not bothered to memorise the number. Besides, the owner was abrupt and rude to callers, and he, Theo, did not want to subject her to his uncouth behaviour.

Cap pulled low over his eyes, a French stick in a brown paper bag tucked under his arm, Lou Cape enters the shop and darts a sheepish glance at Sonya. His last visit was weeks ago, when he said that he was finally overcoming the trauma of the divorce, and this largely through his rediscovery of the pleasure of reading. The smell of fresh bread mingles with the stale odour of books. Can she recommend any recent acquisitions? he asks, placing the bread on the counter. Sonya explains that the difficult times have forced her to cut back on stocking too many books. He understands: everybody is cutting back, trimming the fat, becoming leaner and meaner. Does he regret giving up writing? His face lights up. He breaks off the end of the bread and eats with relish, sprinkling the counter with golden crumbs. In view of what publishers are doing, not at all! He considers himself a free man, as though exorcised of a malevolent spirit. He relates an anecdote regarding Sophocles. When the septuagenarian playwright was asked whether he regretted the waning of his sexual urge, he replied that he had finally escaped from the clutches of a beast which had tyrannised his life. Cape could now relate to the words of the old Greek. Writing was not unlike sexuality; in fact, he often thought that both were somehow inextricably connected. Perhaps they both had their source in will, and that writing was a sublimation of sexuality. Yes, he understands this now, when it is too late. Sex and writing are similar in that they possess the unwary, sap their will, squander their strength, and finally reduce them to dry shells. Writing is like an insatiable mistress. It is no coincidence that inspiration is said to come from the Muse. She is the one who tempts, makes promises, offers bits and pieces, and, having seduced the unsuspecting, destroys their happiness for her own pleasure and conceit. But he has broken free of that vicious circle. At one stage though, he almost leapt from the frying pan into the fire. Having lost his wife, trying to tear himself from the clutches of the Muse, he was tempted to visit next door, but he resisted and vanquished that temptation. He thanks Sonya for having the shop open so early on that fateful day. He breaks off the other end of the bread, extends the stick to Sonya, which she declines, and crunches the hard curved crust. Caught in the torment of writing, he forgot the simple joy of reading as an end in itself. Yes, as a writer he was also a reader, but his reading was always in the service of writing. Now he reads at leisure, for the joy of reading, just as he had done as a boy. At no time is he more at peace with himself and the world than with a book in his hands. At first there was a sense of unease, almost verging on guilt, about holding a book between himself and the world. As a writer he attempted to confront social problems such as gambling, impotency, and youth suicide in his short stories, which had at least helped to bring these issues to the public eye. What could he do about such problems as a reader? Was he turning his back on the world by failing to engage with it? After much soul-searching he concluded that writing fiction was as efficacious as reading in alleviating the problems of the world. Ultimately literature's ability to affect us lies in aesthetics not anaesthetics. He has been fortunate though: his return to reading has cured him of his personal demons, not to mention his wretched haemorrhoids.

After browsing for almost an hour, he returns to the counter with an armful of books. He could have spent the entire afternoon in her wonderful shop, he remarks. This selection should keep him going until next time. Sonya is about to say that there may not be a next time, but holds back at the thought of the 'torch'. Since giving up writing, proximity to books has given him a new vitality. The very touch of a book becomes a life-affirming act. Has she been to the Reading Room in the State Library recently? She ought to go before it closes for major renovations. He was there last week at the invitation of a friend who works as a general staff-member, sorting books, replacing them on shelves, locating special requests. It is a truly awesome and humbling experience to walk into the circular Reading Room and find oneself surrounded by walls of books. He was taken by his friend on a tour behind the scenes, into narrow corridors, tortuous passageways and basement crypts, all lined with books of every imaginable size, from tiny things smaller than a match-box, which require a magnifying glass, to giant tomes which, when opened, were like the gates of paradise or the jaws of hell, depending on your state of mind. The excitement evoked by the tour lasted days. You should pay it a visit, he advises, taking the bread in one hand, a pink plastic bag full of books in the other. They say it will be closed for two years. As he turns to the door promising to be a more regular customer, Sonya goes to a shelf, pulls out two books she thinks he might enjoy and slips them into the bag. Before he is able to question her, she explains that she is planning to introduce a special offer: buy six, get two free. Outside, arms out at an angle, body in equilibrium between bread and books, he looks directly ahead in walking past the brothel.

Sonya wonders whether, like Cape, she too will rediscover the pleasure of reading once this mess is all over. Unlike people who are able to use books in order to block out personal problems, in much the same way as others use alcohol or drugs, she has never been able to concentrate on a book in stressful circumstances. In her case peace of mind and detachment from the demands of everyday life have always been necessary preconditions for the full enjoyment of reading, particularly novels. In fact, since opening the shop her reading has been desultory, skimming over a short story here, snatching a poem there, becoming acquainted with novels through editorial blurbs. Yes, when this is over, she will return to the novel and experience once again the flow of narrative that is able to overcome the current of real time; the power of imagination that is able to warp space as though it were a sheet of rubber; the miracle of fiction that is able to empty the stagnant self and fill it with fresh characters. But what of life after the bookshop? What will she do? Go back to teaching? No, that would be a backward step, leading to certain misery. How will she survive on her own? But she is not alone: there is Theo. They will live together, share expenses, help each other. She has loved books, now she loves the very source of the book, the flesh and blood behind the paper. Perhaps she can persuade him to continue working on his dialogues. With a little encouragement he might be able to put together a sizeable collection, which, through her contacts, might be published. As for herself, she might find work as a reader with a publishing house, or as an editor. In the meantime, she would move in literary circles, meet people, offer to write book reviews for newspapers and journals. Together, they would put the painful past behind and make a happy life for themselves.

Shirt sleeves rolled to his elbows, Simkin stands outside the window, inspecting the facade over the top of his glasses, casting glances right at the brothel, left at the funeral parlour. Sonya butts her cigarette and places the ashtray under the counter. He enters with scraping heels, shaking his head. The tenants in the adjacent properties are doing very well. The quick and the dead, he says, looking around the shop. His protruding lower lip is tinged purple: a sign that he has been suffering acute heartburn. Has he been a bad landlord? No. Has he been slow in attending to maintenance problems? No. Has he increased the rent every year? No. Then why is she treating him like this? He cannot allow it to continue. It will soon be resolved, says Sonya. The business is in the hands of a receiver. Simkin closes his eyes and sways back and forth. First the accountant, now this, he complains. And what about the lease? Two years before it expires! And the arrears? Sonya assures him that the bank is doing all it can to sell the business as a going concern, in which case a new tenant will be assigned the lease. And if a buyer is not found? The bank will sell off the assets, recover its loan, and he will be left with an empty shop and a worthless lease. Would he like to take a few books? Not as payment, simply in appreciation of his kindness. Books, he lisps, tying a knot in the orange measuring tape. No. He has never been one for reading, though his life could fill a shelf of books. When he was a boy in Bulgaria his grandfather would take him to the synagogue. He remembers the sound of the chanter reading in song from the Torah as horses and carts clattered on the cobbles outside. After hearing the written word being sung, its reverberations in the dome sending a shiver down his spine, he became bored by the reading at school. To sit bowed over a book, in complete silence, was not only a waste of time but a form of punishment. In fact, he can still recall days when the teacher would punish them with an hour of silent reading for their unruly behaviour. No. Books and he have never seen eye to eye. He left school at twelve and was apprenticed to a tailor in the Turkish quarter of Sofia. Since then he has much preferred the silence of the moving needle to the silence of still print. He is reminded of a riddle his grandfather would tell. What clothes the world but itself goes naked? A sewing needle, he chuckles, and shakes off the memory with a grunt. No. Books are no good to him. He forfeited his old age pension because of this property: it is his main source of income. And now ...

The slight tremor in Simkin's purple lip moves Sonya. She imagines him standing before the building devastated by fire. At his age the shock might prove fatal. In saving herself from ruin, she would have his death on her conscience. Then again, the fire might be a blessing for him. She recently scrutinised the details of her insurance policy. Given the fall in property prices as a result of the recession, the building is well insured, and he is covered for loss of rental income in the event of property damage. In view of the circumstances, his interests would best be served by fire becoming sole tenant for a night. Things will work out for both of us, she says, tapping him on the shoulder. The new millennium is a few days away, and it will be a new beginning for all. At his age he does not share her optimism. He was going to refer the matter to his nephew, the lawyer, but his fees are expensive. He will now refer it to his niece, a very enterprising young woman who recently opened a debt-recovery agency, and who works on the basis of payment on recovery. Sonya asks him to hold off for another month, when they both would know exactly how things stood. Turning suddenly to the shelf behind the counter, she pulls out the hefty five-volume set of *Jewish Folk Stories*. Theo enters the shop, fanning himself with the gold envelope. She insists that Simkin have them. They are rare and quite valuable. He considers for a moment, then, shaking his head, advises her to use them for her own salvation.

Though delighted to see him, Sonya greets Theo with a forced smile and cold hello. Stepping forward hesitantly, he places the envelope on the counter, but she ignores it, turning abruptly to replace the heavy volumes. He taps the counter with a fingernail. Her back turned to him, she is determined to find out exactly how he feels about her and where their relationship is going. His hands touch her shoulders, clasp her around the waist. She feels a gentle kiss on the back of her neck. Where have you been? she asks, turning in his arms. He holds her face in his hands. Do you call this a relationship? He runs a finger along the creases on her forehead. Let's call it off if we can't be frank with each other. He kisses her lightly on the lips. They stare at each other for a moment. Caught in the gravity of his eyes, unable to feign anger, she begins to relent. Two weeks, and not a word! Why? He signals that she has been constantly on his mind. Not so much as a card for Christmas! Was this his idea of a relationship? He will make it up to her. Why has he been so aloof? How could he allow so much time to pass without a word? Turning away, he picks up a book and flicks the pages close to his face. I'm entitled to an explanation, she says, taking the book from him. His evasive look makes her heart sink. She braces herself for the worst. My work, he signals, biting his lower lip. He has been preoccupied with another dialogue. But wasn't this meant to be the last? asks Sonya, picking up the envelope. Yes, he started them in the hope of making an impression on her, but they have gradually outgrown his initial intention, taken possession of him, until on Christmas eve he was struck by the realisation that everything has been a slow preparation for what will be the twelfth dialogue. What kind of preparation? she asks, alarmed by a sudden intensity in his eyes. One that would allow them to consummate their love and enter the new millennium as one flesh. As she knows, he has had a vague presentiment for some time, and on Christmas eve it was realised in the form of a vivid dream. No, more than a dream, it was a vision, a revelation, a visitation by the logos, the Muse, the Holy Spirit.

Sonya is disturbed by his eyes, blue as an acetylene flame, and the feverish glow on his face. His hands work quickly, at times unintelligibly, as though kindling a fire instead of conveying a message. Now and then she grasps him by the wrists in order to slow him down and make his message comprehensible. It occurred at 11.43, he signals, biting the tip of his tongue. He can still see the red digits glowing in the dark like the eyes of a beast. He had been reading about Savonarola, and must have dozed off with the book on his chest, which may have inspired the vision. Has she heard of Savonarola? He was a Dominican monk and moral reformer who lived in Florence at the time of the Medicis. Among other things he foretold the death of Pope Innocent VIII, and the collapse of the Medicis' power. He set up a theocracy in Florence which incurred the wrath of Pope Alexander VI. At first moved by his forceful sermons on the need to repent and return to the spirit of the Gospels, people took up his call to do away with the vanities of the world. In 1497, at the height of his popularity, he urged people to burn such excesses as wigs, playing cards, objects of pagan art, and profane books. Shortly after this, he was excommunicated, which had the desired effect of alienating many of his followers. Accused of treason by his fellow Florentines, he was hanged and burnt as a heretic. Savonarola's teachings have impressed him greatly; in fact, they are far more relevant today than five hundred years ago. The emptiness of spirit in many people's lives is being filled with material excesses, especially computer products. His vision arose from these thoughts and feelings. It happened in a blinding flash, just as a camera snatches an instant from the flow of time, or an unexpected glimpse of the sun leaves a bright image every time we blink, so every detail of his vision has been burnt into his memory.

He becomes thoughtful for a moment, hands extended toward her, palms full of afternoon light, face radiant with a kind of beatific glow. And the nature of the vision, Sonya asks in trepidation. A dialogue, he replies, eyes brimming with tears. A source of ineffable joy. It will be the culmination and fulfilment of all the other dialogues. When the vision passed and he found himself in his room again, it was as though he had been embraced by a holy flame that melted his body and liberated his soul. Who are your characters for this dialogue? She must be patient a little longer. If he is to record it in a way that does justice to the word, it means he will again be busy for the next few days. He promises to deliver it on the eve of the new millennium. It will be like nothing she has ever read, and it will serve to bind them together in body and soul. The hot tears evoked by the vision have scalded his eyes and opened them to the truth. Now, wherever he looks, signs of the Apocalypse abound, though not in terms of a struggle between the abstract notions of good and evil, as much as between the word and the number. The computer, as an embodiment of the number, is in a global war against the word, the logos, the Holy Spirit. In less than a generation, in various guises and making all sorts of promises, number has turned many people from the book of life. The Internet and World Wide Web are snares intended to catch unsuspecting minds like butterflies, and once the mind is caught the body is doomed to servitude. Promising unlimited information, knowledge, power, the number will in fact plunge mankind into a new dark age, just as happened about the end of the first millennium. And how will this occur? By number turning on itself. He can envisage the chaos that will be unleashed by nothing more than two zeros. As 99, the numerological symbol for amen, clicks over to 00, there will be universal discord, conflict, anarchy, Armageddon. In the beginning was the word, and in the end the number. Has she noticed how rapidly the Tree of Knowledge is proliferating? You walk past a vacant block one day and see children playing, almost overnight a silver tree springs up with satellite dishes for leaves, drawing not the silence of light, but deals, chatter, advertisements. And everyone is drawn to the silver tree. Come, it announces, taste of knowledge and you will be like God. Now, more than ever, people must dedicate their lives to the word: it must be kept sacred and protected from the onslaughts of the number. Now, more than ever, it is time to live the word, to restore it to its rightful place. Now, more than ever, the word must be read correctly, and this can only be done through love. She will be his perfect reader. He agrees with Socrates: just as the lover is closer to the divine than the beloved, so the reader is closer to the word, the logos, the Holy Spirit, than the writer. She will restore and redeem him through the act of reading. Has she planned anything for New Year's eve? No. He would like to spend it with her. She suggests they go to a restaurant.

The city will resemble a madhouse, he signals with sharp gestures. Will he come to her place? He would prefer to spend the night with her in the shop. It is only fitting that she read his last dialogue in the company of books. Sonya is about to protest, but he silences her with a kiss. Another few days, he signals, and caresses her face. Holding his bony wrists, she feels the strong throb of his pulse. Did she read the previous dialogue? It was very engaging. They are all interesting and well written. He should consider getting them published. She would be more than happy to assist him. He has managed to overcome that temptation. Number is at the heart of publishing: digitising the word, quantifying it as a commodity, packaging it as an article for profit. No, he signals emphatically. She has been the sole inspiration for the dialogues. They are for her eyes only. He wrote them because he loves her, and through them hopes to have his love returned. The one on the counter is the last of its kind. Her love has opened his heart to the word. When they next meet she will read a dialogue inspired by the Holy Spirit, for which he has been prepared and made receptive by her love.

Taking her hands, he draws her behind a row of shelves, where they drink the full meaning of each other's lips, taste the electricity at the tip of each other's tongue, probe the dark secrets at the roots of speech. He must go, he signals tenderly. There is so much to be done and so little time left. She caresses his hands, kisses the text of his palms, the print on his fingertips. He kisses the lines of her forehead, the rosy petal of each eyelid with its fine purple veins. I love you, he signals. Sonya grasps his hands once again, but he gently pulls away and leaves.

She watches him through the first O in BIBLIOPHILE (which also circumscribes the front of the body piercing salon) as he runs across the street, his hands now fists of determination. What is she to make of his talk of the new millennium? Caught up in her problems she has hardly given it a thought. Are his apocalyptic views a reflection of his own fears and uncertainties? Is it a sign of mental instability? Or has he been reading Revelation? She has never been religious, though she went through a phase at about fifteen when she read that terrible book. Sensitive to the word, her imagination shaped by reading rather than television, she experienced almost palpably the book's vivid images of doom and destruction. They had an unsettling, disturbing effect on her. For weeks she was filled with despondency: if the world as she knew it was going to pass away, what was the point in anything? Her days were clouded by sorrow, and her eyes would fill with tears at the thought of being separated from her mother's voice, from her beloved books, from the shape of her hands which had changed so suddenly from those of a girl's to a young woman's. Her nights were restless, full of apprehension, with strange beasts leaping from the dark and dreams of conflagrations shaking her from sleep.

At the time she was unsettled by a recurring dream, which even now still finds its way into her sleep, whose source she has traced to startling images from Revelation. Surviving the swells of an ink-black sea that threatens to engulf her, she finds herself on a pebbled beach of what appears to be an island. A walled castle crowns the peak of an austere mountain rising steeply from terraced fields, vineyards, olive groves. At a mere wish of wanting to be up there, she is in the heart of the castle, a rocky grotto, in the presence of a radiant figure seated on a throne, holding up a jewel-studded book in his right hand. Suddenly, a call goes out: Who is worthy to open the Book of Life and read its contents? Whoever finds their name written in it shall have everlasting life, the others will suffer the fires of Gehenna. An endless line of people files past the throned figure, each taking the book in their hands and trying to open it. The sun and moon melt into each other, the stars fall like leaves, and still no hands are pure enough to open the book. Her eyes well with tears of sadness. Suddenly it is her turn, and the book is larger than life. She is surprised by its weight and the warmth of the silver covers. Summoning all her strength, she tries to part the covers, but the book's seven seals hold fast, like congealed blood to a penitent knee. Why? she cries aloud, tears falling onto her hands, sparkling on the silver. She has opened countless books, and now that salvation resides in this, her strength is not up to the task. As she begins to sink in despair, her hot tears trickle onto the seals, softening them. In an instant the book yields and opens almost of its own accord. Bowing over it, she is at once bewildered by an alphabet she has never seen before. The characters are almost pictorial, strange unions of the human and angelic, letters and numerals, the natural and ideal. How is she to read it? Recognise her name? What must she do to render it accessible? A voice answers: 'Renounce your eyes, become the name you seek'. In a blink, she is inside the book, and the silver covers become gates closing upon her, shutting her in complete darkness. Overcome by dread, she attempts to cry out, but her voice fails and she wakes gasping for breath. From that time she has avoided the Bible, not only because of the unease caused by Revelation, but more so because it regarded itself as the Book of Books, thus dismissing and invalidating all other books.

She considers closing the shop and reading the new dialogue without interruption in the back room. But she recalls the advice passed on by the 'torch': to avoid suspicion, she must maintain appearances, keep the business going as though nothing were the matter. As a knot tightens in her stomach, she lights a cigarette and opens the envelope.

The following meeting may well have taken place in St Petersburg toward the end of 1880. But if literary scholars should adduce irrefutable proof to the contrary, this would not exclude the possibility of the meeting occurring in the not too distant future. How? Is this to be a fable? A piece of post-modern fiction? A flight of fantasy? Not quite. A shadow's thickness away from the third millennium, we have been brought up on good doses of atomic physics, and the neurons of our imagination have been set spinning by Heisenberg's uncertainty principle. Theoretically, we could propose anything concerning matter, time and space, and the equations of quantum mechanics (the equivalent of Newton's laws of motion applied to atomic particles) could be used to calculate the mathematical probability of our propositions. For example, consider the train which killed

Anna Karenina: according to quantum mechanics, it is not impossible for that very train to have thundered through the author's study just before he wrote that terrible scene. Imagine the consequences! The distraught woman would have been spared her gruesome fate; while the author, struck by this train from out of the blue, would not have met a bitter and lonely end in the provincial railway station at Astapovo. Furthermore, consider the vase which Myshkin, in The Idiot, *broke the instant before his epileptic seizure. Quantum mechanics maintains that it may suddenly appear on my writing table, perfectly intact, even though the fragments of the original vase existed only in the author's imagination. One must not be too quick to dismiss as fanciful what is about to unfold. If the meeting between the esteemed literary figures did not actually take place, that is only in that plane of time and space called historical reality, and as we know there are infinite possible planes, which means that the meeting may yet happen, for, as the practitioners of mind power know, the very process of imagining an event increases the probability of its occurrence.*

According to the new Old Calendar nailed to the back wall of Sonya Gorenova's bookshop it should be the night of Epiphany, 1881. Braced against the snowing dark, you left the warm bookshop, crossed the brooding Neva crowded with barges, hurried along Nevsky Prospect clattering with covered droshkies and tingling troikas, bowed past the overwhelming statue of Peter the Great, and now find yourself at the corner of a four-storey building whose windows have been unevenly bricked up. Down a flight of greasy steps, and you enter a basement tavern with an oppressively low ceiling. A few men are leaning on the bar, gazing with heavy eyes at their reflections distorted by a mirror cracked from top to bottom. Others sit at tables covered in checked oilcloth. Slurred and slowed by alcohol, conversations drone against the persistent hiss of overhead lamps. At the back of the tavern, two youths are playing billiards on a table covered in stitches and scars.

Sitting alone at a table, a robust man of about fifty is reading a book by holding it up to the lamp with his left hand. He is wearing an overcoat and a muzhik's frock gathered at the waist by a broad belt under which he has slipped his right hand, as though restraining it from some impropriety. His face has the leatheriness of an old boot that has marched through the Caucasus in many military campaigns; his cheekbones are bright as apples; his eyes, blue, with a slight Asiatic slant; and his beard, streaked with white, cascades down his chest.

The front door opens, and a gust of snowy wind announces the arrival of a frail-looking man. Hands deep in the pockets of an overcoat buttoned to his neck, hat partly covering his ears, he stands beneath a lamp and examines the patrons at the bar. Quivering, the lamp-flame appears to recoil from his face, which has the pallor of the terminally ill. About sixty, he walks with a stoop, his steps uncertain. Shoes scraping the bare floorboards, he approaches the man with the book, who stopped reading and looked up expectantly as the fellow entered. They consider each other for an instant.

— Leo ... Nikolayevich? inquires the newcomer in a hesitant voice that falters at the fourth syllable of the patronymic.

— And you must be Fyodor Mikhailovich, replies the seated man.

His voice is firm, resonant, like an autumn wind passing through a birch grove, causing the trees to strain after it.

He pushes aside an empty tea-glass on a chipped saucer and invites the other to sit down, indicating with a broad palm resembling a ploughed field.

– My apologies, Leo Nikolayevich.

– Apologies?

– For being late.

– Not at all, Fyodor Mikhailovich, he says, raising the book. It gave me the opportunity to read a little: a pleasure I seldom have time for these days.

– Yes, there's so much to be done, and so little time.

A timid creature emerging from its burrow, Fyodor's pale hand reaches out, index finger stained by ink and nicotine. The two hands clasp, shake for some time, then hold each other in stillness.

– I've been looking forward to meeting you.

– Sit down, Fyodor Mikhailovich, sit down, he says, pushing back the chair opposite him.

Preoccupied, Fyodor walks around and occupies a chair that requires both men look at each other with heads slightly turned. Removing his hat, he is shaken by a hacking cough.

– Are you all right?

Leo reaches over the table and taps him on the back. Bent forward, forehead almost touching the table, Fyodor manages to smother the cough in a crumpled handkerchief.

– This Petersburg winter will be the end of me.

– You should go south for a while: Yalta, Crimea, the Black Sea. The warmer weather will cure that cough.

– Travel, Leo Nikolayevich? I barely made it here from my apartment on Kuznechny Lane.

A waiter with a dirty napkin thrown over his shoulder walks gingerly to their table. His fashionable boots, which appear a couple of sizes too small, squeak at every step.

– *Yes, gents.*

In picking up the empty glass, he studies Fyodor as though trying to recall where he has seen him before.

– *What will you have, Leo Nikolayevich?*
– *Another camomile tea.*
– *And a glass of vodka.*
– *Anything to eat, gents?* he asks Fyodor.
– *Pickled cabbage and cucumber, Leo Nikolayevich?*

Leo nods and brushes back his mane of greying hair with both hands. The waiter hobbles away, his bow-leggedness accentuated by the ill-fitting boots. Taking out a silver cigarette case engraved with his initials, Fyodor flicks it open and extends it across the table.

– *I gave them up last year,* says Leo.
– *How long had you been smoking?*
– *More than thirty years.*
– *You must have great willpower, Leo Nikolayevich.*
– *A puff of smoke wasn't going to dictate my life.*
– *It's a matter of temperament. I need them in order to write. Every night, in preparation for work, before shutting myself off from the world between ten and four, I derive great pleasure in making my own and filling this case. At times there's more enjoyment in the anticipation associated with the making than in the smoking. Now and then, when the cough's particularly bad and the physician's doleful words haunt my ears, I reprove myself and try to give them up, but I can't abstain for more than a day.*

With surprising deftness, he strikes a match and lights the trimmed end. Reflected in distended pupils, the flame highlights the badly bloodshot whites of his eyes. He exhales the aromatic smoke away from the table and coughs several times.

– They're bad for your health, Fyodor Mikhailovich.

– Health? Leo Nikolayevich. I've not enjoyed that blessing since my youth, and even then I was always high-strung and feared the worst. I've since become an epileptic. After an attack I walk around in a daze for a week. Smoking settles my nerves and helps make the attacks more bearable. A question of the lesser of two evils, you might say.

– You've endured hardships, Fyodor Mikhailovich.

– Call me Fyodor, please.

– You're right: we should drop the patronymic. After all, we've been keeping an eye on each other's work for a long time.

The waiter returns with their order. Leo attempts to pay, but Fyodor restrains him by gripping his powerful wrist, around which he wears a rosary made of black knots, the sort worn by monks in counting 'Lord, have mercy'.

– You're my guest, Leo. I arranged this meeting.

As Fyodor counts a few coins onto the waiter's outstretched hand, the latter scrutinises him closely.

– Pardon me, sir, but aren't you Mr Dostoyevsky?

– Have we met before?

– No, sir. Well, I suppose we have, in a manner of speaking. I was there at the unveiling of Pushkin's statue when you spoke in honour of our great poet. Your speech hit the nail right on the head, sir. Right on the head.

– I'm pleased you liked it.

– Liked it! I'm no book man, sir. Fact is, I couldn't read my own name if it stared me in the face, but I nearly smacked someone on the mouth because he didn't clap when you finished.

Leo and Fyodor laugh.

– No joking, sir, and I didn't have a drop on the day.

Now what's he want? The old miser's always on my back. He's got no feeling for my poor feet.

He picks up the tray and mutters under his drooping moustache while going back to the counter, where a stocky man in a striped apron follows him with a stern look.

— Yes, Fyodor, I must also offer my congratulations. Your stirring speech was reported in the papers.

— It was one of those occasions when enthusiasm got the better of everyone present.

— And you made up with Turgenev there and then?

— Years of bitterness swept away in an instant of mutual forgiveness. That's the Russian soul for you, Leo.

— Yes, it's easily stirred by noble sentiments. Perhaps that's where its greatness lies.

— And its weakness. Once stirred, the Slavic soul is sometimes incapable of distinguishing good from evil. Swept away by demonic forces, it would follow a false prophet, knowing it was being led to the abyss.

Dropping their cues among the balls, the billiard-players start abusing each other. Those at the counter turn wearily, as though annoyed by the disturbance. The verbal conflict spreads from taunts comparing one's nose to a cucumber and the other's ears to a shovel, to denigration of family members, to the state of the roads in their respective villages. The waiter intervenes and threatens to throw them out if they don't stop squabbling.

After blowing on the steaming tea, Leo sips with a faint whistle, holding the glass between his thumb and forefinger, whose nails are clogged with red dirt. Fyodor swirls the vodka in an agitated manner and drinks it in one mouthful.

— You must be wondering why I arranged this meeting, he says, wiping his whiskers with the back of his hand.

— It's been long overdue, Fyodor.

– *I wasn't being morbid in my letter, Leo. Given the state of my health, I don't think I'll see out the winter.*

As he lights another cigarette the match trembles in his slender fingers.

– *Go south, Fyodor. The sun will warm and relax you.*
– *It's too late for that.*
– *No. The sun's full of regenerative power.*
– *You feel nature very strongly, don't you?*
– *I'm happiest in the country, especially when I'm working in the fields. I'm not ashamed to tell you, I shed tears of gratitude every spring.*
– *You're fortunate, Leo.*
– *St Petersburg has ruined your health.*
– *It may have ruined what fragile health I possessed, but it has given me something in return – a vision.*
– *At the expense of health? Is it worth it? It's like a pact with the devil.*
– *God, the devil, who knows?*
– *We must distinguish, Fyodor.*
– *The older I become, the less I'm able.*
– *My experience has been the contrary. Passionate in my youth, I condoned war, killing, and all the excesses of the flesh. I believed that the sanctity of experience transcended questions of ethics and morality. Life was a feast meant to be enjoyed to the full. The world had the freshness of the Garden of Eden before God appeared on the scene. But when my teeth started to decay and the fire in the blood subsided, I began to see things more clearly. There is a moral order, Fyodor, and I found it by bowing to the earth. One sustains and strengthens my body, the other my soul.*
– *That's where we differ, Leo. Your writing springs from an excess of strength and wellbeing, as though your pen were*

a plough or an axe, and, of course, you depict the side of truth which conforms to strength and vitality. But there's the other side of truth, the darker side, accessible only through sickness and suffering, and then by a mind full of doubt and uncertainty. The strong are irresistibly attracted to the earth, as matter is attracted to matter. The sick, on the other hand, not as bound to the earth, are more receptive to things over and above the world. Please, don't misunderstand me, Leo. I'm not advocating morbidity and decadence, simply trying to convey my experience. A new state of consciousness opens to me after an epileptic seizure which I can only describe as beatific.

– When spring comes, it comes for both the strong and the sick. Truth transcends man and his ephemeral emotions.

Fyodor has become slightly agitated. With a fork bent out of shape, he tries several times before piercing a slice of the pickled cucumber. Like the earth-clawing roots of an oak tree, Leo's fingers are crossed on the closed book.

– And my work, Leo? Is it without merit? Are my visions nothing more than the deformed children of a diseased brain?

– You've written some good things, especially the one about prison-life.

– The House of the Dead?

– I was deeply moved by the spirit of friendship in a place full of oppression and degradation.

– And my other books?

– They have their moments.

– Crime and Punishment?

– I found it too claustrophobic, Fyodor. My temperament needs open spaces. I couldn't breathe in those crowded tenements. And the main character was so introspective, I was often lost in the confusion of his thoughts and emotions.

— *I always endeavour to be more disciplined in my writing, but I've never had the health or good fortune to remain on top of my material. Epilepsy, financial hardships, domestic problems: they sap my strength, so that characters and situations often slip from my grasp. Have you experienced that? A character will suddenly become assertive and start making demands on you, the writer.*

— *What do you mean?* asks Leo, grating his fork against the plate in piercing a few strands of cabbage.

— *Just before commencing* Crime and Punishment, *for instance, I found myself face to face with Raskolnikov, not imaginatively but in reality, as real as you're sitting there, or so it seemed at the time. I don't know whether it was simply a case of the imagination overstepping its limits, or an hallucination due to the anxiety of living under the threat of imprisonment. It was at a time when I'd been contracted by a publisher: the deadline was approaching and I hadn't written a thing. Whatever, Raskolnikov stormed into my study in the early hours of the morning and demanded his rights. I won't go through with it, he shouted. I got up from my desk and tried to pacify him, thinking at the same time how thin and dishevelled he looked, far more than I'd imagined. You've got no right to make me do it, he protested. I refuse to murder anyone, even that miserable old woman. He slumped into an armchair and folded his arms in defiance. I stood directly in front of him and tried to adopt an authoritarian tone. You're behaving very unreasonably, I scolded him. I want no part of it, he insisted. You've got no say in the matter, I countered. He sprang to his feet and threw up his arms. It's my life we're talking about, he shouted. I noticed that his shabby overcoat was torn at the armpit, and I wondered whether I should include this detail in the story. Stop acting like a child, I said sternly. After all, it's only a work of fiction. My life's no fiction, he retorted. It's as real as yours. Please, Rodion, I said in a softer tone. And I actually pleaded with him, Leo. At that moment he had the better of me. I was afraid he'd rush out and never re-appear. Please, consider my predicament, I entreated him. Creditors are breathing down my neck, and they'll have me thrown in prison unless I come up with a story. So, that's your game, he snarled triumphantly. You want to use me as payment for your gambling debts. You want to send me to Siberia so you'll be spared debtors' prison. How Christian of you, Mr Dostoyevsky. I was speechless for a moment, Leo. I realised my stand was morally indefensible. I would have conceded, and allowed him to disappear into the St Petersburg night, but I was suddenly struck by the thought that he was subject to literary destiny, just as I was subject to a higher destiny, and that if I asserted myself, he'd be compelled to acquiesce. Listen, Rodion, I said, fixing him with a severe look. You really don't have a say in the matter. The pen's an instrument of fate, and I'm holding the pen. Then I'll go back to my attic, he threatened. To my thoughts and theories. I'll return to the being I was before you dragged me onto the stage. I'll lock my door and open for no-one. It's too late for that, I persisted. The wheels of creation have already been set in motion. I'll tell the authorities that I was simply a puppet in your diabolical scheme, he said with a note of resignation. I'll accept full responsibility, Rodion, I assured him. Yours will be the crime, mine the punishment. With that assurance, Leo, I finally managed to mollify him. He returned obediently to his room, and I was able to start work.*

Fyodor looks plaintively at Leo, as though expecting some judgement to be made against him. Leo's forehead contracts to a number of deep, horizontal furrows.

– Your mind must've been over-taxed, Fyodor.

– There's no other explanation, is there?

– My characters never overstep the bounds of fiction.

– That's evident from your writings, Leo. I admire your masterly control over characters and situations. Not a word out of place, not a superfluous detail, not a gesture that doesn't express psychological insight. You're a great artist, perhaps Pushkin's successor.

His tea now cool, Leo takes a few longer sips and follows this with a generous forking of cabbage and cucumber.

– Art? Artists? What does it all amount to, Fyodor? Where's the permanence of it all? The present concept of art as an end in itself is nothing but a passing fashion, arising from vanity and self-indulgence. Whenever I ask myself why I wrote those so-called works of art, I'm always confronted by the stark reply: Leo, you wrote from vanity and the empty praises of people whose aesthetic tastes you satisfied, people who've never done an honest day's work in their lives. So tell me, Fyodor, how can anything worthwhile arise from such obviously selfish motives?

– Then what I've heard is true, Leo?

– What have you heard?

– That you've renounced literature.

– There's more to life than literature.

– And Anna Karenina? War and Peace?

– There's not an honest line in either of them. They did nothing for me, except fill my pockets and feed my vanity. They were a bad influence, particularly the first one, on thousands who read them.

– You're being very hard on yourself, Leo.

– The truth always strikes our most vulnerable areas.

– And now you're convinced that truth and literature are incompatible?

— *I'm convinced that literature must never be an end in itself; that it should be a stepping stone to the truth of the prophet and the sage. I see the aesthetic as one of the three stages of human development: the stage above the purely sensual, though the two are often difficult to distinguish, and very often the precondition for the religious state. I led an aesthetic life for a long time, Fyodor, but always sensed that it was somehow incomplete. Critical acclaim and words such as 'masterpiece' couldn't appease this feeling of dissatisfaction with myself and my work. Last year I saw the truth: my work was incomplete because I, the creator, was incomplete. In a moment that almost overwhelmed me, and from which I'm still recovering, I realised that I had no inner conviction, no belief, that Leo Tolstoy, the public figure and proclaimed genius, was really nothing but a bag of bones.*

— *That's one of the reasons I wanted this meeting, Leo: to discuss the demon of despair that assailed you. Its talons tore at my entrails for three years, until I found the strength to overcome it in the teachings of the Gospels.*

— *Yes, nods Leo, picking up the book. It seems that one person turns to this and reads it because he has been cast into a living hell by external circumstances; while another, because his inner life reaches a point where he must hide his own belt so he's not tempted to hang himself.*

— *May I see it?*

Fyodor opens the book to the page marked with an oak leaf.

— *The Sermon on the Mount?*

— *If only we'd follow those few precepts, Fyodor. The salvation of the world lies in them.*

Fyodor reads in silence for a moment, holding the book up to the light. A sharp crack scatters the billiard-balls. Finishing the tea, Leo bites a slice of cucumber.

— *'Blessed are the poor in spirit: theirs is the kingdom of heaven.' I've often wondered about those words, Leo. How do you interpret 'poor in spirit'?*

— *Poor in spirit?* he sighs, his fingers twisting the ends of his beard. *I suppose it's a condition when the self's subdued and humbled by suffering and despair.*

— *And 'theirs is the kingdom'? 'Is' and not 'shall be'? What do you make of that?*

— *The kingdom of heaven is realised through the love of one's neighbour.*

— *You're a great humanist, Leo.*

— *What's your reading of the passage?*

— *I agree with you, though only to a point. For me 'poor in spirit' refers to a condition of sorrow verging on despair, and, as you know from your own recent experiences, despair is a state closer to hell than heaven. When it descends and darkens the light of day, a man loses his way and falls into the abyss that was formerly concealed by his ego. At such times a man's thoughts and feelings are directed inward, rather than toward his neighbour. And yet, something happens in this state that suddenly and unexpectedly gives rise to a fleeting glimpse of the kingdom of heaven. I'm talking about a personal vision, Leo, one that has nothing to do with one's neighbour, and which arises from one's Night of Gethsemane.*

— *Is heaven so close to hell?*

— *At times they're separated by nothing but a thought.*

— *Paradoxes, Fyodor. What about one's actions? Morality? Responsibility?*

As Fyodor returns the book, Leo takes it; both their hands hold it so there is an instant when it is impossible to determine whose hand is giving and whose receiving.

— *That's precisely where we differ, Leo. You've chosen to live and work according to Christ's second commandment; and I, perhaps due to my temperament, have chosen the first.*

The waiter returns, wiping his hands on the stained napkin.

— *Everything all right, Mr Dostoyevsky, sir? Sorry about those two jokers. Warned them, I did. Told them serious things were being discussed here. Are they still too loud? Just let me know if they are, I'll show them the door.*

— *No, no, everything's all right.*

— *Discussing literary matters, are you?*

Fyodor nods. The waiter smiles broadly, exposing a gap in his front teeth.

— *This gentleman a literary personage, too?*

— *I used to be,* replies Leo, flicking open a watch attached to a green, frayed ribbon.

— *Never had the chance to learn our Russian alphabet. Fact is, I wouldn't know the difference between 'Zh' and 'Sh' if my life depended on it. The patrons of this establishment are just as bad, so I manage to pick up a few scraps of knowledge by listening to educated gentlemen such as yourselves.*

— *You're quite welcome to sit and listen,* says Fyodor.

— *That's very kind of you, sir, very kind, but he wouldn't like it one bit.*

He glances over his shoulder. The stocky proprietor, apron tied almost around his chest, mouth open perhaps due to the weight of a fleshy lower lip, directs the waiter to attend to something with a nod of his neckless head.

— *Care for something else, gentlemen?*

— *I've got a ten o'clock train to catch, Fyodor.*

— *Then we must be going.*

In pushing back his chair, Fyodor accidently knocks his

glass, which shatters on the wooden floorboards. He springs to his feet and apologises to the waiter.

– Don't worry about nothing, sir. Happens all the time. I'll clean it up before you can say Nebuchadnezzar.

He dashes off, and returns with a scoop and scrawny broom. Leo puts the book in his pocket and fumbles under his thick beard with the top button of his overcoat. Fyodor's face darkens and contracts in watching the waiter sweep the fragments.

– There you go, sir. Nothing to it.
– Take this for the trouble.
– It was no trouble, Mr Dostoyevsky, sir.
– Please, I insist.
He accepts the coin reluctantly and opens the door.
– It was a pleasure to meet you, sir, a real pleasure.
– Good night.
– And God bless you and your friend.

Outside, the wind is howling, swirling snowflakes around the gas-lamps. A horse harnessed to a droshky turns toward them as they climb the steps to the street. Wrapped in a blanket, the driver straightens up and unties the reins from the foot-rest.

– Cab, sir?
– You take it, Leo. I'm not far from here.
– Will we meet again?

Fyodor casts a troubled glance from under the brim of his hat sprinkled with snow. Leo brushes his hair and pulls on a black knitted cap over his ears, the sort worn by monks setting out on a long pilgrimage. Suddenly, Fyodor embraces Leo and they press each other's cheek, moving from one to the other and back again, like the icon depicting the embrace of Saint Paul and Saint Peter. On the third touch of their cheeks, Fyodor holds Leo by the shoulders and whispers in his ear.

– I've envied you for years, Leo. Your success, your intelligence, your exquisite writing. You were my bête noire. The sight of your name in print in the morning paper would blacken the rest of the day. But this meeting has cured me of that, and I feel reconciled to you, like a brother.

– We writers are vain creatures, Fyodor. Yes, I used to keep an eye on your work, too, and then only to compare it with my own. We are brothers, Fyodor. Brothers born of Mother Russia, brothers in suffering, brothers in death.

Leo attempts to step back, but Fyodor clings to his powerful shoulders.

– No, Leo.

– What is it?

– You mustn't look at me.

– Are you all right?

– There's one more thing, Leo. The main reason for this meeting, and I must whisper it.

– You're shaking.

– Did you receive a letter from Strakhov?

– Your biographer's petty minded and envious, Fyodor.

– He wrote to you about ... the little girl? The public baths?

– Yes. No doubt he got those sordid details from your debauched character Stavrogin in The Possessed.

– Ah, Leo, there's something I must tell you.

The horse snorts a cloud of vapour and rattles its halter in shaking snowflakes from its head.

– It's getting late, Fyodor. I have a train to catch.

– All my major characters make a confession – it's now time for their creator to make his.

– I really must go, says Leo, trying to free himself from the tightening grip.
– Please, hear me out.
– I'm not a priest.
– You're a kindred soul.
– It's only a matter of time before I'm excommunicated.
– Better excommunication than damnation.
– Don't place such a heavy burden on me, Fyodor.
– It's horrible, horrible.
– Such confessions are between God and you.

His back turned to the droshky, Fyodor drops his arms and nods in resignation. Advising him to take care of his health, Leo climbs in with remarkable agility. The driver shakes the blanket, throws it over his head again, and whistles sharply at the horse, prodding it into a trot. With a moment's deliberation, Fyodor sets off in the opposite direction. After a dozen steps the chaos of snowflakes has almost disintegrated him, leaving only the vapour of his breath.

Running her finger on the last sentence, Sonya notices a few pricks and scratches on the back of her hand. From pruning the roses in the backyard, she thinks. Perhaps the rose tempts the flesh in order to satisfy the thorn's thirst for blood. Beauty in the service of blood. Love and pain go hand in hand. Two of the scratches form a cross or a lower case 't', and would almost pass unseen but for the sunlight on her skin. What is he working on now? And why so secretive? Is this really the last of his dialogues? The thought saddens her: she has looked forward to each as though it were a love letter. They opened her heart to him. In seeing his light-blue handwriting she has felt the joy of looking into his eyes, in holding each dialogue she has held him, in reading them she has felt him entering her. They have been the substantial source and nourishment of her love, and now, at the prospect of their end, she fears a diminution in the intensity of that love. Yes, he was profoundly hurt by his previous love affair, and perhaps he has concealed and protected himself in these dialogues, and this might well explain why she was so drawn to them, and through them, to him. Reading between the lines, she holds him tenderly with her eyes, assuages his anxiety, loves him to the point where she shares his pain.

Xenia flits past the window and enters the shop. Sonya has seen her several times since their first meeting, but each visit has been fleeting, between engagements. She has rushed in, spoken of her problems, bought a book by a Russian author, and dashed out. From these brief encounters, Sonya has pieced together the circumstances responsible for her present situation. After leaving her husband, she thought of returning home, to her parents, with whom she had not corresponded since her arrival in this country. But she was destitute. Not knowing the language, there was little chance of finding work, and without work she could never go home. The priest and the community had helped, but she was a proud person, and could no longer accept their charity. One evening, when she was at her lowest point, to avoid doing something desperate, she went to the church and knelt before the altar-screen. As she was praying, she noticed an icon of Mary Magdalene washing the feet of Christ. A light shone for her: she did not have the language, but she had looks and a good body. She would use these to make money, not just for the ticket back to Russia, but enough to provide a comfortable life for her parents. They had packed their hopes in her suitcase: their daughter's marriage to a wealthy man would allow them to leave Russia for a better life abroad. Yes, she would use her body to make it up to them. And her faith? It would remain inviolate. Magdalene had been a prostitute who repented of her past and led an upright life. Her task would be more difficult: she would sink into prostitution and, while there, retain the faith of her ancestors until circumstances permitted her to rise from the degradation. It would not be forever. A year, and she would have enough to return home and make a decent life for her parents and herself. A year of forced labour, not in a communist prison in Siberia, but in a brothel in a country of deserts and freedom and opportunity. At times though, when things got the better of her, she was sustained by the conviction that the life of the soul transcended the body, and that a time would come when, having passed through the fire, she would look back on this experience as a bad dream.

Wearing a skirt that reveals the strong movement of her thigh muscle just above the knee, Xenia strides to the counter, her patent-leather stilettos pecking the floor. Could Sonya recommend an erotic novel? She is expecting a new client any minute. A wealthy, retired lawyer who derives pleasure from having women read to him. He has grown tired of both French and German, and now wants to listen to erotica read with a Russian accent. They say he is very generous to women whose reading he enjoys. Sonya goes to a bottom shelf against the back wall and slips out a translation of *Sanine* by the Russian Artsybashev. Xenia has not heard of the author, but is more than pleased with the recommendation. How much is it? she asks, reaching back to scratch her well-defined calf with the book's spine. It's a gift, replies Sonya. A small contribution toward her journey home. Perhaps she might take the book to Russia, where it was burnt when it first appeared at the turn of the century. Fire and revolution are in the Russian soul, says Xenia. The Books of the Nobility were burnt in the seventeenth century. Gogol destroyed the second part of his *Dead Souls* in a fireplace. The communists burnt everything that did not conform to their ideas. May you read to the lawyer with a tongue of flame, says Sonya. Laughing, Xenia thanks her and hurries out, her heels clicking even when she is out of sight.

the TWELFTH *dialogue*

The last day of the second millennium, Sonya muses, standing in the doorway of the shop, sawing the key's jagged teeth on her chin. It is nine o'clock, and, waiting for Theo, she has remained open longer than usual. He did not say when exactly he would come, and she has spent the time between customers looking out the window, heart leaping at pedestrians with the slightest resemblance to him. The days since his previous visit have been full of doubts, questions, misgivings – all arising from her feelings for him. His two-week absence has, if nothing else, tested her love and found it much stronger than she would have thought possible. It has been a long time since she has felt so attracted to anyone. The affair at university crushed her, made her mistrustful of men, and she retreated even further into her burrow full of books. And now, by a fortuitous conjunction of events, just as she is being forced to surrender her books, along comes a man to fill the void in which she would otherwise have found herself. But what are his feelings for her? If only they could spend more time together, she would fathom his thoughts and emotions. She recalls his promise, and his vision. Has he completed his work? There seemed to be so much urgency about it, as if it were a matter of saving his soul. What if he has not completed it? Would he come and tell her? Or would she be stood up? He appears to have an obsessive side to his nature: he might work through the night, forgetting their meeting. No. He will come. The new millennium was too much on his mind. She has prepared herself for the occasion: bought a new outfit and shoes, had her hair cut and styled, and used a little make-up on her eyes. Having spent all day in the shop, she will try to persuade him to eat out somewhere, to celebrate the new millennium along with the rest of the city.

The last day of my books, she thinks, wheeling in from the footpath the small trolley marked: SPECIALS. She locks the door and turns off the panel of lights along the front window. Once again the feeling of anxiety gnaws at her stomach, but she dispels it by reflecting on how the warmer weather during the past few days has enhanced the festive mood percolating throughout the city. Even now, the blazing sunset caught in the upper-storey windows across the street resembles the flags and banners which used to be hung out on special occasions. A sense of anticipation has been evident on the faces of pedestrians and customers. Ironically enough, the shop was unusually busy today, busier than it has been in months. People have flitted in and out, buying their holiday reading, in a state of excitement, as though time were running out. Not one person came in to browse: all rushed in, chose their books in a hurry, and rushed out again, on their way to another errand before the close of business.

Yes, there is a sense of anticipation about this evening's festivities: people everywhere are preparing for parties, dinner-dances, fancy dress balls, street gatherings. With restaurants booked out and hotels decked out for gala events, one would think the country is no longer in the grip of a recession. The city has organised a spectacular light and sound show, followed by fireworks that will crack and shatter against the sky like champagne bottles launching a new *Titanic*. Tonight, bitten by the millennium bug, people will forget their problems, their debts, their mortgages, their isolated lives. They will meet as families, friends, neighbours, communities. Others, mainly the young revellers, will pour into the heart of the city that will throb with the might of the crowd. And yet, at times running parallel with this excitement, there is the feeling of apprehension: helplessness at time slipping away, the fear of growing older, the uncertainty of entering a new millennium. One must not be alone tonight, for fear of being reduced to zero. Tonight, perhaps more so than at any other time in the last thousand years, this underlying apprehension will drive people to seek strength and certainty in numbers, and to celebrate as never before. Who knows, perhaps the fervour of tonight's excitement is directly proportional to the depth of the anxiety at the core of existence.

And Sonya also feels this anxiety. Against the expectation of seeing Theo, of reading his new work, of celebrating the third millennium, of consummating their love, she faces the stark reality of the 'torch' and the imminent destruction of her beloved books. He came to the shop yesterday. From Zitta's description of him as a real professional, she had expected someone in a suit and carrying a briefcase. Instead she was surprised by a shabbily dressed man of about thirty, who looked as if he had spent the night sleeping on a park bench, covered in newspapers. His walk was prominently pigeon-toed and he carried an army disposal bag strapped over his shoulder. Short (verging on dwarfish) and unshaven, he placed what appeared a scrap of smouldering charcoal on the edge of the counter, and, extending a plump hand with stubby, blackened fingers, introduced himself as Photius, stuttering his name. Struggling, at times closing his eyes and contorting his face in expelling a thorny word, he explained that he was a heavy smoker and had run out of matches on his way here. He happened to be walking through those huge gardens on the other side of the river, and there was not a shop in sight. Craving a smoke, he asked one person after another, even stopping a few puffing joggers, only to meet with nothing but frowns and looks of disgust, as though he were a leper. Growing more desperate with each step, he found himself near the war memorial. Had she been to visit it recently? It was an impressive monument. All those names and places engraved in gold sent shivers down his spine. He was often drawn to the Flame of Remembrance as an adolescent, especially at dusk, as the flag was being lowered and the bugle filled the evening with golden sunset. His thoughts one with the flame, he would imagine himself in the hell of battle, dying for his country in an act of bravery. Today, though, his heart raced ahead of him at the sight of the large metal dish containing the flame. He took out a cigarette, but the flapping gas-fed flame was beyond his short reach, and even if he managed to get close there was a real danger of being burnt. The proximity of this inaccessible flame made his craving unbearable. A crow called from a nearby tree and snapped a twig in flying off. He ran to the grassy slope, and there found a dry branch long enough for his need. Returning to the flame, he reached up with the branch. But just as it began to ignite, a soldier appeared out of the blue, grabbed him by the collar, snatched the branch from him, snapped it in two, and stomped on the glowing end with a black boot. Threatened with prosecution for violating a national symbol, he was sent on his way with a stern warning and a rough shove.

By now every cell in his small body was crying out for the same thing. As luck would have it, he happened to walk across an area set up with barbecues and quantities of firewood beside each. One of them had been recently used. Poking about, he picked out a stick of charcoal, blew life back into it, and enjoyed his cigarette. Walking through the city with the charcoal in his hand, he must have lit another dozen in making his way on foot to the shop.

As though the strain of recounting this were too much, he picked up the charcoal with his fingertips, blew it red, and used it to light a cigarette. Sonya took one from her packet. With a nicotine-toothed grin, he offered her the charcoal, but she shook her head and used the lighter. He was glad to be in the company of a fellow smoker, he stammered. It would make his work far easier by serving as a possible cause, and provide plausibility when the time came for her to make a claim. Nodding, head disproportionately large for his body, he walked around the shop as though planning the job. Here and there he ran his black hand over the spines, as though reassuring them that it would be painless, or stopped to open a book and feel the quality of its paper, or bent the covers of a hardback until they cracked and touched. His presence, his toady hands on her books, filled Sonya with revulsion. She felt like ordering him to leave, telling him that she would face her fate, even if it meant losing everything, but she swallowed her words in bitterness, conceding that her rescue lay in his dwarfish hands. Yes, he stuttered, returning to the counter. The job would give him a great deal of satisfaction. He had never done over a bookshop, but could picture it all clearly. An hour, and it would be all over. By the time the fire brigade arrived, the fire would have run its course, and they would find nothing but small ashy crows flying about. As for the arson squad, they could not prove a thing, even if they suspected foul play.

As though frustrated by the exertion of forming his words, he tossed his bag on the counter, unstrapped its buckles, and took out a few sheets of paper in a plastic folder. He wanted his clients to know something about him and the quality of his work, for which he has prepared a sort of curriculum vitae. Would she please read it. In his line of work, it was important for him to know that his client had unqualified confidence in him. In many ways he fed off that confidence, like an artistic performer, and it allowed him to complete a first-rate job. If, after reading the material, she still had doubts, he would leave, no questions asked. Sonya accepted the folder. The presentation suggested it had been professionally prepared using the latest technology: the text was double spaced and, judging by the shining letters, laser printed.

CONFIDENTIAL

(a short story)

Call me Photius. Unlike young Ishmael who set out to see the watery parts of the world and survived the wrath of Moby Dick, my journey of self-discovery has taken me through fire. Ah, I can hear your curiosity in the way you're rustling the sheets. It's an unusual name, you're thinking. Is it a Christian name? A surname? A middle name? First, let me say it's a pseudonym. In this line of work – professional arsonist – one must be intangible as the material with which one works. My real name? Don't bother asking. I wouldn't tell you anyway, not for all the Holy Fires of Greece. In fact, I seldom use it these days, and when I do it no longer feels part of me. As for Photius, a name of my choosing, conferred in a baptism of fire, you might say, it's certainly not Christian, but of pagan origin, going back to my earliest, mythical ancestors. It's neither a surname nor a middle name, but one that's both first and last, beginning and end, a perfect mean.

I was born in a state capital of this country in 1970, in an inner suburb whose last syllable rhymes with joy. My parents, both honest, hardworking factory-hands, left Greece in the early sixties, but Greece never left them, and this, I believe, was a decisive factor in determining the path I'd follow in life. My earliest memories are of fire, and even as I write this, I feel as if those memories are branded in my mind. From my father, for whom the sun shone from the very arse of old Hades himself, I heard the myths of the great heroes, beginning with the greatest of them all: Prometheus, the fire-giver. I've always considered his name, meaning 'fore-thought', to be a corruption of Pyrometheus, meaning 'fire-thought'. Father would relate the myths and legends in Greek, the only language permitted in the house, and this had the effect of transporting me to another time and place. Sitting on his lap, my head on his chest, I'd feel his voice resonating against me, carrying me off to a distant land, a place where men strove with gods. What is one's identity, if not the impressions made on us by our childhood heroes? For me they were: Prometheus, to whom I still trace my ancestry; Heracles, whose apotheosis was attained through self-immolation on a pyre of oak branches and the trunks of male wild-olive; Alexander, who set fire to the great palace at Persepolis to avenge the destruction inflicted on Greece by the Persians a hundred years earlier.

As a boy I wanted to emulate Prometheus, to be the guardian and giver of a new fire – one that would raise mankind from the darkness, even at the risk of offending authority and being imprisoned. Like Alexander, I wanted to carry the torch as a sword, to destroy not one palace but all palaces and churches and parliament buildings, to free mankind from all the old oppressors and lead it into a new world order. And like Heracles (once, when I referred to him as Hercules, father reacted angrily, as though I'd blasphemed, denouncing the Anglo name, saying that it diminished the greatness of the hero), I wanted to use the new fire as a means of personal salvation: climbing onto the pyre, I'd transform my body into pure soul.

My first memories of the living flame centre around the open fireplace in the living room, where father told me his stories. My parents had recently bought the house. Uneasy about living with a huge debt, they skimped on many comforts in order to pay it off quickly. Where relatives were ripping out the old fireplaces and installing ducted heating systems, father, undeterred by their taunts to modernise, would scour the neighbourhood's lanes and factory-yards. I can still see him coming home with a stack of building beams on his shoulder from a factory which had just been demolished. Friends made fun of us, called us peasants, jeered that we couldn't afford proper heating. Being shy by nature, with a blush that made my face resemble a red-hot coal, I was at first embarrassed by father's actions. Later, though, when I understood the true significance of fire, I saw him as a kind of servant of the flame. Yes, he was saving money, but he was also liberating the flame from wood that would have otherwise been buried in a tip.

Those winter evenings were so cosy. We didn't have a television because father refused to allow the English language into the house. I didn't mind: there was more than enough laughter and entertainment from the many friends and relatives who visited, more often than not, unexpectedly. I'd sit with them before the fireplace, watched by grandparents in black and white photographs on the mantelpiece, as they sang and recalled colourful stories about the old days. Happy as those times were, I was happiest when alone with my parents: with mother humming over her embroidery, and father, prodded by my insistence, relating once again (it always sounded as though for the first time) the exploits of my favourite heroes. On such occasions, the metaphor 'tongue of flame' became a real thing. Staring at the flames, I sensed that father's words did not come from him but from the fire: a twisting tongue of flame reached out to me, licked my face and hands, told me about my heroes in a language that went back to a time before speech, back to the sound of lightning splitting a dry oak and setting it ablaze, back to the blackness before charcoal.

It's disconcerting to think that, in this electronic age, one may pass through childhood without direct experience of fire. Many observations convince me that early contact with this natural phenomena enhances both the mind and the imagination, and that children deprived of such contact are the worse for it. There's no better image to represent the mind than the flame: both are restless, both immanent in matter, both transform and spiritualise the physical world. I wasn't allowed to play with the fire in the living room: my curiosity was checked by father's warnings of the house burning to the ground. But things were different in the laundry, which was located in a shed in the backyard. As we had neither a washing machine nor a hot-water service, mother heated water in a large copper cauldron encased in cast iron and stoked with wood. Here, in the steamy little shed, as mother's red hands scrubbed and slapped and twisted the washing in the trough, I would sit on a stool before the mouth of the heater, prodding the fire with the poker. Don't play with fire, she'd warn from time to time, wiping the mirror above the trough with a frothy hand to see what I was doing. But I knew that she didn't mind my presence. I was her helper: bringing wood from outside, tending the heater, keeping the fire humming and the water steaming through the cracks in the wooden lid. It was at this time that I was first burnt, not seriously, but enough to learn that fire doesn't distinguish between friend and foe, between good and bad, between heaven and hell.

As I grew, so did my fascination with, and reverence for, fire. Being Greek Orthodox, though not very devout, my parents took me to church at Christmas, Easter, and the occasional wedding and baptism. I was indifferent to the glassed icons that people kissed, the smoky incense, the dome-filling chants. But the candles! They'd catch my attention and transfix my thoughts throughout the entire service. Entranced by the flames before the altar, particularly those on the table set with dishes of wheat in memory of the dead, I saw all manner of things. One instant they were steadfast compass points, directing souls to a better world; the next, arrowheads, straining for the flesh of the wicked. In the body of the flame I saw Christ and Prometheus embracing as blood brothers; in the tip, a host of angelic orders rejoicing in the Dance of Isaiah; in the black, twisted wick, the damned ascending to heaven. On occasions when a door opened and the flames stirred, I saw the fallen angel Lucifer, the light-bearer and older brother of Prometheus, emerging from the abyss of his punishment and pivoting on a point of golden light. Why was hell represented by fire and brimstone? And why were candles sanctioned in church while Lucifer, sometimes called Satan, was anathema?

I was thirteen when these questions began to trouble me. At the same time, struggling with puberty and self-doubts, I was afraid of the future and uncertain about my place in the world. Who was I? What was my purpose in being alive? I was introverted and, in retrospect, pathologically shy. I'd blush and feel my heart throb to bursting whenever the teachers called the roll. Who knows, perhaps that's why I've chosen a pseudonym: a new name, a new person, a gradual forgetting of those painful memories. Short for my age, with a face that looked mature (even then people commented that, perhaps because of my snub nose, I reminded them of Socrates), I was neither good at sport nor at ease with girls. As for school work, I disliked most subjects, except history and science, which nourished my interest in fire.

It often happens that in times of greatest difficulty, a solution will flash out of the blue. And so it was with me: the purpose and meaning of my life appeared unexpectedly on Easter Saturday of that year. It was midnight, the resurrection service was in progress, and though the church was full to the point of suffocation still more people squeezed inside. I was struck by the thought: should a fire break out many would be trampled to death in the rush to the three exits. The droning chants of lament, the heavy smell of wax and incense, the tingling of coins in the collection plates – this was all too much for me. Noticing my complexion changing, my father fanned me with a newsletter and advised I go out for some fresh air. The churchyard was filling with late arrivals, each holding candles wrapped in silver foil which would shortly serve as a protective cone around the flame. Revived by the chilly air I climbed onto a concrete retaining wall and waited for the amplified service to end. From my elevated vantage point I pondered the press of people: men and women, young and old, they had left the comfort of home and gathered in the dark as a single body, with a common will, to one end. Above, the sky was clear, the stars were sharp, remote, yet somehow connected to what was happening.

The lights suddenly went out, plunging the crowd in darkness, enhancing the stars, the constellations, the Southern Cross. A murmur of expectation rose from the crowd. From the church a single candle appeared in the doorway, raised high in the priest's hand. Instantly, drawn by this solitary flame, the crowd moved forward and a host of blind candles strained to touch the flame, to have their sight miraculously restored. The flame leapt from wick to wick, multiplying rapidly, each a perfect clone of the original which remained undiminished. In a few minutes the yard was full of glowing faces. The chant 'Christ has arisen' filled the night. Hands, foil, plastic cups, guarded the flame as though it were life itself. Overcome with a feeling of being the darkness that received the light, I began to cry, and through my tears the stars seemed reflections of the candles, while heaven became the here and now. As people dispersed, anxious to return home with their candles still alight, to crack the red eggs of the resurrection and break their week-long fast, I remained on the wall, vowing to dedicate my life to the service of the holy flame.

But how was I to serve fire? Through the church? Become an altar boy? No. I was far too shy. Besides, I wanted to serve it in my own way, as Prometheus had done. Express my reverence for it through gratuitous acts of arson? Go out at night and burn the surrounding hedges of wealthy properties? Set the school alight? Start a bushfire on a day of total fire ban, when the countryside was tinder dry? No. I'd read about pyromaniacs: I wasn't one. Such people were generally introverted, using fire to compensate for feelings of inadequacy, and to attract public attention to themselves through their pathological identification with fire. Such wanton destruction filled me with revulsion. I wanted to use fire to benefit people, not highlight a shadowy ego. For this I decided to undertake a thorough study of fire. This would be an initiation, my apprenticeship to Lucifer, my preparation for a higher calling.

Scraping a bare pass in my final year at high school, I went to university and enrolled in a degree course in Fire Prevention.

I figured that an understanding of the nature and containment of fire would better prepare me in its use and propagation. In my element, as it were, I took my degree with honours and embarked on a doctorate, researching the mystery surrounding the famous Greek Fire in the time of the Byzantine Empire. This was an incendiary weapon invented by the Byzantines for naval warfare. Using long tubes, they projected a pitch-like substance at enemy ships, which burst into flame upon hitting the water. The composition of the substance was known to only a few, and guarded so zealously that, upon the fall of Constantinople, copies of the parchment with instructions for its preparation were thought to have been burnt, so that it would not fall into enemy hands. The doctorate absorbed me for three years. I researched the available literature, then set about working in the laboratory, alone like an alchemist, mixing substances by trial and error, searching for the combination that would react with water, the nemesis of fire, to produce spontaneous combustion. As a result of hard work and good fortune, I succeeded; or rather, having served my initiation, the mysterious nature of Greek Fire revealed itself to me.

I saw this as the first stage in my quest for enlightenment, and its successful completion confirmed my worthiness to serve fire. Understandably, my initial reaction was to submit my results, gain the doctorate, and secure a position as a lecturer. But when my elation subsided, I thought deeply about what I had found. The Byzantines, my ancestors, had taken this secret to their graves, and here I was preparing to announce it to the world. It would be a violation of their memories. The Fire had been revealed to me not for personal advancement, but for the protection of those virtues which the Byzantines defended for over a thousand years. I was now the guardian of the Fire, and in this capacity was compelled to keep it secret, using it only when circumstances demanded.

I didn't submit for my doctorate: it now seemed trivial beside the honour conferred on me by those higher powers that revealed the secret of the Fire, even though I had no idea of when and where and under what circumstances I would use it. A restlessness crept into my life. I argued with my father, who couldn't understand why I'd abandoned my studies and the prospect of an academic career. Of course, I said nothing to him or anyone else about the Fire, but defended my action by saying that I needed a break and would return to my studies with greater vigour in a year or two. I worked sporadically at odd jobs, though more to appease my father than for the sake of money. When would I use the Fire that seemed to be fuelling my restlessness? Would I see a sign? Hear a voice? Somewhat of a disenchanted loner before the Fire, I became a silent recluse in guarding its secret. I must say, though, knowledge of the Fire enhanced my self-esteem, which had been so low I used to recognise people by their shoes rather than their faces. It was as if a new identity was forged in the Fire: I felt sure of myself, empowered, confident to face the world and leave my mark when stars and candles conjoined. Unable to put up with my father's harangues, I began wandering the streets. It was at this time that I found solace in smoking.

Late one windy Sunday afternoon, after walking through the city since morning, I happened to find myself waiting for a tram outside the central fire brigade. Striking a match for a cigarette (yes, smoking was a health hazard, but I was prepared to live with this, for it was heaven to my soul), I was stunned by a large mosaic on a side wall of the brigade's newly constructed building. The towering figure of Prometheus was depicted in bright colours, as though draped in flames, dispensing his blessing to an assembly of smaller figures. The mosaic went through me like a lance of lightning. This was what I had lost sight of in recent years! The exemplary greatness of Prometheus! There he was, cemented to brick (worse than being chained to rock), with a flame (not blood) gushing from a wound torn in his side by the setting sun (not a vulture's claw); despite this, he still found the strength to minister to mankind's need, and to admonish me for not using the Fire I'd been given from the depths of oblivion. Several trams rumbled past, but I didn't move. There was a sign in this fortuitous encounter, and I had to grasp it, or spend the rest of my life shuffling the streets, like a windswept newspaper in search of a flame. How long was I there? Ten minutes? Two hours? I don't know. But I studied that mosaic square by square, in all its minute detail, working myself into a state where I envisaged all sorts of fantastic possibilities, not least of which was the idea of reading fire. Stone and fire, I thought. Stilling the flame. What if a flourishing fire were photographed. Who knows, there may be something cabbalistic in that still image: the shape of a letter as a key to the future, the outline of the soul, the very face of God, or Lucifer, one interchanging with the other as in certain ambiguous pictures.

These thoughts and ideas were scintillating, but they didn't lead to anything definite, and I chastised myself for having succumbed to them at a time when more important matters had to be resolved. Turning to walk off my excitement, I noticed a statue of Christ fixed to the wall of a small church across the street from the mosaic. It was a bronze work, darkened by traffic fumes, with an inscription: INVICTIS PAX. A fire of red roses had been kindled just above the crucified feet. I had observed this statue many times in passing on the tram, though with only cursory interest; today, however, under the strong impression of the mosaic, I saw the blackened figure of Christ reaching out for my help. As the younger brother of Prometheus, he had been rejected by the city, which was driven by the material fire of commerce and industry. His fire, the ethereal light of his life and teaching, had been reduced to this cold, black statue. Suddenly, it was incumbent on me to redress the situation. The fire of Prometheus and the Greek Fire were one and the same. To be truly worthy of using what had been revealed to me, I must bow to the fire I'd witnessed that Easter night in the church. In a flash, I saw that I must visit Jerusalem during Easter week, to witness the Holy Fire descending from heaven in the Church of the Sepulchre.

Mad, that's what my father called me. And maybe I was, but there was no changing my mind. I read a dozen books on the subject of the Holy Fire, and a week before Easter set off on a pilgrimage, by plane, to the Holy Land. I left with the belief that this would be the decisive event in my life, and I wasn't to be disappointed. Under Greek Orthodox administration, the Church of the Holy Sepulchre was packed with pilgrims from all parts of the world. Holding an unlit candle, making no progress through the impenetrable mass of people, I squeezed to a position beside a window, on whose narrow sill half a dozen young men clung to each other for a better view of the proceedings. People had been standing for hours, and by now the sense of expectation was feverish. When the Bishop of the Fire appeared in glittering robes, the sight proved too much for some, who fainted and had to be carried out with great difficulty. A procession escorted the bishop three times around the sepulchre, and then he removed his robes and entered it, with the door being closed behind him. By now the crowd was in a frenzy: some screamed, others confessed their sins, while others shook as though seized by epilepsy. A lull filled the church as a priest climbed to a small opening in the section of the chapel above the sepulchre. Holding a few candles in a protective metal frame, he waited to 'catch the flame'. The lull subsided to momentary silence, and then a light appeared from the opening, accompanied by a cry from the crowd which pressed blindly toward it. The priest received the flame from the bishop, who had in turn received it from heaven, and raised the candles like a victory torch. In an instant he was surrounded by a forest of candles, all desperate for the Holy Fire. In the frantic rush, flames were extinguished as people pushed forward to light theirs from candles closer to the source. Others, in a state verging on hysteria, purified themselves of sin by passing clusters of flame over the exposed parts of their body, including their face. Lighting mine from that of one of the men on the sill, I remained pressed against the wall, waiting for the crowd to leave, holding my breath against the smoke heavy with wax.

Finally, as though a vice had slowly been loosened, the crush eased. Candles glowed in the narrow lanes as I returned to my hotel, managing to keep mine still alight. I placed it upright in a glass and lay on the bed, exhausted by the ordeal. Was it a Holy Fire, descended miraculously from heaven? Or had it been the work of the bishop? These and other questions swirled in my head as I gazed at the motionless flame, hovering in a state between waking and sleep. Now whether what followed was a dream or a vision, I can't say, but its impact was powerful, altering forever the course of my life. Where it had been cast in gold, suddenly the flame began to quiver as though due to a breeze, and yet the sheer curtains were still. Ripples of light radiated from its point, forming a halo like those in the icons. I tried to grasp it, but my hands felt as if nailed to a rock. The halo expanded and soon embraced me, dissolving my body in liquid light. After a moment of absolute stillness, the flame fluttered again and split in two, becoming a snake's tongue. I braced myself for a painful sting, but a warm caress slithered over me and covered my body in a new skin. Glowing intensely, the flame was now a leaf twisting to detach itself from a twig, an instant later a wing beating to free itself from the black wick, then a dove flying toward me. Its sharp, pearly beak scratched the soles of my feet, my palms, my forehead. I felt the outline of letters (the ones on my forehead were in mirror image) but couldn't make sense of them. And then the flame was still again. I sat on the edge of the bed, heart beating, forehead covered in sweat, convinced that I'd experienced the last initiation in my preparation to serve fire.

I stayed in Jerusalem for another week, keeping the flame alive by transferring it from one candle to another. Was it from earth or heaven? It didn't matter. The experience had made it my Holy Fire, and I knew that my future depended on it. But how was I to take it home on the plane? Oil, I thought, recalling the icon chalices. Fill a jar with olive oil, transfer the flame onto a small floating wick, and, concealed in my hand-luggage, it would burn for the duration of the flight. No, it was too risky. Not that the flame would be detected by X-ray machines, nor that the luggage would ever leave my hand, but the jar might be disturbed through a jolt caused by air turbulence and the flame extinguished. I wrestled with the problem for the next few days, until a small Arab boy accosted me in a crowded market with an offer of American cigarettes. Yes, I said, and bought a dozen packets. I'd light a cigarette from the Holy Fire and chain smoke all the way home. But would it be the same as a live flame?

Why not? There was nothing more than a perceived difference between a flame on a wick and the same flame burning strands of tobacco. In the latter case, the flame would be made even more personal in that it would be sustained by my breath.

For more than sixty hours (there were delays and missed connections) a cigarette didn't leave my fingers. As my seats were in smoking sections of the plane, I felt quite relaxed for most of the journey. The only time I became a little tense was in the presence of officials in no-smoking areas, but even here I found it easy enough to avoid detection by concealing the cigarette in a cupped hand behind my back. Once at home, I lit a candle from my cigarette, restoring the Holy Fire to its rightful state.

Such were the beginnings of my profession – no, vocation. I now use fire in alleviating the suffering of humanity, although I always take into consideration a person's plight before undertaking to help them. Am I a criminal? Was Prometheus a criminal? Was Lucifer? Christ? They were all punished for their benefactions. And if the same fate awaits me, so be it: I'll take courage from my heroes. But I'm careful in my work and a good judge of character. Experience has taught me to avoid people whose intentions are selfish, who are motivated by greed, for they debase the Holy Fire and cast its servant in hot water.

I now possess three distinct Greek Fires, each of which I use as circumstances demand. There's the fire of Prometheus and Byzantium, with which I torch factories, warehouses, furniture showrooms. Last year when the Olympic Flame was being run through the country in preparation for the coming Games, I managed to steal a light from one of the runners. This I use on places related to the body: homes, restaurants, clothing shops. Finally, there's the Holy Fire, which I reserve for art galleries, bookshops, music shops, and, yes, the occasional house of God.

Allow me to conclude by saying that, as we enter the third millennium, I hope to devote myself exclusively to the third fire. If there is to be an Armageddon, it will be in the form of a great conflagration, one that will redeem matter and raise it to the purity of primal mind.

Sonya returned his curriculum vitae, expressing genuine admiration for his passion and dedication. He apologised for not being able to give her a copy: it was a sensitive document which might land him in trouble if it fell into the wrong hands, though he had taken the precaution of disguising it as a short story, adding the disclaimer that any resemblance to a living person was purely coincidental. He then stammered and struggled through a few perfunctory questions in order to determine her suitability as a client. His large head nodded and shook, while his bulging eyes rolled from her, to the street, to various parts of the shop. All the time, Sonya checked a feeling of loathing: a reaction to his grubby hands, his brown teeth, the way he held the cigarette between his third and fourth finger. In contrast to this ragged, comical, slightly misshapen figure, her books were precise, serious, with compact bodies, perfect spines. She shuddered at the thought of them being devoured by his Holy Fire. How could she have allowed herself to be drawn into such a scheme? And drawn she was! An inexorable force had taken hold of her: the force that draws the moth to the flame, the body to fire on a winter's day. But it was not too late to call it off. A word, and she could still save her books. Yes, she would lose everything she owned, but retain her integrity and conscience.

He must have sensed what she was thinking, for he drew deeply on his cigarette and stepped closer. She saw herself doubled in his eyes: a tiny figure caught in a black circle. Yes, he appreciated her empathy to books, understood exactly how she must be feeling. It was only natural, this attachment to things. He had seen it many times. People who were all fired up at first suddenly got cold feet. This was often a sure sign that they were not meant for his services, and he was honest in his opinion. Occasionally though, particularly in dealing with artistic temperaments, it simply meant that a person of noble sentiment had to be reminded of their higher calling. He adduced the case of a middle-aged painter who, threatened with imprisonment over failure to make matrimony payments, sought his services to set fire to an exhibition of his work which had been insured for well over its value. The day before the torching (he visited all clients the day before, to sound their state of mind and, where necessary, steel their nerves) he found the painter in tears. He could not go through with it, he cried. The paint was like his own blood; the canvases, his own flesh. Photius managed to calm him. He should not forget his higher calling. Yes, he would sacrifice these works, and with them a precious part of himself, but the true artist in him would rise from the ashes, like the Phoenix, and go on to paint greater works by virtue of having passed through the Holy Fire. And so it happened. The painter's nerve was strengthened, and the exhibition went up in a well-confined blaze. Avoiding not only prison, but the slightest taint of suspicion, he went on to win a national prize for portraiture, with the judges commenting on how his former realism had been augmented by a startling spirituality reminiscent of El Greco.

She should consider what was at stake, he said, pausing to read the impression his story had made. One must look beyond the material thing, the here and now, and live for the sake of the soul. There was nothing more precious than the soul's freedom. Was she a writer? No. Had she ever thought of writing? Some years ago. Why had she held back? Lack of talent. N-n-n-o, he beamed, as though about to play a trump card. Burning these books would liberate her soul, and she would one day go on to write books of her own. He smiled and winked. Was he being facetious? Ironical? Or had this little prophet of fire read her deepest thoughts?

He went on to stammer that he prepared for each job thoroughly, and the present was no exception. Did she have a section on art? A book on Michelangelo's work? Puzzled, Sonya found one and gave it to him. It was the sort sold at museums and tourist stands. The front cover had a statue of a naked woman reclining against the backdrop of Florence. Licking a nicotined finger, Photius flicked the glossy pages and, stopping at a colourful painting, invited Sonya to look at the unfamiliar work titled: Sistine Chapel – The Erythraen Sibyl. Was she aware that books featured prominently in the Sistine's paintings? Sonya had never noticed. She ought to take time to study them. Of the four Sibyls and their sacred books, he was most attracted to this one, not because she was the loveliest, but because of her relationship to the book. Unlike the others, who seemed to guard their books jealously, she had it open for all to read. He pointed to a cherubic child above the book. What was he doing with that torch in his hand? asked Photius. Was he about to light the oil lamp for the Sibyl to read? Yes, he grinned, but there was more. That torch was not only for illuminating the page but also for burning it. Half-turned to the book, the gentle Sibyl seemed to welcome the torch both as a means to knowledge and a source of liberation. Having read the sacred book, she would go out into the world and live the word. He paused to catch his breath. Then, as though struck by something, he alternated his attention several times from her to the Sibyl, and commented on the similarity in their profile. Sonya blushed. In referring to the painting, he wanted Sonya to see that the word was a means to the world, and that just as the Sibyl had gone beyond her book, so Sonya must find the courage to part with her collection. As though giving her time to absorb the example, he lit another cigarette and folded his short arms. She stared at the painting: the Sibyl's graceful manner, her fingers turning pages to the back of the book, the cherub straining to light the lamp. Things happened for a purpose, she thought. This little fellow had introduced her to the Sibyl, and there was an instant attraction. Where his appearance had caused Sonya to have misgivings about the fate of her books, the Sibyl's poise (despite her manly arms) and classical calm dispelled those fears and strengthened her resolve.

W-w-e-ell? struggled Photius. Sonya nodded. She would not regret it, he beamed. Yes, there would be a little heartache at first, but it would pass once she entered the third millennium through the cleansing arch of the Holy Fire. There, her soul unburdened, she would be free to partake of a more abundant life. Grasping the vision that came through his fractured words, Sonya nodded again. He extended his plump, black hand, and they shook. What was in the back room? He was pleased by the fireplace. It would have been very useful if it were a winter job. He opened the door to the backyard, looked around, and appeared to make a mental note of something. Could he have a key to the front door? The job would be done tomorrow night. New Year's eve, the end of the millennium, celebrations, fireworks – the conjunction of events was very auspicious. Sonya gave him a spare key. Slipping his arms through the bag's straps, he got himself into a tangle. Sonya assisted him. Th-th-a-anks, he grinned. He picked up the charcoal, blew on it until it glowed, and left with a spring in his pigeon toes.

Sunset's blaze has subsided, crimson clouds have turned to ash, a star gleams through the gaping upstairs window of PLAMEN'S GRILL – and yet still no sign of Theo. Her foreboding grows in proportion to the excitement on the street. In the heavy traffic loud with horns and music, people are dressed for parties; pedestrians embracing bottles of alcohol laugh on their way to restaurants; youths on skateboards speed toward the city; a group of revellers frolic past in fancy dress, some as clowns, others skeletons. Should she turn off the lights and wait for him in the back room? A few more minutes. Another cigarette. She passes a finger across the blue flame. It will be just as painless for the books. Tonight she needs him more than she has needed anyone. She wants to be caressed and comforted by him as Photius releases the tongue of Holy Fire onto her books. She wants to be held tightly, to enter the new millennium with him and start a new life together. But what if he does not come? She subdues an attack of anxiety by turning to the Sibyl. The book and the flame. Body and soul. Is the first letter in the Sibyl's book Q? She looks closer. Yes, painted in gold, almost faded. As for what follows, it has either been obliterated or nothing more was ever written. The open pages are covered in a network of fine cracks, as though the book has aged and is about to crumble. She studies the Sibyl's profile. Is there a resemblance? Or was it Photius's way of drawing her in? But there is something puzzling in the Sibyl's manner of reading, in the expression on her face. Yes! Her attitude is like that of a person looking into a mirror. The book and the mirror: both reflectors. One reflects the outer; the other, the inner. Maybe true reading occurs only when the text mirrors the individual's thoughts and emotions; in which case we never learn anything new, only that which is already within us, dormant, waiting to rise, but only at the silent call of the right words. Sonya has experienced this on many occasions: the deja vu evoked by a certain text; the self-recognition which, from time to time, leaps from the page. Perhaps that was the secret message contained in the Sibyl's book: discover yourself through reading.

She turns to the window: the last of twilight dies from a ragged cloud above PLAMEN'S GRILL; orange streetlights shimmer the tinselled Christmas decorations hanging between buildings and poles; the traffic is impatient at the crowded tram, at an old woman pushing a trolley, at careless pedestrians whose sights are set on midnight. When will he come? Can the dialogue be so important to him? Would he forego this evening's celebration in order to finish it? Has she misjudged him, as she had her first love? The emotions of that difficult time begin to stir again. A sadness rises at the sight of her faint reflection in the lettered window, as though she would be swallowed by the encroaching darkness. Before anxiety can tighten its knot, she once again seeks the equanimity of the Sibyl.

What should she do with the book? Leave it on the counter to suffer the same fate as the others? Take it with her? One becomes attached to a dress because it has taken the shape of the body, or a bra because it makes a particular impression in the skin, or a pair of shoes because they have been moulded by the roll of the foot. It is difficult to part with such items, even when they can no longer be worn. She vacillates over what to throw out when clearing her wardrobe – and this with clothes, which, at least for her, have always been accessories to being. How much stronger her attachment to books! More than mere accessories, they enter her being, undergo internalisation, connect with her own ideas, become an inseparable part of her.

A truck's horn blasts a figure dashing across the street. Sonya's heart leaps: is it him? A face presses against the window, covering her reflection, making it difficult to distinguish her face from his. Theo! His features are circumscribed by the O as though it were a halo. Greeting him at the door with a kiss, Sonya is pleasantly surprised by his appearance. He is wearing a dark suit, burgundy tie, and a white carnation in his lapel. A tremor passes through her at the pine fragrance of his aftershave. He checks his watch and signals an apology for being late. Still almost three hours before the new millennium. Sonya is suddenly struck by the fact that he is empty-handed. He signals that she looks lovely tonight. Accepting his compliment with a smile, she wonders about the gold envelope? Has he not completed what was to be the last dialogue? She was looking forward to reading it, particularly as he referred to it as a vision of sorts. She can wait. Besides, tonight is not the ideal time for reading. He must also feel the excitement of the evening. Has he dressed like this for her? To go out for dinner? She locks the door. He turns off the lights in the front of the shop and follows her into the back room. Would he like some coffee before they go out? He nods, in a preoccupied manner.

In relating what Photius has planned, precursors

to mid-night's fireworks explode intermittently with a thud. When would Photius most likely execute the job? He was evasive, she replies, though he will probably wait for the festivities to subside and the streets to quieten. Theo cracks the knuckles of both hands and signals that time is on their side. Muffled voices and scraping steps sound from the brothel. They smile and exchange looks. Reaching out for her hand, he draws her onto his lap. She whispers that she is happy being with him, but is afraid of what has been set in motion. The shop, the books – she has worked so hard for them. He strokes her hair. It is much better this way, he signals. They will enter the new millennium unburdened by material possessions, bound only to each other, one in flesh and spirit. She kisses his fingers and palms. Things must be done properly, he signals, and takes out a small jewellery box. She opens it: a pair of gold wedding bands. He does not believe in priests and churches. Would she mind if they perform their own ceremony, with God as both celebrant and witness? What must we do? Sonya asks. They stand. He takes the rings, places them on the mantelpiece above the fireplace, then feels for something in his coat pockets. He shakes his head in annoyance. In his haste he has forgotten his Bible at home. Does she have one in the shop? Sonya reflects a moment. No, she replies, feeling her cheeks reddening. They must have one, or the ceremony would have no meaning. She has one at home. They could perform the ceremony there. He shakes his head emphatically. It must take place in the shop, after which he will show her the last dialogue. Have you finished it? Sonya asks surprised. If she has liked his other work, she will love this one. But first he must run back to his room for his Bible – a King James version. Lately he has been reading it to the exclusion of everything else. The Old English text appeals to him. Uneasy about being left in the shop alone, Sonya tries to dissuade him from going, saying they could improvise, but he insists. She offers to drive him there. His room is not far from here, and he promises to return in ten minutes. Placing his hands behind his back, he smiles and signals something with his eyes. What is it? Sonya asks. She will find out soon. He kisses her on the forehead and hurries off.

Waiting for him in the front of the shop, Sonya is struck by the painful thought that this is her last opportunity for some kind of valediction to her books. The fireworks are becoming more frequent, thumping into the soft body of night. A bright star shoots up above PLAMEN'S GRILL, bursts into a bulbous bloom, and spills its seeds in a colourful shower. Inside, everything is tinged orange by the streetlights – the walls, the books, her hands. She needs a cigarette, but desists for his sake. She must give them up. Yes, that will be one of her resolutions tonight. Walking between shelves, she feels the books with her fingertips, as though taking leave of each one. Tomorrow morning when she comes to inspect the damage all this will be reduced to wet ash. No amount of preparation will harden her feelings for what she must confront. Some perhaps feign shock and bewilderment at such times, to convey to onlookers that this was a terrible act of God. She will not have to put on a show: the gutted shop and smouldering books will devastate her. Forgive me, she says, her attention caught by a movement outside the window. Xenia and an elderly man are walking toward a silver Mercedes parked in front of the shop. Sonya observes them from behind a bookcase. She is wearing an expensive evening dress. Is this the man she has been reading to in the course of her work? Has she kept her faith, or has she found a new saviour? Will she return to Russia? He opens the passenger door and she slips inside, careful not to crease the dress. As the fellow walks around to the driver's side, Sonya locates Tolstoy's *Resurrection* and dashes out. She taps on the window, startling Xenia. Thrusting the lever in gear, the fellow is about to drive off, but Xenia speaks to him and the automatic window slides down. Overcoming a momentary loss of words, Sonya manages an apology. A coloured constellation explodes overhead. The fellow rubs his ear, concealing his face with a large hand. She just wanted to ... wish Xenia all the best for the New Year. And would she accept this book as a small gift? Xenia angles the cover to the brothel's neon sign. Glossy lips part in a smile as she thanks Sonya and promises to visit the shop in the next few days.

If only a lot more could be given away, she muses, closing the door behind her. But the investigators are no fools: they will sift through the rubble, looking for signs of arson. Their suspicion would be aroused if the amount of ash did not correspond to the documented quantity of books. She checks the time: an hour and a half to midnight. She is struck by panic. Where is Theo? Is he playing a game with her? There is time to call the whole thing off. What possessed her to become involved with Photius? Zitta! Another thud, followed by an explosion of red sparks in an expanding sphere. In the orange light from outside, she locates Zitta's card among the papers on the counter and dials his mobile number. He answers, but she can barely hear him against the music and babble in the background. She has changed her mind. She wants to call it off. Impossible! he shouts. This is no game. The stakes are high. He has worked hard to set it up. Does he have Photius's number? It is too late. The wheels have been set in motion. Please! Photius is paranoid about his privacy. He does not have a telephone or a mobile. There is no way of contacting him at this hour. Relax, Sonya, he says, softening his tone. He understands her feelings. Everything will be all right. She should enjoy herself, have a few drinks, celebrate the New Year. He hangs up. No! It is not too late. The wheels of disaster can be stopped. She will wait for Photius, all night if necessary, and call it off, even if ... Theo! He is running to be with her. She must tell him. He stops abruptly in front of the bread shop. A white vehicle wails past, red light twisting, AMBULANCE in mirror image on the front. He bounds across the street and taps on the window.

In the back room, despite breathing heavily from the run, he is still able to convey a sense of the excitement out on the streets. She wants to tell him that she has changed her mind, but he takes out the Bible and draws her to the mantelpiece, where they stand beside each other, as though before an altar. He checks the time: an hour left in this millennium. Opening near the back of the Bible, he licks a finger and rustles the thin pages, stopping at Revelation. Perhaps as a result of a mishap with water, the red dye on the edge of the pages has run into the surrounding border. A shudder passes through Sonya: she hoped for something from Corinthians. Laying the Bible flat on the mantelpiece, he takes the rings from the box and places one on his forefinger, the other on Sonya's. Smiling, he points to chapter 6, verse 12. He wants her to read it aloud while he signals the words. 'And I beheld when he had opened the sixth seal, and, lo, there was a great earthquake; and the sun became black as sackcloth of hair; and the moon became as blood.' He turns to chapter 10, and indicates verses 8 and 9. 'And the voice which I heard from heaven spake unto me again, and said, Go and take the little book which is open in the hand of the angel which standeth upon the sea and the earth. And I went unto the angel, and said unto him, Give me the little book. And he said unto me, Take it, and eat it up; and it shall make thy belly bitter, but it shall be in thy mouth sweet as honey.' Turning a few more pages, he stops at chapter 20, verse 12. 'And I saw the dead, small and great, stand before God; and the books were opened: and another book was opened, which is the book of life: and the dead were judged out of those things which were written in the books, according to their works.' From there he goes to verse 15. 'And whosoever was not found written in the book of life was cast into the lake of fire.' He continues to the next chapter, pointing out the first two verses. 'And I saw a new heaven and a new earth: for the first heaven and the first earth were passed away; and there was no more sea. And I John saw the holy city, new Jerusalem, coming down from God out of heaven, prepared as a bride adorned for her husband.'

The sound of those terrible words is ameliorated by the graceful movement of his hands. Sonya turns to him, trembling, eyes brimming with tears. At last she has found her lover and soulmate. Photius flits to mind, but she dismisses him at once: he will not spoil this tender moment. Outside, fireworks now pound more frequently. Theo closes the Bible, kisses the gold cross on the cover, and offers it to her. Then, taking her hand, he embraces her tightly. Eyes shut, she feels the discs along his spine: they remind her of the indented letters on the spine of a hardback; she responds to his body: it has the physicality of a leather-bound tome; she yields to his caresses: they are as light as the pages of the Bible; she dissolves as he kisses her eyelids, just as she dissolved in the pleasure of reading. The tip of their tongues touch, and a ripple passes through her. Giving and taking, they explore each other's silence. As his fingers unbutton her blouse, Sonya imagines they are conveying a message in a private language, declaring his love in signs that only she is able to read. She unfastens her bra and drops it on the armchair. He hugs her from behind and kisses the lines made by the straps on her shoulders and across her back. His tongue probing her ear more meaningfully than any spoken word, he signals that they ought to make love on a bed of books. She nods. Taking them at random from the shelves, they spread a patchwork quilt on the floorboards. Our bridal bed, he signals, and removes his jacket and tie. Her skirt falls around her ankles. They step barefoot onto the books. She feels a hardback's indented letters under her sole. He caresses her eyebrows, her lips, the curve of her shoulders. She trembles as his palms press against her nipples, cup her breasts, and glide down past her waist, over the line in her skin made by her knickers. For an instant, she imagines herself to be the text, coming to life under the loving hands of a blind reader. He signals that she is more beautiful than anyone he has ever known. Blushing, she loosens the top button of his shirt.

Suddenly, as though alarmed, he grasps her wrists. What is it? she asks, feeling his fingernails. He stares at her for a moment, tense, searching. A heavy door closes with a jolt in the funeral parlour. The fridge, she thinks. But the unease that usually accompanies this jarring sound is now checked by his warmth, his aftershave, his tight grip. He studies her for a moment, then his body relaxes and he strokes her hair. Gazing into his eyes, she begins to undo the remaining buttons. An explosion sounds above the shop, followed by a flare visible from around the edges of the bookcase concealing the window. Astonished by what she sees in the light fractured by fireworks, Sonya slowly draws his shirt apart, as though unveiling a plaque or a work of art. Waxed clean of all body hair, his chest is tattooed in the precise blue script of the dialogues. Staring in bewilderment, she struggles to overcome a feeling of revulsion at this horrible act of graffiti. He studies her intently, with an anxious look, trying to read and interpret her reaction. She removes the shirt and places it over a chair.

Beginning at the base of his neck and going down past his trousers, parallel lines of neat text run across the front of his chest, curve around the ribs, and end cleanly on both sides, as though in right–left justification.

Her initial reaction quickly gives way to fascination. What is it? she asks, gliding a finger over a line between his nipples. My vision, he signals. But why like this? The perfect marriage of blood and ink. Pascal, the French genius, turned from science to religion because of a vision, which he promptly recorded on parchment and wore for the rest of his life in the lining of his vest, directly over his heart. He has gone one better, though not to outdo the sensitive Pascal, but to express his own vision in a manner commensurate with its meaning for him. Her desire for him returns, though now stronger than before. She unbuckles his belt. The last line runs across the lower part of his abdomen, just below his belly button. Suddenly she wants not only him, but every word that is written on him. The vision has changed my life, he indicates, as she passes both palms over his smooth skin. He did a course in tattooing after his accident, and for a while worked part-time across the street. Not having a hand for drawing, he left pictures of hearts, flowers, animals to the owner, concentrating exclusively on the written word. In time he became proficient in a wide range of styles, from Gothic to Roman, from Bookman to Britannic Bold. When clients wanted something in a foreign language, he would have them write it on a sheet of paper then reproduce it on skin in whatever style they wanted.

You tattooed yourself? Sonya asks, incredulous. He nods, glimmering eyes fixed on Sonya's face, reading her thoughts. Over three days, using a mirror, he signals. For three days he kept the curtains drawn, replaced the sun with a sixty watt globe, ate nothing and sipped only water. For three days, alone like Lazarus in his tomb, he transformed himself through the grace of the Holy Spirit. When the work was done he felt as though he were no longer a body caught by the gravity of the world, but a being reclaimed by the Holy Word. He has not shown the work to anyone, and never will. It will always be only for her, his loving reader. In fact, he saw her eyes in each letter-shaping point, their tenderness mingling with pigment and blood. How many writers would bear such testimony for their vision? How many would endure even a little pain for their ideas? How many would give so much as a drop of blood for their words? The word gains meaning from becoming flesh, and he has felt the needle's point giving shape to every letter. Can she now see how the other dialogues were a kind of extended prologue for this? But what is the word without a reader? From the moment he first set foot in the shop, he knew from her eyes that they were destined for this evening. She has become his faithful, personal reader, and their relationship has grown through the word. He would not exchange her for all the fame and wealth brought to other writers through millions of anonymous readers. In watching her read, he has felt a sense of fulfilment, completion, as though his words had found their perfect register.

But that was all a preparation for what she is about to read. This is the eternal marriage of blood and ink. The ideal union of man and woman in writer and reader. Love and logos fused, made indistinguishable in the comsummation of body and soul. Through the miracle of reading she will experience the embodiment of his vision, partake of it, become one with him, in order that they might enter the third millennium together, upright before the Lord. Sonya, my love, read me, he signals, and opens his arms. She hesitates a moment, then steps to him on the shifting books. He presses her to his chest, as though he would imprint her with the text. I love to read lying down, she whispers, smiling. Theo lies flat on his back, arms out to his sides, text accentuated by his skin taut as parchment. Kneeling beside him (she would like to straddle him, but thinks it might somehow violate the text), she caresses his eyes and lips. Several fireworks burst in rapid succession. Here and there a car's horn blares. Laughter sounds from the brothel. Five minutes, Sonya whispers. He removes her watch, drops it in his coat pocket, and lightly traces its impression on her thin wrist.

Having never felt a tattoo, she is surprised by the pin-pricked letters, and imagines the needle, finer than a nib, piercing the skin, combining blood and ink, forming tiny buds that would burst with meaning in a season of love. In recent years there has been a fashionable proliferation of tattoos, mainly pictorial, and the many she has seen on customers seemed to have faded with time, losing colour and clarity. The tattoo before her is sharp in its newness, like a page straight from the printing press, or a manuscript just finished by a calligrapher. It has been done with painstaking care, more meticulously than his other work. He has used a rich blue pigment, which contrasts strongly with the somewhat pale complexion of his skin.

Sonya closes her eyes and glides her tongue over the first line. Theo is right, she thinks. Just as no-one has ever written like this, so no-one has ever read like this. She licks the saltiness of each letter, tastes the fleshiness of each word. As he explores her body with his gentle hands, expanding her being, converting her into his own sign language, she attempts to decipher the first line by feeling with the tip of her tongue. Flesh and flesh, the reader and the one to be read, joined through love in the sanctuary of the word. She will read with her eyes later, but only after knowing the text with her lips, her tongue, her teeth. Here and there, unable to resist stealing a look, she finds herself kissing the word 'Angel', licking 'Fire', biting 'Death'. Apocalyptic, she thinks. It also is written in the form of a dialogue. Should she read it before they make love? But which desire will prevail? Is it possible to read it in the act of making love? To climax with the text? Kneeling, she straddles his thighs and continues to explore and experience the text with her mouth. As though from a ghetto-blaster loud music erupts in the brothel in anticipation of the countdown to the new millennium. His hands are now reading without restraint: her curves, her points, the line of hair from her rounded navel. Who are the figures in this dialogue? Why have they made such an impression on him? Between her thighs, his left hand traces the letter of love. On a line between his nipples she glances 'Satan asks' and on the line beneath 'nods Christ'.

The New Year suddenly bursts open around them: a barrage of fireworks whistle and explode, horns blast long and loud, voices sing in the brothel, laughter sounds in the funeral parlour, pots and pans clatter in a nearby restaurant, a bass drum throbs wildly, while brass instruments shriek and bray. Startled, Theo sits upright. What's that? asks Sonya. They embrace, cheek to cheek, and listen for a moment. Wings beat furiously in the front of the shop. Photius! Sonya cries. She slips into Theo's coat and he scrambles into his trousers. Swinging back the door, she recoils from several flames writhing and twisting in different parts of the shop. My books! she shouts, shielding herself from the intense heat. The work of the Holy Spirit, Theo signals, and puts his arm over her shoulder. Her freedom, their future, is in those flames. No, she screams, terrified by the fire crackling glued spines, spreading along rows, leaping from shelf to shelf, wrapping an entire case in its powerful wings. Sap sizzling and wheezing, several pine shelves collapse, spilling books onto the floor. An impish flame pounces at them, licks the open pages, devours the words, grows powerfully in absorbing them, fuses them into the primal syllable that uttered creation, and flies away leaving a flock of black flakes swirling in its wake.

Sonya glances outside: all hell seems to have broken loose. The silver glow from continuous explosions, together with the steady downpour of brightly coloured seeds, has transformed the night into a garish day. Seagulls shriek like souls lost in purgatory, dogs bark savagely at the bloody moon, car horns blend into a sustained groan. It is as though she is seeing the street for the first time. Pale, blotched with shadows, the buildings sway in the pulsating light. Drawn by a white horse, a carriage clatters past, crowded with figures wearing bestial masks. Revellers, many in fancy dress costumes, are singing and dancing outside the shop, delighting in the blaze, encouraged by a cacophonous band consisting of a boy pounding a drum big enough to accommodate him, three youths bellowing on brass instruments, and an old man in a crimson fez squealing on a sheepskin bagpipe.

Turning to a flame grasping and rustling through a thick paperback, reducing it to flakes in seconds, Sonya is struck by the thought: fire to fire, ash to ash. The mind is like fire, and the ideas in these books are being restored to their natural state. Maybe this kind of destruction is also a form of reading: several hundred thousand words consumed in seconds. Maybe this is the highest form of reading: the redemption of the word through fire. But these are fleeting thoughts: the next instant she is again overwhelmed by the full horror of the holocaust. My God! she screams, pointing at an apparition appearing, cigarette in mouth, from behind a row of shelves which the fire is just beginning to climb. Theo turns to Sonya with a look of disbelief. The angel in my vision, he signals. Photius! she shouts against the whirring flames. Get away from there! He responds with a crooked smile, but remains fixed to the spot, pigeon-toed, wide-eyed, as though dazed. Without warning, a few top shelves collapse and fiery books crash down on him, knocking him to the floor. Holding hands, Sonya and Theo rush to his assistance, but a sheet of flame rises before them, cutting them off from him. Suddenly the heat is unbearable and they are surrounded by flames, the way to the back room blazing. Still smiling, Photius reaches out a small plump hand, as books burn around him. This way, shouts Sonya, pulling Theo toward the counter, over which the flames have not yet jumped, but his attention is fastened on Photius, whose hand is still extended, as though beckoning him. Theo! she screams. My vision, he signals. The angel is calling. He will lead us into the third millennium. Sonya tries to draw him to the counter, but, pulling away, he springs through the tongue of flame and grasps Photius's hand. Theo! she cries, tears streaming, and is about to leap after him, when another row of shelves collapses, scattering books around both men. A rush of wings rising from the crackling books drives Sonya behind the counter.

For an instant, unable to catch her breath from the stifling heat and smoke, unable to utter a sound, she watches helplessly as flames swirl and close in upon the pair. Outside an intense magnesium light rains upon the city, the band plays more furiously, the revellers dance orgiastically. Cigarette still in his mouth, Photius crosses himself three times as his shirt ignites. In an instant he is embraced in beating wings of flames. Theo spreads his arms wide and mouths a silent call, as though summoning Sonya, but she looks on, numb with horror, as a tongue of flame licks his chest, sizzling the skin, shrivelling the text, reclaiming and restoring it to its inspiration and source. A siren screams in the distance. Black smoke smelling of burning cloth and flesh rises from the pair. Gasping, Sonya recoils and turns away, her face almost pressed against the strapped collection of *Jewish Folk Stories* on the back shelf. Having tasted flesh, the flames are now ravenous. More through reflex than volition, she draws what little breath she can, raises the collection above her head and, with a desperate cry, hurls them at the front window, shattering it amid the exploding sky, the music's frenzy, the cheers of exhortation. With a sudden presence of mind, she removes Theo's coat, beats back an aggressive flame, and, barely conscious, rushes for the jagged opening. The sky blooms with dazzling constellations. An angelic figure plays a golden trumpet as other angels hold hands and dance in a joyful circle.

Naked, Sonya falls into the third millennium.